Eve Devon writes sexy heroes, s[...] [...]
afters. Growing up in locations lik[...] [...] [...] [...] [gave]
Eve a taste for adventure; her love [...] [...] [...] [when]
her mother shoved one into her h[...] [...] [to]
keep her quiet during TV coverage of the Wimbledon tennis
finals!

When Eve wasn't consuming books by the bucketload, she could
be found pretending to be a damsel in distress or running around
solving mysteries and writing down her adventures. As a
teenager, Eve wrote countless episodes of TV detective dramas so
the hero and heroine would end up together every week. As an
adult, still hooked on romance and mysteries, she worked in a
library to conveniently continue consuming books, until realizing
she was destined to write contemporary romance and romantic
suspense herself.

www.EveDevon.com

X x.com/EveDevon
f facebook.com/EveDevonAuthor

Also by Eve Devon

THE LIFE-CHANGING MAGIC OF FALLING IN LOVE

EVE DEVON

One More Chapter
a division of HarperCollins*Publishers*
1 London Bridge Street
London SE1 9GF
www.harpercollins.co.uk
HarperCollins*Publishers*
Macken House, 39/40 Mayor Street Upper,
Dublin 1, D01 C9W8

This paperback edition 2024
First published in Great Britain in ebook format
by HarperCollins*Publishers* 2024
Copyright © Eve Devon 2024
Eve Devon asserts the moral right to be identified
as the author of this work

A catalogue record of this book is available from the British Library

ISBN: 978-0-00-830671-7

Printed and bound in the UK using 100% Renewable Electricity
by CPI Group (UK) Ltd

To KW, for speaking the languages of Family and Friendship so eloquently.

Chapter One

THE GUY IN APARTMENT 33C

Ashleigh

As I approach Apartment 33C all the jangly, antsy feelings that sit so uncomfortably deep within me start to soften and inflate into this wonderful fluttery anticipation.

It's always like this right at the start and I love it.

My pace quickens and my heart rate skitters, keen to get in on the action. I've become adept at regulating my heart rate but now I give the skitter rein and experience my heart knocking against my chest wall, helping me feel alive.

At the door to the apartment, I pause and look left and then right. The corridor is empty. Everyone who has somewhere to be is already there, so it's just me and the wisps of excitement I can't quite contain. They spark in the air around me adding to the giddy sensation.

Believe me, I never got to experience this in my previous employment.

I slide on my gloves as my gaze slides over the rosewood door with its gold-plated number '33' and letter 'C' in expensive fancy font, checking I have the right place.

It's so tempting to hang around a little longer and prolong the anticipation.

Bask in it for a while.

But I remind myself I'm on a schedule.

In and out.

Not everyone has the skills, stamina and ambition for this type of work, but everyone is driven by different things, aren't they?

The key I've acquired pushes into the lock silently and with the sound of my heart drumming in my ears, one of my gloved hands turns the key, the other turns the doorhandle and I'm in.

First impressions, as my eager eyes scan, waiting to alight on the good stuff, is of acres of polished light oak floorboards and miles of naked white walls.

As my eyes adjust from the plush low-lit corridor outside to this vast new open concept living area, I scan and re-scan, frowning hard at the barren surroundings.

'What the…?' A snort of disgust escapes.

The good stuff I was promised?

Zilch.

Nada.

Disappointment crashes down.

There has to be some mistake.

The cleaning cart I pulled in behind me is having none of my negativity as it drifts off to the side presumably needing a moment to fully take in the beauty.

I stare at the key in my gloved hand.

It fit the lock.

So maybe this isn't a mistake and I am genuinely expected to spend the next two hours cleaning this place.

Two whole hours? It doesn't even need two whole minutes.

Pristine is an understatement, along with the not-so-subtle aroma of bleach.

Perhaps my supervisor gave me the wrong information? With renewed optimism I rush over to my cleaning cart to pull out the New Client file, whipping off my gloves in the process because let's face it, if I leave a fingerprint on anything at least it will give me something to clean.

Across the top of the file that I designed for Sparkle, the cleaning service I work for, it says: *Apartment 33C, Client Name: George Northcote*

I skip to the salient field, 'Type of Cleaning Service Required', where it is clearly printed: *Weekly 5Star Sparkle service.*

Our 5Star Sparkle service is a deep clean usually reserved for between occupancies which is why I thought I was being promised gross-out level dirt and why I'd brought my gloves with me.

I have to confess, non-plussed doesn't even begin to cover it.

I mean, here I am, revved.

Eager to get stuck in and make a difference.

Help someone.

And instead, the work I was promised is nowhere to be seen.

'Weekly 5Star Sparkle service required, my butt, because, *wow*, are you a liar, George Northcote!'

Saying the words aloud makes me feel a little better until I'm startled by the sound of my phone. What if it's Karma calling on behalf of this George Northcote guy?

Without glancing at my phone screen, I answer with, 'Ms. Rivera speaking.' The need to be unruffled and professional is a given with me … as is the need to mitigate sounding like I've just called my newest client a liar.

'Ashleigh?'

'Ma?' Turns out it's someone way more powerful than Karma. I fumble the phone, managing to catch it before it cracks against the beautiful flooring because even with taking every shift offered and always hustling for more, this is New York City and there's no way I can afford to replace it. 'I'm at work, Ma.'

'And, what, you can't take five minutes out of your day to speak with your mother who's been trying to get hold of you for a week?'

The struggle to not feel guilty is real. 'What is it? What's happened?'

'That's what I want to know. What's happening in my daughter's life? You tell me nothing. No-thing! Your brother and sister phone every week, regular.'

Well, of course they do. At twenty-seven and twenty-three, they've both got it together enough to know what's good for them.

Somehow, at twenty-five, I'm still learning what's good for me.

'...And don't be trying to explain it away as middle-child syndrome because I've been reading the middle child is the one who tries pleasing everyone...'

My ma loves to read.

Unfortunately for me, she mostly loves to read *Psychology Today*.

I switch off.

Not the phone, because, jeez, she'd find a way to teleport here out of sheer worry.

And I don't want her worrying.

There's nothing *for* her to worry about.

But this is the sort of call I'm going to get until I give her full access to all my feelings and all my thoughts.

4

Or I attempt to get my old job back, which I do not want, ever.

I think of the typo I spotted in the latest edition of *Best Home* that I promised myself I wouldn't buy yet did and toy with telling her about my deep satisfaction yet equal frustration at seeing the error. Better not. She'll take my words and run with them … right round to every member of the family and before I know it the new minion sitting at my old desk at *Best Home* will be receiving a confusing Welcome to Your Old Job basket.

Biting my tongue and with only half an ear on my mother's chatter, I walk through the living space of Apartment 33C.

An immaculate L-shaped midnight-blue velvet couch with gleaming chrome legs screams form *and* function. A telescope faces the wall of glass. Creepy and *Rear Window*-y or a romantic way of exploring the city skyline?

I study the perfectly sourced mid-century furniture as I walk around a large desk, its gleaming surface only interrupted by an in-tray containing a stack of perfectly aligned papers. The far wall houses custom built-ins. The large flatscreen is enclosed by ordered rows of books, organised by size and colour.

I sweep my gaze over the modern kitchen where there is precisely nothing on the work surfaces, not even a charger cable.

Disturbed by the lack of personal stuff, I reach out and brush a fingertip over the glossy leaves of a Ficus. Like everything else in this place, it feels artificial.

I snatch my hand back.

It *is* artificial.

Maybe I'm being pranked.

Maybe all the mess I was promised is in one of the two bedrooms and if I investigate, I'll be graced with the equivalent of a rock star's hotel suite? Propelling myself into action I retrace my steps back across the living area and head for the nearest door.

'...And so I need to know there's at least the *possibility* of you bringing someone to the wedding. Not that you'll ever meet anyone cleaning but—'

The door in front of me disappears momentarily as I roll my eyes so hard, they feel like I'm doing advanced eye yoga (which, considering I read an article about goat yoga the other day, is surely a thing somewhere).

I manage to hold back the audible sigh but ... ugh! Why is she never going to believe I can have a good life cleaning? A more balanced life? A happier life?

But this is the stuff of pipe dreams because believe me, if you'd spent your whole life being told: Go to school. Stay in school. Get a career. We sacrifice for you. Don't end up like us – cleaning for other people who stayed in school and got themselves a career...

The fact my folks own their own cleaning business that they've franchised out and employ sixty staff, own their own home, put all their kids through college, but will never believe their work is as valid as others ... well, I'm not on a crusade or anything but underneath it all, it breaks my heart. As well as frustrating the ever-loving hell out of me – wait, finally her words filter through and I say into the phone, *'Wedding? What Wedding?'*

'Your cousin Tina's wedding.'

'Tina's getting married?' I stop myself pushing the door to the master suite open. I'm doing it for this George guy because discovering I've just become the only person in my entire family not married or engaged to be married has my neuroses and insecurities laughing at me like a pack of hyenas and trust me, nobody needs that kind of negative energy in their bedroom.

'You didn't get the save the date card?' my mother asks.

I want to say they probably don't deliver invites that look that posh to my neighbourhood but instead I say lightly, 'Nope. So, when's the wedding?'

'June third.'

'Wow, that's fast.' I wait for her to dish the dirt on the reason Tina's getting married so fast but there's nothing. 'Wait – are we talking about June third *next* year?'

'Of course next year,' she says. 'You know how long it takes to plan a good wedding.'

'Oh my God – *I* could be married by then.'

I do not need the ensuing silence to know I should not have said that.

Flippancy.

Sarcasm.

Surrealism.

None of these are the way to go in conversation with my mother.

'And how will you be married by then when you're not even dating?'

Before Loneliness can gallop in and wallop me over the head, I mentally slam shut the trapdoor into my heart, lean against it a little and look around for something to shove up against it. Maybe my left lung?

'Ashleigh?'

I do some more eye yoga and push open the door to George Northcote's master suite, figuring when one door shuts, another one opens.

'I'm dating,' I respond in defence. 'As a matter of fact, I have a date tonight.' This is closely followed by the shoutiest of shouty voices in my head yelling: Have you learnt nothing?

Now all I'm going to get is—

'For real? Joe – Joe?' my ma calls out to my pa like he's on the other side of the world. 'Ashleigh's dating.' And then to me, she says, 'Where did you meet? What's he like? Oh, wear that dress I've always liked you in – you know the one with the thing… And it won't kill you to wear your hair down once in a while…'

I focus on the room before me so that I don't have to focus on my mother's excited instructions. Colour me surprised – the bedroom is decorated in more Pristine.

I try to be positive. You know those people who have to clean before the cleaner comes round? Well, in my experience that only lasts a couple of weeks before they relax at the thought you might think them disgusting scuzz-buckets, aka normal human beings.

In fact, it's my experience they relax so much that it's usually only another week after that before they're completely comfortable forgetting to tidy away their sex toys. I have knowledge of this because aged six and tagging along with my mother to one of her cleaning jobs, I picked up a vibrator I found in one of the bedrooms and thinking it was the best torch ever, paraded it around the fancy house like I was Nancy Drew before she spied me with it and started talking at a pitch only me and dolphins could hear, about how she was never, *ever* bringing me to work with her again.

'So, what's this guy you're dating do for work?' my mother asks now, her voice at normal pitch but with a healthy dollop of interrogation thrown in.

I stare at the navy-blue silk comforter on the king-size bed in front of me. I have to give her something. My gaze moves from the bed to the navy curtains and the white walls. Aiming for some sort of information low-down, I say, 'He's something in…?' I draw a blank, unable to compute all the angles needed to suggest the perfect job that will lead to no more questions aka no more worry.

I mumble something unintelligible and continue with, 'so I'm looking forward to finding out more tonight.'

I stare at the piece of art that hangs over George Northcote's bed. Its straight edges and blocks of colour match the piece hanging over the couch in the living area.

Where the hell is the clutter? The mess? The dirt? All things I need to smooth out those jangly antsy feelings that have returned.

My gaze zooms in on the one personalised item in the bedroom. A photo frame beside the bed.

The couple staring out of it are posed on a balcony, an inky sky over lit-up hills of honey-coloured houses with umber-tiled roofs as their backdrop.

The crowd seems to have parted for the photographer, or perhaps to showcase the perfect couple. Everyone's dressed up, like they're at a wedding in a trattoria in Sicily.

I hear the romantic sigh leave my lungs and combat its presence with the uncharitable thought that the photo is probably only in here because it matches the décor.

Photo Couple are smiling for the camera, perfectly posed with their arms wrapped around each other and free hands holding glasses of champagne.

I lean closer, not sure I've ever seen a woman so put-together before. Sleek blonde bob. Cheekbones to die for and all with no obvious contouring in sight. Cornflower-blue eyes that probably aren't contacts. A perfect symmetrical smile that is neither forced nor one of those mid-laughs that screw up your eyes and produce a double chin. She's wearing a perfectly tailored navy-blue dress that shows off her tanned body … perfectly.

I blow out a soft whistle.

The man is GQ cover model material in his perfectly matching blue suit.

This time the soft whistle comes out louder and longer like it's sighing in a sort of swooning way.

'Ashleigh?'

I suck in a breath. 'Ma, I'm going to have to call you back tonight, okay?'

'Tonight? I thought you had a date tonight?'

Oh, for – my eyes roll upwards once more as it occurs to me that my mother should have been in the CIA. Heck, maybe she *is* and the cleaning business is a cover.

'Tomorrow then,' I amend. 'I'll call you tomorrow.' I hang up the phone, push it into my back pocket and pick up the photo from beside the bed.

The guy's hair is the same shade of brown as mine but it's styled in one of those I-can-run-my-hands-through-it-in-sixty-three-different-ways-and-each-of-them-will-make-me-look-hotter ways.

His eyes are green and laughing.

His mouth has a sensual tilt and he's looking at the woman his arm is wrapped around like no man has ever looked at me.

It doesn't state a couple live here on the New Client File.

Just a George Northcote.

'Well, just George from Apartment 33C,' I say into the purified air. 'I'd better figure out how to make this place look extra sparkly for you as it seems, on first impressions, that you are a complete neat freak.'

A super *sexy*-looking neat freak, I amend with one last look at the photo.

Chapter Two

AN ENGLISHMAN IN NEW YORK

George

In my experience meetings can fall into two categories. Dull and deathly dull.

Presentations on the other hand, especially where the main objective is to unveil an ad campaign that will land the client, well, I will move mountains to ensure they never fall into either category.

I like to think of them as the place where preparation, creativity and adrenalin come together to create something beautiful.

The presentation I'm currently in the middle of *was* representative of this. Until I realise, I don't quite have a handle on what is happening…

For example, Tim Duggins is either on schedule and talking about algorithms and budgets for influencer marketing and I've suddenly lost the ability to understand Advertising 101, or he has decided to really spark my adrenalin by speaking in Klingon. As he really isn't the type to mix things up during a presentation we've been honing for weeks, I can only conclude the problem lies with me.

Maybe I could concentrate better if my chair hadn't suddenly developed the ergonomic properties of custard.

What. The. Hell.

In a move so mind-bendingly slo-mo I could be in a *Matrix* movie I lean back against the chair's mesh backing. I feel weird. Like I'm falling through space.

At the absurdity of the sensation, I sit up straight, grip the edge of the table and wheel my chair in as close to it as possible.

'What do you think, George?'

What do I think, Tim? I think something is very wrong.

Obviously, I can't say that in the middle of a presentation that's supposed to secure me my next promotion. Can't even allude to it. This is why I need to shake it off and concentrate on nailing the campaign's objectives so the client is salivating to sign with us.

I stare at Tim and realise he's speaking again.

My hearing seems to be coming in and out.

I put this together with the feeling of being off-balance and … okay … what makes most sense is that I have an inner-ear infection?

'George?'

'Sorry, Tim.' I glance at the PowerPoint slide and deliver a sentence calculated to make our prospective client, Mr. Yeong of Yeong Cosmetics, look good. 'Regarding CTA,' I say, 'I agree with Mr. Yeong. "Verbifying" our campaign isn't going to speak to the demographic we've identified – which is why we've come up with a clear market-specific message.' As I illuminate Mr. Yeong and the rest of the meeting attendees on how we went about that, I can't help feeling that the head of the cosmetics company doesn't look like he's been ill a day in his life.

Me neither by the way.

Not since I was thirteen.

So if, by some galactically poor timing, I am to be ill ... well, I can't be.

Not today.

Not in this room. With its glass walls meant to denote status and sophistication but which only highlight the miles of cables needed for the huge projection screen they forgot to build in and the fact that the WiFi signal is rubbish.

God, what is it with this heat? It's pulsing and radiating out of me like I'm some super-hero in a comic tapping into my talent. My face feels like it's on fire and now I am actually worried a colleague will remark on it.

Out of the corner of my eye I see Anya's head swivel in my direction.

Damn.

To anyone else, Anya looks politely enquiring, but if they knew her like I know her, they'd be reading her expression as, *What's the deal, George? Make the deal, George.*

I throw her a smile, clear my throat and man up. 'Now that Tim's gone over the benefits of signing with our agency today, why don't I get to what we're really here for. Let's begin with unveiling our new strapline...' I pause for effect, allowing time for Mr. Yeong and his entourage to lean an anticipatory bit closer to the large screen in front of them. 'Can I have the next slide, please,' I say, and then watch as the screen reveals the new skincare product range with the strapline: *Forever Yeong*.

My focus is razor-sharp once more as I see the small tic of appreciation on Mr. Yeong's face.

He's pleased.

Very pleased.

As he turns to face me and I realise that it's fine to look your prey in the eye but not always appropriate to do it for more than a couple of seconds as that turns it into something else altogether, I'm forced to shift my gaze around the room and when I get to the last of Mr. Yeong's team I let my gaze sort of hang mid-air.

This is a mistake!

It makes me feel strangely removed from reality and my heart starts racing. Crazy-stupid-fast-racing.

I swallow dry air.

The glass walls of the office start closing in on me. My mind scrambles and then settles on the only other plausible explanation.

Oh.

Mate!

This isn't an inner ear infection. I've only gone and contracted claustrophobia. We've been camping at the office to get this presentation done. It was probably going around and I didn't even notice.

Note to self: more working from home again. Lots of merit in working from home, I've always thought. Except, wait, no, I haven't once ever thought that. Why would I? I can work anytime. Anywhere, anyplace.

What the hell is the matter with me?

What's the deal, George? Make the deal, George.

With Herculean effort, I ignore the ringing in my ears and the vaguely uncomfortable feeling in the region of my chest and start doing what I am employed to do. What I *love* to do.

Thirty minutes later or maybe it is only thirty seconds later it's all applause and happy faces.

I watch as Anya gets up from the table to shake Mr. Yeong's hand.

Deal done.

Promotion secured.

It's all good.

Very good.

Tim slaps me on the back and shouts, 'Congratulations,' in my ear.

That's when the pain hits.

Incredible pain.

Not in my ear.

In my chest.

Oh shit.

I have to get out of here.

I lurch out of the stupid *Charlie and the Glass Elevator* style cubicle and head for the actual elevators. I usually take the stairs but even I know sprinting down twelve flights of stairs is the type of exercise that's too little too late to stop a heart attack in its tracks.

Besides. Using the stairs is for people who act on their good intentions. The proportion of people who do that is relatively small and therefore there's every chance I'll expire on stairwell nine and won't be found for weeks.

In the elevator, I punch the button for the ground floor, spin around and look at myself in the mirror.

Huh.

I don't look like my ticker is ticking down.

Not if you discount the paleness in my cheeks and the heaving in of oxygen.

The 'ding' of the elevator has me pushing at the doors to get out, even as I'm yanking my tie to the side and opening the buttons of my shirt collar in a move reminiscent of Clark Kent, except when he does it, he's entering a telephone box not exiting the plush offices where the Harrison Richards Advertising Agency occupies space.

I sort of fall out of the elevator, regain my balance and look about me like a wild man. My only mission: to get out into the fresh air. The beautiful polluted fresh air.

I'm tempted to hurdle the security turnstiles in a single leap, yet even in the midst of a heart attack I fish around in my pocket for my pass and slide it over the little clear window with the infrared laser inside before racing for the revolving doors.

My name is George Northcote.

I'm thirty-one years old.

And I am having a heart attack.

I absolutely cannot have a heart attack.

For a start, the hole that was found inside my heart was repaired nearly two decades ago and I have looked after it meticulously ever since.

Also, I'm British, so a thousand per cent will not want to draw attention to myself by asking for help!

Out on the street, the inevitability of my fate hits, the sound rushes in and the ground rises up to meet me.

Chapter Three

IT'S ALL GOOD

George

The sound of the apartment door closing jerks me awake.

It's dark outside and I squint at the time on my phone. 9pm.

I've been asleep on my sofa for hours.

I test myself by sitting up.

Nope.

The overall feeling sitting on my chest and filling up my head is still one of exhaustion mixed with utter stupidity.

'Anya?' I call out, my voice pathetically groggy. 'Is that you?'

A light comes on and she appears in front of me. 'Who else would it be?'

'Where have you been?'

'Out celebrating the Forever Yeong deal with the client and the team.'

I detect the tiniest reprove in her tone and I'm not going to lie. It rankles. Call me old-fashioned but in the event of a heart attack you'd expect your girlfriend of three years to visit you in hospital, would you not?

She is the reason I upped sticks and came to New York, after all.

I mean, I get why it might have looked unprofessional to run out of the presentation after me, but surely afterwards? A harried hailing of taxi. Sprinting down endless hospital corridors. Some tearful bedside hand holding?

Actually, it wouldn't even have been unprofessional because we signed one of those HR things that lets you state you're in a consensual relationship and working for the same company and not harassing each other in any way.

I can't help myself. As I steer from the foggy awfulness of the day, I say, 'I didn't even warrant a "Hi Babe, just checking in with you – looked like you were having a myocardial infarction during the presentation. Concerned. Love, Anya"?'

Anya drops her bag at the end of the sofa and folds her arms. 'You had a panic attack, George.'

Yes.

The shame of it grabs me by the throat and slams me about some more so that I'm now feeling even more tired.

Not a heart attack.

A panic attack!

Distinct difference.

And the reason for the unrelenting feelings of stupidity.

'But you didn't know that, did you?' I accuse, feeling irritable.

'I did, George. You told me. From the hospital. Would you like some tea?'

'Tea?' I stare, agog. I may be from Old Blighty but what the actual? I end up in the emergency room, fully thinking I'm having a heart attack and my girlfriend returns from partying and offers me tea. 'Is that some kind of joke?'

'No joke – I guess, more a clumsy attempt to soothe. What I'm trying to say, is that, yes, you had a panic attack, but you also took care of it without impacting the deal, which, by the way, I commend you for. I told Mr. Yeong you had to rush to another presentation and got you some extra points for dedication. I don't think we should pay too much credence to the panic. It may affect how you get over it. And we can't have that happening again, can we? You're too important.'

I want to ask to whom, but I have a sneaky feeling I already know.

Suddenly, I crave sinking back down onto the sofa and pulling the throw over my head so I can have an almighty sulk.

Aside from the utter humiliation of having a panic attack at work for absolutely no reason at all, I realise I'm upset and confused that my girlfriend isn't dressed in a naughty nurse uniform, feeding me peeled grapes and offering to binge-watch something she hates on Netflix, with me.

Doesn't sit well.

So I stand up and walk over to the kitchen area for a bottle of the good red I like. I pour out a large glass. There's no point pouring one for Anya as she will tell me she's already had her allotted alcohol units while out playing the perfect business hostess.

'Hungry?' I ask, aiming to let go of the horrid irritability dogging my every move. I haven't felt like this in years. I've worked very hard not to feel like this.

Instead, I favour feeling phlegmatic.

Pragmatic.

Chilled.

Anya smiles. Technically she hasn't been hungry for decades.

For some reason, this rankles too. Probably because I'm suddenly yearning for the comfort and healing qualities of a full English fry-up. Which is weird, because I haven't had one of those since the early years, pre-surgery.

But seeing as I didn't have a heart attack I could totally have one now – a fry-up, that is.

I open up the fridge and stare at the emptiness inside.

Or not, then.

It flashes through my mind that maybe if I kept the fridge better stocked and not looking like something out of a bachelor pad then Anya and I would be better about being a couple. A stab of guilt follows at the thought and I vow to get better at all of this. Perhaps if I purchased some scatter cushions? Make the place more enticing for her to stay over more.

It occurs to me I don't remember the reason why we didn't move in together when I agreed to come to New York with her. There must have been one, right?

I let go of the fridge door and watch it close slowly.

Politely.

My heart skips a beat and I tense. I definitely do not want a repeat of earlier, so I smile, and say, 'Pizza?'

Anya reaches out to wind her arms around me. 'Vegan?'

'Sure.' Anything to feel her pressed up against me.

'What's that smell?'

I rear back for a second. God, do I have the smell of hospital on me?

'It smells,' she wrinkles up her nose. 'Sort of oceanic?'

Oh.

Yeah.

I smile for the first time in hours. 'I think the new cleaner started today. I requested a no-bleach smell.'

This was genius of me as smelling bleach always reminds me of—

'But George, how will you know they've cleaned if you can't smell the bleach?'

I hug her, running my hands up and down her sides, reluctant to let her go. 'I guess we'll have to trust we'll notice if their standards drop.'

'Okay.' I feel her start to relax. 'I'm sorry I didn't visit you in the hospital. I really hate those places – not that it should be about me.' She moves slightly in my arms. Anya's always at war with the restless energy that seems to thrum under her skin like a tuning fork. She leans back and looks up at me, her blue eyes worried. 'You do know I only ever want you to be healthy?'

'I know. It's okay,' I reassure her.

'But I realise how not rushing to be at your side must have come across.' She tightens her arms around me.

I remind myself that Anya does care. She's just very used to maintaining an unflappable front. If I ever tried reminding her of the time she admitted to the sense of powerlessness she felt growing up, she would deny it categorically. Not that I would ever remind her, being as I can totally relate.

I probably scared the hell out of her by rushing out of the presentation like I did.

Scared myself a bit too.

But it's all good now.

I'm all good.

'I'm sorry too,' I say, needing her to understand I don't intend to make a habit of this. 'I have absolutely no idea why I had a panic attack but I can't see it happening again. Now, tell me about the awful jokes Tim Duggins tried telling and how many drinks he had before you had to pour him into a taxi?'

Later we're sitting on the sofa, the pizza box on the coffee table in front of us. Anya has snuck a couple of bites from the last slice which always makes me happy and now as she reaches across to snaffle some more of the good red too, the words sneak out of my mouth, 'Anya, what would you have done if it really had been a heart attack?'

Her pretty blue eyes go round. 'Oh my God, George. Don't even joke about it.'

She turns to nuzzle my neck in the way she knows I love and we settle down to some healthy, restorative Netflix and chill.

Chapter Four

MAID WITH LOVE

Ashleigh

'By the time I'd left there, you'd never know I'd been,' I complain to Carlos when there's a lull in customers. 'And that's not a good thing, by the way,' I add as an explanation.

A day later, sitting at one of the seven tables in the bijou bakery downstairs from my even more bijou apartment, I don't know why I'm still so vexed about Apartment 33C. Other cleaners would be stoked when faced with what essentially translates as a mini-break in the middle of their day.

'Poor Ashleigh.' Carlos pouts for me from behind the bakery counter. 'No one to save for an entire day. It's a wonder you're still standing.'

My jaw drops open. That wasn't where I was going with my musings at all. I was comfortable coming around to the idea that I was fixated on George Northcote's apartment and its lack of mess as a way of not having to think about my cousin Tina's wedding, my mother's forecast that I wouldn't have a plus one a year plus from now and the fact that last night's date showed no promise of contradicting her.

'But enough about work,' Carlos states. 'Last night, details, please.'

Here's where I need to mention Carlos's current side hustle is best described as Project Manager for Finding Ashleigh Love.

It was supposed to be called Project: Finding Ashleigh Someone To Hang Out With On The Weekend, but I guess that's not as catchy?

'Last night? Hmm,' I pause for effect. 'How to describe last night … okay, yes, it's coming to me now…' I beam. 'Last night was … *incredible*.'

Carlos punches the air. 'I knew it. I am so good at this – Oz?' he calls out behind him, 'Ozzie-Baby, I'm taking my break, Our Ashleigh's finally ready to grace us with a sitrep.'

Confession: every time Carlos or Oz refer to me as 'Our Ashleigh' my palms get all sweaty and that trap door into my heart rattles. I find myself wanting to tell them about the typo in *Best Home* magazine, but if I didn't want to tell my mother, I hesitate in telling them. I'm not sure they'd get it – we're new friends and haven't yet developed the sort of shorthand that comes from knowing each other years.

Luckily, I don't have time to ruminate because Carlos is whipping off his apron and dashing out from behind the shiny cabinets of seductive breads and pastries like he's in a parkour event being live streamed.

I'm habitually clumsy unless I have a duster or a vacuum cleaner in my hands so I'm always impressed every time Carlos, who looks like he was born on a surf-board, leaps lithely over boxes or around customers to clear tables in the bakery he co-owns with his other half Oz 'Ozzie-Baby' Crannick.

In order to serve the new line of people forming, Oz is forced to come out of the kitchen where his hands knead dough into all forms of delicious addictiveness. While he mutters under his breath at the inconvenience, Carlos slides onto the chair across from mine, plants his elbows on the circular marble table top and leans in, his dancing bourbon-brown eyes imploring.

His eagerness to hear the run-down of last night's date only encourages me and I make my own average brown eyes wide and super-impressed. 'I felt something I haven't felt in ages.'

Carlos sighs with happiness and then leans precariously back in his chair. 'You hear that, Ozzie-Baby? She *felt* something she hasn't felt in ages.'

'I heard,' Oz grunts. 'The whole place heard.'

I hide a grin with a sip of my coffee because no matter how many times Carlos forces Oz into Shop-Front Land, Oz never progresses beyond looking caustically disdainful at having to actually interact with customers.

The customers seem to love it though. Seriously, it's like getting to watch a visual representation of puppies clamouring happily over a dog-hating *hooman!*

Sparing me a quick wink to soften his grunt, Oz begins dumping a selection of the mouth-watering beignets that I started smelling at 5am into a cardboard box with the bakery's name *Oscars* emblazoned across the front in black swirly letters.

Combining their names Oswald and Carlos for business screams 'committed relationship' and to stop myself comparing that to the casual company of friends, I allow myself the distraction of looking at Oz, and the fact that only someone of his size and stature could rock a hairnet.

Believe me, Carlos knows this as well, which is why, I suspect, he cultivates every opportunity to get him out of the kitchen and onto the frontline.

Carlos turns back to me, as does the entire line of people waiting at the counter, expressions all eager anticipation. 'So, dish the debauchery,' he demands. 'What *exactly* did you feel … and how many times did you feel it?'

'Boredom.' I drop the word and all it represents for a date before casually bringing my coffee mug to my lips to take another sip.

'Boredom?' Carlos looks instantly suspicious.

'Yep. That's what I felt last night. *Incredible,* unrelenting boredom.'

Carlos's mouth drops open and I take that as my cue to continue. 'I have to tell you I'm not sure I'd considered it was even possible to be that bored in someone's company.' I put my mug down and then raise my hands to the sides of my temples so that I can mime mind-blown.

Someone in the line laughs but I don't know whether it's at my amazing wit, my obvious misfortune when it comes to dating or Carlos's heartfelt 'Noooo' of disappointment.

In fact, Carlos looks so disappointed on my behalf that I start to feel ungrateful. From the moment the pair discovered I lived alone above their new business they sort of adopted me and while I tried everything I could to run away from their friendship, somehow, possibly through the power of baked goods, they inveigled their way into my cautious heart.

To be honest I wouldn't have survived being in New York without them.

Not after what happened last year.

But I guess you're all wondering why I didn't simply tell

Carlos the teeniest-tiniest of white lies about last night and make out I'd had the best time?

I think it's because he and Oz *have* been so good to me and … maybe, because I really would like to meet someone not already coupled-up to hang out with at the weekend.

Honestly, it's nothing more than that. I mean, sure, my heart gives a little swoon whenever I catch the soft, quiet, lingering looks Carlos and Ozzie-Baby give each other but I can appreciate that and still not want that.

Or need that.

At least not until my mother and my cousin's wedding got inside my head.

'I really thought last night's guy would be Mr. Right,' Carlos says, with a sad shake of his head.

'Oh, he was,' I confirm. 'All. The. Time. Because who wants a little healthy conversation and debate when you can add "When I'm right, I'm right. Right?" to the end of every sentence?'

Carlos winces. 'And that killed any chemistry you felt?'

'What can I tell you – other than it made me wish I hadn't been as harsh about the first guy you set me up with?'

'Such drama over a little bony ankle reveal.' Carlos tuts, remembering.

I shudder. '*Little?* Practically poked me in both eyes, it was so big'—I hold my arms as far apart as I can—'I mean, we're talking at least four inches…'

'Hey,' Oz chimes in. 'No talking about boners in front of the pastries. Or the customers,' he adds as an afterthought.

'*Bony* not boner,' I reply, grinning. 'As in his ankles.' I shudder again. 'Jeans that ended at the calf and brogues with *tassels. Brogues with tassels worn in the pouring rain*. The sound of squelching does not a romantic walk in Central Park make,' I add.

Everyone has a pet peeve, right? It doesn't mean you're not serious about finding someone. It just means it's going to take you longer to find them.

Although, hopefully not a year, I suddenly think.

'You have to stop being so fussy,' Carlos states gently.

Or I could simply put a stop to this and worry about Tina's wedding in a whole three-hundred-and-sixty-five-day *year* from now.

I consider why I didn't stop Carlos when he came up with the idea in the first place but the fact is that as hard as it is to date here in the city, it's even harder to make new friends. Seriously. Everyone single is laser-focused on their quest to meet The One. So, if like me, you suddenly find yourself alone in the big, bustling city because your best friend (also single), has somewhere else she's needed … well, crazy as it sounds, it's easier to find a date-date than a play date.

And after yesterday's conversation with my mother and yes, the aspirational photo from Apartment 33C, I'm thinking I might be ready to put some proper effort in.

'How about I *try* to stop being so fussy?' I ask.

'That's more realistic, I guess. Let's see who I've been keeping in my back pocket, shall we?' Sure enough, Carlos is standing up to take his phone out of the back pocket of his appropriate-length jeans.

He slides the phone towards me, a big grin on his face.

I look down dutifully. 'Um … he's kind of … canine?'

'Huh?' Carlos pulls the phone back towards him and then gets the sappiest look on his face. 'Oops, sorry, that's the cockapoo we're thinking of adopting.'

'Seriously?' I snatch the phone back out of his hands and stare down at the cutest companion you could wish for. 'Oh my god, he's adorable.' I'm smitten and immediately feel a big fat loosening in my heart because imagine having that butter-wouldn't-melt face staring up at you when you got in from work... Imagine all those sunny walks in the park... Imagine it snuggling into the crook of your arm as you doze in front of the TV after a hard day's work...

Imagine it shooting out into the middle of the road...

At the instant wave of nausea, I'm tightening every muscle in my body to shut it down. Absolutely nothing awful is going to happen to a dog I don't even have. I tell myself this another couple of times as with my free hand I start straightening up the sugar dispenser with the creamer jug to perfectly align them in the centre of the table.

Oblivious to my internal catastrophizing, Carlos reaches over and scrolls through a couple more photos. '*This* was the next guy we were thinking of for you.'

I've moved on to gathering up non-existent granules of sugar before I remember the lease on my apartment doesn't allow for pets anyway so I'm already feeling better when I glance down at the photo of a guy in a suit.

Hmm. I'm not swiping left or grasping for excuses at all.

There's a surprised smile on his stubble-chic face as he stands in front of the montage of famous Oscars that I helped to hang on the back wall of the bakery. The inanimate golden Oscar trophy looks like it is sticking absurdly out of the top of his head and on either side of him are decoupaged life-size cut-outs of Oscar Wilde and Oscar de la Renta.

I can't believe a guy that looks this sane (even with a trophy sticking so phallically out of his head) would be single and have agreed to go on a blind date.

'Okay,' I say.

'Okay?'

'Sure, why not?' He doesn't look like a serial killer. He looks friendly and unthreatening.

'Great. Third one's the charm, right?'

'Right.' I wince, flashing back to last night's date. 'But this time, let's make it a foursome. You and Oz. Him and me.'

'If it doesn't work out, I'll date her,' announces the guy third in line.

Carlos swivels to regard the guy so graciously offering himself up to me. 'How much money you make?'

I dribble some of the coffee I've just gulped. 'You can't ask him that,' I splutter and turn to face the guy also. 'He can't ask you that.'

'I make enough,' he says confidently, which immediately puts me off because these days I make enough to make rent *and* buy all the home-decorating magazines I'm addicted to. Naturally, it's made easier on a steady diet of ridiculous hours and ramen, but whose life doesn't feel richer for near exhaustion and noodles?

Carlos narrows his gaze thoughtfully. 'What's the size of your—'

'Definitely do *not* answer that,' I beg Third-In-Line Guy, shooting the woman behind him an apologetic look.

'I was going to say credit score,' Carlos insists, with a grin. 'How many times you been in our shop?'

'Every day,' replies Third-In-Line guy.

'Ha. Every day since…?

Wow. I've never seen Carlos like this. That cockapoo is going to be in safe hands if the endless Dad interrogation is anything to go by although now I'm sort of wondering how Bony-Ankle Guy got past the interview process.

I would love to stay and watch the whole interaction unfold

but I can't be late for work. Getting up from the table, I tune back into Third-In-Line Guy as he admits, 'I've been coming in every day since last week when I moved jobs.'

Carlos's mouth makes an unimpressed downturn. 'We'll talk again when you've been coming in every day for a couple of months and Oz and I feel like we know you.'

'So, this is like a business thing for you two?' I ask Carlos. 'You tell all these guys to come in every day and buy something before I even get a look at the photo?'

Carlos winks and produces a wicked grin that he's cultivated to perfectly match his sun-kissed Brazilian blow-out.

'Unbelievable,' I mutter before adding, 'Make me up a box of those beignets, will you?'

On the walk to work, I try convincing myself I've made such progress lately that going deeper and actually allowing myself to get to know someone properly – allowing someone to get to know *me* properly – won't be as panic-inducing as it sounds.

It's going to be fine.

Really it is.

To reinforce the feeling, I close my eyes and raise my head to the blue sky. I breathe deeply, embracing the gentle breeze and, concentrating, ignore the jarring combination of cars hooting their horns, dogs barking, people shouting and intermittent blasts of motivational-yet-somehow-angry-sounding music. And suddenly, there it is and I smile as I feel cherry blossom kiss my skin.

When I open my eyes and everyone else around me is marching head down, phones out, earbuds in, I want to shout at them to stop so that I can share the petals wafting around in a kaleidoscope of confetti.

But I don't shout. Or even whisper. Can you imagine the response if I started waxing lyrical about nature on a crowded thoroughfare of commuters heading for the subway? I'm pretty sure my boss won't stand for me being carted away by men in white coats as a reason for not attending the weekly meeting to get our rotas, so instead, I focus on how lucky I am to be in a job that allows me to notice the small things.

Life is good.

In fact, life is better than – waaaah!

My heart travels fully into my mouth as I trip on a tree root that has escaped its cement fortress. Fortunately, despite staggering forward like a pastry-armed missile I manage to avoid a humiliating face-planting.

I take a quick look around me, really hoping I only looked marginally like a complete baby fawn taking its first steps and then look down to give the tree root a reproving glare. That's when I notice the white feather on the ground.

Without thinking, I bend down, setting the box down beside me so that I'm hands-free to inspect the feather.

'Hey,' some giant shouts down at me, her five-inch spike of a heel narrowly avoiding the box of beignets. 'What the hell? Does this look like a designated picnic area?'

She barely breaks stride as she click-clacks down the street.

My hand closes gently around the white feather, and I tuck it happily into my tote, perfectly preserved.

Chapter Five

LATE ... FOR A VERY IMPORTANT DATE

Ashleigh

'Y ou're late.'

I look at my watch, and then at Carlos and Oz and then defend myself with, 'By one whole minute. Quick. Call the Dating Etiquette Police.' Then, I can't help but look at the fourth empty chair at the table at Luigi's, the cute little retro Italian we frequent and look back at them accusingly. 'And what a surprise. He isn't even here, yet.'

'He will be,' Carlos says with confidence.

'You said that last time,' I accuse, reaching up to give them a quick kiss hello.

Two weeks ago, Mr. Surprised-Smile Guy, surprised us all by not turning up to the double-date Carlos set up.

It'll be interesting to see what turns out to be worse. The embarrassment I felt during the two hours I sat with Carlos and Oz as Mr. Surprised-Smile Guy left me high and dry in my best little black number and impressively styled hair. Or the cynicism that dogged my every step on the way here that my evening will be a repeat of last time.

Earlier, as I was getting ready, I tried telling myself that worst case scenario, he'll be another no-show and I'll eat Oz's body weight in tiramisu and have a good evening with my friends. But I don't know … I guess what I am learning about going out on these dates, is the amount of energy it takes up.

The energy it takes to meet new people.

The energy it takes to connect.

To make a good impression.

To be myself – wait – no, to be the *best* version of myself.

All on top of working long hours and carrying around enough nervous energy to power an entire city.

Is it really worth it just to have someone to hang out with?

I remind myself of the two intervening phone calls my mother has made now she's discovered I have spare time during my cleaning of Apartment 33C.

'Relax, he'll be here,' Oz says. 'We have visual confirmation.'

'Visual confirmation?'

'You think we'd put you through a no-show again?'

My heart, which I have told strictly *not* to melt on this date, starts to feel gooey. 'So – what – you've got people stationed across the city cataloguing his every movement?'

'Three people,' Oz confirms. 'Triangulated to this exact location. Texting in when they see him.' Oz looks down at his phone. 'Last seen three blocks away. Progress is slow but allegedly he's looking really sharp. ETA twelve minutes.'

'Oh my God, you're serious? You've downloaded an app?' I go up on tiptoes to try and get a look. 'And why are you speaking like an undercover operative? You're not in cahoots with my mother, are you?'

Maybe the bakery is a cover too.

I break out into a sweat.

Mr. Surprised-Smile Guy's really turning up this time.

I should have made more effort.

As if reading my mind Carlos suddenly says, 'Are you wearing *polyester*?' Carlos feels the material of my sleeve. 'You know how hot it gets in here. Polyester does not breathe.'

What can I say?

Tonight, the energy didn't translate to me looking good. That, plus I pulled a double to cover for a couple of staff out sick. My hair is up in its usual ponytail and I have on jeans, and a button-down black shirt that I changed into at the last minute. I shrug and confess, 'I thought he was going to be another no-show and I'd be drowning my sorrows in tiramisu so I went with comfortable instead. And this shirt isn't polyester. It's silk.' I look down. 'Okay, probably not. But either way, let's agree it's understated elegance and shiny-chicness.'

'Shiny-shitness, maybe.' Carlos looks like he is contemplating us swapping shirts but then, after a quick glance to Oz, changes his mind. 'Never mind. No time. Quick, sit down. And look relaxed,' he orders, even as he's busy undoing the first two buttons of my shirt.

'I'm not sure – hey—' My butt misses the chair Oz has pulled out for me and I hit the floor with a thud.

Spectacular.

'With you two as chaperones,' I mutter, 'it's a wonder I'll ever see any action.'

'Ashleigh, I assume?'

I want to say the 'what happens when you assume' thing as a face looms at me at ground level but as I take in the smile on Mr.

Surprised-Smile Guy's face I wonder instead if my polyester shirt has caught fire because it suddenly feels hot in here.

Large, warm hands reach out to easily haul me to my feet.

And so that is how I formally meet Zach Weldon.

Owner of the surprised smile.

Stander-upper of epic proportions.

Okay. One time.

I frown as his gaze sort of gets stuck on my chest area.

I look down and, oh, good lord.

My shirt is open to the waist giving him an eyeful of my non-lacy washed-so-many-times-it's-now-off-white comfort bra.

My hands go to the buttons of my shirt but are beaten to it by Carlos's hands, which Oz immediately reaches over to slap away.

'I-um, hi, so, I'm Ashleigh Rivera, and despite all evidence to the contrary, under normal circumstances I successfully dress myself every day.' My smile is that kind of shy smile as I begin re-buttoning my shirt.

'Hi.' Zach smiles back at me and his smile is tinged with shyness too. 'I'm Zach Weldon, and I have no problem with how you dress. Or don't. Okay, that came out wrong.'

'Sit. Sit,' Carlos insists, clearly delighted with Zach and my flirting prowess. He pulls out his chair and eyeballs Oz to do the same.

The small square table shifts slightly as Oz moves his large frame against it and I notice Zach reach out in time to grab the crutch he's leant against it. It is the perfect accessory to the moon boot he is wearing.

'The broken toe was for real, then?' I ask.

That was the excuse he texted Carlos with two weeks ago to which I muttered words along the lines of, 'If you're going to lie, at least make it a good one,' before ordering a round of shots.

'Actually, it's a broken ankle. Result of a hospital-pass situation on the soccer field.'

Obviously, what I am supposed to do at this point is ask how he is doing – if there's serious damage done – if he plays in an essential-to-the-team position etc.

Instead, what comes out is, 'Soccer? Oh, do you know George?'

As soon as I ask the question, I realise it's ridiculous. It's just that today I may have got a little over-excited on account of finding one whole new personal effect nestled within the shelves of Apartment 33C when I was investigating – *cleaning*. When I was cleaning.

It was another photo of George.

Covered in mud and grinning from ear to ear.

Proof that he isn't the complete neat freak I thought he was.

I think he must be a kids' soccer coach or something because he was surrounded by them, all in front of a goal, each of them also grinning from ear to ear.

'George?' Zach politely smiles as he waits for me to sit down.

Carlos tries communicating something urgent to me with his eyes as he passes me a menu.

I ignore him and concentrate on Zach. 'George Northcote? He coaches a kids' team, I think.'

Zach blinks. 'No, I don't think so. I play with some of the guys from work. So…'

'Sorry. Obviously, you don't know George.'

Across from me, I see Oz mouth to Carlos, 'Do *we* even know George?' and I don't need to look at Carlos to know he is about to ask me who the hell George is. 'Is your ankle painful?' I quickly ask.

'Only when I laugh,' Zach replies, and we all smile.

Chapter Six

EMPTY CHAIRS AND EMPTY TABLES

Ashleigh

I t's about the three-quarter mark of the evening and our desserts have just been set before us when I shout out the word 'gelatinous' in triumph. I fist-bump the air in celebration, nearly knocking my wine glass over in the process and everyone looks at my tiramisu with alarm.

Carlos whispers out of the corner of his mouth, 'Are you having a stroke?'

I look at Zach who looks unsure what to make of my outburst. Concerned for my welfare? Concerned for his welfare? Concerned for the tiramisu? I can't tell.

Damn.

It was all going so well.

I turn to Carlos whose expression clearly states: Make this better.

'Sorry,' I say, taking a huge swig of wine. 'I don't usually shout out words randomly like that. And definitely not during sex.'

'Jesus,' Carlos whispers.

I literally cannot believe I just said that.

Who does that? That was not making it better.

I take another gulp of wine. 'It just came to me. The final answer in George's crossword,' I explain. 'Having the consistency of jelly … ten letters … gelatinous, right?'

'Do you live with George?' Zach asks.

'Oh,' I say. What a bizarre question to ask. I laugh nervously. 'No. Of course not. What would make you think that?'

'Maybe because you keep talking about him?' Oz helpfully supplies.

I shove a mouthful of tiramisu in my mouth and remain schtum.

Just between us though … not only did I discover the photo while I was cleaning, and again, I use the term cleaning lightly, because three visits in and I still haven't had to do anything really, but anyway, there was a newspaper sitting on his desk.

Specifically, in his in-tray.

Bold as brass.

Folded neatly at the crossword.

The one remaining clue in the crossword practically screaming at me, pleading with me to put it out of its misery by completing it.

I love crosswords.

Used to time myself doing them.

I sneak a look at Zach. He is looking marginally more relaxed so I won't tell him that.

I look at Oz.

He is busy devouring his own portion of tiramisu.

I can't look at Carlos for fear of being hauled out on my ass and handed over to the Embarrassingly Crap at Dating authorities.

Help?

I used to be okay at this, I think.

Dating.

I definitely didn't use to get drunk on two glasses of wine because I was so tired.

Or so wired.

When did the nervous energy become my mortal enemy?

Because I swear, I used to be better at making a good first impression.

I was good at flirting.

Great at it.

Before my bestie, Sarah, had to move away, I helped her through all her first-date nightmares. Standing further down from her at the bar so that she could have her moment to shine with a potentially great guy. Feeding her lines via text when she got tongue-tied.

Then, sitting at tables in coffee houses, doing crosswords while covertly making sure she was okay as meeting-in-the-bar turned into a first date.

Me, always having her back.

Her, having mine right back.

My gaze goes automatically to the table behind Oz and Zach.

It is empty.

Emotion hits me like a wrecking ball, making me lurch to my feet, nearly dragging the kitsch tablecloth with me. 'Excuse me,' I mumble. Three pairs of eyes look at me expectantly. 'Restroom,' I mutter, making a break for it.

I stumble my way through the tables heading for the back of the restaurant and push open the right-hand side door.

Inside I stare at myself in the mirror, frowning helplessly.

Should I text Carlos and tell him I'm leaving … out the tiny bathroom window?

If only I hadn't left my phone at the table.

I stare hard at my reflection.

I want this.

I'm ready for this.

Except…

I honestly can't tell if this date is going well or going mortifyingly not well.

I don't even know how I feel either way.

None of the previous dates have gone like this.

Is it because I can't find anything wrong with Zach and it's dawning on me that with my friends here, any excuse for not seeing him again has to be plausible? Real.

I try to envision if I will think about Zach as I slide beneath the covers of my bed tonight. Will there be a smile on my face? Will I be hugging my pillow?

A picture of George enters my head and I think I actually moan in denial.

Or lust?

My heart skips a beat.

Nope.

There's no lusting when it comes to clients.

And definitely not when there's a perfectly good man who's available and whom I've actually met, and is waiting at a red-and-white checker-clothed table just outside my new comfort zone.

I turn on the cold-water tap. Roll up my polyester sleeves and run icy water over the pulse points on my wrists.

The door to the restroom opens and I glance up as a woman, my age, comes in.

'Ashleigh?'

How does she know my name? Probably works for the CIA with my mother. And Oz.

'Yes?'

She passes me a note. 'A guy with great hair asked me to give you this.'

I dry my hands, take the note and open it.

It is a full-blown essay from Carlos.

Jeez.

How the hell can anyone write so much on a receipt for – I turn it over – hair product!

Hon, what the hell? Stop talking about some guy called George. Who even is George? It's not okay to be talking about other guys when you're on a date. That's simple 101 and I know you're an intelligent woman, not some ingénue. (Ingénue! Let's take a moment to high-five my word power being right up there with gelatinous.)

Anyway.

Zach is nice, right? He likes you, right? He likes you even though you're acting like you have a bad crush on some other guy. You could hang out with Zach on the weekend and actually talk as well as have sex. I thought that was what you wanted. I know how hard meeting new people must be for you since —

I stop reading.

'First date, huh?' the note-passer asks.

I nod, neatly folding up Carlos's essay into smooth precise quarters before placing it in my pocket.

'Well, I'd trust your friend. Zach seems nice.'

'How'd you know his name was Zach? Oh. Right. CIA.'

She frowns, holds her hands up and says, 'I wanted to make sure I wasn't passing you something from some psycho-stalker, so I read it. Plus, I'm nosy.'

I smile at her. 'Appreciate it.' I study her casual yet put-together look in admiration. Jeans, shirt, subtle makeup but hair down and killer heels.

That's what I forgot. The heels. Maybe if I hadn't forgotten it wouldn't be so easy to slip into non-date lunacy-talk. 'Are you on a date, too?' I ask.

'Yeah. But he's a total mouth-breather. I was messaging my friend to beg her to stop by and save me when I was stopped by your guy out there. Thought I'd kill a few minutes in here.'

'Sorry about your date,' I say, feeling guilty Carlos was having to save me from myself by writing instructions for me.

'No problem. Got to kiss a lot of frogs, right? Unless this George guy is a prince then I'd definitely recommend you kissing him. A lot.'

'George?' I'm instantly distracted from my teary thoughts. 'I have no idea whether George is a prince or a frog. I have no business knowing.'

'Uh-huh. Well, good luck. By the way, your shirt is buttoned up wrong, did you know?'

I look down.

Good grief, I am so tragic at this. I must have re-buttoned it wrongly earlier. On the plus side, Zach hasn't said a word and how cute is that?

I re-button shirt and sleeves with a new determination. 'Thanks. You too,' I reply as I prepare to go back to the table and repair the damage.

'Hey, us serial daters got to stick together.'

Serial dater?

I just want someone to hang out with at the weekend.

And possibly someone to take to my cousin's wedding a year

plus from now. Someone my CIA-trained family won't read as an individual I've plucked off the street.

As I return to the table and take my seat, Zach says, 'So, neither of these two mentioned what you do?'

'What I do?'

'For work?'

I feel the apology for my strange outburst followed by abrupt exit sort of slip off my face. His reaction is going to be the reason I don't pull out all the stops to get a second date.

I draw in a breath. 'I'm a cleaner.'

'Cleaner?'

'Yep. Cleaner.'

'Domestic, office, or assassin's assistant?'

'Does it matter?'

'Not at all. Just trying to find out a little bit more about you.'

'Why?'

'Okay,' Zach looks mock-confused. 'I need to have it out with my best friend because he definitely told me all those years ago that asking about the other person on a date is considered plain good manners.'

I soften towards him some more. 'Right. He was right. Um, so what do you do?'

'HVAC engineer.'

'Domestic, commercial or … okay, I'm pretty sure that while an assassin may appreciate good heating, ventilation and air-con, it's not a nailed-on requirement?' I ask.

'Nice,' he says, his grin making me feel like I imagined my awful behaviour. Like I'm not a phoney. Like I don't dream about unattainable men because it's safe. 'Do you like being a cleaner, or is that a *dirty* question?'

'There's always a place for *dirty* in my heart,' I flirt back and feel a sort of relaxing going on, not only in my chest but in Carlos and Oz too. I grin, and add, 'I actually love my job.'

'Good for you. Makes the day go quicker, right?'

I decide not to tell him that cleaning legit saved my life. 'And you – you have a passion for um, heating, ventilation and air-con?' Suddenly I'm feeling what everyone who's ever asked me about cleaning might be feeling … because … how is this in any way interesting? Then again. It's New York. Freezing in the winter, boiling in the summer.

'I do,' Zach says, and his tone is simple and uncomplicated, and I like that. I like the sound of simple and uncomplicated a lot.

'You were wearing a suit in your publicity shot.'

'Publicity shot?'

'The photo these guys took of you,' I explain.

'Ah. I was on my way to the bank to get a business loan. Starting up on my own.'

'Good for you.'

'Thank you. It's a really exciting time for me.'

'You really don't mind that I'm a cleaner?'

'Why would I?'

'Exactly. Why would you?' chirps Carlos. 'Another bottle?'

Later, as I unlock the four locks to my apartment, I'm feeling exhausted but happy.

I walk the three steps into my living area and fall onto my bed. There's no need to unhook the curtain and pull it across so there's a divide between my bed and the couch anymore.

I move my arm into the space between the mattress and the small of my back hoping to ease out the kinks from the long day.

At least I don't have to wear skyscraper heels all day. Don't miss that at all, I tell myself before deliberately moving my mind along.

A second date.

With Zach.

He might turn into company on the weekends.

I sit up so that I don't accidentally fall asleep, check my phone for tomorrow's schedule before I set my alarm, then find a text. Janice is still out sick so I reply I'll cover for her, and reset my alarm for an hour earlier.

I kick off my shoes and think, I have to be better at talking like a normal person now I've met Zach. I don't want to mess it up before it's even started.

But I guess I should also be realistic, right?

I mean, what if I can't think of anything to say?

What if he breaks his other ankle on the way to our date?

What if I get stuck in traffic, arrive late and find he's given up waiting for me?

What if?

What if?

What if...

Shit.

Tired as I am, before the endless thoughts can intrude properly, I drag myself to my feet, walk to my kitchen sink, pull on my leopard print rubber gloves and open the cupboard to get the eco lemon-scented cleaner out.

It only takes me a minute to wipe the solution over the tidied countertops, so I open the oven and take out the racks. I soak them and then clean them and then dry them and then stack them neatly back inside the oven and by the time I finish, my breathing is back to normal and the over-crowding thoughts are tamed.

I start peeling off my clothes, taking the time to fold each item

46

before I put them in the laundry bin and then take my Hufflepuff Tee from under my pillow and put it on. I yawn and go to hang my bag on the hook between the potted plant and TV and then remember I put two white feathers in it today.

Smiling I take them out, feel their reassuring softness in my palm and trundle to the hallway console table. The wooden bowl is nearly overflowing with all the feathers I've collected.

Nearly enough for another collage.

The evening wasn't as bad as it could have been.

Not by a long shot.

And who knows how well the second date will go?

It feels like it will go well.

I smile, smoothing my hand over the collection of soft feathers. It feels good to think I'm being looked out for.

Chapter Seven

JOB SATISFACTION RATING

George

I'm standing in front of the Head of the Harrison Richards Advertising Agency's desk, waiting. His EA showed me into the impressively large office, so I'm pretty sure I am exactly where I'm supposed to be, at the exact scheduled time.

Harrison Richards, though, keeps right on typing, his fingers hitting the keyboard assertively.

He doesn't acknowledge me in any way.

It's a power thing, I think.

Old school.

Quite effective if you let it be.

I'm not going to let it be.

I choose, instead, to think about the many things I admire about Anya's father, Harrison Richards.

Halfway through a list of his award-winning campaigns (which handily happen to be framed along the office wall adjacent to his desk) he lifts his head and grins. 'George. It's that time already? Sit yourself down,' he invites, nodding to the chairs in front of his desk. 'I guess you must know what this is about?'

I really hope so.

I mean, I've worked towards this moment since starting in the London office.

Worked hard. And loved every minute of it, so if it's not about this I'm going to feel like a right idiot, not to mention rubbish at my job.

I smile – my most charming and self-deprecating smile, Anya calls it. 'I hope so, Mr. Richards.'

'Please, we're on a first-name basis, surely?'

This is a test, so I smile again and take the seat proffered, smoothing out the tie that Anya picked out for this very meeting. 'How's Mrs. Richards,' I ask. 'I hear she hasn't been very well?'

'Elizabeth?' Harrison frowns. 'Not well?'

I'm sure Anya told me her mother had flu and so she was going to visit her last week, which was why she couldn't make our date night.

'A cold, I think,' I offer.

'Oh.' Harrison looks non-plussed. 'Well, if she had one, she brushed it right off. Elizabeth has the constitution of an ox, that's what you Brits say, isn't it?'

Yes. We say it especially when wandering the corridors of our Downton Abbey-esque houses, insisting we don't need to get one of the maids up to light another fire!

I think about the small three-bed semi-detached house I grew up in on an estate of three hundred identical three-bedroomed semi-detached houses and tell myself that ours might not have been the only one that was clinically spotless inside and increase the wattage of my smile, very much hoping I don't end up in grinning-like-a-buffoon territory. To be fair I've met Elizabeth

Richards precisely once when Anya introduced us at the annual summer charity gala the agency puts on in London.

I'm sure I am not the only one who struggles to feel any real joy in attending charity galas so make it a point not to judge anyone I meet there. Particularly not on their constitution. I remember Elizabeth Richards being every bit as beautiful as her daughter and that she was stellar at knowing exactly what to say to encourage those huge donations.

Anya gets her determination from both of her parents, I think. It is one of the things I love about her – her ability to work three to four times as hard as anyone else. She's had to. Harrison made it very clear she'd get no special treatment working for him and she's always made it equally clear she places the utmost value in that challenge.

Sometimes I do wonder that every minute is about work, but then, if you have to work that hard just to level the field, well, it isn't as if I don't know what that feels like from when I was younger, in and out of hospital and having to work harder just to catch up.

'I've always been impressed with your work, George,' Harrison now says to me. 'From the moment I interviewed you in London, I knew you'd be a good fit. Hardworking. Ambitious. Creative. And when you accompanied Anya back here last year, I had no doubt you were going to hit the ground running and not on her coattails. Your work on the Yeong campaign is outstanding.'

I blink.

I've never had this much praise heaped upon me.

Harrison isn't the type.

Or maybe when you hit that inner circle, he is?

I smooth out a non-existent wrinkle in my tie in the aim of getting it, and myself, to sit more comfortably.

'So, I don't expect this will come as any great surprise to you, the position of Senior Account Manager is yours.'

Brilliant.

Guess I finally caught up *and* got ahead.

I wait for the rush of pride, confidence, happiness, to wash over me.

When they don't, my heart starts racing.

Um … not brilliant?

I think I blink again.

I mean, surely, I do something?

React in some way?

And, dear God, not in this awful, horribly familiar, pressurised feeling in my chest way again.

I can't have another panic attack again.

Can't.

Would rather spontaneously combust.

'George? Don't tell me you're shocked by the offer?'

'Sorry. No.' It is an effort to get my voice out without sounding like I am panting. Panting, for God's sake! 'Of course not. Just absorbing,' I force out. 'I've made no secret this is something I've wanted.'

'You're a pressure player. Knew it from the moment we met.'

My chest tightens and I really, really wish he would stop talking about pressure.

'Anya will have a few junior account executives in mind for you to mentor alongside your team. It doesn't stop now, you realise. I'm expecting more accounts like Yeong Cosmetics.'

'I already have feelers in play,' I reply, hoping that sheer will can prevent the sweat from popping out on my upper lip. 'There's a large hospitality company looking for representation I've had my eye on.'

'Excellent.' Harrison grins. 'I'll expect an update by the end of the week. But for now, go, celebrate. You've earned it.'

'Perhaps a mini celebration and then right back to it.' And by mini celebration, I'm thinking about ordering a large tank of oxygen and sitting in a quiet room with it.

'Speaking of celebrations,' Harrison continues. 'If I can end this meeting on a personal note? I like seeing my daughter happy, George.'

This time it's easy to draw in oxygen as I think about how I intend to make her very happy – when we celebrate tonight. Maybe, as it's a special occasion, she will stay over for the weekend and get relaxed enough that she'll let me do that thing that sort of makes her scream-snort-giggle with pleasure and—

'I have to say, that before she met you, I'm not sure I ever heard my daughter giggle.'

I hope to God that Harrison cannot read minds.

'You make her happy, George.'

'We make each other happy, Harrison,' I manage to say.

'And if there was a bigger celebration to be coming up … of a more personal nature … well, Elizabeth and I wouldn't be displeased.'

Oh.

Finally, I get it.

He's talking about marriage.

As in me and Anya.

Tying the knot.

Getting hitched.

Betrothed.

Engaged.

Am I maybe only being given this promotion so that when Anya and I do get married we look equal within the company?

Openly sweating now.

I hope my new office has adjustable air-con.

I try a laugh.

Which must work, because suddenly I'm being shown out with a camaraderie type hand-slap to my shoulder.

In my new office, I plonk myself down and yank my tie to the side, swiftly unsnapping the top button of my shirt.

It's happening again.

The shortness of breath, the ringing ears, the goddamn awful pressure in my chest. As I sit swamped with sensation, I can remember not one bit of the advice I googled about dealing with panic attacks.

Perhaps some water? There must be a mini-fridge in here somewhere. I jump up and look in the sideboard and, bingo. I take out a bottle of water, unscrew the top and try to remind myself not to chug it thereby adding choking to the list.

It's as I'm bringing the bottle back down to the desk that I notice a square brown leather box with a ribbon tied around it, resting on top of today's *Times* crossword.

Eternally grateful for the distraction, I reach out, sweep the box to one side, and focus on the crossword.

Some of the pressure in my chest eases and I crack a smile thinking how Anya knows me so well.

I love crosswords.

They're one of the few things I brought from childhood into adulthood that I don't associate any negativity with.

My gaze seeks out the longest word in the middle of the puzzle and I read the clue for it.

Roman poet Horace translation, three words

I open the top drawer of my desk and the ubiquitous lone pen rolls into my palm. On the crossword, I draw two heavy lines in the long row of boxes to demark the three words.

Horace... Horace... Oh, I've got it: Carpe Diem. Translation – seize the day

With heart rate nearly back to normal and my breathing coming much easier now, I reach for the leather box that accompanied the crossword.

I might be breathing easier but I notice there's a tell-tale shaking in my hand.

Maybe it's a ring?

No. Anya would never take the lead in a marriage proposal.

She's too traditional.

It turns out so am I as I push back on the knowledge that just because Anya and I have discussed where we'd both like to be in our careers before we get married, choosing when *I* propose means I will have nixed any feeling of being 'levelled-up' beforehand.

Besides, the box can't have a ring in it, anyway. It's far too big.

I rip off the ribbon and open the box.

A very expensive statement watch is nestled inside along with a note in Anya's precise script, saying, *'I knew you could do it. You're going to be great. Love, Anya xx'*

I frown, because honestly the watch is beautiful...

But also, nothing like the simple, leather-strapped analogue watch that my grandfather wrapped around my wrist the day he came to visit me in hospital with a stack of crossword puzzles. The day he sat with me and held my hand and told me he knew I was tired. Understood I was frustrated. Even a little scared. But that the watch, so loose as he put it on my wrist, had magic inside the tiny cogs that kept it going.

That when I felt the cogs were slowing and that time was stretching unbearably it would remind me to use that time to imagine all the great things I was going to achieve when I was better. And then, when it sped up, it meant that I was ready. I was well.

And it was time to live life…

It was time to seize the day.

Chapter Eight

TIME AFTER TIME

George

I pick up the phone to talk to Anya and thank her for the watch.

She answers on the second ring with a 'You're welcome.'

Not, 'Hey, hon' or 'Congratulations', but instead, 'You're welcome' like she hasn't quite got the time to have a full conversation. I glance at my old watch and realise she's probably about to go into a meeting.

'Maybe it'll be me who is saying "You're welcome" back to you tonight,' I tease. 'How would you like to come over to find me wearing nothing but your gift?'

There is a startled silence from her end, reminding me we have that rule about no flirting at work. But still. It's a special occasion, right? I hold my breath, forcing her to answer, which isn't our dynamic but sometimes it's good to try new things.

'That sounds like an offer too good to refuse,' Anya replies and I can hear the smile in her voice.

My heart jumps with surprised pleasure. Maybe I should think outside our dynamic a little more often. Maybe—

'Wait. Tonight?' Anya interrupts my foray into fantasy land. 'I'm sorry, George. I have the Prender launch.'

Shit.

'Why don't you message the gang for drinks?' she suggests.

The 'gang' are the handful of friends we see when we have time. Actually, they're more her friends. And when I say friends – they're mostly colleagues. I guess I could go out for a few drinks with them tonight. The fact it will end up being all about work shouldn't be a turn-off when we'd essentially be celebrating my promotion, and I guess they're never going to become *my* friends if I don't put the effort in.

Out of nowhere, I think of nights out down The Bedraggled Badger pub back in England with my brother and all our mates and my chest gets really tight again.

I try to force a smile into my voice. 'You're seriously turning down Naked George of the Concrete Jungle Where Dreams Are Made for a couple of hours standing around awkwardly high tables eating cardboard canapes?'

'I'm really sorry, George.'

'Stop by after. Stay over tonight.' *Seize the night.*

'Can we make it tomorrow night, instead?'

'Sure.' I try not to let the disappointment show in my voice, being that I am not a petulant child and relationships are all about compromise and, okay, because I am certainly not going to beg, either.

As if she can sense me trying hard, she says, 'I'll make it up to you, I promise.'

'Yeah?' This perks me right up. I wait for further flirting.

Silence.

Apparently, that was it.

'Hey, thanks for finishing the crossword off for me the other week,' I say in a bid to spin the short conversation out as much as I can.

'Huh?'

'Gelatinous. Remember? It was doing my head in to have that one clue remaining.'

'George, you know crosswords aren't my thing.'

'Sure, but did you not leave a crossword under my amazing new watch?'

'Well, I know they're *your* thing.'

I can hear the indulgent tone in her voice but I'm confused. Does this mean, then, that my new cleaner took it upon themselves to finish my crossword?

Doesn't seem quite right.

Should I report it?

On the other hand, it was nice to have it finished.

And the apartment feels spotless and somehow a bit more homey. It probably helps that the aroma of bleach is gone.

I think I'll leave it alone for now.

'So, I have a meeting,' Anya says, 'that if I rush, I won't be late to.'

'Great. Hey – while you're walking to your meeting… I realise both of us are busy at the moment but—'

'George, I'm serious. I really have to go.'

'Okay. But I was thinking, how about we go away for the weekend?'

Silence.

She's hung up on me already.

Not petulant. Not petulant.

But as I put down my phone, I'm staring down at my new watch feeling dejected.

Rejected.

I try to pep myself up. Make tomorrow night about delayed gratification and all the better for it. But if I'm honest, what I really want right now is my girlfriend wrapping her arms around me and sharing this moment with me.

I breathe in sharply. That all sounds more than a bit needy, right?

I shake it off and start composing an email asking the gang to drinks at the sports bar one block over before remembering most of them will be attending the Prender launch and that there's every chance that the only one who will respond is Tim Duggins and ... nope ... definitely not up for listening to him get more and more drunk and less and less circumspect about what he tells me about the dating scene in New York.

I put on my new watch.

Tell myself to get on with my day.

The important thing is that I got the promotion.

Not when I celebrate getting it.

Chapter Nine

THE LEGEND IN APARTMENT 33A

Ashleigh

'I like you, Ashleigh Rivera.'

The matter-of-fact statement from Mrs. Hildegard Lundy, acquaintance of one week and owner of the apartment down the hall from George Northcote, fills me with warmth as I pick up one of her floral teapots made from see-through quality porcelain.

'Usually, people head straight for the dishwasher with all this,' Mrs. Lundy adds with a nod to the delicate china splayed out across the seats-twelve dining room table. 'I'm not sure I've ever had anyone asking how I prefer it to be cleaned before.'

'At Sparkle we pride ourselves—'

The gentle hand on my arm is accompanied by, 'Do you have a problem with people telling you they like you, dear?'

'Of course not.' I feel myself blush. This is all very new to me, having the owner around while I clean, but she's such fun. I've been hearing about how she's been holding afternoon tea networking soirées once a month for the past fifty years and I want to know all the details.

The How Did These Tea Parties Come About.

The Who Attends.

The Whys.

The questions are so reminiscent of the old me that my voice has dried up.

'Good,' announces Mrs. Lundy. 'It's always better when a person can simply accept a compliment.'

I start loading up a tower of teacups to carry back to the kitchen but when I notice Mrs. Lundy traipsing behind me with a stack of matching saucers, I draw the line. 'Oh, Mrs. Lundy, no. This is my job. I'm really very happy to clean these all for you by hand.'

'Nonsense. Helping keeps me active.'

Mrs. Lundy doesn't look a day over eighty, yet I suspect that she is and I guess cleaning helps keep me sane, so, who am I to argue? Besides, the client is always right, so I simply nod my head, but seriously? I don't think I've ever had a client help me clean their own place before. And what a place it is. It turns out that Hildegard Lundy used to be a set designer in Hollywood, hence the fabulous interior starting with about a mile of black and white framed photos of Hollywood's acting alumni. The rest of the place is magazine-shoot ready as well. A coming together of styles and although every surface contains a keepsake, every wall a photograph and every corner a memory, it all screams lived in.

Loved.

It's a joy to clean and I have every faith it will provide me with opportunity after opportunity to forget about my little world and wonder about this one.

It's also about as far away as possible in design and homeliness as Apartment 33C.

To stop myself mulling over the fact that there was another crossword with one last clue left on George's desk this morning and the tussle I had with whether to answer it (I couldn't resist), I ask, 'So is keeping active the secret to your youthful looks and sharp mind, Mrs. Lundy?'

'Well, it doesn't beat a bout of sweaty sex, but it helps.'

The tower of teacups rattles as I put them on the counter next to the sink.

'Does talking about sex make you uncomfortable, dear?'

'Yes?'

'Interesting.'

'I mean, as in, talking about it with a lady I just met who pays my wages, not as in "I have issues" uncomfortable.'

'I see.' Hardly a beat passes before she asks, 'And what's the secret that cleaning saves you from?'

I feel my jaw drop open. 'I—' and my voice has dried up again.

'When you get to my age, you'll discover there aren't really any inappropriate questions.'

'Promise?' I think about all the times I should have asked questions but didn't like to push – think about all the people I should have pushed for answers but didn't and plunge the teapot into the hot and soft, soothing, sudsy water.

'You've accomplished nearly double the workload this morning compared with last week. I'm curious to know if there's a reason for the pent-up energy?'

She remains quietly at my side. Not filling the conversational space, so that I feel no other option than to answer. 'I have something to do after this that I am not looking forward to.'

'Ah. Don't do it, then.'

Revelation! To hear a grownup giving me permission not to do something I absolutely do not want to do. 'I have to,' I say, lifting the teapot out to gently place it on the drainer before taking the stack of saucers into the water.

'What will happen if you don't?'

I systematically wipe the cloth over a saucer, concentrating on the soothing movement. 'I guess I might not be able to respect myself if I don't?' I sigh at the admission. I would never be admitting all this to Carlos or Oz. Mrs. Lundy must be getting me at a weak moment. Relaxed after a sweaty bout of cleaning.

'And why is that?' Mrs. Lundy asks.

I put the saucer on the drainer. Pick up another one, unaware my wiping action is slower as I admit, 'I made a promise to someone that I would do this one, small, easy, thing.'

Not small, I think.

Not easy.

'And what were the circumstances in which you made this promise?'

I turn to look at her. 'What do you mean?'

The sprightly eighty-plus-year-old has a twinkle in her eye as she says, 'Well, if you were kidnapped, tied up and it was a condition of your freedom, that's not really a fair promise now, is it?'

I think I love Mrs. Lundy. 'If only I could put that spin on it. But it was more of a "I think you'd be really good at this and it would really help me out" request.'

Mrs. Lundy looks at me for what seems like an eternity before she simply nods her head. 'And you're the sort of person who follows through.'

I pull the plug to release the soapy water. Wipe my hands.

Want to admit exactly how long it has taken me to follow through on this promise.

'You don't get a lot of that nowadays,' Mrs. Lundy murmurs. 'Impressive.'

'I guess I wish I felt more ready.'

'It can be hard when you build up a time frame in your head for when you think something's got to be achieved by.'

'Right. But I can't keep letting myself off this thing and I think I'll be okay as soon as I get there. You know? Get into it? At least, I'm almost sure. But, what if I'm not? What if—' I head back out to the dining table in the hope I missed a stack of china to wash.

'What's the worst that can happen?'

'I don't know, I guess, I might have a meltdown?' For meltdown read full-on-step-back-to-let-the-crazy-lady-pass moment.

'And?'

'I don't want to have a meltdown in front of people I respect.'

'Ah.'

'Or in front of people who have been through worse than me.'

'One day you're going to have to tell me your story.'

I can't imagine Mrs. Lundy settling for my story being that I'm in a job I love and have a family who, while annoying, make me feel loved and supported. But life's all about nuance and, I've discovered, about how you'll find ways of not doing what you promised you were going to do when it one hundred per cent takes you out of your comfort zone.

I try and accept the fact that the table is empty and I really have no more cleaning scheduled for the day. 'Words of wisdom, please?'

Mrs. Lundy bursts into delighted laughter. 'What makes you think I'm wise, dear?'

'What are you talking about? With age comes wisdom, right?'

'Not always been my experience but let's see...' She brings a finger to her lips and taps thoughtfully against them. 'How about, "Accept that whatever happens, you'll be able to deal with it."?'

'Um...' In theory this is what I've been trying to tell myself. In practice it really doesn't transfer.

'No? Well then, how about, feel the fear and do it anyway?'

'I have the first part down. It's exactly what stops me from following through with the second part,' I admit.

'Wait, I've got the perfect advice,' Mrs. Lundy suggests. 'Don't be a pussy.'

My eyes widen to the size of one of the saucers I've just cleaned. That's just the sort of thing Sarah would say.

'Um ... okay. Don't be a wuss. Just like that?'

She nods her head like it is the easiest thing in the world. 'Just like that.'

'Okay.' This time the word comes out with confidence.

'You can leave now if you like – seize the bull by the horns.'

'Okay,' I repeat to myself. Seconds later and I'm tugging my purse strap over my shoulder before turning around to face her. 'I can totally do this?'

'Totally. And whatever "this" is, I look forward to hearing about it next week, dear.'

'Thanks Mrs. Lundy.'

'Hildy.'

———

Standing outside the hospital, I'm forced to realise my confidence didn't leave Apartment 33A with me.

I don't think I can do this.

Honestly.

I really don't.

All that confidence I felt with Mrs. Lundy.

Gone.

Vanished.

I stare at the front entrance, flyer clutched tightly in my hands. I'm not even sure why I always bring the flyer with me. It isn't as if I wouldn't know where I was going once inside the doors. If I ever make it through the front doors, that is.

I picture the route in my head. Main floor and then up the elevator to the fourth floor. Follow the yellow line marked on the floor and it'll be halfway down the corridor on the right. I wonder if the yellow line is supposed to be representative of The Yellow Brick Road. It doesn't matter, as the final destination isn't Oz, but a place called Really Complicated.

My hands are clammy.

If I turned around and walked away right now, no one would ever know.

Okay.

Hildegard Lundy will take one look at my face next week and know.

This is why cleaners hate it when clients are home when they arrive to clean.

A chuff of breath leaves my body in frustration, leaving me light-headed.

I shouldn't have promised.

I stare accusingly at the hospital entrance and not for the first time in this little charade I pull off every week, I blame Sarah.

It is so completely her fault I'm in this position.

Telling me I'd be so good at it.

Pushing.

Pushing.

Pushing.

And when that didn't work, telling me I might meet someone great while doing it.

It's a credit to the tequila we were drinking at the time that I ever fell for that line.

Like, who am I going to meet on a children's ward?

Other than the kids I would be there to read to, and possibly their parents. Even if, by pure happenstance, some of those dads were single, I'm pretty sure they might have a little more on their minds than flirting with the volunteer readers.

I don't want to do this.

What started out as something small and easy that Sarah knew I had little intention of following through on has turned into something way bigger so that now all I can think is:

Haven't I been through enough?

But what about the poor little sick children?

The exact words Sarah would guilt me with if she wasn't busy elsewhere and could see me walking up and down, wearing a groove in the concrete, and throwing suspicious looks over my shoulder because the hospital feels as if it's creeping closer every time I look away.

She would rush out the entrance in her scrubs, put her hand on my arm, stick out her bottom lip and say, 'But what about the poor little sick ch—'

Damn it.

I promised.

And what the hell am I going to tell Mrs. Lundy when she asks?

She said I looked like someone who followed through.

The guilt at how much that is *not* true settles on my shoulders so that in my next breath I'm thinking, 'Screw it,' and turning around and heading for the safety of the subway that will rush me away from all of this. Next week, if I am asked, I will simply be honest and tell her I didn't do it.

When she asks why, I will *own* my cowardice and I will— aargh! Suddenly I'm turning around and heading straight back to the hospital, flyer clutched to my breast like it's a lifeline.

At the doors, I march myself right on through. The swooshing sound they make continues in my ears as I head for the volunteer station.

One story to *one* patient. That's all I'm reading.

Then I never have to come back here again.

As I take step after wobbly step the only thing that feels solid is my fixed gaze on the floor in front of me. Tunnel vision is the name of the game because if I look up and register my surroundings… If I engage in any way with this overly bright, overly loud environment I will probably pass out.

Anxiety is hijacking my every thought now, making me misremember the super simple directions so that I feel disoriented.

Lost.

So lost.

Someone takes pity on me.

That's how pathetic I must look.

I try to stretch my mouth into a smile that doesn't wobble so that I can concentrate on this new set of instructions and then the person simply walks off and I congratulate myself for fooling them into thinking that I was listening. Absorbing. Instead of what I was actually doing: panicking.

When I feel tears threatening, I'm desperate enough to begin the square-breathing technique I learned in the offices of *Best*

Home magazine – or, to be more accurate, the technique I grappled with perfecting on a daily basis in a toilet cubicle in the offices of *Best Home* magazine.

Those days… Those endless days with my arms stretched to either side of the cubicle walls as if I could physically hold them back from closing in on me – half afraid the counting wasn't going to work, always, always praying that it would because it had to. Because I couldn't lose my job.

Couldn't.

Couldn't.

Couldn't.

'You here for the volunteer reading programme?' a busy nurse asks, never taking his eyes off the computer screen in front of him.

With a jolt, I realise I've made it to Ladybug Ward and am hovering at the reception desk. 'Uh-huh.' My voice sounds thready, not reading-aloud quality at all. I clear my throat. 'I filled out the paperwork downstairs.'

'Great. You brought books?'

'Yeah. I wasn't sure—'

His gaze sweeps me super-fast before settling on something else that needs doing urgently, as he says, 'As long as there are escapist adventures to be had, you're going to be fine.'

'Okay.' Never ever have I wanted more to be a child whose only responsibility is to be told an escapist adventure story.

'You can start with Katey. Bed 5. She's sharp – I wouldn't skip words…'

Anxiety ramps up big time.

Should I disinfect the books with a wipe first? It feels like I should. I want to.

Really want to.

What if I don't and end up giving Katey something worse than she already has?

As we get closer to the bed and my breathing gets all out of whack again and my legs shake, I think that this was a bad idea. A really, really bad idea.

What if I get really attached to Katey and something happens to her?

I'm not even catastrophizing about this as we're in a hospital so it's not at all beyond the realms of possibility.

'Ashleigh?'

I whirl around at the sound of my name, nearly taking out the obs cart beside another nurse who has appeared at the end of Bed 5.

'God – I am so, so sorry.' I can hear the fear in my voice. The panic. The loss of control. The nurse is looking at me like she is very used to seeing people with wild eyes, erratic breathing and who have appeared to lose all control of their limbs.

But on top of that fact, she is looking at me like she knows me.

'It *is* Ashleigh, isn't it?' she asks, smiling. 'I'm Nadine. We spoke at Sarah's funeral.'

Chapter Ten

RAW NERVES

Ashleigh

S*arah's funeral.*

I'd exhale but there's a whopping blockage in my throat.

I believe I mentioned there was somewhere else Sarah was needed.

Yeah…

Truth is if I don't continuously tell myself she was needed Upstairs, by The Big Guy, I will never get past her leaving.

Dying.

Unable to stop myself, I glance up at the ceiling as if I can see through it to the cloudless sky above. Maybe some of her sarcastic words of wisdom will float down to me?

'Ashleigh?'

It's not Sarah's voice but Nadine's that finally filters through. 'Yes, of course,' I manage. 'I remember. I—' Absolutely cannot be here. Among Sarah's colleagues. In her space. It's as I feared. It's too hard. It's too——

'You know Katey, here?' Nadine asks, stepping forward, blocking my exit.

'Um.' I turn around and look at the little girl who has lost all her hair and is watching the interaction between us unfold like it's the most interesting thing that's happened to her today and all of a sudden thinking about someone else is what I need to do in order to let go of that awful day when I had to say goodbye to my best friend. 'Not yet. But I'm hoping to. I'm here to read to you.' I step closer towards her. 'If that's okay with you?'

Huge eyes stare up at me for what seems like an eternity and then she smiles tentatively and gives a nod and just like that, it's no longer, thankfully, about me, but about something as simple as reading aloud to a little girl who must be bored as hell and possibly scared out of her mind.

I'm squashing *Princess Tabitha's Toothy Problem* back into my oversize tote when I spy Nadine approaching again.

'You coming back next week?' she asks with a smile.

I look at Katey for permission and she beams back at me.

'Yes,' I say, lost in the comfort of warm smiles and a little surprised to realise I'm beaming back.

'Great,' Nadine says as I wave goodbye to Katey and turn towards the doors. 'Hey,' she adds, her voice low as she accompanies me, 'I didn't mean to blindside you earlier.'

'That's okay.'

'I miss Sarah. She was a good nurse and was becoming a friend.'

'She had this way of slipping under your skin,' I say, my words feeling full. So full they could overspill out from my eyes in the form of tears.

Not now, I will them. At least wait until I'm on my own.

'So.' Nadine slows just before we reach the elevator. 'How are you doing?'

'Me?'

'Yes. You.'

Horrified as I am by the question, something – maybe the fact that I'm further along this grieving thing than I worry I am – makes me shun my automatic, 'I'm fine,' and decide to be honest. 'Oh, you know… Some days I'm back at square one, other days feel like I've arrived at, at least square four or maybe five. On days like today,' I add with a smile, 'It's a ten.'

'Grief is the shits.'

The statement is so prosaic I laugh. 'Yeah.'

'You get better at dealing with the back and forth of it all.'

I think back to how I dealt with losing Sarah right at the start when grief sucked me right under into its blessed black depths and then I think about the middle, the messy, messy middle and then I think about where I am now – bobbing along on the surface.

'Yeah,' I repeat softly, as I wave "hello" from the deep end and prepare to put my best foot forward again.

———

Looking at the smile on Zach's face, I feel good.

Better than good, even.

I feel present.

Interested in him.

Interesting *to* him.

A girl could get carried away. It has been so long since I have felt anything other than a study in *Hot Mess* but from Mrs. Lundy's out-there pep talk this morning, to leaving the hospital this afternoon with a smile in my heart, to the zingy nervous excitement in getting ready for my date with Zach tonight … these sorts of stand-out days are occurring more and more often lately and how great, is that?

So, before I do what I do and start feeling all jinx-y and ominous about this disclosure, I re-focus on the guy sitting opposite me, determined to stay in the moment.

We've been sitting in a booth in this bar with a cool vibe for a couple of hours now. Simple conversation has been flowing with a healthy side of basic flirting thrown in. Couldn't be more appropriate for a first-second date.

'We should toast Carlos and Oz,' Zach says, lifting his drink, 'for introducing us.'

'Carlos and Oz,' I repeat, lifting my own near-empty glass. 'They'll be so proud.'

'Yeah?'

'For sure.' I nod. 'Of me, especially. You and I have gone through an entire date without me once exclaiming in crossword answers, and look'—I gesture with my hand to my top—'not a button out of place,' I add, with what I hope is a sassy wink.

Zach tips his head in acknowledgement, holding his drink out in another toast. 'A big thank you for not testing my willpower tonight.'

I laugh and shake my head sadly, 'Just what every girl wants to hear.'

He looks contrite. 'That sounded way more chivalrous in my head.'

My grin widens and there's the whole eye-contact thing going on as well.

Yeah … the date is going well.

'Tell me more about this reading to patients programme at the hospital,' Zach asks. 'How did you hear about it? What got you involved?'

My heart gives a little thud at his words.

Or maybe the thud is because he gives such great eye contact.

Either way, I'm all over the first question in the hope that I don't have to go into detail about the second. Guilt nips at me but Sarah would understand me not wanting to mention her on a second date. Wouldn't she?

'Someone was handing out flyers and I had some time so…' I shrug as I say it. Make my smile super bright.

He studies me for a heartbeat longer than I am comfortable with and I immediately second-guess myself. Should I have gone deeper? Can he sense I've just lied?

'Right! And maybe his moon boot is weaponised to help him in his fight against Dates Who Lie. Maybe you'll have to investigate that as you're making out later.'

I blink rapidly. Sarah's sarcasm and laughter are so real in my ear that I almost look around for her. Luckily, I manage to stop myself because acting like you can hear voices or see ghosts is probably not conducive to a date ending well enough that it leads to another.

'Besides,' I tack on. 'We should all give back when we can, right?'

'If I had the time, I definitely would.'

'If you had the time? Isn't that just an excuse though?' The words are out of my mouth before I can stop them.

Damn.

You know what's also not conducive to a date ending well? Lecturing.

'Forget I said that,' I say as he puts on his jacket and I tug my purse strap back over my shoulder. 'I've done, like, one session, and before this my idea of giving back was selling my pre-loved clothes on a vintage clothing app and telling myself I was helping the planet.'

Zach's smile holds firm. 'I really like you, Ashleigh Rivera.'

Wow.

Second time in less than twenty-four hours someone's taken the time to tell me this. I don't fool myself into thinking I'm in love, mostly because I've been drinking sensibly but I feel a bit taller and it's not because I remembered to put on my heels for this date.

As we get up from the table though and head for the door and our separate Ubers, I hope his 'I really like you' isn't going to come with a but.

'I like you, too,' I reply, determined not to let any negative thinking in.

He throws me a quick smile as he holds the door open for us to walk through and I smile back, reassured.

'So…' Out on the street, he shoves his hands into his pockets.

I look up at him from under my lashes. 'So…' This is it. The part where he either mentions a third date, or the 'but' in 'I like you but' comes into play.

'Next Tuesday?' he says. 'Feel like grabbing a meal with me?'

Yes!

Oh!

'Tuesday?' I feel the hours between Friday night and all of Saturday and Sunday stretching out before me like a deserted road. In case I don't get how empty those hours are going to feel, Sarah helpfully appears in my mind's eye, pushing a piece of tumbleweed across the asphalt.

'You got to eat, right?' Zach's voice is charmingly persuasive.

'Um, I'm not sure I can do Tuesday.' *Say it. Say what you want.* 'How about Saturday instead?'

'I can't do weekends.'

'At all?' Oh, the irony. And how am I going to ask Carlos to add such a specific request to his enquiries?

'Weekends, I go home to my family.'

'*Your family? You have a wife and kids?*' I don't consider myself a violent person so socking him in the eye or grounding my heel into his foot doesn't immediately spring to mind. Instead, I settle for staring witheringly at his *family* jewels.

'God no – no, I mean I go home to my mom on the weekends.'

I raise my gaze a few feet. 'Oh?'

'She's on her own since my dad left, so I stop by and check on her.'

'Oh.' That's sweet, really. I try not to think about how tired I usually am on weekday nights and how, once again, I'll have no one to hang out with on the weekends. But maybe … if all goes well, and we progress to lots of dates, well then maybe I could go back to his mother's house with him to hang out on weekends. Or … maybe he could even come back to my folks' house on a weekend. And maybe then, a lot further down the line, of course, we could potentially attend weddings together.

I am so proud of the positive spin I have put on this that it takes me a while to realise he is still talking.

'…I get a home-cooked meal in exchange for doing a few jobs around the house. What about you? You have family, nearby?'

'A couple of hours away. I go back every few months. Keep the visit short.'

'I get it. The longer the stay, the greater the chance you won't want to leave again, right?'

'Right. If the definition of that is actually the complete opposite,' I say with a smile.

'You don't get on with your family?'

He looks like he may have listed getting on with your family as a deal-breaker on his application form and that he might have to have a word with Carlos. How do I explain the intricacies of pushing family away in a bid to show them I'm totally fine since the best friend I lived my whole life opposite to, and with whom I dreamt of living in the city with as we partied while still slaying in our careers, died without warning and left me here, all alone, in the big, bad city?

Surely that's the stuff of third dates?

'I'm joking,' I say. 'I get along great with my family. You're an only child, right?' He nods his head with confirmation and I continue, 'I have an older brother and younger sister who both live in the same neighbourhood as my folks so whenever I go back, I'm seeing everyone. It can get pretty crowded and sometimes the only way I'm allowed exit from the homestead is by being in complete accordance with their life goals for me.'

'I guess that could get a bit much?'

'Hit the nail on the head.'

'So … Tuesday?'

'Sure. Tuesday.' Feel free to roll your eyes at me. I'll be completing my master's in People Pleasing any day now.

He smiles down at me.

I smile up at him.

He takes a step closer to me.

I take one closer to him.

Time sort of hiccups.

Or maybe it's a car backfiring?

And then he leans in at the exact time that I do and we go for the same angle and somehow our noses are bumping and our lips sort of missing each other's.

It is mortifying.

But then he's laughing and pointing at me to go left while he goes right and wow … I wasn't expecting his tongue to slip in straight off like that.

Like, dude! This is only date two.

Sarah would be laughing like a drain at me getting this flustered.

And why the hell am I thinking about Sarah while I am kissing a guy?

In another mortifying twist I must rear backwards or something because we are suddenly apart and then I think he must get it because the next thing I know, he is tugging gently on my hand. Drawing me close … closer … closest.

This time his lips deliver a simple, soft, goodbye kiss. It is so lovely that it has me grinning goofily and I guess Mortification still isn't done with me because my hand misses the door handle of my ride twice before I manage to grab onto it successfully, open the car door, get in and speed off into the night.

Back to my four walls.

And seven long days of the week until our next date on Tuesday.

I've pulled my phone out of my pocket and nearly pressed my mother's number before I realise what I am doing. It's way too early in dating Zach to be sharing with her.

Instead of phoning my mother I bring up the photo I took of the crossword clue George hadn't filled in.

Causing one to lose courage, 9 letters

As I think, I settle back against the car seat, feeling the quietness seep in. It feels louder than before somehow, which is the exact opposite of what I'm trying to achieve by going out on dates but I guess turning up the volume on socialising means laying bare the contrast afterwards.

When the car pulls up outside my building, I see the back kitchen light still on in Oscars. A late-night debrief is exactly what I need to spin my evening out and keep the quietness at bay longer.

'Hey,' I call out as I breeze in, automatically throwing the lock on the door behind me. 'Not only did I style myself for my second date with Zach but I managed to do it in such a way that he asked me out again. I guess also that my amazing conversational skills had a little something to—' By the time I walk behind the counter to the kitchen and note the look of extreme frustration on Oz's face and the flash of pinched hurt on Carlos's, I realise I've walked right in on something. 'What's up?'

'Nothing,' says Carlos, fixing a major grin over the previous expression.

'I don't know what you're talking about,' grumps Oz, reaching for a tub of flour.

The atmosphere is filled with a whole lot of awkward and my heart starts beating faster. I try and do that thing that Mrs. Lundy did, and simply wait for one of them to break silence.

It doesn't work and, if anything, the atmosphere thickens. 'Lovers' tiff?' I ask into the middle distance.

'Sure,' says Carlos.

'Why not,' adds Oz.

Sure? Why not?

What the hell?

I search for something to diffuse the tension and come up

empty-handed. So next I search for permission to demand answers but somehow don't feel I've earned the rights a close friend would automatically assume. Besides, something about their matching closed expressions tells me pushing the issue would only divide them and I don't want to be responsible for causing a further rift.

'Sorry, hon,' Carlos eventually says, 'It's been a really long day. Talk tomorrow, okay?'

It takes me a few seconds to realise I'm allowing him to walk me back towards the door. 'Sure. Details tomorrow?' I manage to get in.

'You know it.'

What I know is that he doesn't mean the details of whatever their argument has been about. I also know that my heart is now doing a serious workout as I try and work out if I am over-dramatizing.

Catastrophizing.

I've never once felt like Carlos and Oz were on shaky ground.

I can't have them on shaky ground.

They're my … friends.

If they hurt, I hurt.

If they're in trouble, I'm in trouble.

As I walk up to my apartment it comes to me…

Clue: Causing one to lose courage, 9 letters

Answer: Unnerving

Chapter Eleven

THE BIG IDEA

George

Exiting the elevator on my floor, my mind is on an upcoming pitch. I can't say I usually mind the fact that my mind is mostly taken up with work. I love the buzz of that new, big idea taking form.

But the problem I have right now is that my capacity to come up with something original, clever and witty that encapsulates a brand of dessert pies seems to have been replaced with an endless stonking headache and I can't settle on the right visuals or emotive language to create a campaign.

For days I've been grabbing at ideas.

Stabbing at them, really.

Leaving them so deflated that a defibrillator wouldn't resuscitate them.

Today's been an especially long day. Technically I should be pleased that after an incredibly tense meeting, I managed to negotiate an advertising spot across all the major networks for the product, but mostly, I'm exhausted.

However, dwelling on how I'm feeling isn't going to get the work done faster so I redouble my concentration on the product's core strengths...

I'm hearing 'happy' music overlayed with laughter as people sit around a large table together. The table should be outside, under a gazebo strung with paper lanterns. The epitome of celebration. Yeah ... a celebration table. Maybe on a private beach? Eating under the stars on a private beach has to be high up peoples' Life Goal lists. Which means I should be able to turn eating Perfect Pies from a niche market life goal to everyone's life goal... The focus should be on the serving platters as they are being passed from person to person and—

'George? George?'

Damn – so close. Finally, the right package of images was coming together. The beginnings of something I could build upon.

But no.

Instead, I'm getting accosted by old ladies outside my front door.

'Hi, Mrs. Lundy,' I say, slightly surprised the weariness in my voice is so obvious.

'Hildy,' she insists.

Sweet old ladies, I amend because truth be told I do seem to have developed a bit of a soft spot for Hildegard Lundy. It has to do with her vast array of kaftans which allow her to move like she's sort of gliding. Bit like Yoda. She's the same age as Yoda, I think, which I find very comforting. Then there's the miles of gold jewellery. Huge hint that she's a bit eccentric. I like eccentric. And then there's the twinkle in her eyes. Yeah, most probably it's the twinkly eyes. Gets me every time. 'Hildy,' I say, making an effort to inject energy into my voice. 'Apologies. I was miles away.' Just because my promotion comes with a team that makes me feel at every turn like my new job is actually more about herding cats, doesn't mean I get to be a dick.

'Apology accepted. Looks like I caught you with your mind on cooking a romantic dinner for that beautiful girlfriend of yours?'

I realise she's staring at the bags of groceries I'm carrying. Suddenly my big idea for Perfect Pies sounds like it came from basic subliminal thought pattern rather than original creative thinking. I bite back a sigh of disappointment.

Why can't I get the idea? The hook? The slam-dunk pitch no one else has thought of.

'Cooking a romantic dinner. Do people still do that? Bit of a minefield these days, isn't it? Food intolerances. Food provenance...' Hmmm, maybe that's what I should focus on with the campaign?

I try to think how I can make a frozen lemon meringue pie that serves ten look romantic. Wait – didn't Tim Duggins come up with a similar idea that I passed on? (I still can't believe Anya palmed him off onto my team). No, his take was more on an older couple's wedding anniversary party. Completely different. Too retro given the client is trying to bring their brand into the twenty-first century.

'Because I haven't seen her around here lately,' comes the sharp observation from Mrs. Lundy.

'Haven't seen who?'

'Your girlfriend.'

'Right. Of course. Well, Anya's been busy with work,' I say in defence.

Mrs. Lundy looks at me like no one could be that busy or am I being paranoid?

'We've both been busy with work,' I add. 'I got a promotion actually.' I'm not sure why I'm telling her this.

'Well, that's wonderful dear but all work and no play makes George…'

'A very dull boy? That's a bit harsh, Mrs. Lundy.' Immediately I'm reminded of my friends not getting it when I couldn't kick a football around the local playing field, and how boring they thought I was.

'Hildy,' she corrects. 'And I wouldn't say "very",' she adds with an eye twinkle that under circumstances where I'm not obsessed with work performance, would tease me out of my funk. 'There's hope for you, yet. With the groceries, you certainly have every chance of turning it around.'

To be fair the groceries are part of my promise to myself to try keeping the fridge stocked with food, plus I wanted to see who usually buys Perfect Pies in the market. I have to be honest. There wasn't a queue forming in front of the freezer unit. I'm going to turn that all around, of course.

'Unless you don't want to turn it around?' Mrs. Lundy's twinkle has been replaced with a hawk-like quality that has me swallowing hard.

'What? Of course, I want to – wait – there's nothing to turn around. Anya and I are in a really good place. The same place we've been in for—'

'The same place? Really, George?' Mrs. Lundy cuts me off with a click of her perfect false teeth. 'Relationships are supposed to grow, you know.'

'And ours is. It's huge.' Huge? How can a relationship be huge? I am really off my game. Not that I was expecting to have to pitch my own relationship to my sweet Yoda-impersonator neighbour after a thirteen-hour day at work and with another few ahead of me.

'I worry about you, George.'

'Worry about me?' The pain in my head pulses. I don't need anyone worrying about me.

'Less so now you have, Ashleigh, admittedly.'

Who the hell is Ashleigh?

'Thank you for recommending her, by the way,' she adds.

Recommending her? Ah. The light dawns. 'Right.' I nod and the movement makes my head pound harder. 'The cleaner.'

'Oh, she's really so much more than that, George.'

Before I can ask her what she means my phone interrupts. If it's Anya she'll understand when I say I have to work tonight but Mrs. Lundy probably won't. 'Sorry, I really have to take this.' I juggle the grocery bags and get out my phone. 'It's probably work.' I offer an apologetic smile.

Mrs. Lundy holds up a hand. 'No rest for the—'

'Wicked.' I quickly insert with a waggle of my eyebrows because there is no way I want her to use the word "dull" again. 'See you again soon, Mrs. Lundy.'

'Hildy,' she says with a wave as she glides down the corridor.

The things we do for love…

Or, at least, for feeling wicked for a while, I think to myself as Anya stares at me across the table, waiting for an answer.

She's only gone and popped the question – no, not *that* question, which weirdly I'd find easier to answer but I don't have time to ponder that as I need to tell her how work is going.

Mentally I go through different answers, weighing up the consequences of each one.

It's not right, is it?

I should be able to answer a direct question about how work is going.

In a bid to try and dodge the question, I start with, 'You know when you called me and begged me-'

'I never beg, George,' she demurs.

'Okay. When you called me and asked me in ten different ways to come uptown for a late-night bite to eat-'

'My meeting ran over. I did explain and if you had work to do, you could have simply said that.'

She's right.

I could have.

But all work and no play makes George…

I think about the weight of work sitting on my desk back at my apartment, now feeling heavier than I could ever bench-press and my heart thuds painfully against my rib cage. I try and concentrate on my girlfriend, sitting across from me. She's put in more hours than me today and looks relaxed and alert all at the same time.

I decide that if dull equals an elevated heart rate as much as wicked does, then I choose wicked. It's just that after working thirteen hours straight and shoving all the fresh food I bought haphazardly into the fridge so that I could rush back out again … only to answer questions about work … well, it doesn't feel wicked so much as it feels like … work.

Hard work.

'Anya, are we in a rut?' I can't believe the words have come out of my mouth and from the shocked look on Anya's face, she wasn't expecting the question, either.

'What? No, of course not.'

She answers so quickly, so emphatically.

So why has my heart seemed to have stopped mid-beat? Like I've suddenly stumbled on a big idea, only this one has nothing to do with my work and everything to do with my relationship?

I try and soften this big notion that has come to me. 'Do you realise when we're not at work, we're talking about work?'

'And there's suddenly something wrong with that? What? You want more, is that it?' Her gaze is assessing me over the rim of the glass she's paused at her lips.

The way her eyebrow is raised, I end up saying, 'You sound like I'm asking for a threesome.'

She scoffs and says, 'Are you saying you wouldn't take up that offer if it was on the table?'

For the first time tonight I smile and say, 'How would that help – everyone we know is from—'

'Work,' she answers and a laugh tumbles out of her.

The sound is fabulous and unexpected and it occurs to me that I haven't heard her laugh in a while. The sound is like being wrapped in velvet so that I feel the tension leaving my head and my heart starts beating faster again, this time for a very different reason. I reach for her hand across the table and stroke my thumb over the pulse point on her wrist. Feel the tiny little jump. 'You want to get out of here?'

'Back to mine?'

I grin. 'That would be a *hard* yes.'

She laughs louder and as we're exiting the restaurant, says, 'So how about them Chelsea United's?'

I try not to think about how my brother would die if anyone referred to his beloved football club, Chelsea FC, as Chelsea United. 'You're really getting the hang of this not talking about work,' I whisper into her ear, telling her how creative I can be with taking both our minds off work when we get back to her apartment.

———

I'm not sure what it is that wakes me hours later, but it takes me a full minute to work out why my navy curtains have sprouted pink flamingos. I stretch contentedly. There's an incredible looseness in my body and my headache's disappeared. I remember I'm at Anya's, but confess, I don't remember flamingos. She must have redecorated.

It occurs to me she's never going to be ready to move in with me if she's still taking the time to redecorate her own apartment. The flamingos are an interesting choice for her, but then again, they're probably more the on-trend decorator's choice. I relax because redecorating to be on trend is very different to redecorating because you are turning your place into a home you don't ever want to leave.

The bed beside me is empty, so I get up, not bothering with clothes, to go and search for her.

I find her working at her desk. No working on the sofa for Anya. She looks perfect as she types away on her laptop. Her soft, silky blonde hair is tucked neatly behind her ears and she looks utterly absorbed in her work.

Work.

Bit of a blow to the ego, if I'm honest. Really thought after tearing up the sheets for an hour she'd be feeling as sated as me.

'Hey,' I whisper.

She jumps but then turns and smiles at me. 'Hey you, I'm feeling, I don't know'—she gives a sexy little shimmy and the shoulder of her silk nightgown falls enticingly off of one shoulder — 'rejuvenated.'

Okay. So this is better. Ego restored, I walk towards her. 'What are you working on?'

Immediately she goes to close the laptop screen but a logo catches my eye and I already know.

'I was playing around with a few ideas...' she explains.

'A few ideas for one of my accounts?' There's a creeping gathering in the centre of my gut, spreading up and outwards like a dust cloud enveloping a city.

'It's not a big deal.'

It *is* a big deal.

I try and make my tone casual because flying off the handle when I don't have all the facts, isn't me. 'Why are you fleshing out ideas for Perfect Pies?' I ask quietly.

'You mentioned you were struggling with it.'

'No, I didn't.'

'You must have.'

I don't want to highlight that there's no way I would ever have told my boss's daughter I was struggling with the first account handed to me after promotion so that leaves one person who could have talked to her about the campaign and I'm now going to need her to say it. 'Who told you I was having trouble with the pitch, Anya?'

'You did.'

My voice is gravelly now when I repeat my question, 'Who told you?'

'Okay. Tim may have mentioned it.'

Tim Bloody Duggins. I nod. Breathe in. Breathe out. Decide breathing is over-rated as it's doing nothing to calm the indescribable anger expanding from the base of my belly. 'So the reason you put Tim on my team is that you had zero faith in me?' I bite out the words. 'Tim is a spy? Your spy?' Jesus, what if it was worse? 'Or your father's spy?'

'Don't be ridiculous. He is neither. I put Tim on your team because he deserved the chance to be on accounts that would challenge him. I have never once expected you to not come up with a big idea. Neither has Tim. You know he looks up to you.'

I can't believe this. I could have been at home. Working on my big idea. I could have come up with the big idea this very evening. Instead, I'm in the beginnings of an argument ... in the nude. Feels weird. Feels ... nope. No way am I going to acknowledge feeling vulnerable. This is ridiculous. I have this. I start to pace. 'I still have a week left before pitching.'

'A whole seven days.'

'You know that's enough time.'

'George.' She says my name so softly I feel the air leave my lungs. 'Do you have it, yet? The big idea? Even the kernel of a big idea?'

My pacing falters. I think of all the ideas I've discarded. Not one gave me the tingles let alone the jolt of electricity I feel when I stumble onto the big one. 'Okay,' I admit. 'I'm cutting it close with this one, but you know I'm good for it. I've never missed yet.'

'But you haven't got *any* workable solutions bubbling away under the surface?'

The fact that I don't answer gives her the answer she's been fishing for all along.

'The agency is a team,' she says, swinging around in her chair to face me fully. She looks me square in the eye. '*We're* a team. Right?'

'Right.'

She nods her head. Crosses her legs gracefully. She is always so calm. 'So then given that, it doesn't really matter who it is that comes up with the big idea, as long as we do come up with one, right?'

'Wrong!' How can she say that? Absolutely it's on me to come up with the big idea. I'm the account manager. The *brand-new* senior account manager.

'Hey,' she soothes. 'You think I don't see how hard you've been working? It's only been a few weeks since you had that panic attack—'

And that she would bring that up right now... 'That was a one-off,' I state emphatically.

Except, it wasn't.

I've been having them regularly.

Like clockwork.

'Well of course it was a one-off,' she soothes again, except … is it my imagination that she doesn't sound as confident when she says it? 'George, you think I don't understand how that could have thrown you for a hot minute? You think I don't know how hard it is to come up with idea after idea? That I couldn't possibly understand the added pressure of the promotion? Of having a new team to manage? You think I don't get how easy it is to go stale—'

'Stale? What the fuck, Anya?' I'm gutted she would even insinuate this. 'I have not gone stale. I couldn't be less stale. Stale is not a word in my vocabulary.'

'But you could use some help with this one account.'

It's not a question. It's a simple, business-like statement.

'I don't need Tim Duggins' help. I can't get behind any of his ideas and every idea *I* come up with he actually checks whether it's an order or a request.'

'I know Tim can be a little … literal, but you won't accept my help, either?'

'I—'

She cuts me off with, 'Because when I take the helm at the agency I kind of thought you'd be right at my side. Or was I wrong about that?'

'That's not for years, yet.'

'But you best bet I'm going to be ready for whenever the time comes, George. It's what I've always wanted. I've been completely transparent about that with you and I've always been given the impression, by you, that it was what you wanted, too?'

'Of course it is.'

'So, what part of me helping you with this one account, actively goes against the end goal, here?'

I sigh because she's right. I have to look at the bigger picture. 'Let me go put on some clothes and you can tell me what you've come up with so far.'

Chapter Twelve

A PIECE OF THE PIE

George

'Twice in one week, Mrs. Lundy. People will start to get an idea about us,' I say as I spot her in the corridor again.

'And why would I complain about people thinking someone as old as time itself might be teaching a handsome young man a thing or two?' She laughs up at me, eye-twinkle at full-flatter sparkle.

I feel my face stretch into what seems like the first smile in days. 'You just getting back from a hot date?' I ask.

'It should be me asking you that, except for the glaring fact that I can tell, very sadly I might add, that you have come straight from work.'

'Really? What makes you say that?'

'You look serious.'

'My work *is* serious.'

'Pensive,' she adds.

Well, who wouldn't be pensive on the eve of delivering a pitch that deep down they weren't fully sold on? To be fair Anya's big idea at least has teeth compared to what I and my team had come up with. And yet if I'm being honest, aren't I still holding out hope I can come up with something better? When I'm not worrying about why I can't come up with anything, that is.

'You also look tired and wan.'

Tired and wan?

As in ill?

I squeeze my eyes shut but can still hear my mother's panicked, 'You look really pale, George. I think we'd better take you back to the hospital, darling. We'll go right now. Don't panic. Stay very calm. Just breathe. In and out while I call the ambulance. In and out. In and out…' With a shudder, I put the memory back where it belongs, in a box marked 'George's Past' and smile down at my neighbour.

'Knife to the heart, Mrs. Lundy,' I tease.

'Hildy,' she insists. 'And if you tell me a date with Anya has you looking like that, I'll be even more concerned.'

'No, it's work. Tricky campaign. But, speaking of Anya, I'm thinking of taking her away this weekend for a romantic break. We've both been working hard lately and we never got a chance to celebrate my promotion and—'

'Are you trying to convince me, or Anya?'

'Neither,' I say, determined to sound determined. 'I'm doing it.'

'Good because when it comes to romantic breaks, "There is no try – only do",' she says with a spookily accurate Yoda impression.

'So, do we think The Hamptons? I mean, there's enough to do there, right? Long walks on the beaches. Antiquing. Quaint little places to eat.' I can't actually believe I'm asking little old ladies for advice on romantic destinations but needs must.

'What are you, my age? I swear ... young people today ... if there's an opportunity to overthink or over-complicate... A romantic break is not about finding the perfect destination or activity vacay ... the only *destination* should be each other ... the only *activity* should be each other. Whisk her away anywhere where you get no reception on your devices and can spend some quality time together. Reconnect. Romantically. Do I have to spell it out?'

'You paint a pretty picture, Mrs. Lundy.' I grin at her. 'So, The Hamptons is a good idea, or no?'

She rolls her eyes but chuckles and adds, 'Hades is a good idea, if it's with the right person, George.'

'Copy that.'

She lays a hand on my arm and gently squeezes and I have the awful idea she feels sorry for me. 'You really do look like you could do with a break. So, don't overthink, don't get hung up on perfecting the details and somehow end up talking yourself out of it, okay? And don't let Anya talk you out of it, either.'

'Book it. Pack for it. Turn up at her place and whisk her away?'

'By George, I think you've got it.' She laughs and as she puts her hand into one of her large kaftan pockets to get her keys out she frowns as instead of her keys she withdraws a plastic dinosaur. 'Oops. I forgot I "saved" one of Davey's dinosaurs from being adopted by his sister's Barbie.'

'Your hot date was next door?' I point to Apartment 33B, where five-year-old Davey lives with his seven-year-old sister, Abigail, and their mother, Julia. I know their ages because my brother's two kids are the same.

'Had myself a spell of babysitting until Julia got home from a job interview. I don't suppose you could return it for me? It took twenty minutes to say goodbye to Davey and if I turn up again it'll only confuse him.'

'Oh, but—'

Mrs. Lundy looks at me like I'm about to say I have work so I smile and say, 'Of course.'

'You'll do it now? Because you know Davey will be upset if he wakes up in the night and discovers it's gone.'

'Yes, Mum,' I tease as I go to my other neighbour's front door and raise my arm to knock on it.

Mrs. Lundy heads into her apartment, and I'm left standing outside the door to Apartment 33B and then suddenly Julia's door is opening and my ears are being assaulted with the worst sound I've ever heard in my life.

The perpetrator of the assault on my ears turns out to be a violin.

I say a violin – as it can't play itself, I'm afraid that I do, uncharitably, lay the blame squarely on the shoulders of the person playing it – young Abigail.

It's amazing how fast small people can make things happen. One minute I'm holding out a plastic dinosaur, the next I'm being dragged by Davey and Abigail through the door and then being shoved onto a chair in the middle of the living area, like a prisoner being exposed to white noise in the hope of getting me to talk.

I can confidently confess that having to listen to beginner's violin practice is torture. As I sit, trying desperately to keep the encouraging smile from slipping off my face, the nerve-shredding notes jumble together in a discordant symphony that I can't help feeling could have been specially composed to play in the background of my pitch tomorrow.

'Abigail, I think Mr. Northcote has heard quite enough of that for now,' Julia says.

I can't help turning my head to Julia and giving her a pleading look that says, 'Maybe extend that to the rest of my life too.' Out loud I say, 'Please, it's George,' and then smile as the correction reminds me of Mrs. Lundy.

Julia looks apologetically at me and mouths the words thank you over the top of her little girl's head as she puts the violin back carefully in its case.

'I really should be going,' I say, needing to rehearse the pitch for tomorrow.

'*Noooo,*' screams Davey.

'Davey, come on,' his mother, Julia, cajoles softly and I can tell it's an effort to keep the tiredness out of her tone. 'I explained Mr. Northcote would only be here for a little while.' She catches my eye. 'He doesn't like it when people leave.'

'I get it, my niece is the same.' I squat down next to Davey and roll up my sleeve to show him my new watch. 'How about I stay here with you for another ten minutes.'

His eyes zoom in on my wrist. 'You're wearing a different watch.'

'Very astute of you, Davey,' I answer, thinking I could do with that kind of detailed observation on my team. 'It is a new watch. See all these dials? I can even set a timer on it – just like on a phone. How about I set the timer for ten minutes and when it goes off, that's when you'll know I'm leaving?'

'Mom would set it for eight minutes,' Abigail helpfully adds in full-on big-sister mode. 'To give Davey a two-minute warning.'

'Even better idea. You want to set the time, Davey?'

Davey nods and immediately works out how to set the timer for eight minutes. As he places it on the floor beside him and goes back to playing with his returned dinosaur, I think of my niece and nephew and make a promise to myself to video chat with them this weekend.

I can book a romantic break with Anya for the following weekend instead. We'll probably all take the client out for drinks after the pitch tomorrow anyway, so it would have been lunacy to try and book something for as early as this weekend.

'Here, at least have a piece of this while you're here,' Julia says and I look up to find a plate of cake being held out.

My stomach grumbles.

Julia laughs. 'Hildy brought some of the leftovers over from the batch we ate at her tea party last week.'

I take a bite and moan. 'Oh my god, that is seriously good.'

'I know, right?'

I stand up and wander over to the kitchen island to investigate the cake box. '*Oscars*? Never heard of it but now need it in my life.'

'Hildy's new cleaner put her onto them. Damn. I forgot. I was supposed to get her cleaner's details as well. I swear if I don't write everything down – wait a minute – I actually *do* write everything down.' She walks over to her phone and scrolls before glancing back up at me with a rueful smile. 'I just need to set reminders to look at what I've written down.'

'As it happens, I know Hildy's new cleaner. Well, when I say know her. I don't "know" know her.' All I really know about her is that my apartment no longer, thankfully, smells of bleach, looks spotless yet feels welcoming all at the same time. She never disturbs anything on my desk and she's a whizz at crosswords. 'I could let her know you're on the lookout for a cleaning service if you like.'

'Do you know if they send the same person each week? It's just that with Davey…'

'Let me check with the company. If they do, I really recommend Ashleigh.'

'Ashleigh. Yes. That's who Hildy was talking about, I think.' She waves the phone at me. 'I neglected to write that part down. I don't know why I'm telling you all this. Probably lack of adult company to chat with.'

'Well, I personally live for talking about dinosaurs and violins. Can I ask you something?'

'Of course.'

'Can you tell me how you progressed from calling Mrs. Lundy, Mrs. Lundy, to being able to call her Hildy? I can't seem to get the hang of it.'

Julia smiles knowingly and says, 'Doesn't she correct you though?'

'Every time.'

'It's confidence. She invited me to one of her tea parties and after that first one, something sort of clicked and I was able to do it.'

'Tea parties?'

'Like an old-school afternoon tea. Glamourous. Lots of delicate china. Tiny food.'

'Why would you want the food to be tiny?'

'I guess it makes it easier to eat while you network. That's what they are really. Networking events.'

'Oh. Right. Now you describe it, I think I remember Anya being invited to one.' I try to remember if she told me about it afterwards, but I'm coming up with nothing so perhaps she didn't attend.

'Anya?' Julia asks.

'My girlfriend,' I explain. 'It wasn't long after I'd moved in.

Mrs. Lundy saw her in the corridor – come to think of it, I don't know why I wasn't invited.'

'Well, not to be un-PC but you're the wrong gender.'

'Wow, who knew Mrs. Lundy was sexist?'

'I think it's more that she has a mission to redress the balance a little.'

'Everyone deserves a piece of the pie,' I murmur.

Julia takes my plate and hers to the sink and runs the faucet over them. 'Never mind a piece of the pie, do you know how hard it is to even get a seat at the table? That's what Hildy's networking tea parties give you. The confidence to take your seat at the table. It's why I just now went for a promotion I didn't think I'd be able to get and got it. It's why as soon as I get these two into bed tonight, I'm celebrating with more of this cake and a long bubble bath. Sorry TMI.'

To be honest I'm not listening. All I'm thinking is… A piece of the pie… Perfect Pies… A seat at the table…

I think I may just have stumbled onto a big idea.

A really big, really good, fabulous idea.

Electricity is pulsing through my veins.

Sirens are going off in my ears.

Actually no, that's the alarm on my watch.

I register that Davey is now standing politely beside me, waiting for me to leave.

Talk about good timing because I need to be back in my apartment working on this brand-new pitch for tomorrow. This is how we bring Perfect Pies into the present. Not by focusing on a nostalgia piece. But by… Yes, I'm picturing a party now. Or a conference. Some sort of company event that's thanking everyone for their hard work and raising profits and all of them get a piece of the pie. Maybe it's a not-for-profit and there's pie for everyone

… or the seats aren't necessarily at a table … or it's a glass-top table and … there's something here.

I know it.

Can feel it.

'I'll leave you to your celebrations,' I say, shooting for the door. 'I have work, anyway. Thanks for the cake and the inspiration.'

'Inspiration? Me? Well, you can thank me by practising calling Hildy, Hildy.'

'Right.'

'Aren't you forgetting something?'

I look up and see that she's holding up my watch for me to take, and there's an endearing smile on her face. I grin and take it from her, settling it on my wrist as I turn and walk to my apartment.

I hear the elevator doors ping. Hildy's probably off on a hot date but to be honest, I give it no more thought. I'm too busy thinking about how I need to get this new pitch written and then call my team.

Refocus our energy for tomorrow's meeting.

My heart is thumping crazily inside my chest, but, oh, how bloody fantastic it feels!

Chapter Thirteen

ONE, IS A LONELY NUMBER

Ashleigh

12 Across: The state of being alone, 8

C*rap!*

I know – that's only four letters.

As the rain pelts down outside, and inside the chatter of other coffee shop customers pushes in on me, I tug the crossword puzzle closer. Shifting on the hard chair, wanting to look at one with my surroundings, I realise Crapola is a letter short but for eight letters I could write 'very crap' in the little boxes instead.

It's tempting but with a sigh absolutely no one in the café will notice, I write down the correct answer which is: *solitude.*

I feel like rebelliously writing in the margin that solitude doesn't always equate to loneliness. For example, I can sit here, happily on my own at this table for two instead of on one of the stools at the chest-height bar area facing out onto the street and not feel in the slightest bit lonely. Or, okay, if not *happily* sitting here, then, at least contentedly.

I sip my latte and ponder happiness versus contentment.

Contentment is better, right? A steady course with a destination, rather than a quick-fix high you can cheat yourself into, in the endless pursuit of happiness. Contentment feels more adult. More realistic than always trying to be happy.

A bout of hilarity erupts from the table next to me. Two teenagers laugh deep from their bellies, shoulders shaking, as they try to catch breath. The friendship they share is palpable. Forged in shared memories and support for one another.

I stare back down at my crossword, my vision bleary. Sometimes the loss of Sarah is so acute I can barely breathe through it.

No matter how many chores, museum visits, cinema trips, picnics in the park, hours in the library and coffee shop crossword breaks … Saturdays are hardest for me. Steeped as they seem to be in togetherness and socialising.

I persevere because what else is a girl to do? No, really. What else *is* there to do on your own in the city?

I might as well confess the only words I've uttered aloud today are: *One for Screen 5. Hey, you dropped your wallet. Latte with a white chocolate and macadamia nut cookie – to eat in.*

This afternoon, at the movies, I opted for the last showing of an intense thriller in the hope I'd be so engrossed I wouldn't feel I was filling time until facing an empty apartment. But as the couple seated near me chose to get their exhibitionism on in full high-definition surround sound, with no one to share a raised eyebrow with, a giggle with, or make matching vomit faces with, it was a very uncomfortable experience. Although now of course I realise if I'd complained to staff, it would at least have been another human interaction.

I glance at the woman sitting at the table directly across from me. There's a small smile playing about her lips as she types away on her laptop. I shouldn't study her but I do, hoping to somehow learn her secret. Absorb it by osmosis because how does she do it? How does she straddle the line between feeling exposed and feeling invisible?

Before Sarah died, I'm not sure I was ever conscious of being alone. She was always one message away, one call away, one minute away from walking through the door at the end of a hard shift at the hospital.

I should stop feeling sorry for myself.

Definitely stop thinking about all those times my mother tried to warn me to make lots of friends. Sarah's mother probably tried to do the same for her. It's not that we epically failed at that – it's more that we didn't even contemplate it.

I glance at my phone. I suppose I could call my mother. Or my sister. Or my brother.

Or I could go sit in Oscars where I could avoid giving my family the impression I'm lonely. Also, the coffee and cookies would be better. Carlos and Oz might be on their one day off together but I could have an end-of-shift gossipy chat with their other member of staff.

Small talk will help.

Small talk will save me.

Plus, I would be exactly twenty-seven steps from my apartment, yet legitimately outside in the world.

I hook my pen over the dog-eared cover of my pocket-sized crossword puzzle book, pick up my phone, shove my arms through my jacket and head for the door.

By the time I'm nearing Oscars, I already know it will be closed. The subway was shut. Rat on the line or something. I didn't stay long enough to read the notice. Instead, I chose to half-walk, half-run the couple of miles, as I concentrated fiercely on not ploughing into one of the other millions trying to escape the steadily falling rain.

Woman on a mission, that's me. Get to Oscars and escape from being too in my head. A place where it's not always Home Sweet Home. I mean I work hard to make it comfortable and homey but sometimes it feels full of spiky furniture, catastrophic scenarios, and a sort of embarrassed feeling for not being able to find a new tribe.

'Ooomph!'

I come to an abrupt stop as I crash into an immovable object right outside the bakery. As I register the cartons of milk lying on the floor between me and the rock-like obstacle I look up, up, up and oh … a smile breaks out on my face. 'Ozzie-Baby. My knight in chef's whites!'

'You should watch where you're going.'

I don't even question what he's doing here, I'm too thankful for the serendipity. 'You going to let us in,' I say. 'Or stand here in the pouring rain crying over spilt milk?' I bend to pick up as many cartons of milk as I can carry.

'I'm going to let *me* in. You probably have somewhere you need to be.'

Wow, bad mood alert. 'What are you doing here on a Saturday night anyway?'

'Choreo,' he answers flippantly.

Undeterred by the mood – because, hello? Daily occurrence

with Oz – I grin up at him. 'Okay, what are we choreographing? I have some moves. I can help.'

'No. No. And no.'

I squint through the rain at him and see that he really is dressed in his chef's whites. 'You're here to bake?'

'Funny that.'

'But it's a Saturday.'

'I'm aware.'

'But you – where's Carlos?'

'Out.'

'Out?'

'You don't see him here, do you?'

Call me Captain Obvious but I've an inkling about the reason for the blacker-than-usual black mood. 'You'd rather talk about anything else at all, wouldn't you?'

'I'd rather not talk at all. I'm here for some peace and quiet. Some—'

'Solitude,' I whisper, finally getting it. One man's anathema is another man's panacea and all that.

'And the light dawns. So, if you don't mind?'

'Right. Message received and understood. I'll be getting out of your hairnet now. Enjoy your alone time. If you need anything…'

'Bye, Ashleigh.'

———

Thirty minutes later, I'm sitting crossed-legged on my floor, wet hair wrapped in a turban, sweats on, *contentedly* re-folding the contents of my underwear drawer, when there's a knock at my door.

My first reaction is confusion because it's been quite the while since anyone knocked on my door. When the sound comes again, sharper this time, I get up and stare through the spy hole.

All I can see is white cotton and it takes another knock on the door followed by, 'Ashleigh, are you in there or have you gone out again?' for me to turn the locks and yank open the door to stare up at Oz.

'I have not gone out again,' I reply.

'So, have you changed your mind about needing company?'

'You want to come in?' That's so sweet and yet the very idea fills me with horror. I don't need Oz seeing how much time I take to fold my underwear on a Saturday night.

'And break some of your hobbit furniture just by sitting down?' he asks with a shudder. 'God, no. Grab your keys and come down to the kitchen.'

I emit a peal of excitement that is quite embarrassing. 'Can I re-arrange your stock?'

'My kitchen does not need re-organisation.'

'Please?'

Oz sighs. 'If you manage not to make me regret breaking my one night on my own in months to help keep you company, I *may* let you align all the labels on the racks of ingredients.'

'For real?'

'Well, no actually. Not if you're going to salivate all over the place, like that.'

I grin, grab my keys and follow him downstairs, outside and into Oscars.

Inside the bakery, something smells amazing. 'What are you making?'

'Bourbon and black cherry brownies. First batch is in the oven. Going to start on the second, now.'

'You are a baking God.'

Oz smiles for the first time and I walk over to the gleaming racks of industrial-sized ingredients and start twisting jars so that labels line up. It's super-satisfying.

Behind me, Oz's large hands are occupied stirring cherries in a pan of bourbon over a low heat. The aroma, combined with the hot, sweet smell of baking chocolate is more soothing than any amount of folding laundry.

After what I consider an appropriate length of companionable silence, I say, 'Hey, Oz?'

'If you want a glass of bourbon, help yourself.'

Totally wasn't what I was going to ask but I wander out of the kitchen and return with a glass. Oz raises his eyebrow at the size of it but I smile and say, 'We'll share,' as I pour a double and offer the glass to him first.

After a brief hesitation, he shrugs his gigantic shoulders and takes a sip.

I take my own sip and as the heat of the alcohol warms me, I gather my courage and try again. 'Hey, Ozzie?'

'Uh-huh.'

'What were you and Carlos arguing about the other day?'

'Other day?'

'Tuesday. I'd just got back from my date with Zach.'

'I don't remember.'

'Don't remember arguing or don't remember what you were arguing about?'

Oz sighs. 'You know when I decided to take pity on you – thanks for the massive guilt trip by the way – and help keep you company tonight … it wasn't so you could ask your endless questions.'

'Okay.' I pour another double into the glass. 'Coming in hot,' I warn and slide it down the steel counter towards him. It stops in the middle of the island and we both stare at it. 'Pretty sure I can rule out a past life running a saloon in the Wild West,' I declare.

This produces a chuckle that lifts my heart as Oz reaches for the glass and whistles a few notes of 'The Good, the Bad and the Ugly'. He turns the heat down on the pan of infusing cherries and sets a timer before taking another gulp.

I imagine Sarah whispering in my ear, '*Do you feel lucky, punk?*' and I decide I do and ask, 'So, where is Carlos, tonight?'

'Out seeing an old friend.'

The way he says it flat and sort of final has my heart thumping. 'And you weren't invited along?'

'I wasn't.'

'Rude,' I empathise. 'So, is that what you were arguing about?'

Another sigh. 'If Carlos wants to go out with old friends on the one night off we have together a week, he's free to do so. I don't keep him chained in the basement.'

'I suppose it's the one night off he has a week, period.'

Oz ignores me and opens the oven to take out the first batch of cookies.

As a distraction, it works because as the top of the chocolate brownie mixture cracks, my mouth starts to water. 'Oh my God, they look and smell amazing. Can I help you make the next batch?'

'Will you stop asking questions if I show you?'

'It's called conversation.'

'Right. So why aren't you out with Zach tonight?'

'He goes home to visit his mom on the weekends.'

Oz snorts.

'What?' I say staring at him. 'You don't think he does?'

'What do I know?'

I frown. 'You think he's out *seeing an old friend*?'

'Or a new friend?'

Wow. The thought had never occurred to me. 'You're too pretty to be this cynical, Oz.'

'Hey, if you say Zach's at home with his mom, who am I to say he probably isn't.'

'Who are you? You're my friend so I would say that gives you the right to be interested, concerned, and in other words, have an opinion.' My statement is bold and steals my breath but what am I supposed to do? Go through life without any new friends? It's why I asked Carlos and Oz to help me find someone to hang out with on the weekend. 'I guess it doesn't really matter either way where Zach may or may not be tonight,' I add, 'since I hardly know him at all and don't have any claim on him.'

'But if you did, how would it make you feel?'

I stare at the batch of brownies. 'Like if I wasn't invited out to see this old friend, I would probably invite myself along, so that I could really see what was going on.'

Oz busies himself with measuring out chocolate, his actions swift and practised, his voice low and careful, as he says, 'And what if he told you where he was going and you happened to find yourself in the exact same place only to find he wasn't there at all?'

I can't stop myself from reaching out and putting my hand over his as I clear my throat and say, 'Well, then I'd guess I'd want to bake brownies.'

He nods as if this was all he needed from me. 'Here, take this silicone spatula and fold the ingredients together.'

I copy him and think about everything I know about Carlos and as I hand the bowl back over to him, venture, 'You know, there's likely a plausible explanation he wasn't where he said he'd be.'

'It must be exhausting being such a Positive Polly all the time.'

I wince because, honestly, it is a lot of hard work but, for me, it's still better than the alternative. 'I just can't see it,' I add, carefully.

'What, Zach lying to you?'

'No, Carlos lying to *you*. I know he's loud and you're not. I know he's sociable and you're not. But you balance, you know? Plus, I see the way he looks at you, even when you're huffing and puffing about being made to serve customers. He loves you. He's *in* love with you. He—'

'He's done it before.'

The words are said so softly that, at first, I think I've misheard until I look at his face.

'Cheated,' he admits. 'When we were first together. Before we lived together. Before we started this place together.' His jaw is set rigid, his eyes bleak. As if he's been stewing about this for hours and has worked his way around to being embarrassed not to have seen this coming. When I stand there silent, trying to take it all in, his smile turns rueful. 'Damn bourbon has my mouth running.' He puts the cap back on the bottle and stores it on a high shelf before bringing his hands down to the counter and hanging his head. 'He'd die knowing I'd told you all that.'

He's right. Carlos is a super-proud person. I scrabble for something helpful to say, feeling woefully rusty at supportive-friend talk. 'Don't make it sound inevitable, Oz. People change when they find their person. It's not just this place I don't see him jeopardizing. You – him – you're a unit. Settled. He's settled with you.'

'You make me sound about as exciting as an unfrosted cupcake. Be honest, Ashleigh, does Carlos really look the type to settle down? Maybe it was wrong of me to expect him to be able to. Maybe *I* need to change.'

'Into what?'

'I don't know … maybe … someone open to an open relationship?'

'Um … wow … okay … but has he asked you for that?'

'No, but if it means I get to be with him…'

I feel myself frowning. 'Aren't there a lot of rules with an open relationship?'

'I'm good with rules.'

'So am I but I'm not sure I could be that open. I guess I'm more of a person meets person kind of person.'

'Careful,' Oz says. 'Those small-town roots you try so hard to hide are showing.'

I tilt my head and consider him as he deftly slices the first batch of brownies into equal portions. 'Don't try pretending you're any different, Oz. What I meant was if Carlos hasn't ever brought this topic up with you, then I think it's because he is too. I could have sworn you were heading for traditional cookie-cutter domesticated blissful marriage and kids.'

'I thought so too. He made me think so too but now—'

'But now you need to have a conversation with him.'

'Maybe.'

'Oz, there is no "maybe". You want to sort this out with him, right?'

He turns away and while my heart thunders heavily that he might not sort this out and then what will happen, he reaches for some more ingredients and asks, 'You want to have kids? Get married?'

I blink at the rapid deflection. 'I-I don't think about it.' I really don't. Too busy striving to stay in the present where it's so much less complicated.

'What, never?' Oz asks, a look of disbelief on his face.

'Well, sure, when I was a kid.' I don't really want to talk about this. Don't really want to think about all the times Sarah and I sat up in the tree house in her backyard, thinking … dreaming … manifesting our futures. 'My parents have always had this great marriage and so I guess that was my foundation and,' I admit, 'I fell fully for the fairy tales.'

'Me too.'

I smile and raise the glass in a toast. 'But you're right about small-town roots. My home town might as well be called, *Weddingville*, seeing as almost everyone there marries their college sweetheart and settles down in a starter home a couple of streets away from where their folks started out together. It's all very—' I draw a blank.

'Copacetic?'

I smile and nod. I remember as Sarah and I got older we talked about what jobs we wanted, what careers. It's a shock now to realise our plans never included what came alongside or after our flashy city lives.

'So, if Weddingville fulfils a lot of fairy-tale criteria, you're still here because?' Oz asks.

I feel guilty. Why wouldn't he be confused when I've been participating fully in Operation Find Ashleigh A Boyfriend?

'It's ironic,' Oz continues, letting me off the hook for an answer, 'that you had to leave your home to escape settling down before you were ready to, and I had to leave mine to find someone to settle down with.'

'But how great that we both found it right here?'

'I don't know. Maybe a city is too big a place to keep it – sustain it?'

I swallow. 'You can't leave! This is your home now. You have roots here. With Carlos.'

'*Maybe.*'

Chapter Fourteen

PROPHECIES AND PROMOTIONS

Ashleigh

'27A on Northside are separating.'

I'm standing beside Jamal, one of Sparkle's longest-serving employees, as he says it and right there my ability to be present in the Monday morning rota meeting sinks without trace as I go right back to worrying about Carlos and Oz and the way Oz said "maybe" on Saturday night.

At the end of the evening, right before he handed me a box of brownies to give to Zach on our next date, Oz apologised for insinuating Zach was out with someone else on weekends and told me I was a good friend. I can still feel the butterflies exploding out of my chest like they'd been shot from a confetti canon. All I could think was that I was a crap friend for internally catastrophizing about him and Carlos separating and him leaving.

Or both of them leaving.

Leaving me here.

On my own.

'27A Northside are *always* separating,' Adeena, another cleaner, states.

Jamal shakes his head. 'For real this time. They haven't slept in the same bed for weeks. Then there's the card from a divorce attorney. Flopped right out onto the floor when I was emptying the trashcan in the second bathroom. Right along with an empty tub of next-level face cream. She's ramped up the retinol percentage by a gazillion and no one's switching up their beauty regime that much and sleeping in another bedroom while thinking they're staying. I'm waiting on the request for a Sparkle 5Star Service deep clean because no way he's affording that place on his own.'

I agree with Jamal's summation. It's an unfortunate fact that your cleaner usually knows what's going on in your life before you, your therapist, or in this case, your lawyer, might.

If I could get a look inside Carlos and Oz's place, I could get a better handle on what's going to happen to them…

No.

I have to stop this.

When I popped into Oscars this morning I didn't get to speak to Carlos because it was so busy, but I did get a cheery "Morning Beautiful" and a flash of his flirty grin to set me up for the day. He looked as carefree as always. So, see? It's going to be fine. *They're* going to be fine. Nothing bad is going to happen. They're getting a dog together. They're getting their happy ending. I'll probably end up asking them to find me a date to their wedding. Become godmother to their kids. They'll move to a big house in the suburbs—

Every muscle in my body tightens and then tightens some more as I realise everyone is staring at me.

'Ashleigh…?' Rhonda Sparkles, my boss, says. 'You're up.'

Rhonda, possibly as a way of mitigating her last name, is way scarier than my boss was at *Best Home* but being as I like this job, and I like Rhonda, I feel sick I wasn't paying attention. I'm sure there was something I needed to ask at today's meeting. 'Um...' I look around the room and as I see Janice I remember. 'Hey, Janice, how are you with snakes? Can you deal?'

'Sure. Every woman has to a time or two, sweetie. You want me to deal with one for you? Is that what has you looking so upset this morning?'

Interested eyes bore into me and I'm mortified there's been a slip in my cheerful, professional demeanour. I hate thinking anyone might see me upset. Might worry about me.

Or be unsure of me.

Pasting what I hope is a relaxed smile onto my face, I explain, 'No, I mean snake as in actual reptilian kind. I'm pretty sure 4A The Clouds is getting one. I saw articles on how to look after them when I covered for you last week. Also, they asked me to clear a perfect vivarium-sized space above the chest of drawers in the kid's bedroom. You know how the 4A parents are – they're absolutely gonna get him one for his birthday.'

Janice screws up her face. 'Lordy, no. I cannot deal. Can we swap? You do 33A and 33C on Tuesdays, right? I could do yours and you could do my 4A and 4B?'

'Sure, I – wait,' I can't imagine not getting to chat with Mrs. Lundy anymore. It's not as if I could pitch up at her apartment for a visit if I'm not there to clean, is it?

And give up cleaning George's apartment?

No. Way.

The thought of another cleaner working out what it is he needs over me working it out? Because there has to be something. Some way in which I can improve his home for him. Every week I go and every week the place looks the same. And every week it intrigues me more. Because if you don't really *exist* in your home where is your escape? Where do you get to be *you*?

I refuse to believe that clinical, soulless place is providing that special breathing space every person needs. Not to mention I've fallen in love with completing his crosswords for him.

I scrabble for something to say and stammer out, 'Y-you wouldn't enjoy cleaning 33C. OCD off the scale. Honestly, pernickety doesn't begin to cover it. And every week it's something else. Something ... *weird*.'

'Weird?' Rhonda interrupts, her police-commissioner hawk-like gaze zeroing in on me. 'We have reporting methods for "weird." You know I have a zero-tolerance policy for "extras".'

'Oh no,' I rush to say, 'not as in "let me watch you clean naked" weird.'

Rhonda's shrewd gaze sharpens to a laser beam and I feel the redness creep from my neck to stain my cheeks. Wow, was that the wrong thing to say. 'What I mean is, weird as in needing to use bleach that doesn't smell of bleach and, plus ... he's *British*, so, you know...'

'Huh?'

Janice isn't wrong in her confusion because there's nothing that I can think of that's wrong about being British so I just leave my statement hanging until finally, with a look on her face suggesting she's embarrassed to be the only person on the planet who doesn't know about the thing with the British, says, 'Ooohhh,' and slowly nods her head up and down knowingly.

'Exactly, right?' I say, my voice getting higher and higher. 'I couldn't do that to you.' I stare down at the rota, wanting to make this better. *Needing* to make this better. 'Adeena, you take your mom to physio on Tuesdays, why don't you swap with Janice?

Save you having to cut back across traffic and Janice, you'd be closer to the L train for getting home.'

Adeena looks over at Janice. 'That would really help me out. Okay with you?'

'Long as there's no reptiles, I'm good. Thanks, Ashleigh.'

'No problem.'

'Right, if that's everything?' Rhonda says and then after a brief pause, 'Ashleigh, can I see you in my office, please?'

My heart travels into my mouth like it's in a reverse-drop ride at an amusement park.

Am I getting fired?

'Do you need to answer that?' Mrs. Lundy asks as my phone goes off for the third time since arriving to clean for her this morning.

I definitely don't.

I'm in an exceptionally good mood after not getting fired yesterday and in all likelihood answering the call will put a damper on that.

'That's okay, Mrs. Lundy. If it was work it would be a different ringtone.'

Mrs. Lundy smiles from her chair. 'So, who's behind the 'Danger, Will Robinson!' ringtone?'

I feel bad as I sheepishly answer, 'It's just my mom.'

'I see.' She lets the phone continue its clanging chimes of doom warning for a beat and then checks, 'It won't be any sort of emergency?'

I plug the vacuum into a wall socket in the dining area and wave my hand dismissively. 'I can see why you'd think that, but, honestly, if it was a real emergency, she'd have my brother or sister phone or she'd message me.' I'm about to add she's only calling because she thinks I'm at George's with nothing to clean and therefore have free time on my hands when I remember my new rule about not mentioning him.

Bad enough Rhonda sat me down in her office and asked me some searching questions about if I was really okay and still happy to clean George's apartment. It took ages for it to sink in that she was asking because George had recommended me for an additional job – cleaning his and Mrs. Lundy's neighbour's apartment, 33B. In response, I'm pretty sure I made things worse for myself by glowing. With pride, obviously. Let's not make this weird.

I guess my reaction *was* weird though. I put it down to surprise that someone whom I've never met, and who I don't understand how I could leave an impression on when I literally walk in to clean his apartment and leave it looking no different to when I arrived, should have noticed me doing enough of anything to recommend me?

'Do you have family, Mrs. Lundy?' I ask as I roll the vacuum over to the Persian rug that the elegant rosewood dining table sits so regally upon.

'Hildy,' she corrects. 'Not anymore. Why do you think I meddle in so many lives?'

My finger pauses on the switch. 'Trust me, your kind of meddling the world can do with. If it wasn't for your pep talk last week, I would have stood outside that hospital for the millionth time and not gone in. The fact that I did, when all the other times I'd chickened out, is down to you. Honestly, now I've done it once, I'd go every day if I could.'

'Every day?'

I catch Mrs. Lundy's expression as I switch the vacuum from

hard-floor setting to carpets. 'You don't think the hospital's missing a trick not extending the volunteer reading programme to weekends?'

'I guess that depends – do you have a burning need to spend the only time you get off from your job at the hospital? Because I'm on the hospital board, so could probably arrange it.'

'You are?' I'm even more glad I followed through on my promise to Sarah now but instead of making an idiot of myself and asking if Mrs. Lundy really could arrange it so that I had a legitimate commitment on the weekends, I judiciously start vacuuming. When I've finished, I ask, 'So what do you do on the weekend, Mrs. Lundy?'

'Hildy,' she patiently corrects again. 'Let's see, most Saturdays I play checkers or dominoes in the park with Alfred.'

'And is Alfred, your, um…' I tail off, unable to think of a suitable term. This is where I could do with a crossword clue to provide the answer because "boyfriend" sounds so wrong when you're Mrs. Lundy's age.

'Let's just say,' Mrs. Lundy continues with a grin, 'Alfred and I play out our thing on a giant gameboard and enjoy ourselves immensely. Naturally, I often distract him with my'—she does a little shimmy so that the multicoloured glass crystals and metallic thread on her kaftan shimmers—'gaming prowess. Of course, he has cataracts, but he pretends!'

I laugh with delight and wonder if Zach and I have the potential to move from a couple of promising dates into something deeper. Probably not if we never get to see each other on weekends.

I'm looking forward to seeing him tonight. Should I tell him about Carlos and Oz and ask what to do to help, or would that be too deep? I've forgotten what third-date discussion material is appropriate. It flashes through my mind Sarah won't be there to grab me by the shoulders and stare into my eyes and tell me not to do anything she wouldn't do and then laugh dirtily.

'…Then I usually head to the senior centre for a bite to eat,' Mrs. Lundy adds, a twinkle in her eyes. 'Get the gossip. Start some gossip…'

I shake off the melancholy. Force myself to remember I'm looking forward to a simple date tonight with a guy I'm enjoying getting to know.

'Sounds like fun,' I say, depressing the switch to make the vacuum cord retract. To prevent any enquiries into what I do or don't get up to at the weekends, I ask, 'How did the cakes from Oscars go down at your afternoon tea?'

Her face lights up. 'They were a hit. I'll be ordering from your friends' bakery again. Do you know if they offer a full dinner service? I have the hospital charity board coming next month to go through some upcoming fundraisers. I find it often goes better with good food in front of them.'

'I'll find out for you.' *Wow, what if Carlos and Oz suddenly had so much work on it would be madness for either one of them to leave?*

I turn and look at the dining table I polished earlier. 'How many would the dinner be for?' I ask, picturing crisp linen settings with some of Mrs. Lundy's patterned china from the matching rosewood display case in the room.

'Let's see, if everyone attends, twelve.'

'You know what would be good? A cherry blossom arrangement as a centrepiece. Maybe some moss at the base? Nothing too tall – if you're going to be talking money, you're going to want to see the whites of everyone's eyes, right? Heavy flatware. Crystal votives. The blush pink of the cherry blossom with the fresh green of the moss, would look wonderful on the rosewood. Fresh as spring. Perfect for looking forward, right? Things always seem more possible in the spring.' I grind to a halt, embarrassed by my enthusiasm.

'You're good at creating ambience. Why aren't you out in the world decorating homes, or designing?'

'Oh. No. That's not me.' The words rush out of me in quick denial. 'I mean I used to—' I stop myself. Mrs. Lundy's skill in getting a person to over-share is considerable. 'I like reading about the latest decorating trends, you know?'

I think of all the articles I wanted to write but never pitched at *Best Home* because I was too nervous, too scared, too worried about being laughed at and then last year when I was too … too…

I heave in a breath. Time to bring this back to what I do now. 'I guess you'll need wait staff? Sparkle could probably help you out with that,' I say without thinking. 'Sorry, that was really presumptuous, I'm sure you have contacts and a company in mind.'

'Wouldn't hurt to take a look at another company – especially if it's a recommendation.'

'It would be a new service for us, but my boss is always looking to expand her business.'

What is wrong with me?

How can I possibly walk into Rhonda's office to turn down the promotion she offered me and then immediately suggest Sparkle start offering silver service as part of its business model?

Yeah … that's why Rhonda asked to speak with me yesterday. After I agreed to take on 33B she *then* offered me a promotion to cleaning supervisor.

'Will you be servicing George later, dear?'

'Will I…?' At Mrs. Lundy's words I think I'm going to have to re-vacuum to pick up the mess left from my jaw hitting the ground a second after my eyes, now way too large for my eye sockets, pop out onto the floor. 'Of course not. If there's going to be any servicing later,' I croak out, 'it'll be of Zach. My boyfriend. That is – when I say boyfriend, what I really mean is we've been on two dates. This will be our third.' I start moving around the room like a trapped butterfly. 'Is a third date "servicing" time? I don't know. Why don't I know? I swear I used to know.' The formal dining room starts to feel stuffy as I contemplate (and for contemplate, read: panic) the reality of going on a third date with the same guy. Because at what point, specifically, do we start to talk on a deeper level?

About the big things that have shaped us.

About how sometimes I'm not always fine.

Sometimes I'm still a bit of a mess.

Which I'm pretty sure, isn't pretty.

'But then, if it is – *you know*'—I go back to thinking about easier things—'then, shouldn't it be mutual "servicing"? I don't need to be getting into something that isn't mutual. This is all so exhausting.' I stop and turn to look at Mrs. Lundy for understanding. 'I was just looking for someone to hang out with on the weekend. But then my mom—' I break off with an exasperated sigh. 'With the whole my cousin's wedding—' I break off again. 'Which shouldn't matter because who cares, right? If I go solo, I mean? Let them talk.'

'I meant will you be servicing George's *apartment*, later?' Mrs. Lundy says, gently.

Shit.

'I knew that.' I nod my head like a bobblehead. 'I absolutely knew you meant that.'

Chapter Fifteen

IMPENDING JUNE!

Ashleigh

The moment I push open George's apartment door, I feel the change. Instead of the clinical, efficient atmosphere, the energy is fizzing with discord.

In the living area, I stare at the scene before me. For George to have had such an effect on his environment, something bad has happened and I'm not talking the existential type of crisis naked to the invisible eye because, believe me, there's plenty of physical evidence around.

An empty takeout container strewn across the usually barren kitchen countertop.

A half-empty coffee mug by the sink.

Torn-out pages from magazines overflow his in-tray and litter his desk.

Stacks of food and lifestyle magazines on the floor under his desk.

For George, this is a next-level cess-pit standard.

In fact, the sight of such carnage has me so concerned I immediately head into the bedroom to check he's not lying unconscious.

He isn't, thank goodness, but from the looks of it, George definitely hasn't been sleeping.

The bed is usually made before I get here but today the sheets are rumpled and the comforter is half-hanging off. George's latest bed companion doesn't seem to have been his girlfriend. Instead, it looks like he's had the starring role in an orgy of work and coffee binge drinking, with the paperwork and mugs deciding to hang around for seconds.

I leave the papers cascading across the bed like a white-water river of thoughts and head into the bathroom.

It's also empty of bodies, which is more good news, but I stare forlornly at the wet towel left on the floor.

Oh, Mrs. Lundy was right to be concerned about him.

That was all she'd meant to convey earlier when I'd so colossally misconstrued her question about servicing. Of course, after my mini-meltdown, I'm pretty certain I've now also managed to make her worry about me.

Thinking about how I must have come across has me shuddering all over again. I don't know why I got so panicked, thinking about a third date with Zach. I've been feeling so good about being in control. I mean, if I don't want to – if it's too difficult, or I'm not ready – I don't *ever* have to talk about losing my best friend.

And yet how could I never talk about Sarah? It's hard enough to understand why the entire world isn't talking about her.

Missing her.

Mourning her.

Sadness wells up and I swallow it back down, heading back

out to the kitchen to make a start. Tears may be the best cleaning fluid for my heart but probably not for cleaning countertops.

I just wish I knew the etiquette for when, on a date, it's okay to bring up why I don't have a best friend messaging me every five minutes to check I'm safe. But I don't even know how to start the conversation.

I thought I was ready.

I'm so not ready.

By the time I'm wondering what to do with the torn-out magazine pages on George's desk, I'm feeling better. The physical exercise of washing all the floors in the apartment has given me back a better grasp on perspective.

As my hands trail loosely across glossy photos, I see that George has been using the magazines like an inspirational mood board. Either that or the multiple photos of pies means he has a fetish that's getting out of control. I did say it only took a couple of weeks until clients got relaxed around their cleaners.

A quick glance at the wastepaper basket shows more photos so I'm going to go ahead and decide that the ones left on his desk are the ones he wants to keep and I start gathering them up into one pile.

It's as I'm shuffling the pages together to stack neatly in his in-tray, I realise there's no crossword for me to complete. Disappointment hits hard and before I know it, I'm going through the rest of his papers on his desk, trying to find it, fingers trembling like an addict craving their next fix.

He has to have left me one, surely?

I selfishly dismiss all evidence he's going through a work thing and probably didn't have time to leave the last clue for me as I methodically double-check the papers again, searching for it.

Maybe I should leave a crossword for *him*?

To help.

Before I second-guess myself, I'm heading over to my cleaning cart, pulling out my bag from the bottom shelf and diving into it for my paperback copy of *The Times* Crossword Puzzles. I flick through for an empty one and tear it from the book.

Back at George's desk, I'm searching for a pen to write in the margin: *In case you're in dire need of a crossword fix.*

I open the top drawer and that's when I see the painting. Now, I don't want to mock anyone's artistic abilities but it's obviously been done by a child so I can't help it – I pull it out for a closer look. It's a picture of a white cottage on a cobbled street with an oversized sign beside it. I'm trying to decide what the animal on the sign is as I turn it over and see the message: *To Uncle George, We thought you might be missing your visits to The Bedraggled Badger with Daddy so we painted it for you. Lots of Love, Millie and Tom.*

Well, how cute is that?

Obviously, he put it in the drawer to protect it before starting work but I can't help thinking it should be displayed where all children's paintings are best displayed, on the fridge. I'm about to put it back in the drawer when I see the newspaper with the crossword underneath it. I pull it out and realise he's completed it. More evidence he's feeling stressed? But, stuck on a large sticky note after the fold is a crossword clue with a note from him.

For putting away my dry-cleaning last visit: gratitude 5,3

I'm sorely tempted to write my answer as *Spank You* and add a question mark, instead of *Thank You*, but after becoming acquainted with how it feels to have my eyes pop out and my jaw hit the ground, I understand how uncomfortable an experience that can be.

Oh, yeah, also how inappropriate.

Instead, I grab one of his pens and write in the answer and then I add some boxes above and below the letter 'o' and write my own clue:

add a contraction before you lay out the mat, 5,7

I smile as I put the crossword in the centre of George's now tidy desk. Will it be crossing the line to add another little note encouraging him to hang his niece and nephew's painting? How could he not be cheered up from seeing that every day when he got in from work? Plus, if he stuck it to his fridge door it might remind him to buy some food every now and then.

Yes, I peeked inside his fridge.

And, yes, removed all the unopened out-of-date food.

And, yes, it does mean he's been left with only a bottle of wine, a chunk of parmesan and a quart of milk.

I'm really not sure he's going to notice so I refuse to feel worried about it as I head off into his bedroom to finish cleaning.

A couple of minutes later I head back to my bag for the box of brownies Oz gave me for Zach. I don't need to be worrying this much about George having no food to eat.

I'm back in the bedroom, smoothing the comforter on his bed when the 'Danger, Will Robinson!' ringtone interrupts.

Fishing my phone from my pocket I answer, 'Hi, Ma.'

'Why haven't you been answering your phone?'

'I'm busy. You know, doing what I'm supposed to be doing in the middle of a Tuesday morning, working.'

'I … you're sure? You're not just telling me what you think I want to hear?'

The fact my mother sounds as if she has donned actual kid gloves has me starting to worry. 'What's up?'

'First, tell me what has you so busy. I thought you said this guy's apartment was sterile and soulless?'

'It was.'

'Was?'

I'm disconcerted to realise I'm grinning like a Cheshire cat.

I know.

So wrong.

It's not that I'm happy that someone's life is potentially in turmoil. It's more the feeling that I'm finally being treated to George's inner life.

Maybe he's starting to trust me – trust that I will clean up the mess he's left.

I can't tell you how gratifying that is.

Mostly because it's my job.

But also, I don't know … it feels good.

Like I'm being given the chance to really help.

'I think Mrs. Lundy was right about George,' I say in a gossipy, confidante kind of whisper.

'Who's Mrs. Lundy?'

Eye roll.

Only my mother could pick up on the new fact rather than the way I said it.

'My friend,' I answer defensively.

'Honey, you don't call friends by their last name like that.'

Busted.

'Mrs. Lundy is becoming my friend. Her first name is Hildy and we talk every week.'

'Every week, huh? Like at a regular time?' I hear her take in a breath and hold it and I brace before she releases it in a stream of exasperation. 'Ashleigh, it's bad enough you're doing this job. Now, you're thinking these clients are your friends? They're not your friends, Ashleigh. They're your employer.'

'And I can't be friends with my employer?' I think about my boss at *Best Home*. Yeah. No. That isn't a good example. I think about Rhonda and how she's not exactly friendly but more, sort of, motherly. Um, not a realisation I need right now when on the phone with my actual mother.

'You can be *friend-ly* with them,' my mother continues, 'but there's a difference. You know there is. Do you really think this Mrs. Lundy wants to know about your life? That if you were in trouble, you could call her up and she'd be there for you? That you could go out drinking together?'

'Yes. Yes, and yes,' I answer emphatically.

'And how old is Mrs. Lundy?'

'Don't be ageist. Friends are friends.'

'And when you're at a bar doing shots and some guy starts coming on too strong are you going to have to wait for Mrs. Lundy to walk over to kick him into touch with her walking frame?'

'Hildy would totally do that for me,' I say defensively.

My mother snorts and my voice takes on a peace-making tone worthy of working for the UN. 'Ma, you can have friends who mean different things to you. Not everyone has to have that one Ride or Die friend. Come on, you always used to tell me to have lots of friends.'

'I did. You used to ignore me.'

'Maybe I'm listening to you now.'

'It's just that you did have that Ride or Die friend.'

'Exactly,' I say super-brightly. 'I'm not interviewing replacements, Mom.'

'You're really doing okay?'

'I know you worry, but yes. I'm meeting new people. I'm enjoying my job. I'm dating…'

'How are things going with Zach?'

'Good. Really good. I have another date with him tonight.'

'At least you're not sitting in that tiny apartment at the weekends, now.'

'Um … right.' I can't do it. Can't tell her we only date during the week.

'So, bring him back here this weekend.'

I need to move. Disperse the nervous energy. Why does she always know exactly what to say to nudge me a little further down the line to Losing-It-ville? 'No, I'm not bringing him there for the weekend. We've only just started dating.'

'But you said it was going well.' She says it so reasonably.

'And I'd like it to continue going well,' I counter.

'He does exist?'

'Relax. He's real. He's an HVAC tech who's starting up on his own. He's been in Brooklyn for four years. He doesn't have brothers or sisters. His folks split last year. And I can't bring him home this weekend because he visits his mother on the weekends.'

Long silence.

Really long silence and then, 'He visits his mother every weekend?'

'Yes.'

'And you have proof of this?'

'Oh my God, you're just like Oz – Oz, another bona fide friend – you probably know him from the CIA.'

'The CIA? Are you even remotely able to have a serious conversation anymore?'

'Zach is that nice he goes home to check on his mother every weekend. I believe him. I'm a good judge of character Ma. I get that from you,' I add as a sop.

'Well, he's going to have to make arrangements for someone else to sit with his mother for the wedding in June.'

'I'm not going to make him organise that a year in advance.'

'No, I mean, *this* June. It's the reason for calling. I—'

'Tina's moving her wedding forward to *this* June? Way to bury the lead story, Ma! So, what, honeymoon deal too good to pass up? Pregnant?'

'No, I shouldn't have told you like that. I should have – it's just that – this is going to come as a shock, I think. Your father was right, I shouldn't be telling you this on the phone. You were supposed to come home for the weekend – finally – I mean I get it when I invite you and you don't because that's what you're supposed to do. You're supposed to be busy that you don't need to come home every weekend and visit your folks but if you had just come home *this* weekend, I wouldn't have to tell you on the phone.'

'Just tell me.'

'Jasmine's engaged.'

'What?' I sink down onto the bed I've just made.

Sarah's sister is getting married?

'Shelley-Ann and I wanted to tell you together, in case – you know—'

'What?' I repeat but my voice is hoarse so I don't think she hears.

'This June – Jasmine's getting married this June and so it's very happy news and you'll be invited and—'

'Ma. Stop. It's fine,' I force the words out. Force my face to stretch into a grin, because that's supposed to help you sound fine, isn't it? 'You're right. It's happy news. It's good the family is getting to celebrate something after such a tough year. It's good, it's…' I trail off. I can't believe Sarah's sister is getting married. To who? Her sister just died. Who gets married one minute after their sister dies?

There are tears rolling down my cheeks, I know it.

Sarah would have been so happy for Jasmine.

She'd have loved it.

She'd have been jealous as hell, but she'd have loved it.

'You're invited,' my mom says into the phone. 'That's what I wanted to tell you – to prepare you – to expect an invite.'

'Of course. Don't worry. It's happy news. The happiest for them all. Of course, I'll go to the wedding.'

'And maybe it won't feel so … that is, if you're there with Zach, it won't be such a stark reminder Sarah isn't there – I mean of course they'll mark that she isn't, you know mention it in the toast and so-forth because they wouldn't want to omit her but maybe you won't find it so difficult if you have Zach by your side?'

'Maybe.'

The feeling I've worked so hard to conquer – the feeling I haven't felt in months – slides into my conscious and then spreads through my body so that my eyelids feel heavy, my limbs weighted and all I want to do with every fibre of my being is sink into bed and sleep.

Sleep for a thousand years.

Sleep while some other version of me – some better version of me – figures this all out and gets herself further forward in life again. Further past it all.

It's the wanting-to-sleep feeling that scares me the most.

And thank God for that fluttering, stuttering fear catching alight until it's a hissing, raging wildfire that gets my heart pumping madly and my breath catching horridly so that to escape I'll do almost anything.

I hang onto the fact that I have something better than just anything.

I have cleaning.

And Carlos and Oz.

And Hildy.

And the reading programme at the hospital.

And Zach.

My life is filling up again...

And the guilt is crippling.

Chapter Sixteen

FEELERS, EGGS, AND IRONS

George

'You've reached the voicemail for Anya Richards, please leave a message…'

Damn it.

No sooner have I put down my phone than I'm picking it up again to contact the one person in the company with total access to the diary management system and able to get through to anyone … our Departmental Overlord, aka, our Departmental PA. As soon as she answers, I say, 'Kate, it's George. I see that Anya's booked solid but I need the next available five minutes of her time. It's urgent,' I tack on, although it's entirely probable Kate's worked that out from the tone of my voice.

'Let me take a look … okay, yes, I see where I could carve out the fifteen before 2pm. Is that okay?'

I glance at my watch. One whole hour from now. 'I guess it will have to do.'

'Do I need to book a meeting room?'

I'm tempted to have Anya summoned to my office but I know exactly how that would look to Kate, so I say, 'I'd appreciate it, thank you.'

The first time Anya made it up to see my office, well, blink and you'd have missed it. She was right, of course. It would look weird to staff if she was suddenly seen up here a lot. Despite us having the same job title these days, being the boss's daughter is something she's careful not to shove in anyone's face and also why she chooses to stay with her team in the open-plan area.

Should I have turned down the corner office when I was promoted? I mean, if HR was asking what I thought about hot-desking, my answer, of course, would be "Hot-desking? *Soooo* many benefits. What's not to love?". But as anyone who's ever remembered halfway into their commute that they forgot to book a desk for the day will actually tell you, hot-desking sucks!

'Okay,' Kate says. 'I'm seeing the main pod is free and I'm booking it now. What shall I title the meeting?'

I'm tempted to call it the Actual Shit Hitting the Actual Fan meeting but instead I say, 'Perfect Pies Update.'

'Of course. Nice talking with you, George.'

The moment Kate ends the call I go back to giving the email on my screen my full attention.

The longer I stare, the faster my heart races and the more my breathing can't quite catch onto a regular rhythm. I don't understand how it could be that the contract I've been chasing for months is now dead in the water.

Except of course, I do know. I know exactly how and why the Perfect Pies account is dead in the water. The feeling of it all is sitting on my shoulders like a piece of prime real estate called Missed Opportunity.

What happened is that we went the wrong way with it.

Then nosedived.

Crash landed.

And flatlined.

I'm so angry about it all.

Furious even.

Especially as I'd been so sure about the direction to take.

I commit the entire email text to memory so that I can no doubt repeat it to myself verbatim when trying to get my solid eight tonight.

How do I get my head around the fact that I've failed?

Failed.

It's a new experience.

It is not a nice experience.

I try and think about what I'd tell a member of my team in this position – feeling dejected. Defeated. Immobile with shock. The words, "Not every campaign will pan out. The trick is how you pick yourself up and crush the competition to get the next one. In a contracting market you need to be even more commercially aware. Even more savvy. That means ensuring you have more than one egg in more than one basket. Keep those feelers out. Have many, many irons in the fire…"

But as the newly promoted Advertising Account Director and therefore responsible for bringing in business and increasing revenue streams and building winners and having awards under your belt, let's be frank … that kind of psychobabble is complete bullshit, isn't it?

Because how's it going to look to Harrison when he learns the first major account that I was supposed to bring in … the example I was destined to set … is dead in the water?

How's it going to feel knowing I've suddenly acquired a great big question mark about me above my head?

Because he doesn't care about how many feelers, eggs and irons I have out there – not when that's just standard business practice. No, what Harrison requires from an account director is the ability to lead by example.

My jaw aches with tension because it was understood I wasn't only as good as the Forever Yeong account.

It was understood I was more.

I swivel around in my chair but the cityscape brings no comfort and worse, no creative thinking sparks how to turn this all around.

I close my eyes only to picture units of Perfect Pies being depleted on a national scale as the winning advertising company propels the company out of the stratosphere because they understood their client's needs and, oh yeah, how to not fail.

I wrench open my eyes and see I still have fifty-seven minutes until I meet with Anya. I think about all those hours stuck in a hospital bed when I was younger. Learning how to be patient. Learning how to dream. Learning how to get ready to take my leap forward and make those dreams a reality.

They seem so far away from me somehow.

Blimey.

Has all my success made me soft?

I heave in a breath, determined to pull myself together and re-set. I need to start making notes on the team talk I'm going to have to give when I disclose that we didn't get the account I had them all working through the night on last week.

Fiercely I set about describing how to never stop creating opportunity – how to never stop creating, period, when I become aware that my left shoulder is tingling.

Really tingling.

I press into the nerves and muscles and note that the area feels hard. Like I'm super tense … or like there's an obstruction?

Left-hand side is heart.

The words on my document swim in front of me and I leap to my feet to pace.

While pacing I stretch my neck out. Rotate my shoulder. Clench and un-clench my hand a couple of times.

Okay, that's feeling a bit better.

I'm fine.

Right?

I try to analyse if I should go back to the hospital and get checked out again. What if they tell me they made a mistake? That I really do have an issue with my heart again.

What if they don't?

I need to trust the doctors at the hospital.

My heart is fine.

The twinge is just a manifestation of the panic.

The stupid panic that's ridiculously holding me back from all that I can be and all that I want.

Why does it keep happening?

I breathe in and out a few times as if I'm some sort of prize stallion.

I need to do better at this.

I can't be like this when I land the next big account.

Thank God for this office.

This private space.

Oh, that I could stay in here all the time.

Of course, if I stayed here all the time, I wouldn't need a cleaner.

That thought brings me up short.

As does the notion I'd miss her – not least because I wouldn't be able to swap any more comfortingly corny crossword puzzle clues.

I think back to finding the clue she'd added onto the one I'd left her.

Make a contraction before you lay out the mat, 5,7.

I know I'd smiled as I wrote in "You're Welcome".

I'd still been smiling as I opened my fridge and found she'd discarded all but three of the contents. Let me tell you, even Google can't come up with a recipe for parmesan, milk and wine. Thankfully she also left me a box of brownies.

It was while eating my second brownie that I made a decision. I was going to leave another couple of crossword clues for her in the hope she'd leave some for me.

After my *third* brownie, I went hell for leather and left a note to go alongside them.

If you're going to throw out perfectly edible food, (sell-by dates … shmell-by dates) at least give a person the chance to re-stock. I see on your company website it lists basic food shop as a weekly service so I've gone ahead and signed up. Food-wise I like everything. Except that weird squirty cheese you all like. I'm from England … I like cheddar. Cheddar comes from a cow. As opposed to squirty cheese which seems to come from e-numbers and I defy anyone to tell me otherwise. Proof of otherwise does not constitute simply squirting squirty cheese from a tube onto a plate and leaving it in the fridge for me – after all, how would I know the shmell-by date?

FYI cheese isn't all I talk about. As I'm sure you're perfectly aware, all we Brits actually talk about is the weather. The winters here are worse, by the way. George.

PS You omitted to put a shmell-by date on the brownies. For my own safety, I ate them all in one go!

Okay. I'd written more of an essay than a brief note but by the end of writing it I was feeling mellow and for some reason had the feeling she wasn't the "judgy" type.

She wrote me a reply.

I have it with me.

It's not what you're thinking. It's because it's attached to the crossword we're creating.

Dear Mr. Northcote,

Please ex-cheese the impertinence but wake up and shmell the Camembert. In my experience Use-By Dates

The Use-By Dates is underlined twice!

are perfectly acceptable clues in preventing a person from getting food poisoning, or worse, your cleaner wondering why you live on your own but buy food for two??

That part of her note made me think maybe she was a little judgy, but then I smiled again with what came after:

Waste is awful and you should give: Dutch Cheese, Red Rind, 4 letters, about it

I actually chuckled out loud as I wrote in the answer: *Edam* and then added my own note in the margin to say I did, indeed, give 'a damn' about waste, which was why I believed in writing in the margins instead of using another piece of paper.

The rest of her note says:

I'm very happy to stock your fridge with weekly essentials and as the service doesn't kick-in for another week, could I take the opportunity to ask am I buying food for one? Or for two? Also, I get you're probably busy with work and stuff, so can I suggest a few fresh things that are quick to make? Maybe a pasta dish? An omelette? I appreciate it's none of my business but sometimes cooking a simple, healthy dish is really relaxing. Ashleigh.

PS I don't mind weather if it's changeable. That way if it's the kind you don't like you're reminded "this too shall pass", right?

I liked the sound of cooking something simple that would help me relax at the same time, so I added in between the lines of her note that that would be great – but could she also attach a recipe or two?

Tonight, I'd planned trying to make pasta arrabbiata – I think that's what her recipe called it. After the day I'm having, I'm really looking forward to unwinding. Not thinking about work for a few minutes.

Guilt stabs at me.

Not thinking about work?

Am I insane?

But then I think of the trouble Ashleigh has gone to, to put food in my fridge and to write out a recipe for me, so I'm going to go ahead and treat myself to making the pasta and if I happen to think about work while I'm doing it, then I can call it working too, right?

I re-read Ashleigh's postscript.

It's very prosaic, especially if I take it in the context of this feeling of failure passing.

I breathe deep.

No tingling in my arm.

I remember Mrs. Lundy mentioning she was glad I had Ashleigh and that she was 'so much more than just a cleaner.'

She is.

And her note has fired me up to go into my meeting with Anya where I'm going to turn this day three-hundred-and sixty-degrees around.

Chapter Seventeen

WHEN YOU FAIL TO PREPARE...

George

Anya is already sitting in the main pod with its see-through walls as I approach. I focus on her and not the fact that the last time I was in this room I had my first panic attack. She's on her phone but as she sees me, she ends the call and smiles, beckoning me into the room.

Why does it feel like I'm about to tell my boss I've failed instead of telling my colleague or my girlfriend?

Do it quick, I tell myself. But I've barely stepped across the threshold when Tim bloody Duggins walks in right behind me.

'I'm sorry, Tim,' I want to turn to Anya and roll my eyes in a "Who does this punk think he is" kind of way but manage to stop myself. 'Whatever it is will have to wait. Anya and I are about to start a meeting.'

He nods and grins in the most grating convivial way that he has. 'About the Perfect Pies account, right? Anya copied me in on the invite.'

I pivot to face Anya. 'You did?'

'Of course,' she says looking cool, calm and collected as always.

'Have you invited all my team?' I ask. I'm aware of the slight emphasis I place on the word "my" and as Anya's lips press together ever so slightly, I see the inflection hit home.

'Only Tim,' she replies casually, increasing the wattage of her smile. 'I thought as he did a lot of the work on the pitch, it was only fair he got the update at the same time.'

Oblivious to any undercurrent Tim rubs his hands together and heads for the mini-bar. 'Champagne all round, then?'

'That's a negative,' I say.

'What?' There's a look of utter disbelief on his face as he comes to an abrupt halt. 'You didn't get the account?'

'*We* didn't get the account,' I correct.

'I don't understand,' he says and admittedly I feel sorry for him because it's not like I don't understand what he's feeling.

'They're going another way,' I say, shoving my hands in my pockets. 'It happens.'

'What other way could they possibly go?' Anya asks. 'You laid out your concept clearly—'

'No,' I correct again. 'I laid out the campaign *you* came up with.'

In the silence, Anya stares at me, assessing me. Assimilating. 'I see,' she says after a beat. She smooths down the line of her navy-blue pencil skirt and then looks at Tim with a warm smile that has me frowning. 'Tim, would you step out, please?'

'If you're sure?' Tim replies.

I catch the look of concern he gives her. What exactly does he think is going to happen here? And he does know he works for me, right? Not Anya? Because if he wants to swap to Anya's team, I'm all for it.

At least I think I am because wait a minute… Call me paranoid but does that look he gave her mean something else? Is Tim under the very mistaken impression there's a fissure in Anya and my relationship? Is he seriously hovering on the sidelines waiting?

I stand tall and stare Tim down until, finally, he gets a bloody clue, and as he backs out of the room says, 'Of course. I'll um, let you guys get your meeting on. Like, no worries.'

As the door swings shut behind him, I sigh and say into the silence, 'Why does that guy not do your head in? *Like*, completely!'

'So,' Anya says, ignoring my comment. 'We're doing the blame game? It's *my* fault you lost the account?'

'No. Yes.' I throw myself into the chair opposite hers as the disappointment glues itself to the failure already sitting on my shoulders. 'It's mostly mine.' I need to be honest. 'But don't worry, I'm going to fix it.'

'Fix it?'

'I should have insisted we went with my concept of everyone getting a piece of the pie.'

'We agreed it was too risky. Too eleventh hour. You hadn't had time to do testing and we had a solid idea ready to go.'

I hear what she's saying yet looking back I don't know why I didn't insist harder. For longer. I mean, of course I was vocal on the subject. That morning before the team from Perfect Pies arrived at our offices no one could have doubted my passion for the idea I'd come up with. I'd had my team working on it all night, for heaven's sake. I was one hundred per cent confident in it.

But maybe not in myself?

That's what has me so furious.

Why would my gut instinct pack its bag and move out the minute I had one lousy panic attack? I've never second-guessed myself like that before. Never. Then, I go and get the promotion I've been working towards for over a year and... bam ... confidence has left the building hot on the heels of gut instinct?

'Anyway,' I say, striving to keep the anger locked in. 'Lesson learned because I'm going to go back to them. Lay out the approach I was going to take—'

'George, let it go. I know it's hard. Getting that account would have been great for the agency but you pitched – and didn't get it. No one gets a do-over in this business and I really don't advise letting the agency look like it's desperate for business. You have other campaigns. Pursuing other options, chasing other leads and working on what you do have, will ease the sting. Believe me. I've been there.'

I don't believe it. Is Anya seriously quoting back to me my own psychobabble bullshit about recovering from disappointment?

And she hasn't been where I am.

I doubt her equilibrium has ever once wobbled let alone allowed itself to feel as if it's been picked up, chucked in the washing machine, and put on a fast spin.

'And how exactly is that leading by example?' I ask.

'You have to trust your team to bring in business now.'

'Like Tim?' I blurt out. 'You must be joking.'

She looks at me like she doesn't know this version of me.

And why would she?

I've always been secure in my work.

Confident.

It's what she needs to see now, I realise.

'Look,' I say, determinedly. 'I wanted to let you know the initial decision they gave me because it was your idea and I thought you'd want to know. I *am* going to go ahead and give them the opportunity to hear my idea. I believe in it that much. I want the account that much. I want to succeed in this job that much.'

'And there's nothing I can say to persuade you otherwise?'

'There isn't.' I'm so disappointed in how this meeting has gone, I don't know where to begin, except with why she would even think she had to persuade me otherwise. You don't give up on something just because it didn't work. You just don't. If I'd done that when I was younger then, no way would I be here now. 'I'll let you know how it goes.'

'Okay.'

I stand up to leave but hesitate as she gently calls my name. When I turn to face her, she asks, 'Shall I stay over tonight?'

It's asked as if she's sensed the way to tidy this all conveniently away and I find myself sighing. 'I don't know, Anya, I'm really tired.'

'We can't allow a little work disagreement to come between us.'

I should agree.

Compromise.

'I thought we were a team?' she adds.

Right up until we lose an account and then it's my fault but I'm supposed to just chalk it up to experience and move on? What if it happens again?

So far, this promotion isn't working out at all how I thought. Instead of feeling invigorated and inspired and *inspiring*, I feel quiet and off my game.

'If you come over tonight,' I tell her, 'there's an embargo on talking about work.'

She licks her lips and I see the flash of panic before she nods her head, and says, 'Good plan. We'll make it about us. A romantic night in.'

At the knock on my office door, I look up to find Anya and automatically glance at my watch. It's gone six o'clock. How did that happen? Oh yeah, a series of phone calls to my contact at Perfect Pies, followed by a couple of hours studying the projected revenue for the quarter, followed by crafting at least ten iterations of the perfect team-building email.

Anya making the effort to purposely stop by my office to collect me for our evening makes me ashamed I even felt a twinge of paranoia over her and Tim. Some of the tension of the day lifts from my shoulders. We can chill over a glass of wine and make that pasta arrabbiata. Hmmm, actually not sure that's vegan? And now I feel a bit guilty that my cleaner has shopped for things I'm, once again, going to waste, thus perpetuating the myth that I don't give 'a damn' about it. Hmmm again I'm slightly disconcerted to find myself thinking about my cleaner when my girlfriend is standing in front of me. I grin warmly at Anya, right up until I take proper note of her expression.

'Please don't hate me,' she begins.

My happy heart performs a handbrake turn, crashing into my chest wall and you know what? I'm getting tired of the endless workout it's getting lately. 'Anya—'

'My meeting's been rescheduled,' she states with a hurried

step across the threshold. 'It's in Tribeca so it'll take me ages this time of day and I have to go. I have to.'

'Anya—'

'Say you understand.' Her voice has a plaintive note I haven't heard before. 'I really was looking forward to us spending some time together.'

'It's all right. I have some work I should do anyway.' Pasta arrabbiata for one, and a head-start on tomorrow's work. Is that really such a bad way to spend my evening?

'You do? Oh, that's great. I mean – you know what I mean.'

Well, right now it feels as if she means that it's great that we both work twenty-four hours a day because then we never have to put the effort into anything else but I'm probably being churlish now.

'I'll make it up to you,' she insists.

'Don't worry about it.'

'Did you manage to arrange a meeting with your contact at Perfect Pies?'

'No need as it turns out.' I push down the added disappointment. 'They've already signed with The Triple A Agency.'

'That was fast.'

I really don't want to focus on it, given that The Triple A Agency is our biggest competition. There'll be other contracts. Ones I'll make sure I don't let slip through my fingers. It's what I promised myself when the reality there was no way of turning it around finally sunk in.

'George, it's their loss,' she gently tells me.

'It really is. But not to worry. Plenty of other accounts—' I break off as I notice Tim hovering in the doorway.

'And I'm hoping to bring in another,' he says, obviously

overhearing what I'd been saying. 'Wanted to run my initial thoughts by you.'

Why is he looking at Anya, instead of me? But even though the last thing I bloody want is to have a meeting with Tim bloody Duggins, I did send out the team-building email this afternoon.

'Sure Tim,' I say, injecting as much positivity as I can into my voice, 'come on in and we'll go through what you have.'

'Great,' says Anya, looking super relieved she can shoot off to her meeting. 'So,' she whispers, catching my eye over Tim's head as he pulls out a chair and sits himself down like he's settling in for the duration. 'We're good?'

'We're good,' I say with a nod and then with a glance to Tim who I now notice is craning his neck to get another look at her, I shoot out from behind my desk, reach her in two strides and with a 'There's just one more thing,' I do something that I don't care is verboten in the office... I wrap my arms around her and kiss her.

Thoroughly.

The gladiator in me beats my chest happily as she softens against me and then kisses me back enthusiastically.

'Stop by after your meeting,' I then softly say although not so softly Tim couldn't hear. 'I don't care what time it is.'

She nods and with one last adoring look leaves the office.

At least, that's what happens in my head. Obviously in reality, I don't plant one on her in a blatant attempt to shove our relationship firmly in the face of a member of my staff. In a relationship or not, there are office rules against that sort of thing.

Chapter Eighteen

FOOD FOR THOUGHT

George

I t's no good.

Uttering an eye-staggeringly, jaw-droppingly impressive amount of swear words that only serve to wake me up further, I throw back the covers and stumble in the darkness, out of my bedroom.

Sleep is impossible.

Trust me, I even tried that marine tip about pretending I was either floating in the ocean staring up at a blue sky, or imagining being cradled in a velvet hammock.

Neither work.

Nothing works.

Except maybe more work?

At this point I may as well.

Bit hungry, I think, rubbing a hand over my stomach while padding over to the kitchen. The pasta was good but I should have made more, or at least not forgotten about it while working, so that I was forced to eat it cold. I open the fridge and see that I also seem to have eaten all the cheddar Ashleigh got me. Grabbing my phone from the counter I decide to google where Oscars is as what I really need is some of those brownies. I note the location and then realise it's 3am and so they're probably shut.

With a sigh I head over to my desk, sit down and reach over to switch on the lamp. Tim's notes about the account he's hoping to land are in front of me. They're not too bad. His strategy isn't risk-free but didn't I used to like risky? Or, as I used to call it when I had his job, boundary-pushing and creatively innovative.

Was I right to tell him to tone down and re-focus on some of the product's strengths? To be honest I'd have preferred not going after another client in the food industry but as Tim took the time to point out, we didn't get the Perfect Pies account, so what's the problem?

Noodles.

That's what the account is for.

To be specific, sweet noodles.

As in for dessert.

I crick my neck left and then right. Pull out a piece of blank paper. Grab my pen. And, for kicks, (and, let's face it, to keep my ego intact), prepare to brainstorm other ideas. Creatively innovative ideas.

Ten minutes later I haven't come up with anything half as good as Tim. I push back from my desk, drop to the floor and do fifty press-ups to get the blood pumping. Back in my chair for another ten minutes of brainstorming and, nope, still nothing.

I open my desk drawer and take out the crossword puzzle Ashleigh left me.

There are three clues left.

I've been rationing them.

Briefly I consider leaving her a clue about sweet noodles but can't help feeling however many letters the clue was for she'd turn the answer into a distinct: *Yuck*.

I make this giant leap of intuition because it turns out that that was the answer to the clue she wrote for me, to let me know her opinion on tasting Marmite for the first time. I mean, I get it. Marmite isn't for everyone. Maybe sweet noodles for me are like Marmite is for her?

I wonder what Anya would come up with for this campaign and realise her angle would be whichever provided the best evidence for uptake. Is this where I'm going wrong? I'm running my department like an extension of my old job. I'm doing less direct work on the creative side and finding that transition awkward.

I put the crossword back in the drawer until I've come at this pitch from every angle but after trying all my usual methods of word association and listing lifestyle indicators all I've done is heavily circle the best social media platform to utilise where in one search I immediately see lots of different takes on sweet noodle dishes. It's already a case of target audience being targeted.

As my palms try and mash my eyes into the back of my skull in an attempt to banish the fatigue, I don't know … I can't help feeling that lately, this all feels so … *irrelevant?*

My heart thumps heavily and then, at the sound of my phone, I jump a mile. I swear if I didn't have an issue with my heart before, I'm doing everything to give myself one now. What the hell time is it anyway that my phone is ringing? I squint at the phone screen.

5am.

Terrific.

Nothing to show for two hours' supposed work except a feeling of consuming negativity.

'Yes?' I bark into the phone. I hear my tone. Alsatian dog? Most unlike me.

'So, have you put a ring on it, yet?'

Hearing my brother, Marcus, immediately some of the negativity dissipates. Except, hang on a minute, being asked if I've "put a ring on it," is never a line I would have expected my brother to utter.

Not only that, answering that I haven't put a ring on Anya's finger *yet* forces me to think about the fact that she didn't stop by after her meeting and it never even registered.

'Bro?' Marcus asks.

'What? No. No, I haven't put a ring on it, yet.'

'Well, I have!'

'What?' I'm confused. First because I have shouted and it's way too early in the morning to be shouting. And second because it's not always that easy to snap out of work headspace.

'I've asked Jules to marry me and she, fabulous woman that she is, has said yes.'

'But why?'

'She's pregnant.'

'Again?'

'Of course. Bloody obvious how potent I am to anyone who comes near me, isn't it?' he declares and as I turn my chair around to face the early morning light glinting off the rooftops it's getting easier and easier to leave my work headspace. There's a happiness that he's going to be a dad again seeping through and its refreshingly worlds away from my work.

'But why do you need to get married?' I ask, intrigued, because of the two of us I'm the more traditional.

'A few weeks ago, some kid started having a go at Millie at school, about how she and her brother belong to parents who, wait for it, *aren't even married*! You know how hard that would have been for Millie…'

I do. Millie feels everything keenly and finds it especially difficult to cope when things come at her from left field or aren't the same every day and just the thought of her being upset has me wishing I was back in England and able to give this schoolground bully quite the talking to.

'It was all sorted out with apologies issued and so forth but, Jesus, George! How is it possible that seven-year-olds can be so narrowed in their thinking, these days?'

'Probably belonged to some warped A+B=C ideals-pushing weirdo-parents,' I say in solidarity.

'That's what I reckoned. Not that there's anything wrong with being married before you have kids, is there, and Jules is incredible with how she helps Millie not dwell on things. But later, doing the whole debriefing thing we got to talking and realised, well, I have a better job now… She has a better job… There's actually money left over at the end of every month, so why not do the deed? What's stopping us?'

'And this is what you really want? I always thought you steered away from conventionality?'

'Yeah, well, it's hard to be conventional when a wedding costs money that's better spent on your baby. Not that Tom coming along when he did was a mistake,' Marcus is quick to say and I realise that for him it was really that practicality beat convention. 'Besides, you know Jules has always been the one for me. She's going to look beautiful in a wedding dress.'

'You've always been the one for her, too, despite me thinking she should have had more sense,' I tease.

'What, because she didn't go for you?'

This genuinely shocks me. 'Why on earth would she have gone for me, Heartless George?'

'Whoa. It's been that long I forgot everyone used to call you that.'

'How could you forget when you still have a scar because of it?' I picture him looking down at the knuckles across his right hand.

'It's what Jules was first attracted to – me looking like a "bad boy", so I should thank you. I should thank Steve too for teaching me how to land a left hook. I still say somebody moved that lamppost otherwise I'd have felled Dave for what he said to you that day. Anyway, of course I was going to jump in and defend my brother.'

Your *big* brother.

Still echoed, didn't it?

The wound of having my younger brother fight on my behalf when it should have been the other way around.

My mother's friends, when allowed into the house, that was, used to say "Poor George" at me being stuck inside so much but I used to think "Poor Marcus" because he was the one always being told to be quiet because I was resting. Or being told to go and have a bath because he'd been outside and who knew what germs he was carrying in and when was he ever going to learn his brother was poorly?

'What do the parents say?' I ask, knowing it was pointless to pick at old wounds.

'They're over the moon. Specially if it means their pride and joy is coming back home for it. You'll be my best man, won't you?'

'Um … yeah?' I answer, thinking about how much I used to enjoy telling them about working in London and New York.

Wait a minute… Used to? Surely, I'm just having a few bad weeks. No one's job is perfect twenty-four-seven three-six-five.

Marcus says, 'Don't sound too excited, will you?'

'Sorry.' I get my head out of my arse and concentrate on the point of the call. 'Course it's yeah. Wouldn't miss you getting married for the world.' I think of Marcus's best mate, Steve. 'But you know … if you wanted Steve for best man duties…'

'I want my big brother. End of.'

'Then consider me at your side aiding and abetting. Stag do at The Bedraggled Badger is a lock. The kids sent me a picture of it the other week actually. Tell them both more pictures please.'

'Will do. Oh, and you'll bring Anya, of course.'

'Of course.' I'm quite proud of the fact that the hesitation was undetectable.

'Might give her ideas … wouldn't be such a bad thing, would it?'

'How do you know we don't have ideas of our own?' I ask, thinking of the five-year plans we love making.

'Please. If it was left to the two of you, you'd marry your careers, not each other. We all thank our stars your jobs are at the same place – if only because it means you might accidentally bump into each other and remember to have sex every now and then. Kudos on the promotion by the way. Exactly how big is that whacking great big pay rise?'

'Oh, it's disgustingly huge,' I say, grinning.

'Good. Although let's be honest, we can all do with more money, but it's not what makes the world go round, is it?'

'Isn't it?'

'Well no. According to some wise-arse in Millie's class it's love … and marriage … *before* kids.'

'So, you're smashing it in retrospect then.'

'Will be and couldn't be happier about it. You'll definitely be able to get the time off?'

'Nothing is going to stop me coming home for my brother's wedding. Nothing.'

'And Anya? Can work spare the two of you at the same time?'

First my kid brother was practical. Then conventional. And now realistic? I try to remember the last time Anya and I had any vacation together and remember Sicily and grin. I know we didn't have such a serious workload back then but we still worked like we did. Work hard. Play hard. I grin some more. 'We'll be there. You can count on us.' There was no way he was letting his brother down like he had so many times when they were younger.

'Cool. Very cool. All right bro, I'm aware of the time out there, so I'll let you get suited and booted. Say hi to Anya for me.'

'Will do. Bye.'

In the sudden silence I stare at the city skyline.

My kid brother is getting married.

My kid brother is a dad nearly three times over.

I'm on track for all of that, I reason.

In a solid relationship, aren't I?

Got the promotion, didn't I?

I rub a hand over my heart.

Anya and I never did get our romantic break. What could be more romantic than a summer wedding in an English village. And I already know I have Harrison and Elizabeth's blessing when it comes to getting engaged. Maybe Anya being around my niece and nephew, seeing a pregnant Jules, being at a wedding … maybe she'll want to speed up our own plans. Maybe forgo another promotion in pursuit of a wedding?

Now that was sweet noodles for thought!

Chapter Nineteen

IN A PICKLE

Ashleigh

'These look fun, right?'

I'm holding up a packet of fridge magnets for Zach to see. I've dragged him into my local bodega to show him the startlingly full range they have for sale. After this, the plan is to head to Oscars for something sweet before seeing a movie tonight.

'They look … cheesy?' Zach says, glancing to them while his hand hovers near the magnets in the shape of gigantic pickles wearing super hero capes.

'Cheesy is exactly the look I was going for. George is going to love them,' I say, as I study the wheels of plastic cheese with magnets stuck on the back. Who needs sensible matching colour-coordinated fridge magnets when you can have these? They're perfect for displaying the artwork his niece and nephew send.

'George has weird taste,' Zach says.

I love Zach for not getting weird on me whenever I mention George. Not *love*, love, obviously. We're only on date eight.

Yep, date eight and still going strong, going by the fact we've made plans for next week and the week after.

I'm still really tired by 10pm but I'm drinking more coffee so that's helping.

I'm also making sure I mention the names of all the other clients I clean for. Equal anecdotal regaling is key to Zach not thinking I favour one over the other. This might be going overboard, but then I really like seeing him laugh when I tell him about some of Mrs. Lundy's amazing stories.

Before heading over to pay for the cheesy magnets I reach out and grab the pack of cape-wearing pickle magnets. 'For you,' I tell Zach, grinning absurdly at him. 'Because the heart wants what the heart wants.' We're still grinning madly at each other as we leave.

We're holding hands.

I can't remember if he grabbed mine or I grabbed his or we naturally found ourselves holding hands but it feels…? I draw a blank and revert to worrying I still haven't told him about Sarah's sister's wedding.

Or, in fact, Sarah.

I'm super worried I won't be able to talk about either without getting upset and spooking him and now with the big day only six weeks away, if I want Zach to come with me, I need to find a way of broaching the subject.

I've been practising this sort of approach: *'Zach? Would you like to come to a wedding with me? It's just that my best friend, Sarah … I must have mentioned her. I haven't? Um. Well, that's because she … um … died … anyway, her sister is getting married and I have an invite that includes a plus one. It'll be a fun night – weekend, it would actually be for the weekend and we'd be staying at my folks' and … I really haven't mentioned Sarah to you? When? June 8th. Oh … when did Sarah die? Last year. I'm completely fine about it all.'*

Yeah. No. You see? Sounds too heavy, going from dinners and movies and cape-crusading pickle magnets to staying at my folks for the weekend so that we can attend my dead best friend's sister's wedding.

'Hey,' Zach says, thankfully interrupting my introspection. 'I forgot to ask, what happened when you told your boss you didn't want the promotion?'

'Oh, um, I think it went well.'

'That's great.'

'Uh-huh. I ended up suggesting someone else for the position and she was happy with that.'

What actually happened was that the moment I entered her office proffering the box of honey and orange madeleines from Oscars, Rhonda correctly guessed I was trying to sweeten my delivery on turning down the promotion. She shoved the swear box that sits on her desk into a drawer and then let loose a slew of profanities that eventually ended with a lecture about how her bones ached and she was looking to retire next year and I was ruining all her plans.

After that, even though the thought of being stuck in an office over being able to keep sane – I mean, being able to clean – horrified me, the people pleaser in me would have accepted the position right there and then which is why it was so fortunate I'd had a long talk with Jamal beforehand.

Of course, the minute I suggested Jamal would be better for the position she let loose another slew of profanities because she understood that probably meant he needed the money if his daughter Letitia had taken off again leaving him with her two kids to take care of.

It all worked out okay in the end because we were in complete agreement about helping out Jamal. But one really weird thing though… Right when I thought I'd got away with not having to talk in any way about why I choose cleaning over being stuck in an office she told me that 'While it was a good thing how much I looked after my friends, I was allowed to take opportunities for myself because, let's face it, I couldn't be a cleaner all my life.'

I can only hope that me slamming into the door frame on my exit was construed as my usual clumsiness instead of feeling I'd just been T-boned by a freight truck. I mean, where does it say I can't be a cleaner all my life and why did she say that thing about looking after my friends like she did? What exactly is wrong with that? Looking out for your friends is the very least you should do for them, right?

I concentrate on dodging the people coming towards me while still maintaining hand-holding contact with Zach. 'So, tell me what's happening with *your* work,' I ask as we near Oscars. 'Have you told them you're leaving, yet?' He's going to need to if he ever wants to start up on his own, surely? It's definitely the first question my mother is going to ask when she starts her interrogation – I mean her healthy-but-in-no-way-justifiable interest in him and his future … apropos *our* future together.

'Nah, I've pretty much decided to stay where I am,' Zach says.

'Stay?'

'As in not leave,' Zach says casually.

We get separated as a crowd comes towards us and then suddenly Zach's right beside me again, grabbing my hand and holding on tighter.

It feels … comforting?

I blink and try not to force myself to endlessly check what I'm feeling. All I should be focused on is being in the moment with him. 'But I thought you'd been accepted for a loan?' I ask him. 'That's a really big deal.'

'Yeah. But I've been thinking if I start up now, I won't have as much time to check on my mom, to see you, to, you know, have a life? When you start your own business it's full-on from the get-go. Do I really need that in my life right now?'

'Sure, but if not now, when?'

'I don't know. Sometime in the future. When it feels right.'

'But what's changed, really? Since you deciding to go for it, to getting the loan, to now, I mean?' I'm aware I'm asking the type of questions I hate but I don't get it – he seemed so passionate about it when he first mentioned it.

Please, please, I think, don't let it be because of me coming into his life. That's a lot to put on a person you've just met.

I stare up at him waiting and I think he's going to say it and I'm going to be left wondering how I feel about that and it all seems too soon. But then someone knocks into me from behind and he swings me out of the way and the moment is lost, or is it?

I mean, if I don't want to, I don't have to let this go. How am I going to get to know him better if I don't keep asking questions? I don't need for us to bare souls on the middle of the street exactly but I wouldn't like him to think I'm not interested, either.

'You can't let other people stop you from what you really want to do,' I say.

'But do I really want the hassle?' Zach says as he pushes the door of Oscars open.

It occurs to me if you're really passionate about something you don't let "hassle" stop you but then I get distracted by the fact that there are no customers in the bakery.

A second later and I'm realising why. They've all left on account of the shouting. Zach and I exchange a worried look before heading straight back to the kitchen area where Carlos and

Oz are standing either side of the prep bench with chests huffing and jaws clenching.

'Um, guys?' Zach asks trying to get their attention.

I don't think it's Zach's voice so much as the ripple of air we discharge as we move into the tiny space that has them turning in unison to face us both.

'This is all your fault,' Oz snarls at me.

Chapter Twenty

MORE CONVERSATION LESS RUNNING

Ashleigh

I stare up at Oz. 'What the what, now?' How could his and Carlos's arguing be my fault?

'*This.*' Oz points between himself and Carlos, then points at me. '*Your,*' then waves his arms about, narrowly missing one of the sets of stacked bowls on the edge of a shelf. '*Fault.*'

None the wiser I turn to look at Carlos.

'We got an offer to cater a swanky dinner party,' Carlos explains.

'From Mrs. Lundy?' I whoop. 'But that's great—'

'But this one,' Carlos says, pointing in the love of his life's direction, 'says he won't do it because we're a bakery not a Michelin star restaurant and how the Pastry Gods will never let him hear the end of it.'

'But, Ozzie,' I say.

'Do not Ozzie-Baby me,' Oz tells me. '*He,*' this time it's Oz pointing his finger at the love of his life, 'already tried that. I'm a pastry chef. If *she*—'

'Mrs. Lundy?' I ask.

'If *she* wants a few pastries to serve afterwards, okay, but Oscars isn't some pop-up kitchen—'

'I'm aware of that, Oz,' Carlos says.

'Are you? Really?' Oz turns to face Carlos. 'Because it's not like you're ever here anymore.'

'Not this again.'

'Yes, this again.'

'Don't make this into something it isn't so you can have an argument about me taking one night every now and again—'

'That would be a night *every* week. Do you really think I believe you're going to see an old friend who's,' Oz finger-quotes, 'going through some stuff'? How naïve do you think I am? That sort of excuse may have Ashleigh believing *you*,' he says, breaking off to give Zach a thunderous look.

I blink. 'Wow, way to bring us into your personal argument, Oz.'

'Maybe we should go,' Zach says looking uncomfortable.

'Don't you dare,' Carlos tells us. 'You leave and this will descend into another argument about something that isn't even a thing, instead of us discussing a profitable business idea. Oz, come on, this is a great opportunity. We could prep most of the food here. We have the van for transport. Mrs. Lundy can give us the kitchen for the evening. I'm sure Ashleigh can help us out.'

'Of course,' I say. 'You don't even have to pay me.'

Oz throws his hands up in the air dramatically. 'You both think it's that easy? You two do it. I'm out.' And for such a big man, he gently breezes past us all and out of the bakery.

'Out?' Carlos asks, swearing under his breath. 'What does that mean? Oz? Oz, what do you mean you're out?' Carlos takes off after him leaving Zach and I alone in the bakery.

'Sorry about that,' I say into the silence.

'It's not your fault. I didn't have them down as drama llamas but that was intense.'

'It wasn't that bad.' I try and laugh off their argument.

'The trials and tribulations of running your own business. Kind of what I was talking about earlier. At least we both have jobs we can have a life alongside.'

'I guess.'

As if he can sense I'm feeling bad for my two friends he pulls me into his arms. 'Don't worry, they'll smooth it out.'

'I guess,' I repeat, only softer because I *do* worry. I've seen them bicker, both tired from a long shift at work or one of them in a funk. That's life, right, and maybe if I hadn't had that evening with Oz and seen him as upset as I did, I wouldn't be so worried because one look at Carlos just now and he's definitely hiding something.

'And, hey.' Zach leans down and kisses the tip of my nose. 'It doesn't have to spoil our night, which I was really enjoying in case I forgot to tell you.'

'Me too.' I smile up at him. Not the kissing the tip of my nose part – feels yuck if I'm honest – but everything else I was enjoying.

He leans down and kisses me on my lips this time and then leans back and looks towards the doorway. 'How long do you think before one or both come back?'

'I'm not sure. One of them will figure out they need to lock up. I guess we wait until they figure it out. I think we're going to miss the movie.'

'I can deal.' He kisses me again.

And again.

And as his lips trail lazily down my neck, I suddenly realise what he's doing and a second before he hits the spot that always makes my knees weak, I jump back. 'Wait a minute. You want to get it on in our friends' bakery?'

'Too weird?'

'After they've had a really bad argument?'

'It could disperse the negative energy?' he says with a hopeful wink.

'I don't know.'

'Right. No.' Zach immediately takes a step away from me. 'I mean I figure we've been out a few times now but if you're not ready, I don't want you thinking I'm some pushy jerk.'

Oh. That's sweet. 'I do want to,' I tell him. 'I do, it's just that—'

It was just that what? Why am I not throwing the catch on the door and jumping on him? Why am I not taking him by the hand, whispering in his ear that I "know a place" and walking up the stairs to my apartment which is *right above this place*?

That's when it hits me. He doesn't even know where I live. I don't even know where he lives. We go out to dinner once, twice a week. Sometimes a movie as well. And we talk. Easy talk. Fun talk.

Definitely no talk about business loans.

Or Sarah's sister's wedding.

Or Sarah.

'Hey,' Zach says. 'I don't want to add extra drama. I'm good with casual and taking things slow.'

I swallow. That's the second time tonight he's mentioned not being a fan of "drama". 'How about on our next date we plan on going back to your place afterwards?' I find myself saying.

'Yeah? You like plans, huh?'

I feel my nose wrinkle as I bat my eyelashes at him. 'They have their advantages.' I mean, it's been a while since I've felt spontaneous... Worrying you're one step away from an anxiety attack tends to remove that ability. As does exhaustion in an intern role where your main skill is to demonstrate you'll do anything, anytime, because you're indispensable and available to move into a permanent job role the moment you're asked. But that was before I was so busy being spontaneous at work that I forgot to check my phone for messages and missed the fact that my best friend was lying in hospital dying.

'I can work on getting the place to myself for the evening,' Zach murmurs. 'The guys owe me anyways, especially when I put these bad boys on the fridge door,' he adds, holding up the paper bag containing the pickle magnets.

'That's right ... you said you share with three others?'

'Yeah. You must share as well but maybe it would be easier at yours?'

'Except my bed is in the living room,' I automatically answer.

What? Technically it is and I don't want to have to deal with telling him why I don't sleep in the bedroom that now stays empty down the hall. Not here when Carlos or Oz could walk back in at any moment.

I've been wanting to feel lighter, haven't I?

This would be good for me. It's okay to move forward with my life again and with Zach there's this uncomplicated pull. 'Organise your housemates to go out for the evening next week,' I whisper, aiming for what I hope is a super-sexy and confident smile.

Suddenly the bakery door is thrust open and Carlos is standing inside with the biggest wounded-bear look on his face. 'I lost him,' he declares, slamming the bakery door shut behind him.

'*What?*' I must sway because I feel Zach's arm come around

me. All I can hear is another voice in another time. Sarah's mother, Shelley-Ann, saying over and over, 'We lost her. We lost her.'

'I thought I was fast,' Carlos says as he sinks down onto a chair, 'but apparently, Oz can run faster. Shit.' He puts his head in his hands and I snap out of the past as everything in me wants to wrap my arms around my friend like I couldn't wrap my arms around Sarah's mother.

I think about how my life is filling up again and how hard it is to leave Sarah behind.

I think about how I want these new friends to become old friends and that the only way that's going to happen is if I invest.

I'm already invested, I realise, because I hate seeing Carlos upset like this.

'Go,' I whisper to Zach.

'You're sure?'

'I'm sure,' I say with a nod and a quick kiss to Zach's cheek. 'Let me know what night next week, okay?'

When it's just me and Carlos again, I flip over the sign to say "Closed" and then head over to the coffee machine. I start pushing levers, pulling knobs and waving a coffee cup under various openings until I hear Carlos sigh, and get up to walk over and rescue me, or, at least, the machine.

'I can't afford for you to break this,' he says, nudging me out of the way. 'Go sit down, I'll bring us two.'

'Unless you want the really good stuff?' I ask, heading over to one of the corner tables. 'I know where Oz keeps the liquor.'

'You do?'

I nod. 'Oz and I hung out when you were out with your friend who's…' I finger-quote like Oz, 'Going through some stuff.'

Carlos stares at me and then seeming to collect himself, collects two cups from a shelf.

I hope he's not going to regret not going for the hard stuff. 'You realise Oz thinks you're helping this person through his stuff in an entirely non-platonic, intimate and sexual way?' I watch his shoulders tense but when he doesn't say anything, I add, 'Are you having an affair on him?'

Carlos gives his full focus to bringing the coffees over to the table like he's me and can't navigate empty space and my stomach churns because what the hell will I say if he admits he *is*?

'I'm not having an affair,' Carlos says, sitting down opposite me. 'And deep down, he knows I'm not, either. He knows I'd never do that to him—'

'Again?'

Carlos goes completely still except for his face which looks like it's desperately searching for haughty disdain and, instead, is only able to find crestfallen. 'He told you.' He whispers it and it's not a question. It's a scar of hurt stretching tightly over a mass of shame and I feel awful, just awful.

'Don't be angry with him,' I plead. 'He felt hideous when he realised it had slipped out.'

Carlos throws himself back in his chair, shoving his hands into his pockets. 'And now you think I'm this "get it wherever I can" guy. Or someone who doesn't know how to appreciate what they have.' He says it all defiantly but he's watching me intently.

'I really don't. But to check … this friend you're—'

His gaze narrows even more. 'Please do not finger-quote at me again.'

'*Helping through some stuff*, isn't waiting in the wings for when you announce to Oz you want an open relationship?' I take a sip of my coffee and then send him what I hope is a piercing yet friendly eyeballing.

Carlos looks genuinely shocked. 'That's what Oz thinks? I'm not into sharing Oz with anyone.'

'That's good because Oz went to that place you said you were going and waited for you. He waited for you thinking he was going to have to watch you with some other guy. It might have been worse for him when you didn't show up at all.' I pause and then lean forward to ask, 'So, tell me what you're doing that it's easier to make him think all that of you again, rather than tell him the truth?'

'Is this the part where you try and "save" me?'

'Damn right. You and Oz are my friends and if you think for one minute that I'm going to leave one of you behind… That's not me.'

Anymore.

Wow. My mouth has gone dry and I have to divert my hands from going to my cup when I notice them shaking. As I lay them as casually in my lap as I can, I wait, watching Carlos watching me as he debates internally whether the risk of telling me has enough reward.

I'm honestly about to declare him the winner of the standoff when he says, 'I'm at business classes.'

'Well, Jesus, Carlos, how can you do that to Oz – wait – what?' I've been so primed to receive the worst kind of news that it takes me half a minute to compute and then, 'No. I don't get it. How is that even a thing?'

'I—' he breaks off, then breathes deeply. 'Do you know how difficult it is to tell Oz things sometimes? He's so talented … but also so … in his own head. He doesn't always see what's going on around him. And then, when it's pointed out, he gets upset he didn't see it and then can't create at all and it's a crime for that man not to be able to bake.'

'You have him up on a pedestal.' I recognise what Carlos is saying but what's so hard about getting someone to really listen to you? But then I realise Carlos probably did try that. Over and over. And so why wouldn't a person give up?

I feel a bit sick.

As I study Carlos, really study him, I see how tired he looks – how defeated. 'Why can't you tell him you enrolled in a business class?'

'Because I lied to him.'

'About cheating on him with another guy?'

He pushes his coffee away as if he's lost his appetite. 'I'm talking about after. I lied about how much experience I had running a business like this. I thought starting up the bakery would be something we could focus on together. A fresh start. And it was. Except now we're losing customers every day and we're running out of money. *His* money. His money that I sold him on getting a return on.'

'But you're rammed every morning.'

'It's the early morning rush and then it tapers off.'

'So, the fact that you had no customers earlier wasn't because you two were arguing?'

'Please. Seeing us arguing would probably up the entertainment value. You know how everyone loves Oz once they get a look at him and you've also seen how hard it is to get him out front. Besides, he's not some performing monkey. He's the talent and I'm the – I don't know what I am. I thought it would be easier than this and I'm not sure Oz gets it – sees it – you know?'

Now the veil has been lifted I can see how overwhelmed he's been feeling. I reach over to lay my hand over his. 'Oh honey, seeing my folks run their own business, trust me, I know how hard it is. But isn't it more that you're not letting Oz see it? Maybe if he did—'

'He'd what? You heard him earlier? He's not interested in catering one dinner party, let alone making that part of our business.'

'You're panicking and I totally get it but if you tell him why—'

'Do you have any idea what he gave up to do this with me?'

I squeeze his hand. 'Everyone gives up things in life to move forwards. Did you ever think that maybe he wanted to give whatever it was up anyway? For the chance to do this with you? And now that he has, I'm pretty sure he'd want to know the extent of the problems so that he can help you fix it.'

'It's not that simple.'

'It really is.' I say that like I really believe it. Like I don't know that there are a gazillion grey areas that we all use to complicate things when we want to. My hand leaves his to creep up to my thumping heart, beating a heavy drum and bass beat trying to get him to see that the risk of saying it has to outweigh not saying it. It just has to. Because it's such a crappy feeling being the last to know something. And you always find out in the end.

Always.

Only sometimes when you do it's far too late to do anything about it.

'You're already working to find a solution to the problem, Carlos. Tell him. He'll respect you more for it.'

'What if all he hears is that I've lied to him again? What if he—'

'I know a lot about sifting through What Ifs and the only What If you need here is … what if you *don't* tell him and you lose him because when he works it out, and he *will* work it out, he loses all respect for you? Because what if he feels like you thought he wouldn't be able to handle it – that you never even gave him the opportunity to rise to the occasion? That's worse. So much worse.'

Carlos blows out a breath, shifts his gaze from his coffee to staring out the window before he says, quietly, 'You're right. I know you're right.'

'You'll tell him?'

He nods his head carefully.

'When?' I ask feeling like a kid demanding to know when a parent is going to Think About It. 'You should do it now. Tonight. As soon as you see him. Don't leave this, Carlos.'

'It's okay. I'll tell him. Thank you … I needed to hear all that. You're the only one of our friends to wade in, you know?'

They probably don't have as much to lose, I think, but say, 'Don't think you're getting off lightly. My turn … before you came back to the bakery, I think I agreed to have sex with Zach. Next week.'

'I'll get the bourbon,' Carlos says and I wonder if it's to celebrate or to help calm me down.

Chapter Twenty-One

KEEP CALM AND BUSY

Ashleigh

'Apatosaurus, diplodocus, stegosaurus, triceratops.' I stare at the plastic dinosaur in my hand. 'So, then what are you?' When it doesn't burst into a fully animated introduction, I'm forced to grab my phone and bring up the list I made last week. 'Let's see, long snout, smooth spine, oh, right … you're the *irritator*. I'll try not to hold it against you,' I tell it as I slide it onto the shelf between the diplodocus and the stegosaurus.

There.

Five-year-old Davey Montford's collection of dinosaurs is exactly as it should be, standing proudly on the shelf that runs the length of his bed – except now the shelf underneath them is dust free.

Win-win.

And a total turn-around from last week when it hadn't been stated in the New Client File for 33B that Davey's dinosaur collection, along with everything in his bedroom, needed to be kept in strict alphabetical order or he wouldn't be able to function.

I still can't believe that thanks to George recommending me I now get to clean all the apartments on the thirty-third floor of The Clouds. This one is a headquarters of frantic family life and I love restoring order to it for them.

I sweep my gaze between the list and shelf to double-check I got the order right. The last thing I want to do is upset Davey, or his mother, Julia, who was kind enough to label last week's episode "first-clean teething troubles".

My gaze snags once again on the Irritator, reminding me I'm irritated with myself. I've been rushing around all week and, as yet, haven't had time to properly check if Carlos has told Oz about the problems with the bakery. Talking about the business while standing in line in the premises isn't ideal so other than my whispered, 'How did it go? Have you told him?' and his rushed, 'It'll be fine' I don't know any more and all efforts to catch a glimpse of Oz in the kitchen have been thwarted.

Has Carlos told him?

Is everything going to be okay?

Tomorrow I'm determined to get the lowdown if I have to hold over his head not telling him about how it goes with Zach tonight until he does.

Tonight, with Zach. The nerves jangle in my belly.

To distract myself I head into Julia's bathroom to doublecheck every surface sparkles. Extra supply of freshly laundered fluffy white towels on the heat-rack – check. Mirror streak free – check – whoa… I take in my reflection, hoping the shadows under my eyes are from the bathroom light, rather than proof of sleepless nights.

I guess Rhonda rattled me with the "being a good friend"

comment followed by the "you can't be a cleaner all your life," comment, and what with worrying about Carlos and Oz as well, for more nights than I'd like to admit, I've been having trouble sleeping again.

I lean further forward to inspect under my eyes. I'm going to need concealer for my date with Zach.

After reading Carlos the riot act about talking to Oz, did I take my own medicine and tell Zach about Sarah or about the invite to her sister's wedding?

I did not.

Instead of having a conversation about this thing that I can feel growing bigger between us, I decided to check out how big his thing was first – that's right – I prioritised sex. Decided talking about Sarah and being with Zach are in no way connected, but that talking about Sarah will get me upset and I was allowed to have some fun first. At least, I hope it's going to be fun?

I'll tell him after.

Well, not right after, obviously.

That would be weird.

But soon after.

I'll find a way to bring it up in conversation.

Why am I so nervous?

Maybe it's that I prefer sex to feel less scheduled? I know I said I was good with making plans, but I don't think I've ever once had to plan when to have sex.

At least his housemates are going to be out. There's nothing worse than waking up in someone's bed, finding your way to the kitchen, bumping into a stranger and making awkward small talk while trying not to draw their attention to the fact your underwear is half-hanging off the couch.

This way I'll know my way around the place before I emerge from a bed in the morning.

At least I hope it will be the morning.

What if we don't … work?

Why is this so difficult?

I sigh into the mirror.

At least "why" is different to "what if".

I square back my shoulders.

It's going to be okay.

And if it isn't okay, I'll figure it out.

Because *I'm* okay.

All I need to do is keep busy and not freak myself out, which is why I'm so grateful I have an extra shift volunteer reading at the hospital this afternoon. I'll be able to get that done and head back to my apartment with just enough time to shower and find something to wear before heading over to Zach's.

For the sex we'll be having.

I draw in a deep calming breath and … oh … thinking about calming reminds me. I scurry out to my cart and pull out the bottom drawer. I push aside one of the new company tabards Jamal handed out this week. They say Sparkle all over them in silver and gold on a background of fluorescent white and I don't think I was alone in thinking it looks like some sexy lab coat. I was supposed to put it on when I got here because there was no way I was going to wear it on the subway. Not because I'm embarrassed about where I work but because I was worried the sheer glare coming off it would be too much for people. Anyway, under the tabard I take out the little surprise I brought for Julia to re-create getting that *High-End Spa Feel At Home* article I was reading.

Back in the bathroom I take the glossy bamboo leaves and strands of natural twine and spray them with a spritz of gorgeous-smelling bergamot and rose essential oils – perfect for relaxing. Now for the tricky part as I tie one of the leaves around the bottle of handwash using the origami-style instructions from the article. It's meant to look like a kimono obi belt afterwards.

When it doesn't spring apart after a few seconds I give a little leap of pleasure and move on to the other bottles in the bathroom. I stand back, happy with the results. The room feels less simply clean and functional and more invitingly relaxing. Which is great because, having noticed the book *Doing All The Things While Still Retaining Your Sanity*, that was lying on her bed last week, I figure if there's one thing the hardworking, single mother of two deserves, it's a little gift of spa-like pampering and relaxation.

'…And I get to go home next week, Ashleigh. *Home.*' Katey hugs her arms to herself, while beaming proudly from the end of her hospital bed.

'That's the best news, ever, Katey.' I'm beaming right back at her, my heart fat with happiness as it sits inside my chest.

Earlier as she was reciting her favourite chapter from the book we've been reading together, I sat beside her thinking about how easy-breezy I'd found it to sail through the hospital's entrance doors and walk up here to the Ladybug Ward. As if I'd been doing it for years. I'm so grateful to Mrs. Lundy for using the right words to get me to follow through.

And now even knowing that sometimes the patient isn't going to get to go home I'm not going to let that stop me from turning up every week. Sarah was right. I'm kind of good at this.

'…I'm gonna get to play with my dog, Bert,' Katey says. 'Wanna see a picture of him?' She pulls out a photo from the bedside locker beside her and thrusts it into my outstretched hand. 'I can't wait to give him the biggest hug. I asked my dad if Bert could sleep on the end of my bed the first few nights and he said "Absolutely", not even "We'll have to see". No way would Mom have said that. Promise you'll never tell him that?'

'Promise,' I say with a laugh.

'I'm going to miss you.'

A lump forms in my throat. 'I'm going to miss you too, but seeing this picture of Bert here, I know you're going to be in the best paws!' I hand her back the photo. 'I want to thank you too because you've helped me so much with my visits here.'

'Uh-huh, you hardly ever miss out words now,' she says, nodding her head. 'Maybe I'll tell *Tabitha's Toothy Problem* to Bert? I'm coming back for the Read-A-Thon, so I'll get to see you then, right?'

'What's the Read-A-Thon?'

'It's where we all get dressed up as our favourite character from books and read and we get sponsored and it's for charity. It's on the noticeboard on the wall outside the ward.'

'Well, that sounds amazing and you can count on seeing me here.'

'That's so great because I didn't see your name on the list so I went ahead and added it for you. How will I recognise you? Who will you come as?'

'Hmmm, I'm going to have to let that be a surprise.' Aka, whatever the shop has left in my budget.

Chapter Twenty-Two

ANONYMOUS SARDINE IN A SPARKLY TABARD

Ashleigh

Who *doesn't* love sitting on the subway, with a giant bush between their legs?

Wow.

That sounded so wrong. To clarify, I'm currently sitting on the packed subway with an overly large, let's call it, "mature" potted plant between my legs. To be honest I'm not sure anyone has noticed on account of being squashed in like a sardine. An anonymous sardine due to the unwritten rule about avoiding eye contact.

I'm on my way to The Clouds to deliver the plant to George's apartment. Considering I'm supposed to be on my way home to get ready for tonight, I don't know what possessed me.

Okay, the Read-A-Thon made me do it. It's scheduled for the morning of Jasmine's wedding. I'll make it work somehow but it made me think about how I still haven't told Zach about the wedding. Nerves that were gone while reading to Katey came

185

back tenfold and somehow, instead of getting on the subway, I found myself standing in front of a stall of plants for sale when it hit me. Getting George a plant – a *real* plant – to replace the fake Ficus he has, was exactly what I needed to do.

I'm worried he won't get the joke because it references something we were talking about or I guess *writing about* would be a more accurate description. Alongside the habit we've slipped into for leaving crossword clues for each other, there are now sometimes notes that we staple to the page when we run out of room in the margins.

It's becoming quite the little book. A jumble of crossword clues. Recipes. And thank you notes the like of:

Ashleigh,
Thank you for the 8Across, push/pull effect, 7. They're acutely...
14Down, Another word for cheesy, 6

I'd grinned as I'd written the answers "magnets" and "kitsch", into our crossword.

and add a certain 17Across, French, 4 words, 2, 2, 4, 5 to the artwork, and overall apartment décor.

17Across, "Je ne sais quoi", had only come to me as I was getting into bed that night, and I'd wished *acutely* I'd been able to message him the answer. Instead, I'd had to wait until the following week's visit to write the answer and leave him a note that said:

George,
I've included a New York cheesecake with this week's grocery basics.

How are you liking New York anyways? Is it super-different from where you lived in England? I've never been to England but hope I'll get to visit, one day. Where would you recommend – apart from The Bedraggled Badger, which looks like somewhere everyone should visit.

George's response had been:

Ashleigh,

The Bedraggled Badger is a dreadful place – as least that's what we tell anyone who mentions it looks halfway decent. My brother is holding something over the pub landlord that makes him charge an exorbitant fee for anyone wanting to pose for a selfie on the premises. It's the only way it'll retain its specialness. In fact, maybe I should get rid of the picture my niece and nephew painted for me – you know, destroy all evidence. Except, what would I then use the fridge magnets for?

PS 3am's random thought: Do you ever think about what it would be like if there were bridges between high-rises so that you didn't have to go all the way back down to the ground to get to the next one? It would mean being permanently surrounded by great views (my favourite thing about living in The Clouds). The views don't appear to help with insomnia but they're restful to gaze at.

I'd thought about the postscript for days after reading it. Specifically, about the fact that he's not sleeping. I could have mentioned de-cluttering, because a tidy desk equals a tidy mind but his place is clutter-free. In fact, maybe that's the problem. I responded with:

George,

When I can't sleep, I clean. Although I just realised in telling you to try that, I could be talking myself out of a job. I could tell you maybe to get on with some work, but it looks like that might be the problem? So I'm going to go out on a limb and suggest something more Zen. Have you thought about a hobby? Maybe: 33Down Japanese art of growing dwarfed trees, 6

I look at the tree between my legs. Let's hope he doesn't think this is part of the bonsai I was suggesting … unless he wants to invent Bonsai for Giants? The thought makes me snort out loud.

I wrote a postscript to him as well:

PS: I like the views from up in The Clouds too. I love the vibrant, pulsing, sense of being alive that's so tangible at ground level, but there's a serenity to the views from up high. Bridges, huh? I've always wondered about cranes you can summon like elevators… where you step out onto one and it swings you around to the next building. But I guess there's the oxygen issue … probably need a lot more of it. Suddenly, your fake Ficus is looking even more redundant!

PPS I've sprayed a little lavender oil on your pillows to promote sleep. Let me know how it works out for you.

He never did answer what he thought about living in New York. Maybe he doesn't have an opinion. Maybe he's only here on a fixed-term contract. Maybe our book of crossword clues and notes and recipes and impressions will come to a crashing stop.

At that thought, I try telling myself there'll always be another apartment to clean, right?

When he did eventually add another note, it read:

Ashleigh,

This morning as I watched the sunrise chase shadows across the cityscape, I thought about those time-lapse videos you get of light playing over mountain ranges (they always appear on ancient music videos or indie films to depict the passage of time). Anyway, it made me realise why I love the skyline so much. It reminds me of being in the mountains. But I guess at least in the real mountains you get to breathe in the fresh air. Maybe if our bridges and cranes were planted with trees like The High Line? You were right about work, but I'll figure it out. I got a promotion, so I think a little less sleep is to be expected. The jury's still out on the lavender spray.

PS More cheesecake, please.

Confession: I'm not the only one to have read this latest note from George.

It fell out of my bag and Carlos picked it up. To say the look on his face was *enthusiastically eager to discover more, 4 letters* (Answer: avid) was pure understatement.

'What?' I'd said, trying to snatch it back to tuck safely away again. I'd only bought the papers back with me so that I could concentrate on a crossword clue. At Carlos's "Tell me everything right now" face, I'd attempted a shrug of indifference. 'It's just a note from George.'

'Sweetie, this is not a note you leave a cleaner. Notes to cleaners go along the lines of, "Derek shat on the carpet, again. Sorry."

'I really hope that Derek is a dog in this scenario?' I'd replied.

'*This,*' Carlos had waved the note around in the air like he was announcing it to the world, 'this, is more like a sonnet.'

'Don't be ridiculous,' I'd snapped, jumping up, surprisingly athletic, for once, to snatch it out of his hands, vowing to never think of having joint custody of the clutch of papers again, even if I had contributed to fifty per cent of the notes.

I shouldn't feel relieved that Carlos and Ozzie-Baby's latest arguments have distracted Carlos enough that he hasn't mentioned the note again and as the subway lurches to a stop my brain is taken up with more pressing matters ... like how the hell I'm going to get this plant into George's apartment.

I'm pretty impressed with myself for getting my cleaning cart out of the amenities room and using it to wheel the plant to the service lift and then into George's apartment.

In the lounge, I study the artificial Ficus in the window and then study the plant I've brought. Is it my imagination or is it super difficult to tell the difference between the two?

But who wants fake when you can have real? Other than the fake one being about a ton lighter. It's probably some universal truth that people only ever purchase real plants just *after* they have been watered.

I walk over to remove fake Ficus from its cast-concrete pot. I really hadn't thought this through because now I'm wondering what I'm going to do with it.

I suppose I could take it to Zach's as a gift.

'Here, I brought you this fake Ficus, now let's have the sex.'

Not sure how that would be received.

Also, if I removed it from George's apartment I'd technically be stealing. Although can it legitimately be called stealing if it's a fake?

I head back over to my cart to get real Ficus. But as I stagger across the floor with it, I feel my foot go out from under me as I slip on the water that's dripping across the floor.

I go one way. Real Ficus goes the other.

Ever start something you then wish you hadn't?

Wet and claggy soil leaves a trail that if I don't clean up quickly will probably stain. With a sigh I get to my feet, testing my ankles, because I'm not sure Zach would get the irony if I had to miss our date because I'd broken mine. After a few wincing steps I'm all good and get the bleach and cloth out of my cleaning cart.

I return the real Ficus to a standing position, inspecting it for damage. It looks all wonky now. Forlorn even.

Scooping up the spilled soil I squish it back down around the base of the trunk and then drag it over to the window. Poor thing. It's been through a lot in a short space of time. It'll need a little extra care. I hope George is up for the responsibility.

I take a step back to check out how it looks in its new home and that's when I stand on the bottle of bleach. Safety cap, my ass, because more profanities as the top explodes off and thick detergent squirts everywhere like it's a special effect in a horror-movie blood-bath scene.

I drop to the floor, so busy spreading cloths out to halt the liquid slurping all over the beautiful blonde oak, it takes a while to notice the bleach has soaked into the knees of my jeans, the detergent sticking to my skin when I stand up.

Great.

I can't stay in these. For one thing, I absolutely wreak of bleach.

Why couldn't I have made a mess at Mrs. Lundy's? At least I could have borrowed one of her amazing kaftans. If only I was wearing my Sparkle tabard … oh … wait … I put it on, shucking out of my jeans and realise it's going to be quicker to spot-clean the worst of the bleach off and then throw them in the dryer but it's going to put me back at least an hour.

I'll have to go straight to Zach's and pray he doesn't care I don't look like I've made an effort. Maybe he'll think I'm so eager to be with him, I rushed straight over from work?

The nerves come back so I start scrubbing the floor harder. To calm myself I think up names for Ficus. It needs to be something I could write a clue to for George to work on…

Something that starts with Ph or F, right?

'Phineas the Ficus?' I wonder aloud.

I blow a strand of my hair out of my eyes as I glance up at it.

Doesn't look like a Phineas.

'Finn? Finlay?' Suddenly I hear George's front door open. 'Fu…?'

Chapter Twenty-Three

THE INCIDENT

George

D espite the colossal amount of alcohol I've consumed, it's no exaggeration to say that this has turned out to be:

Literally. The. Worst. Day. Ever.

After letting myself into my apartment I weave along the corridor, I assume with the intention of finding either my sofa or my bed. Can't seem to work out which but I definitely want one of them to provide the oblivion I seek.

Still can't get my breathing under control.

Really thought the alcohol would help.

Big no.

Have this horrid feeling I'm permanently on the verge of a panic attack.

Probably still in shock.

Hours after the incident.

My breath continues to shudder in and out of me as my mind

continuously loops on the awfulness of the day and what has transpired.

But wait a minute – what's this? My next laboured breath simply stops in my throat as my gaze zeroes in on the woman in my apartment.

On all fours.

In some blindingly white lab coat that doesn't even cover her... As my oxygen runs out, I'm not exactly sure what I was expecting the final thing I saw to be, but hands-down I wouldn't have come up with a pretty brunette in a super-sexy lab coat.

I don't understand. And my mind can't quite catch up to my mouth as I stagger across the living area, hand outstretched, presumably to introduce myself to the angel I can only assume my brother has arranged for me with some warped idea of cheering me up.

Wouldn't have been *my* first thought if Marcus had called *me* to drunkenly state he'd be attending my wedding solo on account of having broken up with his girlfriend ... and that that wasn't even the worst of it.

But then that's Marcus for you. Champion of thinking outside the box. Have to commend him on his ability to spring into action as I'm not sure it's been even an hour since I phoned him from the bar.

Still ... on my last breath or not ... manners dictate I at least introduce myself to the woman who's let herself into my home. Unfortunately, that's when her leg suddenly kicks out in an efficient slicing motion and then the next thing I know, I'm dropping to the floor like a sack of spuds.

'What the ... *ow*?' I hear a deep groan and realise the sound has come from me.

'Holy guacamole—' The brunette switches position on the

floor and suddenly she's exceptionally up close and personal, her huge brown eyes staring deep into mine. 'Please say I haven't given you a concussion. How many fingers am I holding up?' She waves her hand madly in front of my face making me feel unbalanced despite the fact I'm lying on the floor.

I try and focus as her voice turns sympathetic. 'I had to put you on the floor, George. You do understand that, right? I mean, you can't just reach out to touch whatever you feel like touching … not when it's an actual live person.'

'You're not some absinthe fairy I've summoned?' I croak out, embarrassed on so many levels, the most important one being that I can't work out what the hell is going on. 'You're real?'

'Oh, I'm as real as it gets, George.'

'I see.' Except I don't. Still unable to grasp the situation fully as the logic of walking into my apartment and being confronted by Tinkerbell in some *Weird Science* fantasy, meets the insurmountable fact that there's no way Marcus could have organised this from across the pond.

'It's me, George. Ashleigh.'

'Ashleigh?' My mind scrambles. Then, I'm pretty sure my eyes goggle. 'Wait – *you're* Ashleigh?'

'As you live and breathe,' she says with a nod.

I really wish she hadn't mentioned breathing but then all I can think is … oh … shit … was I about to accidentally come on to my cleaner?

I breathe in sharply.

Open my mouth to apologise.

That's when I smell the bleach.

Sweat pops out on my upper lip and nausea hits bad, making the alcohol sitting in my belly bubble up.

Heat suffuses my face and I feel spacey.

Weirdly spacey, like I'm going to pass out.

Yep … definitely going to lose consciousness…

Any second now … as soon as I finish huffing and puffing around the cramping sensation in my heart. This isn't good. Like, at all.

And I've sunk to a new low if I'm using the word *'like'* the same way as Tim bloody Duggins.

Damn it.

I hit my chest.

Hate this.

Like, *really* hate this.

'I—' Need to explain. 'I—'

'Wow. Okay, George, let's get you sitting up.'

Suddenly Ashleigh's hauling me into a sitting position and gently pushing my head towards my knees. I want to say the whole, hey, you can't just reach out and touch whatever you like, you know, but I can't form words on account of concentrating on inflating my lungs.

'It's okay,' Ashleigh says. 'Are you asthmatic?'

I think I manage to shake my head.

'Which means I'm pretty sure you're hyperventilating – having a panic attack. But it's going to be fine. We're going to sit right here on the floor and breathe together.'

'I—' She makes it sound so easy as she takes hold of one of my hands and enfolds it gently between her own.

'Don't worry about talking right now.' In a flurry of movement, she's letting go of my hand to rummage in her bag and then, either I've entered the hallucinatory phase of oxygen deprivation or a chocolate glazed doughnut really does bounce off my knee and land on the floor between us.

I look to her for confirmation and realise she's holding a paper bag, presumably for me to breathe into. I've seen this in the movies and make a grab for it but she holds it away from me.

'No longer the perceived wisdom, George,' she declares. 'Instead of you breathing into it, I'm going to move this paper bag slowly up and down and you're going to breathe in while it goes up and breathe out as it moves down. You have one job … follow the movement of the bag as you breathe.'

'I—'

'It'll pass, I promise you. In and out. That's it,' she encourages me. 'That's exactly right.'

Her voice is soft but firm.

Patient.

As if there's all the time in the world for me to catch my breath.

Minutes pass as we sit on the floor. Her rhythmically moving the bag and me tracking its path, gradually realising the name on the front of it is one I've come to recognise: Oscars.

More minutes pass and gradually the hideous pressure in my chest alleviates and I feel like I can catch a breath, hold onto it, and release it before reaching for another.

'We must have gone past the five-second rule by now,' I finally mutter.

'Huh?' The bridge of her nose wrinkles cutely as she frowns.

I point to the doughnut lying between us on the floor. 'Five-second rule. Can't eat it now.'

She follows my gaze and then grins. 'Ha! You're funny, George. I didn't know that about you. Keep watching the bag. The doughnut stays where it is until I clean up. The last thing you need right now is to confuse your system with a sugar-rush.'

Yet more time passes and it occurs to me I would do a lot to stay in this brave new world. This magical world, where it's just me and Ashleigh, sitting on the floor together, breathing. I maintain my gaze on her tai-chi cloud-hands movement of the bag like she instructed and allow myself to believe I only have this one job. This job of watching the bag and letting the breathing come in and out of my body.

And all the while she acts as if it is no big deal.

As if everyone goes around one step away from this.

As if she really hasn't saved my life, or at least saved me from face-planting into the sofa and passing out from panic and alcohol consumption.

The more my brain starts to function past it all, the easier it is for the humiliation of the day to take its seat at the top of the table.

'Don't,' Ashleigh says with a firm shake of her head as if she can sense it banging on the door of my brain. 'Don't let yourself go there and don't you dare apologise. If anyone needs to apologise it should be me. I'm not supposed to be here. You would never have expected me to be here. All you did was walk into your own apartment, George. I'm so sorry I triggered you into having a panic attack.'

'Not you,' I murmur as she brings her hands to a stop and lays them and the bag gracefully in her lap. 'It was the smell of the bleach. Been a while since I smelled it and it was the final straw on an indescribably shitty day.' And just like that my heart skips several beats and I think blind panic must enter my eyes because Ashleigh leans forward and grabs a hold of my hand again.

'Sometimes the hungry panic wants another bite so let's try this instead,' she soothes. 'Name three things you can see.'

'Huh?'

'Real fast, tell me the first three things you see.'

'Um, a plant. Another plant, wait—am I seeing double?'

'Keep going, one more.'

My gaze shoots back to her. 'You,' I say.

She blinks and then rushes on with, 'Now name three things you can hear.'

'Hear?'

'George.'

She sounds a little exasperated but I like it. Like hearing her. So, I try harder to please. 'The whir of the air-con, the hum of my drier … and … you.'

She blinks again as into the new silence the drier clacks off.

'I'll explain about that in a minute,' she says, waving her free hand in the direction of the drier. 'Now name me three things you can touch.'

'The floor,' I say and then something else catches my attention, and my free hand automatically reaches out to pick the unexpected object up. 'A white feather?' I glance at her to check this isn't some new twist of my imagination and see that she's staring down at it too. I can't quite work out the expression on her face, but I realise the hand still touching mine, has tightened. '*You*,' I whisper, moving my hand so that it's now gently gripping hers.

'What?'

My answer must permeate because her startled gaze bounces straight up to mine and I notice the tip of her tongue come out to swipe over her bottom lip. 'I can feel you,' I repeat and then realising how that must sound, I add, 'I mean – you know – not as in what you thought earlier but as in—'

'The tips of your ears have gone red. Did you know they do that?' she says and there's a new light of confidence back in her eyes. 'I think by your breathing it's started to work. Congratulations on bringing yourself successfully back into the present.'

I blow out a breath and it feels utterly normal. 'Thank you.'

'No problem. How do you feel? Probably like you could sleep for a year, right?'

I ignore the fact that as she's been talking, she's smoothly extricated her hand from mine. 'Yes. How do you know all this?'

'Oh.' She efficiently plucks the white feather out of my other hand and shoves it into her bag before picking up the doughnut and rising to her feet. 'I have some experience. How about I make you a cup of tea?'

I flashback to when Anya offered to make me tea after the first time this happened but this time it somehow feels more like out of concern and a real need to help me feel better. 'Actually, that sounds really good.'

'I can't guarantee it'll be as good as the kind you get back home but I'm prepared to give it a shot.'

'I'm sure it'll be fine.'

She glances up from depositing the doughnut in the bin and I can't help but feel a certain kind of way about her padding around my place barefoot with a short uniform on. It's a good visual.

I shake my head at myself because I'm pretty sure I'm not supposed to be thinking that but I guess, the day, the panic, all of it has me shaken and stirred.

Ashleigh disappears from view and I realise it's to retrieve something from the drier.

'I want you to know that I don't usually do my laundry at clients' homes,' she says, shaking out a pair of jeans and then shucking into them. 'This is strictly a one-off. Spilled bleach on them. Oops, shouldn't have mentioned the 'B' word.'

My mouth stretches into a grin. 'It's okay. I really do feel better now.'

I'm not sure what I expected my cleaner to look like … to be honest

I never once thought about it when I was writing notes and crossword clues. I feel bad realising that the clues and notes were more for me. A sort of coping method and reward for getting through the day.

'So why does the smell of bleach trigger you?' she asks as she peeks in cabinet after cabinet looking for tea-making things.

Without even thinking about it I find myself admitting, 'My mother would use it to clean the house every day.' I don't want to make my mother sound weird so I add, 'It was because I was a sickly child. Had a heart issue – all resolved now.' Even though I've rushed over the words I can't believe I said them. I've tried to make it the least relevant thing about me, so the words feel alien on my tongue.

I steal a glance at her but she still has the same kind, interested expression on her face. The perfect kind of interested, as in not getting off on the confessional. I swallow and stretch my legs out. 'My mother wanted to do her utmost to make sure that no added germs would get in and make me worse.'

She nods, and finishes dunking a teabag. 'Makes total sense.'

It did? Just like that? No more questions asked?

I wait a bit, braced, but this angel simply gets on with making me a cup of tea. 'You should make one for yourself,' I insist. 'Or a coffee. Or your beverage of choice.'

Your beverage of choice?

So smooth.

'Okay, I'll try some of this tea, maybe.'

She brings the tea over, passes it to me and then goes back to make hers. 'So, what happened today that you tried to get drunk, which, FYI, is darn near impossible when you're amped-up on panic.'

'Noted.' I take a sip of the boiling hot breakfast tea and find myself sighing before I say, 'Today was just your average cluster-fuck, I guess.'

'Not sure there's anything average about you, George. But...' She makes a rolling motion with her hand. 'Continue...'

'There was an incident at work.' God. 'I was involved in an incident at work. I – what's the most embarrassing thing you've done at work?'

I see her shoulders rise and then carefully lower back down. She takes a sip of tea and ignoring me, says, 'Is that what happened to you, today? Something embarrassing? We've all done embarrassing things at work.'

'Yeah? But what's the worst thing you've ever done?' I probe. 'Drop a client's Rolex down a toilet? Mistake a can of deodorant for furniture polish? Because I have to say it would have to go a long way to beat mine today... Oh, yeah, I should mention mine also includes criminal activity.'

I watch her eyes go round and nod my head. 'Yep. Me hyperventilating – not for the first time today.'

'Oh, George, hyperventilating isn't a crime.' She bites down on her lip thoughtfully and then says softly, 'But anxiety can make us do the worst things.'

'Like assault someone?'

'What? No ... oh my god, you *assaulted* someone?'

'With a bowl of noodles.'

Chapter Twenty-Four

ALL THE GORY DETAILS

George

'With a...?' Ashleigh leans forward on the island unit, her mug between her hands. 'Okay, I'm going to need you to expand on that.'

She doesn't look scared.

Or disappointed.

So, humiliating as it is, I'm glad I clarified about the method and weapon.

'It was during a campaign pitch,' I say.

She makes another continuing motion with her hand. 'More of those pesky details, please.'

I sip tea, reluctant to allow the incident to unfold again in my head, let alone report it to a stranger.

Not a stranger, I think. Still. 'I don't think I can. It's utterly humiliating.'

'To my knowledge humiliation never killed anyone. Did anyone go to hospital?'

'No.'

'Then it can't have been that bad. Is anyone pressing charges?'

'I don't know.' Hadn't even thought about it as I fled the scene of my crime, or rather, skulked away from it.

'If your phone or email isn't blowing up then probably not. So, what happened, exactly?'

'I shoved Tim bloody Duggins' face into a bowl of noodles for perving on my girlfriend.' There. I've said it. I check my breathing, surprised to discover it's remained relatively normal.

'Sounds like he deserved it,' Ashleigh surmises.

Wrongly, unfortunately. 'Only it turns out it wasn't perving,' I state. 'I mean, it isn't actually considered that when the two people in question are together.'

'What? They got it on together in the middle of a meeting? I hope you reserved a noodle-dunking for your so-called girlfriend as well.'

I like that she looks indignant on my behalf. Anyone else I was explaining this to would be waiting for a punchline. I guess at least I can be grateful I didn't actually punch him. Not that I would ever. I don't think. Haven't been in a fight since … um … ever. Left that to my little brother, didn't I, on the occasions when I was too ill to do it for myself, which were way too many to count, I remember darkly. I close my eyes briefly as if to make sure I don't dwell on what I can't change and then realise I'm still only halfway through my sorry tale. 'No – sorry I was in the middle of a meeting,' I explain. 'I was sitting in on Tim bloody Duggins' pitch for sweet noodles. I'm a Senior Account Director for the HR Advertising Agency – *was*.' I wince because I'm pretty sure I don't have a job anymore.

Without the panic, and without alcohol helping me to justify my actions, the seriousness of it all slams into me. How I've basically thrown my career away, which, when I'd woken up this morning, was the absolute opposite of what I'd planned.

Immerse myself in work, had been the plan.

Land a new account, had been the plan.

Fill my day until I could come home exhausted and fall into bed without allowing thoughts of what Anya and I had agreed to, to derail me in any way, had been the plan.

'Oh, I've heard of them. Did you do the—' Ashleigh breaks off, taking in the bleak expression on my face. 'Sorry, not relevant right now. Continue…'

'I'm not sure what to say.' I pull my legs up and lean forward to rest my forearms on my knees, holding my mug of tea comfortingly. 'Except, I guess, you know that phenomenon where you see something once, and then start seeing it all the time?'

'You mean as in dead people?'

That makes me rock back slightly. 'Whoa, so not where I was going with this. You *Sixth Sense* see dead people?'

'No of course not – that would be totally weird, right?' She brushes it off with a laugh but also goes bright red before hurrying on with, 'So, you saw something and then kept seeing it wherever you went?'

'Right. The two of them together. Tim bloody Duggins and my girlfriend. For weeks now. Everywhere she was, there he was. And, okay, yes, I'll concede that as we all work together technically the odds are pretty high, but I guess I began to think it was more than coincidence. And then, right before the pitch meeting … well, usually when you see two people holding hands, you're perfectly within your right to assume more, right? A level of intimacy?'

'Absolutely.' She nods her head but then stops abruptly. 'I mean, well, I guess, *we* were just holding hands, so…'

'Damn. Good point. Unfortunately, without that insight, I had Tim and Anya, holding hands at her desk, playing on loop in my brain during the meeting. There's no excuse really. One minute I was listening to Tim deliver his pitch – smarting a bit because it was good – and then the next thing I knew I was standing over him with an empty bowl of congealed noodles in my hands, watching them slide satisfyingly down his face.'

Ashleigh takes a breath and then whispers, 'Wow.'

'Quite.'

We're both quiet for a moment and then she says, 'Is your girlfriend the one you have your arms wrapped around in the photo beside your bed?'

'Anya.' I nod. 'She is. *Was*.'

'Was?' Ashleigh purses her lips in sympathy. 'Surely she could forgive you for making an assumption – I bet if she'd seen *us* holding hands—'

'The thing is … not only was I wrong in assuming she and Tim were together, thus dumping a bowl of dessert noodles over his head for no good reason – although to be fair, I've always thought he's a colossal dick. But being as I'm supposed to be a grownup – a newly promoted grownup at that – pretty sure I'm supposed to know that while I can *think* someone is a colossal dick, I'm not supposed to highlight that in a meeting. Especially one where we're supposed to be on the same side.'

'But you thought he was hitting on your girlfriend.'

'*Ex*-girlfriend because here comes the irony… We broke up last week.'

'You did?'

'Yes. A technical detail she reminded me of immediately after the bowl-crowning incident when she rushed in to ask what the hell was going on. She couldn't understand, you see. How could I behave so strangely when we'd agreed we were going to handle our separation politely and respectfully and not drag it through the gossip mill at work. She thought I understood… She'd made sure that I was all right about it all—'

'All right about it all? What? The? Actual?'

It feels good, so long after the fact, that here's finally someone who understands the whole adding-insult-to-injury deal of her saying that in front of everyone. 'You're sweet to get so indignant on my behalf but considering I so misconstrued their hand-holding, which, apparently shouldn't have affected me considering we had broken up, and shoved a bowl of presentation dessert noodles over Tim bloody Duggins' head, in the middle of a pitch meeting, and *then* had my relationship breakdown aired in said meeting, and ultimately started staggering about clutching my heart like a loon before she had to help me out of the glass-walled room – did I mention that by the way?' I wince at the memory of watching everyone's guppy-like faces soaking up the drama. 'Not only did the potential new clients see me full-meltdown, but so did everyone on the office floor. One minute I was inside a glass-walled room being stared at, the next I was on the outside of it staring at my co-workers staring back at me like if it wasn't the top agency in the city, they'd be whipping out their phones and filming me dying—'

'Having a panic attack can make you feel like you're dying,' Ashleigh confirms gently.

'I *was* dying – or at least my career was. Right in front of everyone.'

'Wow.'

'Yeah.' I place my empty mug down beside me to shove my hands through my hair and release a series of sighs that could build an entire bridge to rival the ones in Venice and Oxford. 'In one week, I've managed to lose my girlfriend, my job and my dignity.' I close my eyes to try and deny the reality.

'I know a bit about losing dignity,' Ashleigh says quietly.

'You do?' Immediately intrigued, I open one eye to stare at her. Her eyes are lowered so that they're focused on the contents of her mug. 'Oh, that's right,' I say. 'You alluded to it earlier. Well, I'm going to need you to expand fully on that if you want to join me in my pity party. If you need a drink to tell me, there's a bottle in the cupboard over the sink.'

'I don't think we should drunk-compare right now. Alcohol won't sit well on top of tea and besides, technically I'm still at work.'

'I won't tell if you don't tell and at least you have a job.' God, what am I going to do if I've lost my job?

'I'm sure if you go in and explain to your boss? Fall on your knees? Beg?'

'You're exceptionally good at pulling all the gory details out of a person. I left out the part where my boss – Mr. Richards – the head of the agency … is also my ex-girlfriend's father.'

'Double-wow.'

'Yep.' I like how she manages to convey so much understanding every time she utters the word "Wow" but then a new thought occurs. 'Hey, I know you said you were still technically at work but don't you usually clean my place on a Tuesday?'

'Right. So technically I'm not still at work. I stopped by to bring you—' she hesitates. 'It seems so silly now.'

'You stopped by to bring me something?' I think of all the little things she's been doing for me over the last few weeks. The thoughtful touches. How I'd been feeling cared for.

'It's nothing. Well, maybe, I guess you'd call it a gift?'

'You brought me a gift?'

Ashleigh runs her hands nervously down her jeans as she steps out from behind my breakfast bar. 'Not so much a gift as something to help.'

'It's not more lavender oil, is it?'

She walks over to one of the plants and imitates jazz hands over the top of it as if to present it in the manner it deserves. 'Meet … well, you'll have to name it. I was thinking of something beginning with an "F" or a "Ph." But not everyone loves alliteration. So, you know, whatever you want…'

She's nervous.

So sweetly nervous that I have to tear my gaze away from her and force myself to stare down at the plant.

'You still haven't told me what it is?' I say, charmed that a stranger would think to get me a plant to look after.

Not a stranger, I remind myself for the second time.

We've exchanged notes.

Compiled crosswords together.

Held hands.

'It's a Ficus plant,' she says. 'I bought you a Ficus.'

'Ah.' I nod my head. 'Thank you.'

'It's a real one.'

'Well, you weren't to know that taking responsibility for something living tends to add more stress when you don't have a job.'

'I could see if I could return it—'

'No. I want it. Thank you. Fern?'

'Fern?'

'Yes. Fern the Ficus.'

Her mouth drops open. 'You can't name it after another plant. It'll get issues. It's already had somewhat of a rough start.'

'Did you save it from something, too?'

'No, I did not save it,' she says, rolling her eyes. 'Contrary to popular opinion I'm not on a mission to go around "saving things".'

'Wow,' I say back to her.

'Sorry. Something someone said to me the other day that was so far off the mark as to be...'

'On another planet?' I offer.

She relaxes, flashes me a grin and says, 'It was only when it arrived here and I dropped it and then put it wonkily into the pot that it began its shaky start.'

'Feels like Fern and I could be kindred spirits,' I say, thinking back to arriving in New York and how this feeling of being on shaky ground has been following me around ever since. Bit of a revelation that I haven't been feeling on a solid footing for so long. But why? I'm working to a plan. A plan I came up with. The plan to get me exactly where I wanted to be. I don't get it but also, really don't want to think about it right now. 'I'm sure you didn't mean to hurt F—'

'Not Fern. Anything but Fern,' she counters.

I grin again. 'You said I should go for alliteration.'

'But I was thinking more along the lines of Fergal. Fifi.'

'How about Fiduciary?'

'Fi–' She looks horrified. 'No. Absolutely not.'

'I've got it.' I click my fingers and leap to my feet, energised. I head in the direction of my desk wanting to write it down for her. 'How about, sixteen letters, dreamlike, shifting appearance. Wait – where is our crossword compendium – ha! More alliteration. I'm sure I left it on my desk. Maybe I left it in the bedroom.'

'Um. So about that,' she says as I'm rooting through the papers on my desk, a feeling of dread developing in my belly as I stare at the work folders. 'I kind of have it.'

My head shoots up to stare at her.

She's in her bag, rummaging again. 'It's not stealing. I mean I wrote half of it. I just took it to…' She produces it with a flourish, holding it out for me as she blows a strand of hair out of her eyes.

'Work on the last clue?' I ask gently.

'Yes. Is that okay?'

'Of course. Maybe we should come up with a new rule. Whoever is working out the clue gets to keep the—'

'Crossword compendium?'

'Yes.'

'Okay. Then, I'm hanging onto this so that I can write down… Sixteen letters, you say? Dreamlike? Shape-shifter?'

'*Shifting appearance,*' I correct.

'Well, I'll work it out. And then, if I like it, I may let you keep it as a name.'

'Thank you.'

'You're welcome.'

'No.' I take a step forward and note the look on her face that suggests she's about to hear something she won't like. I need to say it though. 'As well as thank you for the plant, *thank you* for being here – for saving my life this afternoon – this evening.' I yawn suddenly. How long have we been here talking?

'Why don't you go and take a shower and I'll make you something to eat?'

'What, because I'm some invalid?' My eyes widen as the words snap out from me. To coin a phrase: Wow. Way to thank someone in one breath and reject them in the next. 'Sorry. I guess it's all catching up with me and I'm feeling weird. I never tell people about my…' I point to my heart. 'Changes how people look at me and I hate that.'

'All I was thinking was I'd hang around a while longer because we're sort of friends now, aren't we? And it's really no trouble to make you something to eat. Think of it as part of the Sparkle service, if you like. I did put most of the food in your fridge, after all.'

I'm wondering why I don't want to be on my own to lick my wounds. I should be working out how to mitigate the fallout from today but… 'I don't have a lot of friends in New York.'

Something flashes in her eyes. 'Me either.'

'So, I guess I'd like that. You don't have anywhere you need to be?'

'No – oh damn, wait, yes, I do. But don't worry, I can bail. I'll message my, er, friend, while you take a shower and then I'll make us something to eat. I don't know why but I'm in the mood for…' Her eyes take on a devilish glint. 'Noodles. You?'

I mimic plunging a knife into my heart. '*Way* too soon.' Halfway across the living area I stop and turn back to her. 'Am I going to be triggered every time I see noodles now? How long do you think the misery and the feeling cold all over at the memory will last?'

'Oh, only a day or two. It's really not that big of a deal.'

'Really not that big of a deal? Did you hear any of what I said happened?'

'I did but, hey, at least you didn't pee on your boss.'

I burst into laughter at the absurdity, feeling another relaxing in my heart. And then I take in her expression. It's sort of hesitant with a bead of … No. No way … she did not. 'You did not pee on your boss.' I snort.

'I did. And not to save her from a jellyfish sting!'

Chapter Twenty-Five

THE EX-FILES STARRING MOULDER AND SCURRY

Ashleigh

With that cliff-hanger hanging in the air (and I honestly cannot believe I admitted to that or that I'm now going to have to tell him the whole sorry tale) I wait until George has closed his bedroom door before getting out my phone.

Zach picks up on the second ring. 'Hey you.'

'Zach? Hi. I—' Um, what do I say that won't make him feel how easy it was to tell George I could bail on tonight?

'Why are we whispering?' Zach asks. 'Ooh, sexy times? Nice.' His voice drops too so that I have to press my ear tight to the phone as he says, 'What's your ETA? I bought wine. Oh yeah, I also got candles.'

He sounds his usual easy-going Zach but there's a tiny element of nervous-excited breathlessness in his voice and it's adorable. Listening to him now, I can't understand how I allowed myself to get into such a state about spending tonight with him. I take a big breath and say, 'Zach, I'm afraid it's not so much sexy-times as I'm really sorry to do this to you times … I can't make tonight.'

'Oh. Okay. What's up?'

'I—' Am I going to lie? It feels like I'm going to. My big left toe is tingling in the way it's done ever since Sarah's mother caught us both coming in from drinking at Billy's house and gave us a million chances to tell the truth but I stuck to our well-rehearsed lie right before my grand exit which featured me stubbing my big left toe on the kitchen doorframe before throwing-up Billy's dad's warm beer. I could hardly walk for a week afterwards which meant Sarah got to spend lots of time hanging out with Billy and I got to hear about it. Lots.

But why should I lie now? As I draw circles with my toe on the hardwood floor all I can think is why would Zach want to feel as if I'm choosing another guy over him tonight of all nights?

Not that helping George is anything like that at all.

I glance to the bedroom and decide to simply tell the truth. If Zach doesn't like what he hears, well then, he won't like what he hears.

'Zach, I'm actually with George. He's had the worst day ever. Is dealing with some bad news and I'd be a really crappy friend if I didn't stay and let him talk it out.'

'Oh. So, rain-check on tonight?'

'Yeah. I'm really sorry.'

'Hey, it's an emergency, right?'

'It really is.'

'Then, no worries. I can head out to where the boys are.'

I can't actually think of anything to say so I repeat, 'I'm really sorry.'

'We'll reschedule. You do want to reschedule, right?'

'Absolutely. For sure.' I wince as I hear how over-bright my voice sounds. 'You want to find out when we can get your place to ourselves again?'

'Sure. Any nights you can't do?'

It's funny, isn't it? How once you've scheduled *it*, you can't go back to before. No more dates where it may simply happen naturally. Only this meeting of diaries. I wonder if George and Anya synced work calendars and then wonder why Anya ended their relationship and why George decided to be fine about that? I wonder if he realises his heart is sick or broken again, but this time not from something physical?

'Ashleigh?'

'Um ... I think I'm free every night.'

'Cool. So, I'll let you know?'

That was it?

I should be pleased my boyfriend is so easy-going that when his girlfriend tells him she's spending the evening with another guy he's so understanding about it.

So unaffected.

So cool.

'Wait—' *Boyfriend? Girlfriend?*

My mind is so scrambled thinking about those two words that it takes me a minute to realise I asked him to wait. I lick my lips. Try and compose myself. Filling up my life again means dealing with life again. It's spring, right? That time of new beginnings. I don't want this to be the only thing the call was about. I promised myself I'd give more of myself to things. To do that authentically I have to be braver. 'Um, so there was something else I wanted to run past you when I saw you tonight?'

'Sure, what was that?'

'So, you know I do the volunteer reading at the hospital? Well, there's this read-a-thon—'

'Ash, that's not really me, reading to a bunch of kids. I mean, I'm happy to do something else.'

'No. That's okay. I mean, it's good you're happy to do something else because after the read-a-thon…' I squeeze my eyes shut. Clutch the phone tighter. 'There's this party after. Lots of music. Dancing. Drinking. We could even stay over?'

'Sounds good.'

My big left toe starts tingling again. 'It's a wedding,' I admit and imagine Sarah looking down on me from Upstairs, running around on some sort of cloud, wings flapping in excited congratulations. 'It's the sister of my friend. It's – she's – well, I have this plus one invite and it would really be good fun.'

'Okay.'

'Okay? You'll come?'

'Yeah.'

'I—but that's great. Really great. Oh, you have no idea how long I've been wanting to ask you.'

'What, am I an ogre? You should have asked me. If I didn't want to do it, I'd have said no.'

I grin. Not an ogre but a rare find. An uncomplicated person. 'Hey, Zach?' I whisper, half hoping he'll tell me to come over later. After I finish being a friendly ear to George. 'I really am sorry about tonight.'

'Emergencies happen. Hope George is okay. I'll get back to you with a date, okay?'

'Sure. Okay.' And then I'm listening to nothing but the sound of my big left toe squeaking that I didn't tell him about the fact that the Read-a-Thon and Wedding is on a Saturday.

The night sky has an overlay of dull yellow light from all the buildings by the time I realise I haven't heard any sound coming from George's bedroom for a while. Should I check on him? Damn the efficient soundproofing in these apartments. I didn't even hear the shower go on and off. Surely if he'd crashed to the floor, I would have heard?

I pace over to George's bedroom door. I could knock and inform him it only took me twenty-five minutes to work out the answer to the sixteen-letter clue and that there's no way I'm giving permission to name the Ficus *that*.

I lean forward and press my ear to the door.

Nothing.

I raise my hand and knock.

Nothing.

Steeling myself, I turn the handle and open the door.

George is sitting on the floor, his back against the bed.

He looks lost.

Lost in thought, I think.

His hair is still a little wet from a shower.

He looks gorgeous in touchable-soft grey jogging top and bottoms – *miserable*, I mean. He looks utterly miserable.

It's all finally caught up with him, hasn't it?

'Hey, you want to forgo food and have a sleep?' I ask as I walk over and, picking a pillow up from his bed, hold it out for him to put behind his back. 'You don't even have to move off of the floor.'

He starts a little, surprised by the intrusion before brushing a hand over his face as if to wake himself up. 'How long have I been here mouldering?'

'A while but that's fine. You're allowed to moulder a little,' I add, my voice soft to match the light. 'I phoned my friend. I'm

217

yours for the night.' The words hang in the air as I feel my eyes go round and my face get red.

'You don't have to scurry?'

His eyes are intense. Time to move the subject right along. 'I haven't made anything to eat yet in case you needed sleep first.'

'You're very kind.'

'I'm thinking about how I would have liked someone to be around me when—' I break off.

'When you peed on your boss?'

'How much to forget I ever said that?'

'Oh, you couldn't afford it,' he replies and it's good to see the trace of a smile now. 'Stay and talk to me?'

In his bedroom?

'Um … okay.' I end up sitting down next to him, stretching my legs out in front of me.

'Did you expect to come in here and find me an incoherent puddle on the floor?'

'Absolutely not,' I state, staring straight ahead at the wall.

I feel George turn his head to look at me. 'Did you come in here and expect to find me asleep?'

'Little bit.'

'Would you have watched over me while I slept?'

I turn my head to look at him. 'Little bit,' I admit again.

After a quick grin for me, he goes back to staring straight ahead. 'Like I said, you're very kind.'

'You want to tell me what happened between you and Anya?'

'Will you tell me about peeing on your boss if I do?'

I roll my eyes. 'Yes.'

He stares down at his hands for enough time that I wonder if he's going to speak at all and then, quietly, says, 'There's not really that much to tell, which now that I think about it, about sums up

218

the last few years. Basically, Anya said she wasn't in love with me and didn't think I was in love with her, either.'

'And she came to this conclusion because…?'

'She saw me coming out of my neighbour's apartment being handed my watch like I was leaving after getting dressed.'

I can't help it, I burst into laughter. 'Clearly, she's never met Mrs. Lundy. I mean, the woman is a phenom but also, what, like four-hundred-and-eighty years old?'

George's laughter is soft, making his voice sound deeper as he asks, 'You call her Mrs. Lundy too? Not Hildy?'

'Oh, I've tried but back to you and Mrs. Lundy having a torrid affair.'

'As it turns out it was my other neighbour's apartment Anya saw me leaving.'

'Julia Montford's? Yes, I suppose that would look a bit different.'

George nods. 'Anyway, Anya saw me as she was about to step out of the elevator but what shocked her wasn't me looking like I was getting dressed and leaving another woman's apartment. What shocked her was that she didn't care.'

'Couldn't the fact she didn't feel jealous also mean she trusted you? That she saw what she saw and yet knew categorically that you would never cheat on her?'

'That's what I said. She said I was missing the wider point.'

'Which was?'

'That even if I'd been having an affair, she wouldn't have been crushed because she wasn't in love with me and that, deep down, I had to know I wasn't in love with her either. Have to say that rankled, being as I moved halfway across the world to be with her. That's when she said I actually moved halfway around the world for my job.'

'And did you?' I ask quietly.

'I really hope I didn't because I don't like what that makes me.'

'We're all only human,' I say.

'But I'd rather be a good human than an evil human, if you know what I mean?'

'Totally. Though sometimes we can be good and still make mistakes. Also,' I hesitate but then add, 'sometimes it suits the other person to allow us to make those mistakes, you know? She didn't have to let you move all the way across the pond to be with her, did she? She obviously at some point thought you were the perfect match for her. In that photo you have, she looks happy. You look happy. Like you're having fun. With each other.'

'I guess.' George shakes his head a little and then says more assertively, 'No, you're right. We did have happy times together. It's what made me raise my sword—'

'Your sword?' I interrupt, raising my eyebrows at him before glancing down to his lap.

'Metaphorically speaking,' he answers, his smiling eyes suggesting he knows I'm only trying to keep him from getting too sucked back under. 'And don my armour to fight for her.'

'It says a lot about your character that you fought for her,' I say. 'Proof of being a good human.'

'Except, in the end, she made it impossible. Carefully, systematically, shooting down all my arguments against us ending. She hates drama. I thought that was why her words were so … devoid of… But the more she didn't waver, the more it began to dawn on me that she really meant it. Had spent hours thinking about how to tell me. And you know what killed me?'

'What?' I whisper, feeling so bad for him.

'That not only had she left me no chink, not one weak area for me to chip away at, it was that, well, there was not one ounce of—'

'Passion?'

'Yeah.' He turns his head to look at me. 'Passion.'

Wow. Before I know it, I'm reaching out to lay my hand on his thigh because I need to show him that that sucks. It hovers and I have to force myself not to touch him but to simply say, 'Everyone deserves passion.'

'I think so too. Anyway, suddenly I'm mid-argument thinking about my brother and his fiancée and the wedding that's coming up for them. And how he has this family and their wedding is going to be a celebration of that love, that family, that bond. And how everyone will be celebrating with him because they see it, you know? And I'm arguing to stay in a relationship where we pitch up to this celebration and everyone there is going to take one look at us and know that if I'd plucked someone off the street to go with me, they'd look more invested. And what is *that* about?' He pauses and then says, 'God, I have to attend my brother's wedding solo.'

'What is with the world getting married, right now?'

'You too?'

'I have one coming up in a couple months and another a year from now and I'm dreading both.'

'Because you don't have a boyfriend?'

'Because … it's complicated. But hey, I'm sure your family will get it. You can play the wounded knight and get left alone.'

'Or endure the pitying looks. The George-is-a-failure looks.'

'You are not a failure for not being in a relationship.'

'What about if you're not in a relationship and not employed, either?' He shakes his head and another sigh leaves him. 'I know you're right. But when I'm there it's not going to feel like I know

221

you're right, is it? It's going to feel like everyone's watching and asking, is George okay? His poor heart. We knew New York would make him ill again.'

Wow.

Life can sure feel complicated sometimes.

For instance, if only I'd been a coward for longer and not this second asked Zach to go with me to Jasmine's wedding because George would have made the perfect plus one, being that he totally gets it.

'I thought you said your heart was fixed now?'

'It is. Although, despite the doctor's reassurance, there's nothing like the weeks of anxiety attacks I've been experiencing to make me feel like it isn't.' He blows out a breath, and my gaze is drawn to the corded muscles of his neck as he throws his head back and stretches. 'I've been sitting here trying to work out if everything with Anya started before the first panic attack or after. If me having one – so out of the blue – so *unplanned* – was too real for her. A glimpse of something she could never cope with. As if she was putting me out of my misery now, instead of if I really needed her?'

Anger bubbles up into my chest. 'But you don't leave someone if they get ill.'

'Some people do though, don't they?'

The anger sits, fizzing. 'Well, they shouldn't.'

'Did someone leave you like that?'

'No. I – no. But I hate it when a person assumes you won't want to hear something, when actually it's their cowardice that stops them from saying they're unhappy about something.'

'I guess Anya's no coward because she definitely let me know.'

'It hurt you though, so I'm sorry she did that to you.'

'I don't think I'll ever have a heart issue again, despite how much the panic makes me think otherwise but that's not to say I couldn't get something else.'

'Sure. But so could she have. I mean we don't want to go into something expecting that but we want to know that if it does, we'll cope with it because we love the other person, right?'

He smiles. 'I'm beginning to think we never would have worked anyways.'

'But why did the sight of her and that guy holding hands cause you to react the way you did, then?'

'Male ego? Maybe the thing I'm really upset about *is* my job … not Anya?'

'Wow.'

'Quite. So why did you pee on your boss?'

Chapter Twenty-Six

FLOATS LIKE A GHOST, STINGS LIKE A JELLYFISH!

Ashleigh

I laugh. 'You say it like I deliberately chose to.'

'Enlighten me, then.'

'Okay, but I need to move.' I don't think I should be sitting next to him as I tell him. His body heat is too Essence of Invite to Overshare.

As I get up, I promise myself I'll only tell him the actual incident.

Not what came before.

Not what came after.

Although if I don't at least manage some of the before and after he'll have all these questions and what if he asks them quietly? So quietly and sympathetically that I find myself giving it all away, the whole sorry mess of it.

I walk over to the window, drag in a breath, and choose to simply start and see where it takes me. 'I've only been at Sparkle ten months,' I admit. 'Before that—' I press my hand against the windowpane, trying to store in my mind the coolness of the glass against my fingers. It feels fleeting, so I stretch my fingers out so that my palm presses against the glass and I can keep myself grounded.

'Before that,' I begin again, 'I worked at *Best Home* magazine.'

'Because you like words,' George surmises behind me. 'You're a writer?'

'Hardly.' I turn my head to see him watching me but then it's as if he knows watching me will have the words drying up, so after a flash of an encouraging grin he goes back to leaning his head back against the bed. 'I guess I wanted to be though?' I say as he closes his eyes. I turn back to face the window in case he opens them again. 'I couldn't have gotten a better interning role on a better magazine because what I've always also really loved is interior design. It was a dream come true when I got the position. My family and my best friend, Sarah, were so excited for me. Sarah especially because as a newly qualified paediatrics nurse it meant we'd both achieved what we'd set out to. We were both going to be living and working only hours from where we'd grown up but light years away in terms of career opportunities.' I stop, realising I can no longer recall that feeling of heady zestfulness when you succeed in getting the job you set out to get. What came after has eaten away at that innocence. That naivety.

'You know when you're starting out and it feels impossible to work too hard? To burn out. Get it wrong? Except at the same time, it's really daunting?' I murmur. 'The staff are so good at what they do. Better than you. You forget they've been doing it longer. You're so focused on your shot – you think it boils down to one opportunity – one shot to shine. And the environment fosters competition, right? You think it's healthy competition – when you stop to think about it, which you don't. It's a large arena. In a bustling city. It's this pulsing, frantic, fun, thrilling feeling of being alive. It's where you're meant to be. Living your best life.

At first you don't notice you're hobbled by a fear of failing. So afraid because you're so grateful. So grateful to be running around after your boss doing all the grunt level dross that has absolutely nothing to do with anything except making yourself indispensable so that when you've paid your dues … when that sliver of a bone is thrown your way, you're primed to take it.'

'And did you take it?' George asks.

I press my hand harder against the glass. 'No plan is ever really linear, is it?' I state, my voice reflective before turning tight. 'I had to be told it was my shot. My *last* shot. Imagine my surprise to learn I'd already had several handed to me and been oblivious to them. Before having that spelled out, I wouldn't have thought I'd missed an opportunity in my life. But then by that time, I was so different. Tired. A ghost in my own life and a disaster waiting to happen.

'I was like that because—' I swallow so that the words will come out. 'Well, because, before all of that … on one of those days where I was doing all the things at work I *thought* mattered – that showed added value, I phoned Sarah for one of her pep-talks on standing up in a meeting and pushing my ideas forward. I'm not sure when I'd let the confidence slip exactly but I remember going in every morning full of ideas. Determined to pitch them, yet somehow never following through. Allowing instead the potential to be shot down in flames and how that would feel, to grow inside of me.

'When Sarah didn't answer I didn't think anything of it other than I really needed the pep-talk and when I didn't get it, I didn't stand up and push my idea forward. After the meeting I worked harder to make up for that fact. Stayed later to make up for it. It was my pattern. It was only on my way home that I checked my phone and saw all the missed messages. Sarah's mom had been trying to contact me over and over because—'

Can I say it?

I squeeze my eyes shut.

When I open them the view out the window is replaced by my own reflection and a superimposed image of Sarah standing behind me, smiling encouragingly. I know the image isn't real. But it makes me think of the white feather that spilled out of my bag while George was talking earlier and then George asking me if I *Sixth Sense See Dead People* and how Sarah would have found that hilarious and as I blink and refocus so that I'm back to staring out of the window again I find it easier to say, 'While I was running around work picking up dry-cleaning and getting lunch for people and finding out where to get a million gallons of paint from so that I could ombre a wall for someone else's idea for a photoshoot, my beautiful best friend was in the hospital. At work but not at work. She was in the ICU. She'd been in an accident – some scaffolding on her walk to work hadn't been properly secured... She died before she should have. Before I was ready. Although, I guess, how could you be ready, right?'

In the silence I realise I've said all the words.

Aloud.

Not to Zach but to George.

I'm super-grateful for his silence. For how much easier it makes it for me to tell him. But I can't turn and face him. If I see the empathy, I'll get lost in it.

'Afterwards ... for weeks,' I tell him, 'I floated through life. I turned up every day for work but it meant nothing other than I had bills to pay. My boss was the only person I told. She kindly expected less of me and I consistently delivered that for her. And then one day, without warning, she told me about last chances and so I started trying to deliver more. Maybe her words had been designed to shake me out of my grief. They worked because the more I worked, the greater my sense of peace. Nothing made sense without Sarah but I couldn't lose my job. Without it, I'd have to go home again. And I couldn't do that. Not without Sarah.

'The first time I pitched an idea I had an anxiety attack. I examined the anxiety from all angles and put it in its place. I hadn't been sleeping. Was working long hours. Been through something so gut-wrenching I was forever changed by it so it made sense to cut myself some slack. I cut myself some slack the next few times as well. But soon it felt like I was existing on two different planes. The *work* me, focused every minute on looking like I was holding everything down. And the *real* me, who really wasn't.

'I started doing better when I redoubled my efforts at work and when I'd gone a few weeks free of anxiety attacks I pitched another idea on a Baroque decorating trend for the winter – lots of dark colours, with accent floral colours inspired by the old Dutch stili life paintings. Very luxurious. Gothic undertones.

'My boss was enthusiastic – really enthusiastic about me realising this was my last chance, anyways. She wanted me to run every facet of the photoshoot past her. Every draft of the accompanying article. I planned the photoshoot meticulously. Arranged all the materials to be at the studios we used and got in early to oversee the furniture placement. I guess here's where I should mention I'd had this idea… Instead of taxidermy or faux-dermy, to represent some of the still life aspects, I'd thought, how great would it be to get a live animal into the picture? Lots of homeowners have pets. I imagined side-articles on matching your home décor to your fur-baby. I found the perfect animal and spent my lunch hour meeting the rabbit and the rabbit's handler! I mean, sure, I'd expected a more averagely sized cute little bunny rabbit instead of the 5kg giant rabbit but one look at its white fur coat and I was sold. It was going to contrast perfectly with the midnight navy blue walls, the rose and teal toned Persian rug, aubergine velvet Chesterfield sofa and gold and glass coffee table.

'I spent a great deal of time zhuzhing orchids and Spanish moss so that they tumbled perfectly out of antiqued birdcages and then arranged the palest pink peonies and paper-thin petalled dark red poppies into vases. My boss phoned to say she'd been hearing great things about what it was looking like and she'd be along to take a look as soon as she'd finished her meeting…

'I was nervous. Stressed. *Really nervous and really stressed*,' I admit to George. 'I may have taken something to help calm me down. Probably not a good idea on top of all the caffeine to help keep me focused. Anyway. The shoot started off great. I mean I definitely asked the rabbit's handler if Tiny – go figure – would be okay to sit on the sofa. The sofa was $5000 and I didn't need any "accidents".' *Who knew that would come from me?* 'Anyway, Tiny posed perfectly. I started feeling really good. At least *in my head* I did. In reality, I was probably shooting off orders a bit hyper before my boss arrived on set.' I stop. Wince. Force myself to explain. 'Make that definitely sounded hyper because the rabbit started shaking. When my boss arrived, *I* started shaking. That was when Tiny started hopping around. Actually, it was more one small hop for a bunny … one giant leap for a giant rabbit. The photographer thought it was hilarious and started chasing it to get more candid photos. The handler and crew started getting nervous when they couldn't catch it. I started getting hysterical when it nearly crashed into the vase that was on loan from a really expensive furniture store. That's also when I started feeling queasy and light-headed. And then – at least this is what people who were there say – I emitted some weird warrior-woman like cry, leapt forward and pushed my boss. I don't remember the cry but I do remember seeing she was about to step on Tiny. She had these killer heels on and I couldn't afford to get blood on the Persian rug – also on loan from the fancy-shmancy furniture store. My boss wobbled alarmingly before falling to the floor. I grabbed the rabbit, lifted it into the handler's arms and then, absorbing the fact that I'd knocked my boss to the floor, apparently looked like I was going to barf all over the Persian rug. Instead, I went one better and dropped to the floor in a dead faint. I say the floor. It was actually my boss. I fainted on my boss. You probably know what sometimes happens when you faint... And ... so ... that's how I came to pee on my boss!'

Cue laughter.

'So, like I said,' I add. 'you'll only feel cold all over for a few days. I'm completely fine with bunnies now.' In the silence I force myself to turn around and see what he thinks of it all. I take in his closed eyes and the fact, that now that I've finished my sorry tale, I can hear him breathing steadily. Deeply. 'Wow!' All that and, 'He sleeps,' I whisper in disbelief.

Chapter Twenty-Seven

MESSAGES FROM HOME

Ashleigh

I'm sitting on my bed absorbed in finishing my collage when my phone rings. Even with the weekend stretching before me, there's this new energy I have that's magically turned all the hours into a pocket of time I don't even worry about how to fill.

'Hello?' I answer, holding another feather to the canvas, toying with where to place it.

'Mom's worried you've manifested this so-called boyfriend, *Dick*, so I've been deployed to check for signs of delusional paranoia.'

'Hey, Joey.' My tone couldn't be less impressed with my baby brother allowing himself to be used as a vessel for acquiring more information for my mother. 'Delusional paranoia, huh?'

'Yep. Aka, tendency to create scenarios filled with unconvincing worldbuilding.'

Jeez. 'His name is Zach,' I correct. 'Not Dick.'

'You sure about that? Needing to look up his name in your notes, over there?'

'You realise you've allowed yourself to be exploited? This latest technique of Mom's – getting the weakest to do her dirty work—'

'Who out of the three of us is the weakest, now?'

'Well, there's no way CeCe would have allowed herself to be used in such a way. Information gathering and reporting back is considered grunt work. Basic entry-level CIA training.'

'You think Mom works for the CIA? I guess that's not actually insane. She found out I added basil to one of her recipes the other day – how, I swear I can't figure it out, but I've had three calls and an *email* about it.'

'And knowing this you allowed yourself to be a pawn in the torture of another?'

'Maybe I just wanted to talk to my sister? Been a while.'

'It's fine,' I reply, not wanting him to feel guilty. 'But when Mom was haranguing you into phoning me you did remind her that I react perfectly averagely to stress now?'

'That would be a negative. I have to follow orders or I'll start getting the Mom Treatment over kids and Terese and I have been married for about five whole minutes.'

'Five whole minutes is long enough, little brother.'

'Tell that to my wife who's up for promotion.'

Hearing about Terese being up for promotion makes me think of George. I hope he's doing okay.

When I left him the other night – after I'd told him about my own Day of Days, (which, the more I think about him sleeping through, the better I feel about it all) – he seemed like he was going to be okay. I'd managed to make him laugh at least.

Some of the laughter had been intentional and some not. I'd

been trying to cover that awkward slice of time when I was in the hallway and he was leaning against the door to his apartment, his hand idly stroking over his heart. It had felt weirdly intimate. Him in his leisure wear. Me in my uniform and jeans. Like I was just leaving him to go off to work or something. After the third time of me asking, 'Are you absolutely sure you're going to be okay?' and him nodding his head, I'd made him give me his phone so I could add my contact details in case he did need something. Passing him back the phone in the quietness of The Clouds' corridor had felt even more intimate and I'd scrambled further for a way to depart and ended up saying, 'Well, it's been sixteen-letters *phantasmagorical*, but I should skedaddle.'

At his delighted expression for me working out the crossword clue, I'd added, 'And no, we are so *not* naming the Ficus that.'

He'd burst into laughter and it had been like a rush of dopamine to hear the rich, throaty sound. Unfortunately, I'd then turned around and in doing so promptly bumped into my cleaning cart.

He'd immediately gone into gallant knight mode and stepped forward to check I was all right, until, clocking the rush of mortified beetroot-red to my face, he had backed away, given a mock salute and turned around to wander back into his apartment, casually waving a goodbye on his way back in. I think I'd heard a low chuckle as well.

'So, is he?' I hear Joey ask now. 'Real?'

George felt maybe like the realest person I'd met in a while. Not hiding that you were struggling when faced with another person seeing you up close and personal – what could be more real than that? Plus, I'd held his hand. Felt his body heat.

Wait.

Joey's not talking about George.

'Yes, Joey, Zach is real.'

'And you're dating? As in, spending time with each other outside the sheets, in public places where sex is frowned upon and so you have to spend the time getting to know each other?'

'Oh my God, Joey, I swear.' It's not an answer but I'm definitely not talking to my baby brother about my sex-life – or lack thereof.

'So, bring him home next weekend.'

'You must be joking. Why would I give you a pass on more Mom treatment about babies?'

'Or is it that he's not suitable "Bring Home to Meet the Family" material?'

'You got me. If you want the truth, he's an unemployed ex-sex addict who I'm completely in love with.'

'*Ex*-sex addict? I feel sorry for you.'

'Shut up, Joey,' I say but I'm grinning as I say it.

'You're going to have to give me something realistic to report back or it isn't me you're going to be getting more calls from.'

'He's coming to Jasmine's wedding with me.'

There's a long pause as he absorbs the gravity of my statement. 'For real?'

'For real. Tell Mom for me. You know, when you're reporting back that I'm fine.'

'Are you though?'

'I really am.'

'I almost believe you.'

'Well, that's already better than all the other times, right?'

'Look, we have stuff the next couple of weekends but how about next month Terese and I hop on the train and come out and see you? It's what, like, only twenty hours, or so, right?'

'It's two hours and it's a great idea, but seriously, I know you're both saving for babies *someday* and I don't even have the space to put you up.' Guiltily my head turns towards Sarah's room lying empty next door.

'We can stay in a hotel,' Joey says.

'It's really fine, Joey. I want you to hear me when I say I'm good. Because I really feel like I am.' Besides, I've only just got Zach to agree to come to the wedding with me. I start throwing in weekends with my brother and sister-in-law and he's going to think I'm trying to rush us into something more serious.

'Ash—'

There's a knock at my door.

Talk about saved by the bell.

'Sorry, someone's here. Gotta go.' Springing off the bed, I walk the three steps to the front door and look through the spy hole.

'Someone, or you?' Joey asks suspiciously. 'If you're banging on your own door in the hope I'll tell Mom—'

'Ashleigh? You in there?' comes the impatient voice from the other side of my door, making me grin.

'Is that him? That's Zach?' Joey asks.

'Like I said, gotta go, baby brother.'

I end the call, open the door and stare up at Oz.

'I brought humble pie,' he says, bringing what actually looks like a key lime pie out from behind his back. 'You going to let me in?'

'I don't know.' I try to look concerned. 'Can you be trusted not to break my hobbit furniture?'

'You want me to stand up the whole time, I will.'

I have to put him out of his misery. 'Oh, come in, you big lug.'

Oz steps into my apartment for the first time and immediately takes up all the space. Putting the pie on the kitchen counter, he turns around and leans against the wall. 'You haven't been into Oscars for a couple of days,' he states.

I try to read his face. See what he makes of the scan he did of the room but the scowl he was wearing when I opened the door hasn't deepened so I relax. 'You here to check up on me?'

'I'm here to apologise about the other day when you walked in on me and Carlos arguing.'

I pat his arm as I brush past to reach up to my one kitchen cabinet and get down my only two plates for the pie. 'You were upset.'

'I was upset with Carlos. It wasn't okay to take it out on you. Or Zach.' He breathes in deeply. 'Have I messed things up for you with him?'

'Not at all.'

'That's not the reason you haven't been in? I feel like I'm the reason you haven't been in. I'm a big guy. I know when I'm angry my size is even more noticeable.'

'Oh, Oz. Obviously, I won't let on outside these walls, but you are the gentlest giant that ever lived. I'm not afraid of you. Not even when you're angry – which you had every right to be. Has Carlos…? Um, has he told you where he's been going?' I pass him a piece of pie.

'To a business class.' He nods and takes a mouthful of pie but it still doesn't disguise his next words. 'What if he meets someone there?'

I lower my fork back to my plate. '*That* was your take-away from what he told you?'

'No, of course that wasn't my take-away. But along with feeling all the other stuff like fear, anger and disappointment over the business… It's easier to admit to a bit of displacement jealousy.'

'Well, you're being absurd. But I guess I get it. He must worry all the time that you'll meet someone in the Pissed Off Pastry Chef Allegiance.'

Looking only a little abashed, Oz replies, 'Cute. But we've disbanded. Didn't have enough members to form the Class of '23.'

I smile around a mouthful of pie. 'Are you going to be the Lone Pissed Off Pastry Chef now?'

'I guess I'm going to try not to be if I'm to try and help save the business. Thought I'd jump right in at the most stressful part for me – the people part. I really thought Carlos didn't get that but it's part of why he didn't tell me.' He leans his head back and sighs deeply. 'How could he not tell me, Ashleigh? How could I not realise?'

'He was trying to let you do the thing that you love instead of having to deal with the business stress. And he was worried you'd think him a failure.'

'Yeah, I get all that but I thought we were good at communicating. Thought that's what set us apart from my other relationships.'

'You're going to need to forgive him, forgive yourself and concentrate on the bigger picture. He *has* told you now. Working together – I know you can figure this out.'

'It's the other reason why I'm here. I was hoping you'd come to this Mrs. Lundy's with me? I need to take a look around her kitchen. Check out the facilities.'

'You're going to cater for her dinner party?'

'And any other her guests may offer us. If I want Oscars to survive – if I want Carlos and I to survive – I need to show him I heard him. That this is on both of us and we can turn it around.' He starts rolling his eyes as he looks at me. 'No. Do not do that hands-clapping-in-glee, thing.'

I immediately put my hands behind my back but can't hold back the giant grin spreading across my face. 'This is going to be great. I already mentioned the possibility of getting wait-staff from Sparkle. It'll be a win-win for both businesses.'

'That would be great. So great. Thanks, Ash—' Oz breaks off and steps across the room to stare at the canvas. Without mentioning my bed, he picks the collage up. 'Hey, this is beautiful. You're making this?'

I nod.

'Ashleigh this is terrific. Angel wings, right?'

I nod again.

'You know we could put this on the wall in Oscars.'

'But it's not an Oscar.'

'Is this a one off?'

'I, um, did a couple before. But I wasn't a hundred per cent happy with them. This one … this one is turning out how I've been seeing it in my head.'

'You could sell this.'

I blink.

I could?

I could use the money to go towards helping repay Shelley-Ann who insisted on helping me out with rent after Sarah died.

'Maybe we could sell art by local artists in the bakery,' Oz muses. 'It's an idea, right? I mean, the Oscars are only on that one wall at the back.' He breaks off as his phone alerts him to a message. He opens the message then shoves his phone back into his pocket, with a, 'Yeah … no way I'm asking you that.'

'Ask me what?'

'Nothing. Forget it. Ignore that,' he says as his phone sounds again.

'You shouldn't ever ignore phone messages,' I say quietly,

unable to help myself. 'What if...' I lick my lips. 'What if it's Carlos with something important.'

He stares at me a moment and then sighs. 'Okay, I'll take a look.' He opens his message and rolls his eyes. 'It's essentially a repeat of the first message.'

'He's okay, though?'

'Debatable,' Oz says and silently holds the phone up for me to read:

HAVE YOU ASKED HER HOW THE SEX WAS WITH ZACH???

My mouth forms the word, 'Oh.'

'I keep telling him you'll tell him when you're ready,' Oz says. 'I mean, you said I didn't mess things up for you with all my "He's not where he says he is at the weekend" but ... it went ahead? Because Carlos said that was how you were spending your evening the other night? When you didn't come into the bakery the next morning, we figured it had gone well – that you were still there. But when you didn't come in yesterday, either...'

'I didn't – that is – we didn't.'

'Didn't?'

'Have the sex. Couldn't.'

'*Couldn't?* Right. Um ... I'll just put...' He starts replying to Carlos's messages. 'She says they couldn't have sex because...?' He looks helplessly at me.

'His penis was too big?' I say and then as he goes to type I put my hand out to stop him. '*That was a joke.* Do not tell him that.' My own phone goes off and laughing I say, 'You should have typed faster. That's probably him demanding the tea on Zach and me. No way he'd ever trust a PG version from you anyway. Oh...'

It's not Carlos.

It's George:

I've worked out why you peed on your boss. You were part of a trial to find some sort of non-bleach cleaner and the experiment went horribly wrong. Before you shrug my hypothesis off, if that isn't what happened, consider there's a well-known drink product that started off as toilet cleaner, so it's not that far-fetched.

I grin and message back:

And being the expert, how would you go about advertising something like that, exactly?

A few seconds later I get the following response:

Well, you'd be the face of the product, obviously!

I message back:

Obviously! Except I already told you what happened. In detail. It's not my fault you fell asleep.

I hesitate but then turn my message more personal with:

How are you doing today?

The response comes back:

Fine. Sorted out lots. Meeting with work on Monday!!

I message:

Great, but how are you doing today????

I wait a few seconds and get:

All good with me, thanks. No need to worry. Haven't even had an inkling of a panic attack. Have a good weekend.

Oh.

That was that, then.

I'll check on him on Monday. After his meeting with work. That would be a legitimate reason to see how he is.

Suddenly I become aware of Oz's openly interested gaze.

'What?' I ask.

'That isn't Carlos you're messaging with. You have a dreamy light in your eyes.'

'I do not,' I scoff.

'Are you sexting Zach, who you didn't have sex with? Is this some quaint courting ritual?'

Time to change the subject. 'How much do you think I could get for the angel wings?'

Chapter Twenty-Eight

TAKING THE DEAL

George

As the elevator whizzes me up to my meeting with Harrison and Barbara-from-Human-Resources, I wish I'd had the gumption to schedule this meeting somewhere more neutral. Possibly Switzerland.

Not that where we meet is down to me and let's face it, this is all part of my punishment, isn't it? The walk of shame through the corridors of the place I once called my second home.

I was up all night preparing what to say to keep my job.

I mean I obviously have a lot of apologising to do but after that? Truthfully, somewhere around five o'clock this morning, my plan became to wing it. That's right. I'm going to wing it in the most important meeting of my life. Maybe I'm having some sort of breakdown?

Where has my resourceful, innovative, and creative spirit gone because if I ever needed to be able to market myself as a sure bet when it comes to being a desirable employee, now is the time to pull that right out the bag…

The elevator doors swish open. Anxiety kicks me in the arse, booting me straight out of the elevator and into what suddenly feels like alien territory. They've definitely been expecting me because I'm ushered straight into a meeting room – thank goodness, not the glass one.

I assume I smile as I sit down. My face feels stiff, my mouth dry.

I try to listen as Barbara-from-Human-Resources outlines the process the meeting will take. This is about my job, after all.

My career.

I definitely hear Harrison talking about how sorry he is that it has come to this. How, if he had known how stressed I was feeling, he'd have made sure I had more support.

I think I frown at this because he's making it seem as if the reason that I dumped noodles over Tim's head was because I couldn't handle the stress of my promotion.

Before I can establish that's the path that he intends taking this meeting down, he's talking about Tim not pressing any charges and that he's certain both parties will be happy with the outcome of this meeting, here today.

He stops talking and I take that as my turn to apologise profusely.

It's the right thing to do.

Even if, inside, I feel smaller and somewhat defeated.

What little planning I *had* done I remember that I'd wanted to use simple, straightforward language so there could be no doubting my sincerity but now as I watch Barbra-from-Human-Resources shift the papers before her and add a few notes on her laptop, it feels as if my apology is somehow lost in translation.

Or that it was never going to make any difference anyway?

I don't even know how I feel about this.

Why don't I know how I feel about this?

Harrison thanks me for my apology and then tells me that obviously I can't work at his agency anymore. Maybe in the future, blah blah… Door's not completely shut, blah blah… But best all round if I leave today. It's a testament to our *past* working relationship that he's prepared to offer me a couple of months' salary if I go today.

Out of respect for the relationship I had with his daughter he'll ensure I'm not precluded from getting another job in advertising before my work permit expires and any new prospective employer would need to fill out the relevant forms, but obviously, I'd need to be mindful… Not approach any competitors. Although, and this is only well-meaning advice, I probably should look for something outside the sector given how I responded to the promotion.

There's a pregnant pause, presumably while I get a few moments to process. To decide.

I say nothing.

Probably due to feeling numb.

And then Harrison's thanking me for all the hard work I put in up until my regrettable outburst, blah blah. He wishes me the best for the future, blah blah…

Let's face it, I'm not surprised. I think it's why I piled all my work files into a bag and brought them with me to hand over today but even so, now the over-breathing starts as I think one thought and one thought only…

Please do not give my promotion to Tim bloody Duggins.

'Of course not,' Harrison responds, making it fact that I uttered the words aloud. 'Anya's going to be taking on the role you were doing alongside the one she already has.'

While this news sinks in, I wait for him to say something – anything else. Specifically, about Anya and me. About how only a few weeks ago he'd been giving me his blessing about joining the Richards family.

But he doesn't say anything and the next thing I know I'm in my office to collect my personal belongings.

I plonk myself down on the desk chair and swivel around for one last look at the view from a corner office. When the back of my neck starts prickling, I swivel back around.

Anya is poised in the doorway.

'Of all the offices, in all the world,' I say in a fairly atrocious Bogart impression.

With a ghost of a smile, she says, 'I know I have no right to ask this, but please don't make things difficult.'

'No drama. Right. I remember.'

'I meant don't make things difficult for yourself. Take the deal, George.'

I flashback to where I think this all started. The meeting with Yeong Cosmetics.

What's the deal, George?

Make the deal, George.

'You thought I was sitting here weighing my options?' I ask.

'Weren't you?'

Some of the numbness turns into the creeping realisation there were never really any options to weigh up. My position became untenable the moment I did what I did. Anya's probably wondering why I'm not hightailing it out of here, tail between my legs. I don't want to disclose that discombobulation has a tendency to slow a person down.

Suddenly I want to ask her why she's always in such a hurry – at work at any rate. Because she certainly wasn't in a hurry to marry me. The insight slams into me. How when I spoke about career progression it was always as a prelude to getting married. Having kids. When she spoke about it, it was simply to run the agency. All the important things that I considered standard like marriage and kids, she considered extras to be tacked on after.

Am I glad the scales have fallen from my eyes? Considering I can see nothing ahead of me, not really.

'You can relax,' I say, tiredly. 'I took the deal.'

'Will you be going back to England?' She swallows like she's worried she's shown her hand and quickly follows up with, 'That is – what are you going to do now?'

I stare down at my hands steepled together. It would probably be easier for her – tidier – if I went home. 'I don't know but I'm sure I'll figure it out.'

With nothing more to say I get up and walk towards her and to my utter mortification a security guard steps out from behind the door. He's obviously been waiting outside, all along.

My ego shrinks to the size of a peanut.

Anya takes a step forward and with one look gets the security guard to stand down, which is even more humiliating. He steps to the side and I step out into the reception area of the top floor of the HR Advertising Agency.

Harrison is standing in the doorway of his office.

Anya is standing in the doorway of what used to be my office.

Harrison's EA stands up from behind her desk.

Even Barbara-from-Human-Resources comes to an abrupt stop on her way to the elevator.

And then, to make it even more of a Tarantino-esque stand-off, the elevator doors swish open and standing there is Tim Duggins.

Out-bloody-standing.

My gaze settles on Anya. Anya's settles on her father.

At least it's not on Tim – whom, I realise, is simply collateral damage.

My gaze sharpens on Anya, because she has my job as well now.

Am I just collateral damage?

I feel sick.

Heartsick.

If I could close my eyes and when I opened them, be back in England, I'd be the happiest I've felt in a long time.

I do close my eyes briefly yet all I feel is that the very last place I want to be, is back in England. Not now the treadmill I've been on for years has come to an abortive stop, turfing me unceremoniously off at Destination Nowhere.

It all hits proper.

All the study. All the career planning. All the late nights and non-existent weekends.

For what?

I take the few steps needed to be right in front of Anya. 'I don't pretend you're sentimental.' I take off the watch she gave me and hold it out for her to accept back. 'Turns out neither am I. Not about this anyway.'

When she stares awkwardly at the watch, I turn and place it gently on the EA's desk, step into the lift and step out of their lives.

———

At the soft knock on my apartment door hours later I find myself lunging across the room to answer it. It's probably Anya come to let me know she's made a huge mistake.

Which is so handy because I've been sitting here thinking the exact same thing!

What the hell was I thinking, not fighting with every breath left in my body to get my job back?

What the hell is wrong with me?

What the hell am I going to do?

But when I open the door, it isn't poised Anya looking heartbroken and desperate.

It's Ashleigh.

She's dressed in her fluorescent white Sparkle uniform as if, were she in normal clothes, I might not recognise her.

Her shiny brown hair is pulled back into its dancing ponytail.

Her huge brown eyes are sympathetic as they burn into my soul.

For some reason my heart does a little flip-flop – must be the reminder of the panic she saved me from.

'Hello George,' she says simply. 'You doing okay?'

'Are you going to be following me around forever now, checking on me?' I should never have told her about my heart. Definitely shouldn't have texted her at the weekend.

Despite the quickly masked hurt in her eyes, she doesn't wait for me to tell her that I'm doing okay. Instead, she brushes past me, bringing a couple of bags in with her, which she puts down on my kitchen countertop.

'What's all this?' I say, pointing to the bags. The quicker she tells me, the quicker I can say "Thanks, but no thanks" and be left on my own.

'I brought you some food. Home-cooked.'

I snort. 'Home-cooked from a deli.' I can't believe I sound so rude but it's as if now this has happened to me, maybe I'll be rude for life. Interesting. Probably get left alone if I was rude all the time so not a total disappointment then.

'No, George,' she says lightly. 'Home-cooked as in slaving away at my miniscule kitchen stove like someone from out of the fifties.'

The aromas from the bags take some of my surly, snarky rudeness as I find myself taking a step closer. 'You cooked?'

'Cooking is budget-friendly.'

'Right. How much do I owe you?'

She pauses in setting out a container. 'Don't insult me, George.'

I feel bad. Not sure I'm that good at this being very rude thing. 'But you looking after me like this… It's… It's…'

'What? What is it?' She finds a ladle in my utensil drawer and then looks up at me and I find myself feeling even worse because she looks suddenly worried. 'Is it overstepping? Sappy?'

I shake my head. 'You, using your personal time like this when I know you don't get much of it. Please, allow me to pay for the groceries.'

She looks relieved as she decants some of the container into a bowl that I didn't even know I had, places it in the microwave and hits 'Start'. 'You really want to compensate me?'

'Yes.'

When the microwave dings, she takes the bowl out. 'Then have some of this soup and tell me how you're feeling.'

I sit down on a breakfast bar stool and drag the bowl of soup towards me. 'First, I guess, numb. Now, after being offered a really sweet deal to quietly make this whole episode go away, instead of feeling relieved, I guess I'm feeling … affronted. Insulted. Humiliated.'

'Wow.'

'Yeah, and, also,' I tip my head to the side so that the new word can roll out into my consciousness… Oh yeah … here it comes now. 'I'm feeling guilty.'

'That's normal, I guess. You acted out of character and you can't understand why. It'll take a little time.'

'This soup is really good,' I say and like that she looks pleased. 'No. I mean, yes. I feel guilty for that. But today … earlier … Anya bought me this insanely expensive watch for getting that promotion and I handed it back to her in front of everyone. I may have added that I wasn't sentimental about it – about us.'

'You were hurt.'

'I was cruel. I… That's not me. Just so you know.'

'Again, you were hurt – are hurt.'

'Am I?' I put my spoon back in the now empty bowl of soup and run a hand frustratedly through my hair. 'I'm definitely confused. I didn't just like my job, I loved it. I worked so hard at it so how could I have thrown it all away like that? My career has been years in the making. Years. And now it all feels such a waste of my life. It feels like my career choice was irrelevant. Do you know how many hours of TV I watched as a kid when I was too ill to do much else? Do you know how many advertisements were included in that TV-watching? All that time on my hands, thinking how I'd make the advertisements better. Thinking how I could help businesses sell their product. And now, I have nothing to show for it at all. Why did I allow Tim to get to me? Confuse me about Anya? Because we were good. We had plans. She got me. She understood me.'

Ashleigh stores the remaining soup in the fridge and then turns and leans against the counter looking lost in thought. Then, she says, 'I thought you said that maybe she didn't? That maybe she bolted because she was worried about your health? That maybe she was using all this as the perfect excuse.'

'I was probably wrong about that. We've been together years. We – why are you looking at me like I'm some poor deluded fool?'

'No, well, it's just … did she rush out after you when you gave her back the watch? Has she called you? Checked in with you?'

But then I haven't called either.

I haven't called because … the truth solidifies quietly inside of me.

It was over, wasn't it?

'Hey,' Ashleigh says. 'You want to get out of here for a while? Get ice cream, then come back and download an appropriately-wallowing-type tearjerker romcom.'

'I'm good, thanks.'

'Come on. It's either me, the ice cream and movie wallowing or…'

'Or?'

'Or I'll suggest to Abigail Montford that you'd like a violin recital to cheer you up.'

'Sadist.'

Chapter Twenty-Nine

A FEATHER FOR YOUR THOUGHTS

Ashleigh

Outside the air is already warmer, and with the traffic mostly stationary, it's verging on feeling sultry. The cherry blossom has long since pooled into soft pink puddles at the base of its trunks, forming pretty doughnuts.

It'll be June before I know it.

June!

Jasmine's wedding.

Since asking Zach to go with me I haven't really thought about it but I guess I should figure out how it's going to feel seeing the whole of Sarah's family without Sarah being there.

But not now. Now is about George. I'm impressed it didn't take too much wrangling to get him outside. I like he's always ready to try to make the best of a situation. Probably comes from spending all that time not being able to do anything about being ill.

As we walk and talk, the sights, sounds, smells are going to help keep him in the present.

And making sure he's okay will help keep me present.

'Careful,' George cautions as I stumble.

Yes. Careful, I repeat to myself as I steer us onto Montague Street. I'm not the poster girl for "saving" people.

'Why do I get the feeling the lure of ice cream was merely a ploy to get me outside?' George asks, his tone absent of rebuke as we walk further down the street.

'Oh, we're getting ice cream,' I promise, smiling up at him. 'In a while.'

We walk a bit further and I try to figure out if people are staring at us because we look ill-matched or if it's because I'm blinding them in my fluorescent lab coat. To gather more intel, I take off the white tabard and tuck it around the handle of my tote.

'Before I fell asleep the other night,' George remarks, 'you mentioned you hadn't been working at Sparkle long. How did you get the job?'

'You do not need to get a job at Sparkle,' I immediately say.

'What's wrong with being a cleaner?'

'Absolutely nothing,' I shoot back. I watch people walking towards us and there's less frowning and more openly admiring of George now they're not being blinded. Yeah, if George worked at Sparkle, Rhonda would have to have multiple conversations with him about how to deal with clients asking for extras. 'I got the job through a recommendation,' I tell him. 'I was cleaning out my desk at my old job and one of the evening-shift cleaners, Jamal, stopped me to ask if I was leaving. When I said "yes" he said that made him sad because I was the only person who never treated the cleaning staff as if they were invisible.'

'God, I feel like I may have done that at work.'

'Hey, it isn't like we want clients taking up our shift

unloading their problems, but a friendly acknowledgement and sometimes a quick two-way chat? That's different. No one likes to feel invisible.' I hear my voice get quieter at this last statement and determine to push away the tightness in my throat. 'I told him about my parents owning their own cleaning company and how I used to help out as a teenager and he suggested I go and see his boss. They had a domestic cleaning service as well and were always looking for staff and the rest, as they say, is history.'

It's amazing how walking in to see Rhonda and walking out with my first shift was the start of a good change. The cleaning was something I knew. It brought comfort, routine, a sense of control. Made me feel I could survive.

Because I wasn't surviving before – not after Sarah died. Not in my job at *Best Home*. Not in our tiny apartment.

Not after going through her things and discovering…

'Well,' George says, pulling me out of spiralling thoughts. 'I'm making a note that whatever I do next it won't involve ignoring cleaning staff.'

'Do you have resources to take the pressure off finding something ASAP?'

'I do but I'm so used to having a plan and working to a plan. It's uncomfortable to realise I need to plot my way through again.'

'Those skills will come back to you.'

'You're very good at this.'

'This?'

'Soothing the soul. Easing the panic.'

'Oh.' It feels like I'm blushing. Or is it that it's so warm out today?

'So now that we're out of my four walls, are we heading for anyplace in particular?'

'I don't know. What's your favourite coffee shop? Favourite store?'

'Other than the grocery store, I'm not sure I've been into any around here.'

'You've lived in The Clouds all this time but never ventured down to the stores?'

'Anything I needed I got delivered. Which I've mostly needed to do because I've been working, working, and, oh, yes, have I mentioned I've been working?'

'Cute.'

'I did Manhattan when I first arrived. And I know more places around where the agency is. Bars. Restaurants. The place I get my hair cut.'

'Well let's explore some.'

'But I don't need anything.'

I snort. 'So other than your office and the surrounding area, some fancy-shmancy places to eat and drink and maybe a couple of Broadway shows, that's the extent of your New York City experience? You've done none of the cheesy sightseeing? You realise when you go back for your brother's wedding everyone's going to ask what all the famous landmarks are like?'

'So where do you recommend?'

'Um … so many places.'

'Which one did you love the best?'

I feel him looking at me but I need to concentrate on where I'm walking.

'You *have* done the cheesy sightseeing thing?' he asks.

I shrug. 'I've been busy with work. So much work. And, oh, have I mentioned work?'

'Cute,' he mimics back to me.

After a few beats, I admit, 'It's not as much fun doing the

cheesy sightseeing by yourself. My brother keeps threatening to visit and so I always think I'll do it then.' I tail off, embarrassed to have let slip that I'm more into sharing experiences than going solo.

'So, let's do some together?'

My head whips up so quickly to check I heard right I nearly bump into a man walking a cat on a lead and George pulls me clear just in time. Frowning back at the sight, it takes me a second to mumble, 'Together?'

'Sure. I have time on my hands now.'

'But I have work,' I remind him.

'We could do something on the weekend.'

'Are you serious?' I don't know what to think about this. Zach already told me he'd done all the sightseeing things he was interested in so I never pushed for anything different to movies or dinners during the week. But after I bring him to Jasmine's wedding, will we be spending more weekends together? Or won't we?

'Serious,' George says. 'But you have to promise me something.'

I lick my lips. 'What?'

'Whatever we do, it has to have the cheese factor.'

I'm going to get to do the tourist thing on the weekend. With a friend. How has this happened? Why has he made it sound so simple?

'Okay,' I answer, because this is okay? I picture Sarah staring down at me with an expression that says, "Why wouldn't it be okay to go out on a weekend with a friend? Isn't this what you've been wanting?" 'Okay, it's a deal,' I add. 'Prepare for cheese. *So* much cheese. Hey, let's go in here?' I jerk my thumb to indicate the tiny store with its dark intriguing window and black gloss woodwork.

'A music store?' George says.

'Sure. We'll go through their vinyl.'

'But I don't have anything to play it on.'

'You could use album covers as art on your walls.'

He looks intrigued and then before we can go further, he stops, bends down and picks up a white feather lying on the ground. He holds it out to me but I just stare at it. 'Oh, sorry,' he says, and thinking I'm looking at the state it's in, he takes it back and brushes some dirt off it, and then hands it back out to me. 'You collect these, right?'

He says it *like it's perfectly normal.*

Like there's no story behind why a person would collect white feathers.

Chapter Thirty

GOING VIRAL WITH VINYL

Ashleigh

I reach out, searching desperately for a way to accept the feather in a way which also makes it look like it's no big deal. No big deal that he even registered its importance to me.

In the end I realise not accepting it will make it into a bigger thing and so I take it from him and sort of smile a thank you while I tuck it carefully into my jeans pocket and then I take his hand and pull him into the shop.

As soon as we're inside I drop his hand from mine and clench my palm against the wild tingle left behind.

How do you stay in the moment if the moment is causing all sorts of What Ifs to ripple through you?

And then it's as simple as paying attention to the soundtrack playing through the speakers. *Saturday Night Fever*. 'You hear this?' I say, grinning. 'Doesn't it make you want to strut?'

A slow lop-sided smile spreads over George's face as he walks over to a bench containing boxes labelled 'Classic Rock.' I try and ignore that there was a bit of a strut in his step.

'So why do I need art, again?' he asks after a few moments thumbing through the records.

I pull out a couple of fantastic Bowie covers and show them to him. 'To replace those boring block paintings, you have.'

'The paintings in the apartment? I never really paid attention to them.'

'Exactly! Interiors should say something about a person. They —' I break off, aware I was about to wax lyrical on interiors that turn dwellings into homes that reflect personality. Given that he slept through my recounting of my past life as a decorating nerd, I don't want to send him to sleep again.

George whips out an album with a giant frog's head on it and holds it up as if it's his head as he says, 'Are you trying to tell me that currently I blend into my background. That I'm...' He lowers the album cover, and his eyebrows bounce up and down. 'Boring?'

I laugh at the absurdity of George looking like a frog rather than a prince. I don't think anyone could describe him as boring. Anya must be one of a kind to have given him up so easily.

As he puts the album cover back and then moves over one aisle to look through some more, I find myself following.

'Look at this gem.' George holds up a cover and must be able to tell by the bemused look on my face that I've never heard of the band because he explains, 'My nephew used to sing this at the top of his voice, usually in a public place causing maximum embarrassment. It will make a really thoughtful wedding present for them.'

'The way you're saying "thoughtful" with that evil smile makes me compelled to tell you, you should also get them something *actually* thoughtful as well.'

George laughs and nods his head. 'What though? I want it to be something the kids will love too.'

'A toaster can be for everyone,' I tease and then, thinking of his niece and nephew's artwork on his fridge, I add, quieter, softer, 'You must miss them?'

'I don't think I've allowed myself to think about it – but yeah.'

'It'll be great to get to visit with them again.' Suddenly I feel anxious for no good reason. So what if he steps one foot back inside The Bedraggled Badger and never wants to come back here. So what if he decides to stay in England forever. If that's the right thing for him then that's obviously what I want for him.

As a friend.

'What about you?' George asks. 'You mentioned a brother. Do you have more siblings? Nieces and nephews?'

'My sister has a six-year-old who wraps me around her little finger with just a look,' I say proudly. 'My brother Joey was just telling me he and his wife want to wait a while but I don't think it'll be that long. Not if my ma has any say in it, anyways.'

'What about you? You want kids?'

I think my mouth drops open a little.

'Um … sure.'

'Sure?'

I frown. Can you really have it all or can you only have bits of it? Bits of it doesn't sound bad, I think. I never saw myself having kids and being a busy senior editor of a magazine. That dream would have to come with a nanny and for me, a nanny getting to see my kids take their first steps while I wrestled with budgets didn't fill me with enthusiasm. I like how my ma and pa muddled through. It was messy. Hard. But career and family all came with a sense of community. I think that's what family means to me. As much as I've thought about never going back home, there is that closeness there. A support network helping in all the ways needed. I can see myself having kids in that kind of setting. Maybe while running my own cleaning business? I don't know where I'm living. I don't know who I'm with, but I can feel it as a possibility. Something that could take root inside me. Something to work towards?

It feels good.

Right.

A goal for the future.

'Yeah, I want kids,' I admit. 'What about you?'

'Sure.'

He says it so much more confidently than I did but I still find myself saying, 'Sure?'

He smiles. 'Yeah. Me and Anya... It's possible she was right. It's possible we were really in more of a *situationship* than a relationship. Deep down I knew there was this massive mis-step between us. But I really do want kids and now I know I'd discuss that honestly if I met someone else.'

'You'll meet someone else.'

'Or will I get so caught up in working again that I don't prioritise that?'

'Maybe you'll meet someone at your brother's wedding?'

He looks at me as if he's deeply considering the idea and then says, 'Bit soon don't you think?'

My hand on the album cover relaxes. I wasn't even aware it had tightened but it was probably the shock of having a deep and meaningful in the middle of a vinyl shop and the strange reality of how easy it is. How natural. How enjoyable.

We go back to contentedly looking through the covers, but my gaze keeps straying to him.

Why can't I stop these furtive sneak-peeks?

I don't need to see what his hair is doing this minute.

Or study his large hands as they flip through the record covers.

I'll count to one hundred before I look at him again.

…twenty-one, twenty-two, twenty-three…

I am so crap at this because I'm now studying the laughter creases at the corner of his eyes and, yes, his hands that are drumming out the beat that's being played through the speakers and now his lips that are moving silently to the words.

'You look like you're about to burst into song,' I tell him.

His gaze slides to mine and then he shocks me with, 'What would you do if I did?'

I tip my head to the side in consideration. Feel my hair in its habitual ponytail slide over my shoulder. My hand moves up to play with the ends of it. 'Depends,' I say. 'Can you sing?'

He grins and it's everything.

'Wow,' I whisper. 'I'm going to need you to sing.'

He snaps his fingers with disappointment. 'Sorry. The moment's passed.'

'Easily solved,' I say and start walking backwards as if I'm rewinding time and damn if he doesn't copy me so that we're forcing people to step to the side as we end up back at the doorway.

And then, damned again, if George doesn't burst into song like he's a singing Tony Manero.

Right here in the shop.

In front of people.

Some of whom, also grinning, whip out their phones and start filming.

I can't believe this is George, singing as he struts down the aisles of the shop like he's in a musical version of *Saturday Night Fever*, pretending to comb his hair back and fix his tux.

So amazingly cheesy yet…

So confident.

So at ease.

Sooo good.

His voice is a rich nerve-smoothing, nerve-tingling baritone layered over the higher pitch of the Bee Gees.

He plucks a plastic daisy out of a groovy seventies-style vase on the checkout counter and passes it to me while he sings and the customers in the shop start to applaud.

I become aware I have the goofiest grin on my face as I accept the flower and press it to my nose to inhale its non-existent scent before falling into a pretend swoon.

I've fallen into an actual romcom musical and I'm not hating it.

I'm loving it.

At the end of the song, having made several rounds of the shop so that he's now back at a different stack of albums, he bows good-naturedly while people applaud, and then he goes back to thumbing through albums, like it never happened.

After a few seconds he looks up to discover that I'm standing in front of him, hip cocked, arms folded and staring.

As I raise my eyebrow he grins again and says, 'Rock choir. For a solid four years. It was a form of therapy and exercise to help, you know, keep my lungs and this thing'—he taps his chest where his heart is—'healthy.'

'Do you belong to one over here?'

He frowns and shakes his head.

'But you must,' I insist.

'I already told you; my heart is fine now.'

'No, George, that wasn't what I meant at all. I only meant – you're good and you looked really happy when you were singing. If you enjoyed it, why not keep doing it?'

He does the cute pushing his hand through his hair thing that shows me he's feeling awkward and conflicted and I don't want to ruin the happy place he found himself in so I tell him, 'Well, just so you don't feel too special, know that I too have an exceptional voice and got to shine in my school's production of *High School Musical*. Check these bad pipes out,' I draw in a breath and burst into my rendition of a *High School Musical* medley and it is … completely awful.

So awful.

Enough awful that people cover their ears which just makes George laugh harder.

When I come to a stop, he says, 'That's quite a voice you have there.'

'Thank you. My brother says I sing like a braying donkey on helium.'

'He's not actually wrong,' he replies but then looks totally ashamed of being so rude until I reach out and briefly lay my hand on his arm to show I'm really not offended. 'You know what talent you have that's better than being able to sing?' he adds.

'What?'

'You can laugh at yourself.'

'Hey, with a singing voice like mine, it's easy to stay humble,' I say hoping I'm not glowing too much.

'Yeah, but how many people can't poke fun at themselves, especially when people are filming. You're not afraid of entering into the spirit of something or of having fun. I'm realising how serious I've kept things lately. Doing this, this afternoon … I feel so much lighter for having a good laugh, so thank you.'

My heart skips a beat. Ever since I left *Best Home* I don't think I've once been able to poke fun at myself or make light of a flaw. I need to celebrate this progress. 'Come on, ice cream time.'

'So, I was thinking,' I say, as I grab my pistachio cone from the guy behind the counter. 'How about we name the Ficus: *two words, five and five "So good they named it twice"*?'

George has already eaten his chocolate and vanilla cone while laughing at how long it's taken me to choose a flavour. He thinks for a moment and then snorts. 'You want to name the Ficus: Ficus-Ficus?'

'What do you think?'

'What do I think? Hmmm.' He regards me and then leans towards me and wraps his hand around my wrist. I feel his thumb press gently against my pulse point and heat pools and I think my ice cream is going to melt on the spot and then I can't really think at all because what is he doing so close that I can see the flecks of brown in his blue eyes?

In the next second, he's audaciously taking a long lick of my ice cream and all I can do is watch his tongue slide out and over in slow, considered concentration. My gaze tears itself away and lands straight on his heated gaze.

'I think not,' George says, after a moment, his gaze never once losing mine. 'No to the pistachio, which, *yuck*, and no to Ficus-Ficus.'

I'm left trying to put my eyeballs back into their sockets so that I can stare down at my ice cream cone.

I totally misread what just happened, right?

He wasn't leaning in all sexy?

I'm mortified to have even thought it.

I'll just take a big old lick of this ice cream and it'll cool me down nicely.

Chapter Thirty-One

DINNER CONVERSATION

George

From my seat at Mrs. Lundy's dinner table I hear a plate smash and stare worriedly in the direction of the kitchen door Ashleigh just disappeared through.

It's clear she didn't expect to find me here at this dinner party.

To be fair, I never expected to be here either, but what's a guy to do when a thousand-year-old lady pops around and begs?

Well, I say beg…

What I actually mean is Mrs. Lundy instructed me in a hundred different ways, all of them adding up to "show me I don't need to worry about you not leaving your apartment for days by attending my dinner party".

Of course, I'd made my own bargain with her before accepting. Stressing that if I caught even one whiff of a matchmaking blind date scenario then she could consider me straight out of there, to hell with good manners.

She'd given me the longest look before replying, 'And why on earth would I do that to you when I know you've only recently come out of your relationship?'

Damn it.

Ashleigh must have told her. Probably asked her to come and check on me as well. Like I'm some sort of invalid.

It's possible Ashleigh and I need to have a chat about not trying to "save" every single person she comes into contact with because it's like she doesn't know her company is enough. Not that I've had much of her company recently.

'But since you've brought the subject up,' Mrs. Lundy had added. (I definitely hadn't). 'Anya was perfectly nice but never right for you. Too married to her job.'

When I'd expressed surprise at her calling Anya perfectly nice because I'd suspected she hadn't particularly liked her, Mrs. Lundy had said, 'Yes, well, and what is "nice" anyway? Nice doesn't fuel life. Nice doesn't incite passion or adventure. Nice is nice is nice. Nice is a good start but you deserve someone who'd walk through fire for you.'

I've got to admit, I'd still been enjoying the thought of deserving someone who'd walk through fire for me when Mrs. Lundy had skewered me with, 'If nice doesn't develop into all of that, then you've plateaued. Knew it the minute the two of you never did take that romantic break.'

Plateaued.

After the surgery to fix my heart, I never thought I'd plateau in anything. Life was for living. Loving. Now, my kaftan-wearing Yoda was informing me I'd plateaued? Which is another reason why I'm here. Getting involved. Not sitting in the apartment on my own, plateauing.

I shouldn't have licked her ice cream.

Ashleigh's not Mrs. Lundy's.

I'm not in the habit of going around licking other peoples' food, even if, the starter tonight of cilantro king prawns enveloped in a puff pastry case, is delicious.

I look again towards the kitchen door and feel myself go hot at the memory of leaning in to lick Ashleigh's ice cream. I don't know what possessed me. Turning something innocent into … heat.

I can only think it was because I'd been having so much fun being around her. How long had it been since I'd had conversation that wasn't work-related? And how easy had it been to talk about everything from where we stood on having kids to what our favourite flavour of ice cream was.

Pistachio being somewhat near the bottom of my list, I'm in no doubt I'd purposely leaned in to take a lick for other reasons. Reasons that rewarded because as the flash had ignited in her eyes, reducing the big, wide world to only the two of us, that crackle of awareness arcing between us had heightened anticipation. Experiencing that had been every bit as fun and addictive as talking about everything under the sun with her.

But now I've ruined something, I think, because back at the apartment she'd become more careful with me. Less playful.

When my brother had video-called to check how I was doing, introducing Ashleigh had been my way of taking the pressure off it only being the two of us. But as soon as she'd moved closer to get her face in the frame, the hyper-awareness had been present again.

She'd rallied more easily. Asking lots of questions about the wedding but after a while, she'd declared it had been great "meeting" everyone but that she had to go and would let herself out.

The apartment door hadn't even closed before it had started.

Who was Ashleigh?

Was she my new girlfriend?

She was pretty.

And funny and creative.

Was I bringing her to the wedding?

So many questions and opinions. I'd had the hardest time getting us all back on safer ground.

Then, when Ashleigh had turned up the following day to clean, I'd got the, "I'm in such a rush today – extra shifts. You carry on with what you're doing and I'll whizz round," speech. Without waiting for me to respond she'd flashed me an overbright smile and put on her earphones. I'd spent the entire time wondering if there was actually any music playing through them.

If I could get up from the table now and go into the kitchen to find her and apologise, I would. Because *what the hell* had I been thinking? I'm just out of a relationship. Am I really so anxious to prove to myself I can have something deeper with someone?

And more than all this, Ashleigh isn't just "someone".

She's a friend.

I don't want to hurt her.

Conversation around the dinner table blends into the background as I feel the wave of anticipation build again, waiting for Ashleigh to come back out of the kitchen dressed in her sexy white shirt and black skirt, carrying dinner plates.

Not sexy, I tell myself.

In the same way her fluorescent white uniform isn't sexy.

What is it with *me* and Ashleigh in uniforms?

I think about her dressed in jeans and a top.

Yeah … no … still sexy.

Hot.

Hot *friend*.

We all have one, right? I should consign it to that.

Anya had a "capsule wardrobe" and every piece in it was smart, stylish, elegant, and buttoned up. A uniform of a different kind.

Ashleigh turns practical and efficient casual dress into something soft and lived in.

Approachable.

The very opposite of stand-offish.

'So, George,' the dinner guest beside me says loud enough to finally get my attention. 'I didn't catch how you're affiliated to the hospital?'

'The hospital?' I hadn't thought there was a subject guaranteed to take my mind off Ashleigh, but I was wrong. I look across the table to our host, Mrs. Lundy, *really* hoping it's a coincidence and that Ashleigh hasn't told her I have a health issue so she's stuck me next to a doctor or something.

Had.

Had a health issue.

Strange that I've not had one panic attack since I left the Harrison Richards Agency.

Not strange – good, I decide.

Great.

Fixed.

Mrs. Lundy catches my raised eyebrow and addresses the room, 'Everyone, I should have explained, George here is my neighbour. George, I'm afraid you're going to find the topic tonight mostly about fundraising for the hospital.'

Fundraising?

Hospital fundraising?

Suddenly I'm a boy again and instead of getting to play soccer with friends I'm being wheeled out or dragged to every cardiology unit fundraiser my parents could organise.

Have I been totally played by my new hot friend and my neighbour with tricks aplenty up those kaftan sleeves of hers?

Chapter Thirty-Two

KITCHEN CONVERSATION

Ashleigh

I n the kitchen one of Mrs. Lundy's perfectly whole plates now lies on the floor in three separate pieces.

My heart sinks, or, rather, does a nosedive off my chest wall to land heavily in the pit of my stomach.

'What happened?' Carlos asks as he bends down to clear up the mess I've made.

I feel awful. This is Carlos and Oz's big chance at working towards keeping their business alive and here I am already causing them fee deductions. I take the jagged pieces out of Carlos's hands. 'I'm sorry. I'll ask Mrs. Lundy to invoice me so you're not out of pocket.'

'Never mind that, I mean, what happened,' he points in the direction of the kitchen door to the dining room beyond, '*out there*?'

I lick my lips nervously. Feel my heart flopping around in my belly as it tries to find solid ground. 'It's George. He's here. I mean, *out there.*' I mimic Carlos's pointing to the dining room. 'I thought this was a fundraiser brainstorm. I didn't expect—' I break off as Carlos's eyes narrow. It's possible I'm babbling. 'I don't get why he's here is all. I mean, he is Mrs. Lundy's neighbour so maybe... But then, Julia Montford's not here... Do I pretend I don't know him do you think?'

'George?' Carlos frowns but then, interest piqued, adds, 'George-of-the-sonnets, George? Let me see him.'

'Me too,' says Adeena, who Rhonda added as the other half of Sparkle's wait-staff team tonight.

Before I know it, Carlos and Adeena have shoved open the kitchen doorway more than a crack and shoved their heads through to get a good gawp.

Oh. My. God. Please let none of the guests notice them. I place the pieces of plate on top of my bag, hoping I'll be able to fix it at home, and turn around to look at Oz. Considering how big a deal this is for him, he looks calm and in control despite the antics at the kitchen door. I guess I'm not totally surprised now that we've eaten this meal about a hundred times while he's been practising but credit where credit's due. 'Thank you for not joining in,' I tell him.

He shrugs as he picks out some micro-herbs from a small container. 'One of us has to plate up.'

I walk over to Carlos. 'Hey,' I fiercely whisper, pulling on his smart black apron strings, 'Catering 101 says no spying on guests at the private dinner party function.'

'Who is George, anyways?' Adeena asks, moving away from the kitchen door. 'Is he the smoking hot guy?'

Oz's hand, complete with tweezers and micro-herbs, hovers mid-air over a piece of perfectly pan-fried halibut as he looks to Carlos for confirmation.

'Oh, he's a hottie, all right,' Carlos confirms quietly. Thoughtfully.

Oz places the herbs and returns the tweezers to the container before wiping his hands down his apron and moving out from behind the counter, presumably to get a look for himself.

'Traitor,' I mutter.

I stay right where I am.

I already know what George looks like, don't I?

And thanks to him invading my personal space and stealing my ice cream I know what he looks like up close and personal.

Very close.

Making it so personal.

'I can't go back out there,' I say, my voice low. 'Adeena, can you serve the mains?'

'If she does, you'll have to do dessert and after-dinner drinks,' Carlos says, walking over to me. 'Does Mrs. Lundy have spare crystal?'

'Very funny.'

'What happened between you and George? Why are you so hot and bothered?'

I choose to answer the last question only. 'It's a kitchen. It's supposed to be hot in here.'

'No. There's something I'm not getting. Something...?' Suddenly Carlos's expression changes. 'Oh, sweetie. No.'

He looks so genuinely concerned for me that my first thought is to reassure him. Tell him that, *no*, this is *not* some sort of J-Lo *Maid-in-Manhattan* deal where I'm falling for the client! That, yes, all right, I have experienced a little world-tilting on account of a few incidents like presenting me with a white feather for my collection. The quirky-nerdy-sexy serenading. Discovering I could do cheesy sightseeing with him on weekends. Seeing him interact with his family. The ice cream licking…

But not to worry because I've dealt with it and he should now consider himself firmly friend-zoned because… Panic revs through me while my brain works overtime trying to remember why but thankfully it's given something else to think about as at that moment the kitchen door swings open and Adeena, Oz, Carlos and I all turn around to find Mrs. Lundy.

'Everything all right in here?' she asks.

'Absolutely,' we answer, in unison.

'Then I think we're ready for the mains. Oz, that first course was outstanding.' And at that, all four of us are alone again.

'Service,' Oz declares in a commanding voice.

On a fortifying intake of breath, I snatch up the large serving tray and aiming for confident, say, 'Okay, load me up.'

Carlos hesitates. 'You're sure?'

'I'm sure,' I say, nodding firmly. 'Wait.' I put down the serving tray and make a sign of the cross.

'What are you doing?' Carlos asks, not looking reassured at all.

Oz snorts. 'Sending up a prayer to the Pastry Gods.'

Carlos rolls his eyes but then, obviously thinking it wouldn't hurt, makes a sign of the cross himself before picking up the tray, passing it to me and sending me back *out there*, to the dining room.

As I serve each guest, I try imagining their homes to stop myself imagining George and the way his tongue—

Damn. I try again, focusing on the guest I'm setting down a plate in front of. Does she live in a modern minimalist monolith or a – damn again – my gaze collides with George's, only instead of remembered heat there's a frozen polite smile on his face.

Has seeing me caused that?

My hands tremble at the thought so I focus on the conversation going around the room, right in time to hear the person beside George saying, '…yes, but the cardiology department needs its own dedicated fundraiser. More than that we need a person who can put together campaigns. Someone who thinks outside the box and can make people sit up and take notice. Someone who—'

'Oh, but George could easily help you with all that,' I say.

It's as I move to set the next plate down that I finally hear the silence.

Wow.

Something tells me I used my actual voice instead of my Inside my Head voice.

I look up to find all eyes are on me as the guest beside George says, 'He could?' then turns to George. 'You could?'

I feel like I've been given the chance to make up for the awkwardness between us. It's on me after all that I've claimed to be too busy to do our cheesy sightseeing. Probably on me as well that he's been staying in his apartment – apart from when I called around this week to do his cleaning and found that he'd gone out. A fact I'd reassured Mrs. Lundy over when I'd then popped in to clean for her.

At the time I'd been relieved. For about ten seconds. After that, I'd missed his company. His apartment had been spotless so me taking my time over it, almost as if I was waiting for him to return, had been even more ridiculous.

Now, as I stare at George it's as if he doesn't seem to know how to take up the opening I've laid out, so I add, 'George's speciality is advertising and marketing – increasing revenue streams, getting the word out about services and products, so that would tie in really well. Same principles, right?'

'Ashleigh,' George's voice is a soft warning but I'm on a roll now. Too intent on helping.

'British,' I explain to the table as I set down his plate. 'Very self-deprecating. But George is absolutely your man for this. And if you only need someone temporarily, he's between jobs, and you did say you were from the cardiology department and—'

'*Ashleigh!*'

George says my name with such portent that I'm forced to use my inside head voice to finish my '—you won't find anyone with more heart to help you out,' statement.

I become aware I'm slightly out of breath and from the look on George's face I'd have been better off breaking the ice between us again by leaving him an amusing crossword clue to fill in.

I don't get why he's looking so upset. He needs a job. This is a job made for him. It's serendipitous. Plus, he'd actually get what patients were going through.

'George, let's talk,' the guest sitting beside him says, looking very interested in capitalising on this new information.

'I'm sorry.' I rush out. 'I shouldn't have suggested—'

'Nonsense,' Mrs. Lundy says. 'No idea is a wrong idea. And it's not as if you don't have a connection to the hospital anyway.'

'She does?' George asks, watching me carefully. 'You do?'

'I—' Oh no. Is Mrs. Lundy going to mention Sarah used to work at the hospital before she ... died? How's George going to feel about that? Apart from bad that he fell asleep while I was telling him, that is.

'Ashleigh's part of the volunteer reading programme for the children's wards,' she says.

Instead of feeling relieved I feel put under the spotlight and, okay, I'm starting to get what George may have been feeling.

'A small way of helping,' I mutter.

'And you *love* helping, right?' George says, his smile tight.

Chapter Thirty-Three

HOLE HEARTED

Ashleigh

'Why are you stealing Mrs. Lundy's plates?'

I whirl around at the question and find George leaning casually against the kitchen countertop, helping himself to another piece of the pecan and toffee roulade Oz served for dessert.

'You scared the crap out of me,' I say. So much for thinking I was alone. The kitchen is the last place I expected to find him. Not that I'd been searching for him. Okay, I had. But only so that I could ignore him. I'm still mad at him. And myself. Hadn't realised I'd given him the power to hurt me with a few curt words about helping people.

Despite George and I being in a weird place, the dinner party has been a huge hit. Mrs. Lundy had us all out of the kitchen so the guests could compliment the chef and watching Carlos beaming with pride at the praise being heaped upon Oz had given me the warm and fuzzies. But now in the kitchen, I'm caught off-guard again. 'And I am not *stealing* anything,' I state, deliberately finishing the act of putting the plate into my bag along with the broken one. 'I broke the first and noticed a crack in this one. I'm taking them home to fix.'

George doesn't say a word but as he stands opposite me, his blue eyes cool and assessing, I know what he's thinking. He's thinking that the evidence is stacking up on my predilection for saving things.

'What are you doing in here, anyway?' I ask, closing up my bag, which then leaves me nothing to do with my hands. There's a breathless quality in my voice and the urge to clean becomes acute so I move towards the sink and start filling it so I can wash some items while the dishwasher finishes.

'It's an emergency,' George says.

'Low blood sugar?' I ask, dubiously, watching him slowly put another forkful of the dessert into his mouth. I take in his open shirt collar and the way his Adam's apple bobs up and down as he swallows. The swipe of his tongue as he licks a crumb off his thumb.

I grab a stack of plates and with trembling hands plunge them into the too-hot water as I imagine Sarah's wicked observation that he's, '*Awful good at eating things.*'

I glance heavenwards and mutter a 'so not helpful' under my breath.

'Hey,' George says, as he puts down his plate and looks around. 'Why are all these containers from Oscars?'

'If you head back out to the party to join the other *guests*, I'll make sure Oz boxes you up another slice of the roulade.'

'The food tonight is all from Oscars? Oz is from Oscars?'

'Oz *is* Oscars. One half of it anyway. The other half belongs to Carlos.'

'The light dawns. You know them. You put them in touch with Mrs. Lundy. And then you got them this gig?' He pauses but doesn't leave room for me to reply before he's adding, 'You know I'm seriously thinking of suggesting to Mrs. Lundy she makes it official.'

'Makes what official?'

'You, as her apprentice.'

I stare at him, my mouth hanging open. 'You think of Mrs. Lundy as some sort of "fixer" because of her networking get-togethers and I get that. But I am not that. The only way I help people is by making sure their homes are clean. It's that simple. I guess if you want to help *me* out though, you could put yourself on the other side of that...' and with my hands still in the hot water, I turn my body sideways to indicate the kitchen door.

'No can do. I've claimed this as a safe space.'

'You're *hiding* in here?' I try to make it sound like I think he's a coward but in the short time I've known George, with everything he's overcome in his life I get the impression he faces things, rather than turning his back on them.

'Damn right I'm hiding in here. The guy that was sitting next to me is Kyle Denton, Head of Cardiology at Memorial. For the last ninety minutes he's barely drawn breath and his sole topic of conversation has been getting me to work for him.'

'I feel so sorry for you what with you needing a job and someone sitting next to you at a nice dinner being in a position to offer you one. An interesting job you could do standing on your head.'

'That's not the point.'

'No?'

'The point is that this is all your fault so you have to help me.'

'Oh, *now* you want my help?'

'What happened to being responsible for me after saving me?'

'You mean apart from the fact that you gave me, and everyone else at the table, the impression you'd had it up to here.' I withdraw a hand from the water, spraying a few suds as I indicate somewhere around his nose height. 'With my help. Or was it simply that you don't think the hired help should speak?'

'Of course that's not what I think.' He bows his head to stare at a lone soap bubble drifting down to the floor. 'You know me better than that,' he adds softly.

'Do I?'

His head whips up to regard me. 'How can agreeing to go on sightseeing tours with you, be treating you like hired help? And what's up with you welching on that, by the way? Where's my promised cheese?'

'I did not promise cheese.'

'I believe the exact phrase was "prepare for so much cheese".'

'You're obsessed with cheese,' I say, but there's a grin forming on my face.

'And you're obsessed with helping people. It's who you are, so I'm thinking I should simply accept it.'

My smile fades. 'Wow.'

'So, help a friend out and let me hang out in here for a while?'

'You do know you could head back to your own apartment?'

'Yes, but that would spoil all the fun you and I are having.'

The atmosphere alters. Thickens. 'Fun?'

George turns so that he's standing as close as he can get to me without actually touching me. 'You're not having fun?'

'I—you—we—' How can we be here again so soon? In this confusing, swirling, exciting place?

The spell is broken the moment the kitchen door opens. I turn to see who it is and George immediately ducks down beside me so that he's hidden by the kitchen island unit.

I feel his hand on the back of my thigh presumably for balance and I have to place my wet hands on the cold countertop to keep steady.

Kyle Denton, the Head of Cardiology, steps into the room. 'I was looking for George.'

The hand on my thigh gently squeezes making me stammer out, 'Um, I think he left.'

'Damn. I was hoping to pick his brains again.'

I clear my throat. 'If you leave your card, I can make sure he gets it.'

'You can?'

I feel the warm pressure from George's hand. 'Sure. I maid for him.'

'You're made for him?'

George's hand tightens.

Sweet. Baby. Jesus.

'What I mean is, I'm his maid? His cleaner. We're friends,' I end with.

Kyle takes a card out of his pocket. 'You'll make sure he gets this?'

He moves as if to come around to my side of the countertop so I hold up my wet hands apologetically. 'Pop it on the countertop and I'll make sure he gets it.'

'Appreciate it,' Kyle says, laying down the card before leaving.

George rises to his feet at the door closes. My thigh still tingles with warmth from the heat of his hand. My heart is beating super-fast. He's close. So close I see he's staring not into my eyes, but at my mouth. For one absurd moment I think he's going to kiss me.

His gaze moves up to mine and our eyes search each other out like the answer to the world's trickiest crossword clue is on the tip our tongues.

George's head descends and then he pauses and suddenly he's stepping back on a sharp inhale of breath and saying, 'Thanks for saving me. Again.'

'Not a problem,' I mumble.

What just happened?

Why did he pull back?

I could ask him.

But what if I got this all wrong?

What if he hadn't pulled back because he hadn't even pushed forward?

What if I imagined the swirling vortex of anticipation licking deliciously at my insides?

'Why did you leave so abruptly the other night?' George asks as he picks up a dish towel and a stack of silverware and begins drying it.

I sneak a glance at him. He doesn't look all hot under the collar and there's absolutely no sign of his heart beating out of his chest. 'I wanted you to have a nice visit with your family. You didn't need me there.'

'That's the only reason?'

I'm such a coward. Even if the adult thing to do is name what happened and move on from it, I can't. I'm already too hot. Too bothered. 'While I was talking to your niece and nephew, I came up with an idea for a wedding gift. I guess it's sort of a piece of art?'

'Yeah? So where do I buy it?'

'You don't. I made it – that's what I went home to do.'

In reality I'd spent a few hours lying wide awake in bed going over and over what had happened between us before, for my own self-preservation, I'd got out of bed, grabbed a new blank canvas and my bowl of feathers and started making a collage.

It had made a change from getting up and cleaning to quieten all those What Ifs so too bad I'd chickened out of giving it to him or he'd have the evidence already back at his apartment.

'You make art?'

'Oh. No. Not really. Or, maybe? I just started. It's – I really like doing it. It's soothing. Oz saw one of them and said it was good. Not that he's an art connoisseur or anything. But he told me I should think about selling in Oscars, like creating a gallery wall or something, so…' I blink a couple of times, surprised at having pushed myself forward when I'd never managed to do that at the magazine.

'And you were inspired to create something for my brother's wedding?'

'You were all so excited and I can tell you're trying to make it as special for them as you can.'

'It's that obvious?' George asks, looking uncomfortable.

'I didn't know you were his best man so it makes sense. But I think even if you weren't it's just who you are – that you'd go out of your way to make it extra special for him because he's your brother – which is super cute by the way.'

'There were a lot of things Marcus missed out on when we were younger.'

'Because you were ill?'

He nods. 'He never complained, and I want him to have everything he wants, you know?'

I definitely know about wanting desperately to make up for something but I don't need to make this about me, so I aim for light and say, 'Like I said, super-cute.' He winces again and I smile and add, 'It got me thinking about family and so I thought why not create a personalised Wedding Family Tree? With all of you in your little nests. Maybe even include the pub, since the wedding is going to be held there?'

'It sounds perfect. I'll take one.'

As simple as that. Sight unseen. 'There are probably other nests I could add to the tree, if you want to give me a list. Important people. Places. Then, if you really like it, I'll think about a price,' I say, feeling brave.

He makes me feel brave.

'The Bedraggled Badger should definitely be on it,' George says. 'It's where he and Jules met and you already know they're having their wedding reception there. Plus, he sort of owns it. Part of it anyway. Everyone in the village clubbed together and bought it and they look after it and run it on a rota basis alongside their jobs. They bought it so that they could make sure they didn't lose their pub, it's sort of like a community thing.'

It makes me think of the community I'm slowly building here. How slowly but surely, I've been forced out of my comfort zone of grief to search for something that will hold me here. Something that turns this big anonymous city with its high-rises that stand tall together yet don't quite touch, into a home where I can stay. Where I can thrive.

'Why did you come here tonight?' I ask George.

'Mrs. Lundy asked me to,'

'You have a soft spot for her.'

'I do,' he agrees. 'And I didn't have anything else to do. All my friends in the city were Anya's friends and so now...' He tails off and adds a lopsided grin and a shrug.

He was missing community. Sure Mrs. Lundy pops in to see him but I've been distant recently.

I feel bad and step closer. I put my hand over his and then

laugh over the wetness and immediately lift it again to pick up a towel to dry them.

George clears his throat. 'So, you read to kids in hospital?'

'Do you know how bored they are? How long the days are for them? How scared they must be?'

He looks at me for so long that I wonder if he's going to answer at all but then he says, 'There's absolutely nothing wrong with helping them, Ashleigh. Nothing at all. It's a good thing you're doing.' He reaches out and re-tangles his hands with mine. 'I wish I'd had something like that when I was younger. I know someone like you reading to me would have helped me a lot.'

Someone like me?

I feel like I should push the feeling of being brave further and ask him but the kitchen door opens and in walks Carlos and Oz. I hurriedly withdraw my hands from George's but not before I see Carlos noticing and frowning.

'George was just—'

'I hear you're Oscars?' George says, stepping forward to shake their hands. 'I love your food.'

'Yeah?' Carlos asks. 'I haven't seen you in our bakery before and I definitely would have remembered you.'

I wince at Carlos's tone.

'I found out about you from a friend who lives in the building. I've been meaning to pay your bakery a visit and after tonight, I'm going to make a point of it.'

'Tell all your friends,' Carlos says, his tone softening a miniscule. 'We could do with all the customers we can get.'

'You're the guy in advertising?' Oz says, oblivious to Carlos's hard stares. 'We could do with your advice. We're trying to get the word out but haven't the resources to spend on marketing.'

'Oh, but George isn't here to dish out free advice all evening,' I interject.

'That's okay,' George says with a quick smile for me before answering, 'You need to get your customers to help you out.'

'How so?' Carlos asks.

'Do you have something like a hashtag frame customers can take a selfie in front of and tag your premises? Or, Ashleigh mentioned you're thinking of doing a gallery wall of local artists? Maybe you could start with that and post selfies on your channels?'

'Ashleigh told you we were thinking of doing a gallery?' Carlos asks, looking mystified.

'It was Oz's idea,' I chime in.

'You need more than one approach,' George adds. 'The crucial question is what do you want from your advertising?'

'More customers,' Carlos answers. 'I figure we can retain loyalty once they taste the goods.'

'Good point. But you need focus. More private chef customers or more walk-ins to the bakery. People hiring a private chef want a very different online experience to people visiting a bakery.'

Carlos slowly nods. 'If it's a private chef it's about the food, if it's someone coming into the bakery, then being online includes our personalities.'

'That's it exactly.'

'Carlos is in business school,' Oz says proudly.

'The main problem is that while everyone loves Oz,' Carlos muses, 'Oz only loves a select few.'

'Then focus your online presence on baking so that when they visit you can turn them into regular customers.'

'I like the sound of that better,' Oz says. 'What do you suggest?'

'Off the top of my head? Well, alongside getting mentions on socials why not offer something like private Bake-Dates?'

'Bake-Dates?'

'An immersive experience. Couples come and learn to bake together. Maybe teach them one of your signature bakes? That way, they heard about it online but then also fall in love with the experience in person so keep coming back and tell all their friends too.'

'That's not a bad idea,' Carlos says and then, turning to Oz, 'Do you think you'd be comfortable being that front of house?'

Oz's smile is soft and makes my heart go gooey as he replies, 'If it helps save the business, with you at my side, I can do anything.'

'I'll help,' I add, without thinking.

'You can. By being one of the couples,' Carlos says. 'You can bring Zach.'

I'm busy maintaining eye contact with Carlos but it doesn't stop me feeling George's interested gaze swivel sharply in my direction.

Wow.

How could I have forgotten about Zach?

'Um, right. I could. Of course,' I say, lamely. 'I will.'

'And George, you'll come too, right? And bring a date?'

Chapter Thirty-Four

AND THE OSCAR GOES TO...

George

The first thing I notice walking into Oscars for its first-ever Bake-Date is Ashleigh. Her hair is loose and falling past her shoulders in silky, touchable waves. She's wearing a dress.

A "date" dress?

'What do you think?' Carlos asks as he greets me at the door and presses something soft into my hands.

I think she looks incredible.

'Does it fit?' Carlos asks.

'Yeah,' I mutter, drinking in the sight. 'It fits really well.'

'You haven't even tried it on, yet,' Oz says, walking out from behind the counter.

I'm confused, until I realise that they're actually referring to the apron Carlos shoved into my hands when I walked in. Hurriedly, I unfold it and put it over my head and as I fumble with tying the strings at the back I ask Ashleigh, 'Where's yours?'

She looks up from her phone, locates a garment in identical

black and gold and smiles shyly at me. 'Carlos had these printed for tonight. I was telling him they should sell them as merchandise. Like a reminder of the experience?'

'Great idea. Here,' I say stepping towards her, 'let me help you tie it?'

'I've got it,' she insists.

'Of course.' I move back to the second bank of tables set up with bowls of ingredients. 'Where's Zach?' The question pops out of my mouth without warning.

She answers in the form of a wide-eyed blink and I guess the innocent-sounding question may not have sounded innocent so much as extremely blunt but hey, I'm more than a little curious to meet this guy she's supposedly dating. *The guy that up until the dinner party at Mrs. Lundy's a couple of weeks ago I had absolutely no idea existed.* Considering all the things we've told each other I'd found the fact she'd never once mentioned him way more interesting than I should have.

'Yes, where's Zach?' Carlos asks. 'Don't tell me he's broken his other ankle. Not tonight.'

'He just messaged,' Ashleigh answers. 'He's running late.'

'Make a habit of that, does he?' I ask.

A scowl forms over her big brown eyes. 'No, he doesn't make a habit of that. He has a work emergency.'

'A work emergency?' I say, sounding unconvinced. 'What does he do?' With my luck he's a heart surgeon.

'He's an HVAC engineer.'

Hopefully not at the hospital. I'm not sure I could take another mention of the place. I'm finding it hard enough that the job the Head of Cardiology offered me keeps popping into my thoughts.

Ashleigh's staring, waiting for me to comment on Zach's job. I end up going with, 'Cool.' Except it's probably something

Ashleigh finds hot? Couldn't be more different to sitting in an office, thinking creative type thoughts, like I do. *Or did.* And my exercise is the gym and to be honest I can't remember the last time I fixed something. I'm not feeling like I'm much competition here.

Not that I'm looking to compete.

'And when is *your* date arriving?' Carlos asks, turning to me.

'About that ... I didn't manage to find one.'

'A guy who looks and sounds like you couldn't find a date? Did you even try?'

'I thought tonight was only a trial?' I say, looking to Ashleigh for confirmation. The fact that bringing a date would have made it more difficult to concentrate on meeting who Ashleigh is dating is completely beside the point.

'An *authentic* trial,' Carlos answers. 'And, hello? Bake-*Date*. The clue is in the title which *you* came up with.'

'Ignore him,' Ashleigh says. 'He's nervous.'

'I like a man who has the confidence to attend solo,' Oz says.

'Thank you, Oz,' I say, puffing out my chest a little.

'Wow.' Ashleigh inclines her head to indicate Oz as she says to Carlos, 'Who knew *he* would be the more diplomatic?'

'You'll have to team up together,' Carlos says, looking unhappy at the thought.

A similar unhappy look settles across Ashleigh's face.

'Fine by me,' I say.

'You can separate when Zach gets here, but we should probably start.' Oz settles himself in front of the counter. 'We're hoping to have at least five couples per event, which means we can't fit in the kitchen all at once, so we'll be using tabletop hotplates and then I'll put your tins in our ovens. The first thing I want you to do is—'

'Question,' I interrupt. 'What are we making?'

'Shit,' Oz says. 'Not shit,' he corrects, blushing. 'Shouldn't have said that. It needed to be something easy and enjoyed afterwards with a glass of something great, so I've gone for brownies.'

'Sounds delicious,' I say, encouragingly.

'Maybe you should begin with a short introduction to Oscars?' Ashleigh suggests, moving to stand next to me. She's wearing scent.

I try to focus on what Oz is saying and not allow the lovely, fresh scent, to wrap around me like some sort of magic potion. 'You should also include a little house-keeping – Health and Safety, allergies, where the restrooms are, etc.'

'Maybe the two of you should run this event?' Carlos mumbles.

'Sorry, consider it read that you've gone through those basics. Oz, what do we do first?'

'One of you needs to measure out the butter into the bowl and the other needs to break the chocolate into pieces and add them to the bowl also...'

'So how did you and Zach meet?' I ask Ashleigh as I'm adding chunks of chocolate to the bowl.

'I thought we were here to learn how to bake?' Ashleigh says. She makes a show of referring to the instruction sheet Carlos handed us but I know she's no novice when it comes to cooking.

'It's called asking the person about themselves,' I explain. 'That's what you do on a date and we're supposed to be helping make this authentic, right?'

'Yes, but we're not – never mind.' She breathes in and then breathes out. 'I should have told you about Zach.'

I watch her efficiently repeat measuring out ingredients for her and Zach's batch of brownies. 'And why would you feel like you needed to tell me about you and Zach?'

'Because…'

She looks so guilt-ridden I immediately soften, 'You're not obliged to tell me anything about your private life, Ashleigh.'

'Okay, now you're making me feel even worse.'

'I don't want you to feel worse. I don't even want you to feel bad. So why don't we go back to the small talk. How did you and Zach meet?'

'Oz and I introduced the two of them,' Carlos answers for her, handing us two wooden spoons. 'That's what we do. We find Ashleigh dates. They get along great. Don't you?'

'Sure.'

I can't work out if its embarrassment flooding her face or something else. 'You don't sound too certain? I guess we'll find out. *If* he turns up.'

A spark flashes in her eyes and her mouth opens but no sound comes out and then we're both concentrating again on Oz.

'Fill your pan halfway with hot water and set it on the hotplate. Take the bowl and set it inside carefully and slowly heat, stirring the ingredients occasionally.'

'Tell me more about Carlos and Oz finding you dates,' I whisper as I stare at the two pans nestled side-by-side on the dual hotplate, 'because maybe they should do this as part of their business. They could call it the Love Bakery.'

'Don't even suggest it,' Ashleigh whispers back while Oz talks about different qualities of chocolate. 'Unless you're ready for dates from hell.'

Interesting. 'But they found Zach for you, right?'

'True. But be careful what you wish for.'

'Zach isn't what you wished for?'

She smiles as if he is but I don't quite believe her. Or am I looking for signs that aren't there? As her friend I want to make sure he's a good guy for her. 'What *did* you ask for?' I press.

She lays her hand over mine so that I stir the ingredients in the bowl more softly. Our eyes meet for a nano-second before she's withdrawing her hand and with a shrug surprises the hell out of me by answering, 'I wanted someone to hang out with on the weekends.'

For some reason her answer makes me extremely happy, until the door opens and in walks Zach.

Thirty minutes later as I try and put the stupid baking parchment into the stupid tin, I spy Zach leaning in to give Ashleigh a quick kiss.

Someone should tell him PDAs are passe. Or maybe he thinks he's staking his claim or something? Either way, treating someone like they're your property is not on.

Oz takes pity on me and comes over to help so that I can finally pour the brownie mix into the tin. Feeling irritable I say, 'You know, these bake-dates don't have to be romantic per se.'

'What? Don't listen to him, Oz, it's going really well,' Ashleigh weighs in.

I guess I should be grateful she's come up for air because if she and Zach are going to spend the next twenty-five minutes that the brownies are in the oven, kissing, then my irritability levels are going to rise considerably. 'I just think that if you make it too romantic some people might get carried away'—I stare pointedly at Zach—'making others feel uncomfortable.'

'But think of first dates – ooh, and Valentine's – Oscars should totally capitalise on that,' she replies.

'For every Valentine's though, there's Galentine's Day,' I counter. 'I'm sure friends would love learning how to bake. Not everything has to be made romantic.'

'You could do wedding anniversaries,' Zach chimes in, making me think no one's getting my point.

'Like I said, think outside the "romance" box. Maybe go for birthday parties.'

'It's important to be able to scale-up and expand on an already successful format,' Carlos says, 'but let's see how successful this is first.'

'Business school looks so good on you,' Oz says, beaming at Carlos before saying to us, 'Talk is good while your brownies are in the oven but you're supposed to be working out how you want to decorate them when they come out.'

'Hey, so I have a majorly important question.' Zach pauses for dramatic affect and then says, 'When do we get to lick the spoon or the bowl?'

'Licking?' Ashleigh shakes her head vehemently. 'There will be no licking,' she mumbles, turning beetroot red so that I know she's thinking about when we went out for ice cream.

'Spoil sport,' I find myself saying. 'And so *unromantic* when, if used properly, *a tongue can wreak havoc.*'

Ashleigh's eyes look like they're about to pop out of her head and I have to tell you I'm now feeling a lot less irritable. Right up until Carlos gives me a shrewd look and says with a hint of warning, 'Maybe that's enough with the helpful suggestions.'

I give him a nod to indicate message received loud and clear. I like how protective he and Oz are over Ashleigh and even though

I've not seen any evidence of Zach being like that with her tonight, that doesn't mean he isn't a nice guy.

I remind myself I'm usually a nice guy and try to get to know him better. 'Ashleigh mentioned you're an HVAC engineer, Zach?'

'Yep,' Zach says.

'He's thinking of starting up on his own,' Ashleigh adds like she's listing his prospects.

'Nah, I told you I wasn't pursuing that anymore, remember?' he says, and then explains to me, 'Too much hassle.'

I'm not sure what to say about his lack of ambition, other than, 'Well, at least you're honest.'

'It's a good skill to have,' Zach responds, making me wonder when honesty became a skill and not a pre-requisite for a relationship. 'Life can get really complicated,' he adds. 'It's good to understand when to slow it down. Chill. You know?'

'So, um, what does chilling involve?' I can't imagine Ashleigh overly complicating anyone's life. Quite the opposite if I think about how much she helped me.

'Nothing better than a game of five-a-side after work,' he says.

'As in soccer? You play soccer?'

'Soon as this cast comes off.'

'George plays as well,' Ashleigh remarks and with a look for me, adds, 'Or have I got that wrong?'

'Not for years,' I admit. 'But I know what you mean about it being great to do in spare time. I used to coach kids at weekends back in the UK.'

'Ah, the photo you have makes sense now,' Ashleigh responds.

I'm trying to understand if it's that Zach doesn't have one jealous bone in his body or if it's complete indifference to hearing that Ashleigh knows what photos I own when it suddenly occurs to me it's as simple as him knowing she's my cleaner.

'Ashleigh reads to kids at the hospital in her spare time,' I say. 'Did you know that?'

'Sure,' Zach answers all easy-breezy. As if it isn't a big thing or something to be proud of.

'Have you seen her artwork?' I ask.

That has him looking confused. Enough to make me think he knows next to nothing about her but then she's filling the gap and talking a mile a minute about how I must miss coaching and how it's something I should get into over here and have I looked into joining a rock choir, yet?

'Or...' Carlos interrupts as Oz brings out the tins of brownies and sets them down in front of us. 'You could spend your spare time telling all your friends about Oscars. Right?'

'Right,' the three of us answer and then it's heads down as we decorate.

Grabbing a piping bag, I start icing a grid pattern and then after shading some of the boxes in, I ice in letters in a couple of spaces until movement out of the corner of my eye has me glancing up to see Zach playfully trying to smear a blob of icing across Ashleigh's cheek.

'You're dribbling,' Oz tells me.

'Huh?' I look to where his gaze is and realise, I'm squeezing the piping bag so hard icing is oozing out all over the floor. 'Shit, sorry.'

'Happens to the best of us,' he laughs. 'Well, no, not me. My aim is never off.'

'Mine either,' Carlos comments, barley managing to hide his smile as he passes me a wad of catering tissue.

'I was distracted by the quality of their decorating,' I mutter. 'Are those meant to be soccer balls you're icing on top of your brownies? How is that romantic?' I ask.

'I'm not sure you're in a position to mock another's love language,' Oz says looking down at my own offering.

'Yeah, what have you gone for?' Zach asks, too busy having a good time to take offence as he leans over to look at mine.

I'm only interested in Ashleigh's reaction as she joins him.

'It's a crossword puzzle,' she looks up at me to check, a soft smile playing about her lips. 'Let's see, you've put in two letter "o's". Oh, 2 down is Love and 3 across is Oscars?'

'Correct,' I grin back.

'Hey, what's the time?' Zach suddenly says, looking first outside at how dark it's got and then at his watch. 'Shoot, I've got to bounce, I told the guys I'd drop in on their game. This was fun though. Ashleigh, you coming?'

'But it's still early.'

'It sucks I had to stay later at work. Can you imagine if I was my own boss? I'd still be working, right?'

'You really can't stay longer?'

'I promised the guys. We're finished here, right? We can bring the brownies with us. Or you can stay and we'll catch up later in the week.'

If it was me on this date with her, I wouldn't leave early for anyone or anything.

'I'll stay and help clear up,' I say.

'It's okay, I promised I'd help. I'll walk you to the door,' Ashleigh tells Zach and I hate how her voice sounds so accepting. So resigned. It makes me want to ask Oz and Carlos where the hell they found this guy because to coin a phrase from Mrs. Lundy, "Ashleigh deserves someone who'd walk through fire for her."

Chapter Thirty-Five

IN A DRESS, GIVING OUT MY ADDRESS

Ashleigh

Carlos and Oz are ready to declare the evening a hot success and launch Bake-Dates but I really don't know what to make of tonight.

I don't know why I wore the dress.

Or wore my hair down.

Or put the perfume on.

'Yeah, you do.' I feel like Sarah would be saying, so all right then, I don't want to analyse it – I only want to enjoy what feels like calm and quiet for the first time tonight as George and I sit next to each other on the fire escape out the back of the bakery.

He clinks his bottle of beer against mine and reaches into the box for another brownie, saying, 'So that happened.'

'It did.'

'I think they might do better with real people.'

'Are you saying we didn't keep it real, George?'

He turns his head towards me and, as always, when he studies me, I get caught up in the blueness of his eyes again and my heart rate accelerates.

'I feel like I did,' he says, quietly. 'Did you?'

It's hard to say. Lately I've been feeling … lighter? Happier. More optimistic. At least until I suddenly become aware of what I'm feeling and then I'm cloaked in guilt. I don't ever want Sarah to think I've forgotten her. Which is part of grief I guess because deep down I know she'd want me to be happy and living a full life. She didn't work as a nurse helping to fix people up, so they could be sent home to be miserable.

'I think it was real, no matter how much I wished it wasn't,' I say.

'What bit would you change if you could?'

'I wouldn't be sitting here in this dress.'

He stares at the top of his beer bottle. 'You regret not leaving with Zach?'

'No, I meant I'd be sitting out here in jeans instead of this dress.'

His gaze flicks up to me. 'It's a great dress.'

'Thank you.' At least someone noticed. I take a pull of my beer and wonder if Zach was more affectionate or less affectionate than usual. He definitely had fun. But then again, he likes being active. It must be hard with the cast on, I guess, but also, why have neither of us initiated a new plan to meet up and get considerably more intimate with each other?

I blow out a breath as I inwardly admit my overriding feeling tonight is embarrassment that in front of my friends Zach put his own friends first when I'd assumed he'd accepted my invite because he wanted to spend time with me and not because it happened to conveniently kill time before something else. The look on George's face when Zach said he was off out somewhere else said it all – even Carlos and Oz exchanged a surprised look.

I don't know… Am I trying to turn Zach and me into something more than casual?

'I suppose I could go change,' I tell George. 'I'm only three floors up so it would take me, like, two minutes?'

'You live here?' George automatically shifts his gaze upwards.

Wow. I'm wondering why I haven't initiated sex with Zach, yet I've still never mentioned to him that I live above Oscars. Then, five minutes on a fire escape with George and I'm divulging all sorts of things.

'So go change and then come back down,' George adds.

'Yeah?' I mean, it makes sense, doesn't it, that this would probably feel less like a date – I mean, that I should be sitting with my *friend* in jeans over a dress?

'Yeah. Hey, you want to show me your artwork?'

'George, are you asking to come up and see my etchings?' The words come out of my mouth in a breathless flirt and I squeeze my eyes shut in mortification but then immediately open them again so that there's no chance of imagining Sarah clapping her hands in delight.

George chuckles. 'I meant, as in, have you finished the piece you're working on for my brother's wedding?'

'Right. Um, not ready to show you that yet.' I pull myself to my feet and smooth my dress down. 'I'll be five minutes – six tops.' Because now I think about it my lips are really dry so I should probably re-apply some lip gloss and brush my hair to make sure there's no flour in it.

I'm out of breath when I sit back down next to him. It's because I've climbed out my window and down the fire escape concentrating fiercely on not falling clumsily at his feet.

'I've been sitting here thinking how great it must be to live above a bakery,' George says, handing me my beer.

'I didn't want to look for somewhere else after—' I swallow and hurry on, 'You're right, it's great here, even if Carlos and Oz only opened Oscars last year. I hope they manage to keep the place going. I'm steamed none of their other friends came to support them.'

'Carlos and Oz look like they're working out what they need to do. And maybe they feel their biggest support – *you*,' he nudges me, 'were here for it so they didn't need anyone else. I suspect your friendship means a great deal to them.'

I stare at the muscles in his forearms as he leans his arms on his knees, his beer bottle dangling casually from his large hands and then swing my gaze to his face again. 'No comment about fixing them or saving them?'

'Nah.' He grins and then adds, 'I'll save that for when you're least expecting it.'

I grin back. 'How's the job-hunting going?'

His mouth turns down slightly. 'It's going. I guess I'm feeling ambivalent?'

He takes another pull of beer and I use the time to choose my words. 'I couldn't help noticing you didn't take that cardiology guy's card the other day – Kyle Denton's?'

'Oh, you noticed that did you?'

'So, I saved it for you.' I stand up, put my hand on his shoulder for balance and feel the heat and strength seep seductively into my bloodstream. Quickly I shove my hand into my pocket and hold the business card out so he has no option but to take it from me and then hurriedly sit back down, wrapping my hand around the cold of my beer bottle. 'Why don't you want to follow it up?'

He sighs. 'I don't want to work at a hospital.'

'Who says you'd have to? It may be work you could do from home.'

'I hate hospitals.'

'Why?' The penny drops. 'Shit. Of course, you hate hospitals. I'm sorry, George. I should have realised. Wow, that dinner party must have been tough.'

'You really didn't put Mrs. Lundy up to inviting me?'

'I really didn't.'

'It wasn't that bad, I guess. Cardiology Guy wants me to come up with a campaign to encourage donations but also highlight heart health and make people understand what the department does. And before you tell me I'd be at least capable of understanding what some patients are going through, I don't want to be reminded of my own journey every day. I've tried really hard not to let it define me.'

'You've never once given me the impression it does.'

'I think … ever since the panic attacks I'm finding it hard to … recalibrate my expectations? A lot of it feels so irrelevant. Maybe the panic attacks were a sign I'm not supposed to be in this line of work.'

'You should at least try doing what you love for someone else first.'

'Why aren't you at another magazine, then?'

'Ouch. Okay, I didn't look for another writing job after *Best Home* but it was different for me. I was only at the beginning of that career and never pushed myself to compete at the level I'd studied for. Looking back, I played at it. My whole life was about studying and then doing anything but cleaning to please my parents. After leaving the magazine, I didn't have time to evaluate what I wanted to do next, I had two priorities: paying my bills and not wanting to go back home. I'm lucky I fell into doing a job that honestly makes me happy. I feel grateful for it, every day. Would it make it easier if I didn't feel like I had to justify what I do? Yes. Does it make me sad that people think it's less important than other jobs? Definitely. But essentially? I'm happy.' I grab a brownie and take a bite. '*Yikes, this is truly awful.*'

'I think that's from my batch, but I appreciate the diplomacy!'

'Oops, um … yum?' I force myself to take another bite which produces a laugh from George that rumbles though me. 'At least if you work somewhere else you won't feel like you only got the position because you were sleeping with the boss's daughter.'

'What the hell?' He turns to me, all indignant. 'I'm damn good at my job.'

'And that reaction is *exactly* why you should look for something in the same field. I never felt that where I was. Seriously though, you never once wondered if you got the promotion because of that?'

'I never did.'

'Wow. It really is different for men.'

'Okay. I did wonder towards the end.'

We go back to staring at the brick wall in front of us and I can't help it, I dig for an answer to what's really been on my mind. 'Maybe you'll get back to the UK for your brother's wedding and feel like it's the right place for you. Maybe you won't want to come back here.'

'That's not going to happen.'

'You don't think you could get a job back home that has interesting challenges, career progression, money and status?'

'Are you trying to get rid of me?'

'What if your brother, on behalf of the village, asks you to run The Bedraggled Badger?'

'Now that would be a cool job. But I'm thinking no to both.'

'How come?'

'It's a question of questions. As in, the endless ones I'd get if I got a job near my family. They mean well but the worry is ingrained. I can't breathe with the "Why are you still working this late at night, how many hours have you worked this week, why do you have to work the weekend? These are inevitably followed by "You look pale. Tired. Ill."'

'You don't think they worry about you being over here as well?'

'But the physical distance forces a different conversation when we speak on the phone. They concentrate on all the positives I tell them.'

'George, do you sit in your apartment in The Clouds and lie to your family?'

'Sure. You think I'm looking forward to telling my parents exactly what happened with Anya? One thing about Anya is she didn't treat me with kid gloves. She didn't worry about me.'

'But that's what people who *really* care about you do.'

'But there's absolutely no need to.'

'I know. And I get what you're saying but—'

'Do you lie to your family?'

'Only to allay fear,' I admit.

'So, we're both liars.'

'I like to think of it more as being considerately protective.' And then before I can stop myself, I'm doing the very opposite of lying and admitting, 'I'll miss you when you go back.'

'It's not for a while yet and I'll only be gone for a few days.'

'Sure.'

'I'm not staying there. I'm coming back.'

'Right.' It's great that he's so sure but when Sarah died, I learned that none of us can say anything with absolute certainty.

What if I trusted the intention though?

'If I *didn't* come back,' he then says, ruining my foray into positive "what ifs," 'do you think we'd keep in touch?'

'Keep in touch so you can lie to me and always tell me you're okay?'

'Would you lie straight back to me?'

'Going to plead the fifth on that one.' Because I definitely don't need to lay it out that I'd miss him again.

'Are we still going to do the cheesy sightseeing thing?'

'Absolutely. I was thinking we could start with Top of the Rock, Rockefeller Plaza.'

'Hmm. Less cheesy, more *really* high up.'

'It'll be great. Plus, for a: five letters: portion of extra cheese and because of your *Saturday Night Fever* tribute I'll take you to Lenny's Pizza first. Or maybe if you're leary of heights, afterwards.'

'Five letters: Portion of extra… Slice? Good one. I'll consider myself in safe hands and leave the full itinerary up to you.'

'I have the wedding this weekend, but I can do after that.'

'Zach won't mind?'

I don't want to tell him Zach sees his mother on the weekend and potentially get laughed at or looked at like I'm gullible or deluded or to be pitied in any way, so I go with, 'No. We're very casual.'

'Casual because you only want someone to hang out with at weekends or because he keeps it deliberately that way?'

Chapter Thirty-Six

I'LL LOVE YOU TO THE WEDDING AND BACK!

Ashleigh

L ife is all fun and games until you're standing outside the hospital in your bunny costume and your date's a no-show.

Where is Zach?

I can't believe I was optimistic enough to think that just because he didn't turn up to support me during the read-a-thon, he'd at least be here by the time we were supposed to leave *for Jasmine's wedding*.

I stare down at my phone.

No missed calls from him.

No messages.

I hug my arms to myself to try and ward off another head-to-toe shiver. That's another thing I don't understand. The weather app said today was supposed to be super sunshiny and hot.

It is super the opposite.

Despite my teeth chattering I try calling him again but when he doesn't answer anxiety adds to the goosebumps until I'm left with one great big humiliating: *What if I'm being ghosted?*

No.

Zach wouldn't do that to me.

Not before the wedding.

With shaking hands, I pull up the app to check my car rental booking because the way my day's going... Okay, there's nothing to suggest it isn't going to be delivered to my place on schedule which gives me an hour to get back, change out of this *ridiculous* outfit, and pack the car. I could then swing by Zach's and pick him up and still do the two-hour-drive in time.

If he hasn't ghosted me...

Dread makes friends with Anxiety and together they skip hand in hand through my system.

I absolutely cannot *not* turn up to Jasmine's wedding. But the thought of having no distraction to stop me getting overwhelmed – worse, the thought of letting Sarah down? All of a sudden this feels like a lot.

My breathing is coming quicker and the oxygen seems thinner as I start pacing to try and find a solution amid what feels like rapidly diminishing options. I need a lifeline. Someone who'll – what *is* that noise? Wow, okay, I've been so busy pacing I almost missed my phone ringing.

'Yes?' I answer breathlessly, thinking I should have checked who it was because why, yes, my mother *has* used my siblings' phones this morning to check I'm still arriving.

'Hey Ashleigh, what's up with the calling?'

'Zach? Thank God. Where are you? Are you on your way?'

'On my way to...?'

I stop pacing.

It couldn't be as simple as he forgot, could it?

'To Memorial for the read-a-thon?' I explain. 'Which is actually over but was the precursor to the *wedding we're going to*?' I feel bad about the sarcasm but it's already been quite the morning on account of my mother worrying and then the mix-up at the costume shop.

'*Oh* … Oh shit, I'm at my mom's.'

'Excuse me?'

Wow. He did. He actually forgot.

'Come on, Ashleigh, it's not like you don't know I come back to check on her at the weekends.'

'I do know that. But we had plans. You told me you'd told her about the wedding.' I don't believe this. I reminded him last week. Should I have reminded him every day in between? What am I, *his* mother? Come to think of it, what kind of mother has he got that she didn't remind him when he got there? Mine would have been all, 'Why aren't you at that wedding you said you were invited to? Why are you lying about going out? I'm worried about you. You need to leave the city and move back and be around your family.'

Now all the times Oz and my brother scoffed at the idea Zach went back to his family home on the weekend, has me wondering, which I hate. To distance myself from the thought I do an abrupt turn around and … *whack*, bounce off someone.

'Sorry,' I mutter, squeezing my eyes shut with mortification as a priest regains his balance and then looks at me with a frown as deep as the East River. I pull the bodice of my costume up higher and start walking again.

'I guess it's me who should be apologising,' Zach says. 'Ashleigh? You still there?'

'Do you have a suit there? How long would it take for you to travel from your mom's place to my folks for the wedding?'

'No, I don't have a suit here and obviously I'm not going to be able to make it to the wedding.'

Why is it obvious? Did he not understand all the times I portrayed the wedding as a bit of fun I was, in fact, deadly serious about him going with me?

'We'll get together when I'm back, yeah?' he says. 'Maybe catch that new movie—'

'You know what, Zach? Forget it.' I can't make more casual plans right now. I need to workshop a solution to a change in plans already made.

I stare down at the entrance to the subway. How did I get here? This gives new meaning to walking off a bad mood as I've no memory of getting here from the hospital. Through a haze of yet more confusion, I wonder if Carlos would let me borrow Oz – wait, scratch that, Oz would not do well in any kind of small-talk, wedding-guest situation, so it'll have to be that Oz is willing to let me borrow Carlos for the night.

'Okay, we'll do something else,' Zach says, interrupting my train of thought.

'No,' I say. 'I meant forget it as in whatever it was we were doing? I don't want to do it with you anymore.'

'Come on, don't make it into such a big deal.'

'It was a big deal to me,' I whisper. I mean, I get that it's all relative but I'm beginning to wonder if anything in Zach's life is *ever* a big deal.

Or is his casual and convenient ability to forget a date that happened to include an overnight stay with me about something else?

Maybe I'm not attractive enough to him? Maybe I'm carrying around too much baggage no matter how much I tried to protect him from it? Have I somehow made this all too difficult for easy-going Zach?

'Ashleigh, we can still have some fun together—'

'I don't think so, Zach.'

'So that's it?'

'I kind of think it has to be.'

'Okay, well, then … no hard feelings?'

'No feelings at all, Zach,' I mutter, ending the call as I walk down into the subway. Although that isn't strictly true as anger fizzes through me because … what? I didn't even warrant the pretence of his being disappointed I called it quits?

Maybe I *am* too much, these days?

Maybe I – wait, no. This is *his* loss.

Everyone has baggage.

Wasn't it George who'd said about evil humans and good humans and how he'd rather be a good one? Good humans help each other carry their baggage – help lighten the load.

Not that I think Zach's evil but I guess what it boils down to is that we barely scratched the surface with each other – certainly didn't get around to scratching an itch for each other.

That isn't all on him because I didn't even try to go deeper with him. I kept meaning to, but I didn't.

As the movement of the subway train lulls me into a sort of quiet shock, I remember how I'd wanted uncomplicated and simple.

And how I totally had that with Zach, yet have thrown it away so easily.

Please, please, please be at home... I pound on the apartment door and when it opens, for some reason, instead of saying, 'Thank you, I could really use your help,' what actually comes out of my mouth is, 'Don't you know when someone's pounding on your door, it's usually an emergency? Were you asleep? It's like, lunchtime already.' I'm of course blaming the stress of not being able to stop time and the knowledge that the wedding is looming ever closer for my rudeness.

Unaware of the need for speed, George simply stands in front of me staring.

Yeah ... instead of the subway leading me to Carlos and Oz's door, it led me here, to George's.

Slowly he looks me up and down and asks, 'Why are you dressed like Bridget Jones?'

Ignoring the Bridget Jones quip I march right on into his apartment. 'It's really not healthy to stay in your apartment all the time.' I turn around in time to see his gaze drag upwards from my fluffy cottontail. A flash of red appears high on his cheekbones which under normal circumstances would produce all sorts of tingles, but I don't have time for tingles right now. 'It's lucky I decided to check on you,' I say and then, going into his bedroom like I have every right, I add, 'I'm taking you out. You'll need to bring a change of clothes.'

'Change of clothes? But I think *my* bunny suit is at the dry cleaners.'

'Cute but can we – *waaah.*' I whirl around to put a stop to the distracting bunny talk not realising he was right behind me and for the second time today clumsily bump full-on into someone only this time it's George and his lightning quick reflexes. I manage to whack him in the face with my bunny ears as I look over my shoulder to check that what I'm feeling is real – George's hands clamped confidently on my ass-et. 'F-forget about the b-bunny costume,' I stammer out.

'Hmmm … not sure I'm going to be able to do that,' George replies, looking at me like I'm asking the impossible.

I feel my cheeks – both sets – get hot. 'You want to, um, let go of me?' For an insane moment I want to recall my words but luckily for my sanity George is stepping back and holding his hands up in mock surrender and I can finally drag in a much-needed breath. 'Look, *this*'—I indicate my whole body—'was supposed to be dressed in full faux fur, okay?'

George's gaze runs the length of me again so that I feel hot and … *hot*, as he says, 'Yet what you have on is definitely not full faux fur.'

'Thank you, I am aware. I nearly gave a priest a heart attack on the way here.' Why I'm highlighting the fishnets and black satin with white fur trim I do not know. 'I was supposed to be the hare from the *Guess How Much I Love You* books. I mean, I should have known something would go wrong because I have previous with giant rabbits, don't I?' I should stop because George was asleep when I told him about peeing on my boss so he can't have any earthly idea what I'm talking about and the crazier I appear, the less likely he's going to agree to go to Jasmine's wedding with me.

I wait for him to catch on but he still looks mystified.

'You know, the *I Love You to the Moon and Back* books? For the read-a-thon at the hospital?'

George's eyes widen. 'You read to kids dressed like that?'

'You say it like I had some sort of choice in the matter,' I say, wrenching open his closet doors and shoving my face inside as some of my anger about Zach spills over. 'When *I* agree to do something, I don't back out. *I* follow through. Ask Mrs. Lundy. She commended me on my ability to follow through just the other week. *I* don't conveniently forget so that it's too late. Do you have any sort of bag in here?' My hands fall on something leather and with a tug I extract a holdall. 'This will be perfect.'

'Why? Are we robbing a bank?'

'No, of course not, why would you ask that?'

He stares pointedly at the bag and then at me. 'You mentioned you were taking me out?'

'Right.' I dive back into the wardrobe and exit with a bunch of clothes I shove into his bag. 'I'm taking you on a cheesy sightseeing tour where cheesy and sightseeing can also be translated as back to my home town to attend my friend Sarah's sister's wedding.'

When there's no response from George, I poke my head back into the closet until the ensuing silence gets too much and I have to look back at him. I lick my lips because he's going to force me to say it, isn't he? 'Full disclosure, it's an overnighter.'

George nods his head as if it all makes complete sense. 'Hence the bag.'

'Yes.' I shove my head back into the rack of clothes. 'I'm looking for your suit but I don't see it.'

'Which one?'

'The blue one from the photo by your bed. You look really good in it.' Wow. So shouldn't have said that. 'I mean not that you don't look good in everything.' Not making this better. Making this very worse. 'I mean – you know it's very clean in here. I should talk to my boss about adding closet curation services. Not that you need it of-'

'Ashleigh, please come out of there for a moment.'

'We don't have time.'

I feel gentle hands on my arms turn me around. 'You want to tell me what's going on?'

I blow out a breath. 'I would have thought it obvious that I'm having kind of a day. I have to get to this wedding. I can't stress enough how much I have to get to this wedding. I have to be at this wedding and be okay that I'm attending this wedding, which right now feels... I – I can't have people thinking I'm not okay. I can't have them worrying. Not today. Oh, also, I knew there was an extra thing to mention... For the purposes of attending this wedding with me I, in fact, also need you to answer to the name of Zach.'

'You were supposed to go to this wedding with Zach and now you're ... not?'

'Yes. You have a problem with that?'

'I have a problem with Zach letting you down—'

'Well, don't worry. He's not going to be in a position to ever let me down again.'

'He *is* still alive, right? Tell me you didn't go weirdly bunny-boiler on him.'

'Relax. He's very much alive and happy at his mother's. Allegedly.'

'Allegedly? What does *that* mean?'

'It means I neither care if he really goes to his mother's every single weekend or not. It doesn't matter. I don't think it ever did.'

'So, you're not all torn up about this?'

'Hello? Bigger problems...'

'Because you seem like you're—'

'I'm not upset about ending things with Zach. What I'm upset about is ever thinking taking a casual date to this wedding would cut it. I cannot make this day difficult in any way for Sarah's family. I'd never be able to live with myself. So, do I seem not my usual calm, positive self? Absolutely. But do I still need to arrive at my parents' house in less than three hours?

Completely. So am I going to have to figure out the rest on the w—'

'Hey, Ashleigh?'

The softness in his voice has me stopping dead in my tracks.

'Give me five minutes to finish packing, okay?'

My smile turns wobbly as for the first time all morning it feels like there's a chance this is all going to be okay. 'Why do you need five minutes? I've already packed for you.'

'And thank you but I'm pretty sure I won't be needing this?' He pulls out the wetsuit I'd randomly packed. 'Unless it's an underwater wedding?'

'It's not an underwater wedding. It's a regular church and backyard wedding.'

'Then put this,' he says pulling out his blue suit, 'in a suit carrier with a white shirt while I get my wash kit together, okay?'

'Okay. Hey, George?'

'Hmm?' He pauses in the act of shoving a pair of shoes into the bag and looks up at me.

'Thank you,' I whisper.

Chapter Thirty-Seven

ROAD TRIP DISTRACTIONS

George

'Give me a couple minutes to change,' Ashleigh tells me, dashing past to disappear into another room.

I stay by the front door of her apartment, my gaze swinging from the couch with the *bed* behind it to the kitchen that's really more of a kitchenette, to the two closed doors in what passes for a hallway, before swinging back to the bed again.

Her place smells familiar – clean and fresh and identical to the scent left behind when she visits my apartment – the scent of an ocean breeze on a warm sunny day. I breathe it deep into my lungs and swear I can feel it tiptoe into my heart looking for somewhere to snuggle. I raise my hand to rub at my heart, still trying to get my head around the fact that less than thirty minutes ago I was woken from a fantasy about Ashleigh *by* Ashleigh. So much for trying to brainstorm job opportunities, I must have dozed off.

Of course, now that I have the sexy bunny visual it's going to be impossible to focus on important matters like finding employment.

I flash back to the feel of her body against mine when she whirled around into me all clumsy-sexy and endearing as hell.

With my glance fixated still on the bed, I bang my head softly against the door a couple of times. 'You want me to load the car while you're changing?' I call out. Anything to distract me from the bed and my thoughts.

'Great. It's everything in the hallway.'

I love that she's zoned a space that's essentially no bigger than a postage stamp. I scan the console table with the bowl filled with white feathers and the bags and packages surrounding it. As I reach up to get a garment carrier that's hanging lopsided off the mirror, I spy two plates and recognise them as Mrs. Lundy's. No longer cracked or chipped, because Ashleigh has fixed them up with some sort of gold paint. I reach out and run my finger over the three cracks. Isn't the whole point of fixing them so that the lines aren't glaringly obvious?

A quiet cursing from the room beyond has me smiling. 'Hey,' I ask, 'you got cannoli in one of these bags?'

'Cannoli?' Her voice is muffled like she's got her head stuck inside a top she's changing into.

I'd offer to help but I sort of like the idea of her having to keep the bunny costume on for the drive. 'I'm thinking going home to your parents might be one of those "Take the cannoli, leave the wetsuit" situations?'

She pokes her head out the bathroom door. 'Ha!' She disappears briefly and then pops her head back out. 'Wait, that *was* a *Godfather* mashup, right?'

I grin, refusing to let my gaze stray down to her still naked shoulders. 'Right. So, do we need to pick up some cannoli on the way?'

'Got it covered but thanks for reminding me – there's a box from Oscars in the fridge that needs to come with us. George?'

'Yes?' I blink. Damn. Eyes strayed. Got stuck on that gorgeous smooth curve of her shoulder. 'Right. Absolutely. On it.'

We've been in the car maybe twenty minutes but from Ashleigh's vice-like grip on the steering wheel, the more miles we eat up, the more the tension thrums inside her.

'Where is this wedding?' I ask, hoping to get her to relax a little. 'Where's "home" for you?'

'Little place outside Rhinebeck.' She glances to the clock on the dashboard as she names the place. 'Shouldn't take more than a couple of hours to get there.'

'On the Hudson?' I ask, getting out my phone to look up the name she mentions.

'Mmmn. It's ... small.'

'And picturesque,' I say, looking at my phone. 'This will be great,' I add enthusiastically. 'It's good to get out of the city once in a while and this place reminds me of the village where I grew up.'

'It does?'

'Yeah.' I wish I could take her back there for a visit. I can see us sitting in the beer garden of The Bedraggled Badger, sinking a couple of pints before walking to my parents' house for Sunday roast.

Woah…

I never hankered for that with Anya. Mostly because we *did* do that once. Anya spent the majority of the visit on her phone before asking if we could head back to London early so that she could finish up some work. I remember my father's deliberate neutral expression coupled with my mother's anxious looks that her son was working too much and not looking after himself. Their worried silence had been deafening.

'I guess I should mention,' Ashleigh says, 'my family can be … I guess … loud would be the word?'

Total opposite of mine then. 'Well, this has worked out well for you. I'm a great guy to take home to parents. Never met one yet who didn't like me.'

This produces a quick laugh. 'I love that you think you're still on your ex's Christmas card list.'

She has a point. 'I suppose Anya's parents have a skewed view of me now but prior to recent events it's all been good. I guess, growing up I spent more time around adults.'

'George, for grownups do you mean medical professionals?'

'Yeah.'

'Then I think you might be okay as my mother gives every impression of being a fully qualified psychotherapist. This, despite the fact her knowledge comes from every magazine and Reality TV expert you can think of!'

She lapses into silence again.

'What's worrying you?'

'Nothing. Um, so you're good with loud?'

'Yep,' I reassure. It feels good to be able to help her and there's method to my madness when I ask, 'So, are we sleeping together?'

'What the—?' Her head whips round to mine so fast I worry I've given her whiplash. Then, with her eyes back on the road, she demands, 'You think me turning up at your door on the verge of a meltdown is my seductive way of asking you to have sex?'

'Well, no,' I concede, 'you probably have better moves than that.'

'*Probably?*' She casts me a swift glance and I grin because at least I've got her out of being too in her head.

'It's for backstory and authenticity when I do the whole'—deliberately I adopt the worst imitation of an American accent—'Hi, I'm Zach and I knew the minute I met your daughter that as well as being really hot, she'd be very cool with me having little ambition in life other than putting the hours in at the day job before kicking around a football with my bros.'

'Oh. My. God. Do not say any of that.'

'Did you know you get a cute wrinkle at the bridge of your nose when you're stressed?'

She flaps a hand at her nose and continues, 'And don't disrespect Zach's work like that. There's nothing wrong with being an HVAC technician.'

'You're right, there isn't. But there *is* something wrong with not wanting to do anything that might cause you a moment's "hassle" in life – his words, not mine. Don't be overly fair on him, Ashleigh. There's going with the flow and then there's avoiding making decisions.'

'Says the guy who's been sitting in his apartment for days, letting perfectly good job opportunities slip through his fingers. Have you thought any more about that job?'

Damn, left myself wide open. 'Yes.'

'And?'

'It's still a "no".'

'But why?'

'Ashleigh.'

'No. Seriously, didn't you say a part of you had been feeling like the work you did lately, felt irrelevant? This would be the opposite of that. Still creative but instead of increasing profits for some corporation, you'd be getting the word out about something that matters. Something that informs and benefits others. That in turn also benefits you and makes you feel like you're involved in something *real*.'

'Are you on some sort of retainer with the hospital?' I ask, trying not to let her words intrigue.

'No, that would be *you* if you took the job.'

'Look, I know you think I'd be perfect for it but—'

'But nothing. I'm not going to let this go, George.'

'Oh, I definitely hear that.'

We lapse back into silence again and I'm left to contemplate why it is that every time she brings it up, the job sounds better? And how is it that every time she does, I can feel my heels digging in deeper? How much of my reaction is down to my heart history and dislike of hospitals and how much of it is to do with because I didn't plan for needing to change jobs?

'You know, maybe I encouraged Zach to let me down.'

Ashleigh's soft statement brings me out of my reverie. 'What the hell?'

'Maybe I didn't'—she blows out a breath—'listen enough? Or only heard what I wanted to hear? Maybe I missed something – some nuance?'

'How could you understand nuance if he didn't give you any context?'

'But what if he told me the context and I didn't hear it because I was busy solving my problem of going to this wedding with a date?'

'Don't do that. He told you he would go with you and then he let you down. This is not your fault.'

'I guess.'

I hate that she doesn't sound convinced and try and take her mind off doubting herself with, 'So, what's my kissing like?'

'How would I know?'

She'd know if I'd kissed her in Mrs. Lundy's kitchen like I'd wanted to. Or on the fire escape outside of Oscars like I'd wanted to. Or in my bedroom a scant hour or so ago when I'd seen how hard she was working to hold it together. Instead, I say, 'I'm pretty sure your family are going to expect you to have kissed a guy you're seeing.'

'Oh. In that case. Your kissing is spectacular.'

Our gazes meet again and she smiles, shakes her head and murmurs that I'm, 'so tiring' but there's no bite to it.

'Spectacular? Noted. And what side of the bed do I sleep on?' I ask.

'That one's easy. You sleep in the middle.'

Damn. Is she answering that Zach does or that she knows I do because she cleans my bedroom? 'So how am I in bed?'

'Hey, if you need to ask…'

'As Zach should I go with spectacular again?'

'*As* Zach you're not going to need to answer that.'

Interesting. Is that because she didn't sleep with Zach? And why am I fishing for information? Why is my chest puffing out a little and a warmth spreading through me? 'I'll just say that the sex between us is good?'

'You're not going to need to say anything because no one's going to ask.'

'You're kidding? That's one of the first questions your sister's going to ask you.'

'No, she isn't.'

'If not her, then your brother?'

'He better not.'

'Well, what do you want me to say if your father pulls me aside and asks what my intentions are?'

'What do you *want* to say? No. Stop. We are not having this conversation.'

'I don't want you to get blind-sided. Weddings do funny things to people.'

'Well, then, I'll just tell them...' She trails off, blows out another breath.

'You'll tell them...?'

Her voice is back to shaky as she says, 'This is a really bad idea.'

'You're going to tell them we're a really bad idea? I don't think that's going to help them not worry about you. This situation has Divide and Conquer written all over it and if we don't give them what they want you can bet innocent-looking Granny in the corner will get the info out of us.'

'You think Granny will be a ringer?'

'Is this the first time you've brought a guy home?'

'Crap,' she says and the next thing I know she's pulling into a gas station, switching off the engine and reaching for her phone.

'Ma?'

'Oh my god you're not coming,' I hear her mother immediately say. 'I knew it. Joe? Joe? Didn't I tell you this was going to be too difficult for her—'

'Relax, I'm still coming,' Ashleigh quickly inserts. 'I just wanted to give you a heads-up I'm no longer bringing Zach but instead my friend, George.' She pauses and with a roll of her eyes, adds, 'I'm not seeing Zach anymore and yes, George is a guy.' I can't quite make out her mother's response before Ashleigh turns to me and with her gorgeous button-brown eyes sparkling, adds,

'The poor guy has been super lonely and I just felt *so* sorry for him.'

I burst into laughter and mouth the word, 'Touché.'

Ashleigh has this ability to make me feel light, whole, happy. It's familiar – as if she's returned a piece of me that I didn't even know I'd lost. If I took that job, I could be around her energy even more.

And explore the spark between us.

Chapter Thirty-Eight

HOME BITTERSWEET HOME

Ashleigh

'You asked for it,' I whisper out the side of my mouth as George and I stand in front of my folks' front porch.

'Actually, I believe it was *you* who asked for *me*,' he whispers back.

Liquid fire ignites inside me as I wonder if I did, in fact, ask the universe for George. Luckily, I'm spared any deep-thinking as family descends the porch steps in a wall of sound and we're collected up as if we're one unit. Bear hugs abound and emotion swells within me.

I try to turn my head to look opposite to the house where Jasmine will have her wedding reception later. The house where Sarah grew up. The house that up until last year I'd treated as an extension to the one I'm standing in front of now.

I can't look. Not yet. So, I risk a look at George. He doesn't look intimidated at all as he claps a hand on my brother's back like he's known him years. But I should have told him more about the wedding. Should have properly explained.

The moment we cross the threshold, I say, 'There's something I need to tell you in private—'

'Sit and have some food first,' my mother says.

'Food?' I forgot about her bat-like hearing capabilities. In my peripheral I notice the good chinaware set out. 'But there'll be food at the wedding.'

'Sit and have a drink first,' she amends.

'And some food,' my father adds, with a "make your mother happy" look at me. 'It's not often we get the brood under the same roof again for a weekend.'

My hand trembles as I set down the cake box. 'Everyone's staying? But where's George going to sleep?'

'You think an add-on built itself while you were away?' my brother, Joey, asks, ignoring the food set out to lift the lid on the box from Oscars. Automatically helping himself to the biggest pastry, he adds, 'He's sleeping in your old room. With you!'

Before I can fully process this, George sits down at the table like one of the family. My sister, CeCe, stares at him and then aims a "Well isn't this interesting?" face at me.

With a sigh I too sit down, telling Joey, 'The pastries are from my friends' bakery, and leave some for the rest of us why don't you?'

'Swanky,' he mumbles around the cream cone.

'So, Ashleigh mentioned *you were a friend*?' my mother tells George as she grabs a plate, puts a pastry onto it for him, and then, as he's about to take hold of the offering, keeps a steady grip on it.

Beginning her interrogation before he has a full belly? Attacking while he's weak from hunger? Classic trap.

I look under my lashes at George. Poor fool. He doesn't even hesitate and answers, 'Close friend,' while delivering a warm smile to CeCe, who I swear *swoons*.

'And how did you meet?' my mother asks.

Please don't tell her I'm your cleaner and confirm every legitimate concern she's had that I've sometimes pretended to have lots of friends who have only, in fact, been people I clean for.

'We met through our shared love of crosswords,' George says.

Wow. Way better than I would have come up with. I'm allowed all of ten seconds to bask in the feeling before Joey snorts, 'Crosswords? Very, um, stimulating.'

'Oh, you have no idea.' George laughs like we share this special sexy crossword deal and okay, I do find our shared passion for them sort of sexy but does my brother need to know that?

'Well, I'm glad Ashleigh brought a date for today however you know each other,' my mother comments and I can't tell if she thinks we're real friends or not. It occurs to me I could never make someone like George up. I'd have never come up with someone so perfect for me.

'Me too,' George says. 'I mean, we all know she could have come on her own, even if it would, understandably, be hard for her.'

Understandably hard for me?

What the what, now?

'Your daughter's very strong,' he says looking my mother straight in the eye, holding his hand out for the plate, and adding, 'but I'm sure you know that.'

'Oh, I do, George,' she replies, with a delighted smile as she relinquishes the plate. 'I do.'

I shake my head to check my hearing.

The statement is bold. Simple.

But the words don't sound simple to me at all. I'm starting to feel like this could all get away from me. I don't have any control over the conversation and I don't like the feeling.

'She only brought me with her today,' George explains, 'because she didn't want to leave me on my own.'

'You're that irresistible, huh, George?' my brother asks.

'It's the British accent,' his wife, Terese, whispers to CeCe.

'I wish.' George chuckles.

I want to look at him so bad. Did he mean he wishes that he was irresistible to me?

'I've been through some stuff recently,' he admits, 'and you know Ashleigh for collecting people up and helping them.'

Oh, crap. He somehow thinks he's here to push me into the spotlight and throw glitter over me?

No, no, no, no, no.

'Leave no man on the field?' CeCe sums up. 'Yeah, she's started doing that.'

I want to run so bad but where would I go?

With every fibre of my being, I wish I could ask Sarah what to do – how to put a stop to this. But there's not even a sarcastic comment floating in on a white charger – I mean feather – and I know why, don't I?

It's payback.

For leaving her on the field.

'And what have you been through, recently, George?' my mother pries.

'Ma, you're going to give him indigestion.' I turn to George. 'I forgot to mention she works for the CIA.'

George looks confused. 'The cleaning company's a cover?'

My mother smiles wryly. 'It suits my daughter to pretend I'm more than an interested mother hen trying to ensure all her chicks are okay.'

'Got you.' George smiles back.

No. I will not have this.

George is winning over my mother?

My world paradigm shifts, turning my breathing unsteady as I let in the fact that George is the type of guy my mother always wanted me to meet. Zach's laid-back attitude would have worried her instantly. The irony sucks.

'The truth is,' George says around a bite of glazed doughnut, 'my job came to an unexpected end and I'm not doing great at deciding my next move. I spent my life working to get where I was in that job and then…' He tails off and shoves another bite of doughnut into his mouth and I'm left looking around the table at my family hanging on his every word. Where's the talking over each other? Instead, he's holding them in the palm of his hand. Holding *me* in the palm of his hand, right up until he says… 'It's hard to describe the panic, but of course with everything Ashleigh's been through, she totally gets that "world collapsing around you, staring into the void" feeling. Her picking herself up after leaving something that was making her ill is inspiring.'

'Ill?' My mother pounces on the word.

'At the magazine,' George explains.

'*Please stop*,' I implore but, apparently, not loudly enough because George carries right on putting his foot, his leg, his entire body into his mouth.

'Recent experience,' George adds, 'has shown me you can legitimately feel like you're dying during a panic attack.'

'You had panic attacks at the magazine?' my mother asks quietly.

I want to die but who would notice because George is carrying on in his jolly, amiable tone, 'Anyway, I'm grateful she left to go to Sparkle. The place makes her happy.'

'I'm impressed you know where Ashleigh worked and where she works now, George,' my mother says leadingly.

'Like I said, we're close friends. The lack of support she had at that other place must have made you all crazy too, right? You go through something like losing your best friend, you're in a new place, and she gets, what, five minutes before they're piling on the pressure. I get that business is business but you still have a duty of care, right? Everyone has their breaking point.'

My skin suddenly prickles with sweat and my heart jackhammers in my chest because, *he knows…?*

He was pretending to be asleep that night?

Had in fact been listening to my every word?

'Anyway, it's their loss because it feels like Sparkle reward for going above and beyond, which Ashleigh consistently does. And it must feel nice to think potentially what you've built can stay in the family? She's incredibly proud of what you've achieved while raising three children.'

I feel my mother's thoughtful gaze as she says, 'Have *you* thought about working for the CIA, George? Because you appear to have gotten a better sense of where our daughter's at, than we have … ever!'

'Excuse us a moment,' I mutter and grabbing George's hand, I yank him up from the table and march outside. Before the screen porch door even shuts, I'm whirling around to face him and I don't even recognise the shrillness in my voice, '*You know?* That night in your apartment you heard every word I said about Sarah dying? About working at *Best Home* and the panic attacks and Tiny the giant rabbit?' At least he has the grace to look guilty as I demand, 'But why didn't you say? Why didn't you laugh when I came to the end of my story?'

'Because it wasn't funny, Ashleigh.'

His statement has me feeling like I'm folding in on myself.

'I mean, yes,' he continues, his voice stupid-gentle, 'you told it all excellently. Have you considered stand-up? It's just I saw right through it.'

'What do you mean it wasn't funny? How many other people do you know who can cause such comical carnage in one day at work?'

'You really want me to be honest?'

I look at him like obviously I do even though I really don't.

He shoves his hands into his pockets and says, 'Yes, your clumsiness is sexy, endearing, charming, funny. But you peed on your boss because you fainted. You fainted because you weren't looking after yourself. You weren't looking after yourself because you'd been told it was your last shot so you overworked right up to it, despite still grieving the loss of your best friend. You overworked and everyone at that place let you. I didn't want you to see—'

I take a step away from him because it all makes hideous sense now. 'You didn't want me to see your pity,' I finish for him.

'No, my anger. I was mad as hell on your behalf. If you'd have heard the false bravado in your voice … trying to make it appear like none of it mattered … that you hadn't been dealt a humiliating blow on top of what you'd already been through.'

I stare down at my feet, my mind racing because while it's on a level of awesomeness I can hardly compute that George has been able to make my well-meaning mother see how well I'm doing, I don't feel deserving. Especially when there's another truth here. 'You have to think about it from my boss's point of view. One minute I was reliable. The next minute'—I stop, lick my lips, and force out the words. 'I didn't ask anyone to help me either and sometimes you have to ask.'

Sometimes you have to shout it really loud even though it's the hardest thing to do. Even if you feel invisible. Because sometimes people are busy going about their business, thinking everything is fine and then, the next minute it's too late and your best friend gets left on the field.

Chapter Thirty-Nine

HOW I MET YOUR SISTER

Ashleigh

A wedding guest hands me the mic and I stare at them as if they've given me a mouldy dead mouse instead.

I have not yet had nearly enough to drink to give a speech to the newlyweds, though it's not through lack of trying. When does the numbing effect kick-in, that's what I want to know?

For the last hour I've been sitting in this marquee where lights shine onto colourful goblets and vibrant centrepiece flowers. I'm surrounded by adults chatting and kids chasing each other around. It's the kind of colour and noise that slams into your carefully constructed grey and forces you to reckon with it. To join in with it.

I really *want* to join in with it – to keep present and not let the emotion of the day overwhelm me but it's impossible when I can feel Sarah's presence everywhere. She was there in the beautiful ceremony in the little church. She's here in the marquee. I bet if I stole away to the tree house beyond this tent, to the place we confided our secrets and hopes and dreams in, I'd feel her there too.

It's not the same.

Not the same as her physically being here and I hate it, hate it, hate it.

Hate that she can't celebrate with her family.

Hate that she didn't get to come home.

I think I hear my mother say, 'You don't have to speak, Ashleigh.'

But I know I do.

For Sarah.

And then George is gently tipping my face towards his. Our eyes meet and he tells me, simply, 'You've got this.'

He's so confident I find myself rising on unsteady feet, my hand clenched around the microphone. My gaze connects with Sarah and Jasmine's mother, Shelley-Ann, and I go blank until I feel George take my free hand, tangle his fingers with mine and squeeze and somehow, I begin. 'I met Jasmine the day I pushed her sister, Sarah, into the duck pond on the corner of Maple and Third. It was a total accident – knocking Sarah into the pond, not meeting Jasmine...' There's good-natured laughter but it's George's deep rumble that helps me form a smile around my words so that they sound less wooden. 'Even dripping wet and smelling of pond weed I recognised her as the girl my age who'd moved in across from our house the day before. Believe me, this was *not* how I'd intended for us to meet and become best friends. I tried explaining it was all Billy Jenkins' fault. If the boy hadn't been so beautiful to look at, I would have been looking where I was going. I even offered to jump into the pond so that we matched. Of course when she said that would be okay by her, I decided we weren't destined to become best friends after all because, *obviously*, she wasn't supposed to agree with me.'

There's more laughter. Maybe George is right about me doing stand-up. 'While Sarah waited for me to jump fully clothed into the pond, she informed me I sucked, the town sucked, her entire life sucked and, *worse*, it was only going to suck harder when her sister discovered she'd,' I raise my fingers to finger-quote, '*borrowed* her brand-new training bra to wear that morning and it was now ruined. Sorry, Jasmine,' I say, sneaking a look at the bride who is smiling warmly at her husband as he smiles warmly at her chest area, making everyone laugh again.

In the warm, convivial atmosphere of the room, I continue, remembering the day as if it was yesterday. 'It seemed my fate was sealed and I was definitely going to jump in and meet my watery end. That is, until beautiful Billy Jenkins rode past us again and Sarah suddenly decided if I could get her sister a date with him instead, she *might* survive the summer. And so that's how I met Jasmine – by sacrificing what I'm sure would have been a long and lasting relationship with Billy, had he ever once glanced my way. Jasmine went out with Billy five times before dumping him, leaving him heartbroken and only more attractive to Sarah and me. But the coolest thing about Jasmine was that she didn't kill Sarah then, or any of the other times the two of us accidentally mortified her, which meant Sarah and I got to become best friends and stay best friends.' I drag in a breath, drowning in sudden emotion and my voice is wobbly as I glance at Jasmine and her new husband, Rob, and then the rest of Sarah's family. 'Sarah would have loved seeing you all so happy. Would have loved being here to share this special day with you. Would, let's face it, probably be a little inebriated by now, and therefore less circumspect about having to wear a bridesmaid's dress in lemon yellow chiffon despite being a ginger. But even in lemon yellow chiffon she'd have looked so stunning that a guy as beautiful as Billy would have wanted to whisk her off her feet. I can't believe she's never going to get the chance to get her Billy Jenkins. Or to get married. Or to do any of the—' I stop, swallow, as I fumble my words. 'Sorry,' I whisper. 'I meant to stay in the present, t-to—'

'To the bride and groom,' George finishes for me, holding up his glass.

People are too slow to respond. Quiet, as they look at one another.

I've somehow done what I didn't want to and changed the energy.

'Um, speaking of presents,' George says again, 'why don't you open this one…' and he gets up, grabs a gift from the gift table and hands it to them.

Even through the sheen of tears I recognise the plain brown paper wrapping. 'George?' I grab his hand in horror as the alcohol inside burns like acid in my throat. 'How is that parcel here?'

'What do you mean? I picked it up with everything else when I loaded the car.'

'You didn't. No, please. I—' I squeeze my eyes shut as the bride and groom open the gift.

You can hear a pin drop.

No, it's worse … I hear Jasmine's quick intake of breath as my angel wings collage is unveiled and then I can hear George whispering, 'Well, damn. I was convinced it was a cheesy album cover with a silly frog on it or something.'

I'm leaning against the treehouse ladder, trying not to hurl when George finds me.

'Ashleigh, they loved the angel wings. If the piece you're making for me is half as good, my brother is going to be one lucky—'

'It wasn't for them,' I interrupt. 'It was for Oscars' gallery wall because who wants a reminder their loved one isn't there on their big day? Bad enough I ruined everything with my speech.'

'You didn't. You acknowledged their loss in a beautiful way. It didn't take away – it gave.'

'Don't be nice to me.' My shoulder digs into the rough wooden ladder. 'You don't get it.'

'Then explain so that I do.'

'I can't. I can't tell anyone.'

'What's the point of having friends if you can't be real with them?'

'That's just it, George. I'm an awful friend.'

Behind me I hear George laugh. 'What a load of bollocks!'

'Well, prepare to be even more bollocksed because—'

'That's not really how we use that word, but—' George must see my hands clench into fists because he says, 'So not the point. You were saying…?'

'I stomp all over what my friends really want and make it into what *I* want. You think I saved Carlos and Oz and Oscars? Well, what if I didn't do it for them, but for me? So that I wouldn't lose them too? And do you know how many times I tried talking Zach into going into business for himself despite him telling me repeatedly he'd changed his mind? That's not being a good friend, George. That's called being selfish. Come on, even you think I'm just trying to "save" you with going on about the job at the hospital?' God, have I been doing that in some warped way of trying to keep George here? That's really bad. 'Good friends listen. I don't listen, George. I didn't listen to Sarah and now she's dead.'

'You can't really believe that.'

'If I'd *listened*, she wouldn't have still been in the city, with me. She'd have been back here. Safe. Like she wanted to be.'

'Safe? Did something happen before the accident?'

'*Me.*' I bend forward, convinced I won't be able to keep swallowing the boiling acid back down. 'I am what happened to her. *Me*, with my grand ideas and my dreams of living in New York City. Big adventure. Living our best lives. Me, who talked *at* her and *persuaded* her and then, once we got there, I didn't hear her. I made her feel invisible. I was too wrapped up in a job, I didn't even do well at. I was too busy. Too selfish. Left her floundering.'

George is silent but I know what he's thinking. 'You think I'm making it up? But I know she felt those things because I read her journal after – afterwards.' Remembering pierces through my skin, leaving me fragile and ashamed. I'd wanted to feel close to her. Hadn't even hesitated opening it. Never ever considering what I might read. Or that I would read something I wished I hadn't. 'It was all there in black and white. How she wasn't really enjoying living in the city. How she didn't know if she could stick it out. How she was thinking of moving back here. How she couldn't see how she'd meet anyone because everyone moved too fast. She felt rootless but she didn't know how to tell me. How to make me hear her…'

'Oh, Ashleigh, honey.'

I whirl around because that voice doesn't belong to George.

It belongs to Sarah's mother, Shelley-Ann.

'No. Oh no, you heard? I'm so sorry.'

'I'll leave you two to talk,' George says diplomatically and as he turns and walks away, I'd give anything to be able to go with him instead of having to tell Sarah's mother that I'm the reason her daughter isn't here anymore.

'Have you been carrying this, this whole time?' Shelley-Ann asks, her voice thick with emotion.

I look into her eyes and it's like Sarah is staring back at me. 'I didn't know she was struggling,' my words feel torn and rushed. 'I should have known.'

'You were living your life, Ashleigh. *Both* of you were. That's all.' Her hands reach for mine. 'You were figuring life out. All its ups and downs, its twists and turns. It's what you're supposed to do. How else could you learn what you're going to like or what you're suited to best or where you'll be happiest living if you don't try new things? If you hadn't suggested New York City, she'd never have thought of it, but if she hadn't wanted to go with you, you'd have gone on your own.'

Would I? Or did I drag my best friend along for support instead of trying it for myself? What were my dreams and what were hers? And did I conveniently and unfairly merge them into something that suited me more?

'I lost you your daughter.' The words tumble out of me.

'No. You showed her she didn't have to stay in one place. I can understand her wondering where long-term should be, but I know she'd never have swapped having all that fun with you. Never. And she could just have easily had an accident here because that was what it was, a freak accident. And yes, it sucks, as Sarah used to say. But, Ashleigh, none of this is your fault. It's the fault of the person who didn't tie in the scaffolding. Sarah wouldn't want you to punish yourself.'

'But I read her journal.'

'Well, so what? I overheard you and George talking just now

and I didn't walk away. Instead, I kept right on listening. It's human. Sarah wasn't caught under your spell, Ashleigh. You didn't drag her anywhere. My daughter had a quiet strength to her, she had to, to do the job she did. If she'd decided she really wanted to move back home, she'd have figured out a way to tell you. She assumed she had more time to tell you properly, is all.'

'I can't – I don't know how to be here without her.'

'Yes, you do – you're doing it. Your mom tells me you're enjoying your job. Making new friends. You're finding ways of being. Of living.' She steps back to take a fierce look at me. 'That's not a lie, is it?'

Will I always question the gap between how much Sarah wanted to go home and how much she tried to find a way to tell me? Always feel a sadness she didn't get to have what I have now … that sense of expansion of my world … of letting in instead of shutting out? Of finding a sense of community and welcoming in a widening friendship group. Wasn't that what being in New York City had always been about, for me? 'No, it's the truth,' I tell her through a sheen of tears.

'I'm glad. And I can tell you she'd have loved your George. I mean,' she leans in and whispers with a wobbly, nostalgic smile in her voice, 'obviously not a patch on Billy Jenkins!'

'He's not my George,' I whisper back.

'Isn't he?' She pulls me in for a hug and then says, 'I want to thank you for letting me help out with rent.'

'Please, it's me who should be thanking you.'

'Your parents would have done the same if it had been Sarah in your position. I needed to feel that connection, but I hadn't thought how it might make you feel tied to the place? So, with George on the scene if you ever want to leave or move him in, I don't want it to be awkward to tell me.'

'He's not my George,' I repeat, thinking about how maybe soon with the artwork and my job I could afford to cover all of the rent on my own but that I couldn't even think about living elsewhere. Not yet. Not without Sarah. But maybe it was time to start thinking more long-term?

'If you like we could revisit the situation every couple months?'

'I'd really like that.'

'One other favour?'

'Anything.'

'Make me a collage like you did for Jasmine and Rob? So that I have some more of Sarah's white feathers?'

'Of course.'

'You don't have to stay away, you know.'

'I know that.' *Now*.

'The way we keep her alive is to be *alive*, yes?'

'Yes.'

'And in that spirit, maybe you should ask George to dance. See what happens?'

Chapter Forty

DANCE LIKE NO ONE'S WATCHING

Ashleigh

I don't know why I thought I'd be able to steal back into the marquee without anyone noticing. I try telling myself no one is watching me but, of course, my family absolutely is.

CeCe is retying the sash around my niece's party dress for the thousandth time today, all the while offering me a fierce smile as she tracks my progress across the floor. Joey is eating from a plate piled with food – go figure – but still manages to fist-bump his heart at me when our eyes meet. My mother... Oh, Lord, my mother breaks from her group and makes a beeline for me until my father gently puts his hand on her arm, and with a look that says "Our daughter has this under control", steers her instead towards the dancefloor.

What made my pa so confident in me? What made George feel the same earlier?

Not that I'll ask George when I find him. But maybe I'll ask him to dance. With me. To a slow song. I mean, I already know the man can move from his Tony Manero impression, whereas I'm not sure I was made for dancing. Not with all the Clumsy inside me. I try picturing what I'd look like throwing some shapes with him but instead what comes to mind is the two of us moving against each other…

And then, adding another whoosh to the heat suffusing my body at the thought, there he is, suddenly turning to face me like he has this in-built radar for me.

The notion is kind of thrilling.

As he watches me walk towards him, I feel as if I'm floating. Maybe it's the alcohol finally kicking in. Maybe it's that after talking with Shelley-Ann I'm feeling so much lighter.

Whichever it is, the floating at least makes it impossible I'll trip over anything.

He's standing with Jasmine and Rob and I wonder what they've been talking about but somehow, I'm not worried. George isn't Zach. He won't run in the event of an intense conversation.

Jasmine has her arms wrapped around the angel wings collage, and, oh, it's as if Sarah is standing right with her, making my heart sigh extra emotionally as it powers through my lungs.

I'm not going to run either.

When I finally reach the three of them, George reaches out, pulls me into his arms, and looking down at me, asks, 'Okay?'

I nod, deciding there's definitely going to be some dance-asking if it secures me more of this wrapped-in-his-arms feeling but then he's looking at Rob and inclining his head towards the bar area and I'm left standing with Jasmine.

'Are you *really* okay?' she asks as soon as we're alone.

There's no point in pretending I haven't been crying but I nod again, clear my throat and say, 'In case you weren't already aware, your mom's the best.'

Her smile turns soft. 'Yours too. She's been checking in on me every now and then. Brought me books on grieving. Gave me details of pertinent podcasts.'

'Oh God – that's Ma, for you.'

'But it was so well-intentioned and somehow always exactly when I needed it. When I met Rob, I got a more formal visit. I think she was deployed to establish if we were the real thing, and if we were, whether it was too soon, you know.'

Maybe my new habit of checking everyone is okay – of helping – isn't only the guilt or fear since Sarah dying. Maybe I'm more like my ma than I thought.

Wow.

Level ten mind-blowing.

'You're wedding toast was my favourite,' Jasmine says, adding with a quick laugh, 'You were right – Sarah would have hated lemon yellow.'

'You wouldn't really have had that as your bridesmaid colour if she was still here.'

'You would have been sent to talk me out of it.' She indicates the collage. 'And I love this.'

'Um, I didn't actually intend to give that to you.'

'What? Why not? It's perfect.'

'George mistook it for your gift when he was loading the car, and so I was surprised when he handed it to you and well,' I remember to breathe, 'I'm so happy you love it.'

'Speaking of George… Of course, I'm officially an old married lady but I got eyes in my head don't I and *someone* has to acknowledge it – George is *hot!*'

I can't help myself. I look over to where he is standing at the bar with Rob. 'Yep.'

Jasmine puts the collage down and folds her arms. When I

don't say anything else she stares like my simple acknowledgement doesn't even begin to scratch the surface of the topic, so I grin and say, 'So is Rob.'

'Right?' Thankfully she takes the opening and runs with it. 'From the moment we met it's like we've known each other all our lives. I'm the one who proposed, did anyone tell you? Rob tried slowing the pace when we got into "serious" territory but all I could think was that saying, you know, about tomorrows and promises?'

'Tomorrow is promised to no one?' I whisper.

'Yeah. It was probably because of Sarah but I had no question marks at all about him.' She leans in to confide, 'I think she sent him to me.'

I blink. Well, why the hell didn't I think of asking her to send me someone? Probably because what I was really looking for was some friends! I think about Carlos and Oz and George and Mrs. Lundy and everyone at Sparkle and Nadine from the hospital – even Zach there for a while. My small but amazing community that means I'm no longer sleepless in the city that never sleeps.

'For sure if it was the other way around,' Jasmine says, 'and within my power, I'd have found someone to send to her.'

'Billy Jenkins maybe?'

'Oh, god, no. Look, this is what he's into now…' She pulls her phone from her wedding gown pocket and brings up his socials.

I stare at the photos and then look up at her in stunned horror. 'You have to prepare a girl for seeing that!' The two of us stare for a second or two longer at the clown shoes and then look at each other and burst into laughter.

'Sarah could never have been with a clown,' Jasmine asserts, then, sobering, she sighs out, 'She'd never really talk about dates she went on in Brooklyn. Always kept her cards so close to her chest, you know?'

'She went on a few,' I confess, realising there must be things her sister didn't know but would like to. Good things. Simple things. Things I could share. 'I'll have to tell you about some of them someday.'

'Yes please. I'm glad she went on dates. Had fun. Was with you.'

I stare at the floor before forcing out, 'I've sort of been feeling like I robbed you all of time with her.'

'Ash!' Jasmine reaches out to clasp my hand in shock. 'Never think that. Ever. It would have been so much harder on us if Sarah had been living a plane ride away from us all. The thought of never having got to the hospital in time or thinking of her isolated somewhere – in her first proper job but living on her own, all alone?' She shakes her head as if even the thought is unendurable. 'Instead, in what turned out to be her last year she was sharing an apartment with you – her best friend in the whole world.'

I don't know how to respond. I'm not sure I'd ever considered there could be an "at least" from their perspective that they could take comfort in. It's going to take me a moment to process. Sort of feels as if shredded wires are getting re-sheathed and redirected to a different terminal in my brain. I reach out to accept the tissue she's holding out to me. 'No, *you're* crying,' I say.

She laughs and sniffs. 'We'll meet for coffee and talk about her, yes?'

'I'd really love that,' I admit.

As we both mop our faces and hug, I sense George and look up to find him watching me intently.

Is it wrong I'm thinking of paying the DJ to play slow songs all night?

It's because being in George's arms makes me feel startlingly alive.

All *womanly*.

Which is because, pressed up all against me, George feels amazingly tantalizing.

And incredibly *capable!*

That intense, watchful look that had propelled me over to him after talking with Jasmine, had never once wavered. It had made my heart pound and my mouth go dry so that I couldn't even form the words to ask him to dance. When I'd licked my lips to try again, his gaze had tracked the movement and something about the muscle pulsing in his jaw had allowed me to reach out and take the beer bottle from between his hands and place it on the bar behind him.

He hadn't stopped me.

And didn't stop me when I grabbed one of his hands, placed it on my shoulder and turning, led him onto the crowded dancefloor.

I'd felt his fingers flex against my naked shoulder, felt his thumb brush along the line of the spaghetti strap of my dress, up into my neck, to the sensitive point just below my ear and I'd wondered if he'd experienced the tremble ripple through me. Or the goosebumps chaser at feeling him so close behind me. So much communicating without using words. Were those really my hips swaying that little bit more with each step, making me think I could do this – move to the music with him.

My take-charge approach was the sort confident women took in clubs but we weren't at a club. And, let's be clear. You don't grind on the dancefloor at a wedding. You dance appropriately.

'This feels like very adult dancing.'

At my words, George's laugh is husky. Intimate.

'Damn,' I say. 'Forgot to use my inside-my-head voice. I just meant, you're very good at this.'

'Thank you.' He flashes the kind of grin I know is going to make me babble.

'It's interesting,' I tell him, absorbing the feel of his hand at my waist, mine on his shoulder. Sensors spark from the surface contact, transmitting loudly to other parts of me. 'There aren't many places these days that call for the traditional dance hold. I bet Mrs. Lundy's waltzed a time or two, but our generation—'

George smoothly changes it up, so that both my arms are looped around his neck and his hands are skimming down over my ribcage, sliding sensually over the material of my dress before coming to rest hotly at the small of my back.

Wow.

'Better?'

'Oh, there wasn't anything wrong with—' I look up at him. 'Yes.' *Even better*. Especially when his thumbs move over my hip bones like that. My fingers curl in on themselves to stop them curling into the hair at the nape of his neck.

'So did they pull you aside at school and teach you how to dance impressively?'

'Nope.'

'Me neither.' But I seem to know how to do this. I mean, Clumsy has seriously left the building.

'Maybe all it takes is the right partner?'

That serious and sexy look appears in his eyes again, making him look seriously sexy.

'Hmmm.' I kind of think that George would be able to dance

like this with anyone. 'Or some naturally born talent on my part because I can't believe I haven't once trodden on your feet.'

'And you must have noticed I have exceptionally large feet,' he teases. 'By the way, you do know what they say about men with big feet?'

I bat my eyelashes. 'Well, duh. Big feet … big shoes!'

He throws his head back to laugh and oh, my, I do like it when he laughs. I like it when he talks. I like it when he looks.

I like it all.

'Now that you've acknowledged your talent *and* my exceptionally large feet,' he says, waggling his eyebrows, 'I think you're ready for some big moves.'

'Yeah?' This word comes out breathlessly.

Without warning he takes my hand and spins me out and back into him.

I laugh, liking the silliness too, as I land against him. 'Hey? You ever think about buying clown shoes?'

His eyes go round with surprise. 'Ew … clown shoes do it for you?'

I snort with laughter at his expression. 'They definitely do not.'

'Phew. You had me worried there that any big move I made could be misconstrued as *clowning* around.'

I punch him playfully on the chest, swallowing hard at the hard wall of muscle. The silliness evaporates and my heart thumps because we're back to something altogether *more*.

'Hey, George?' I swallow nervously.

'Hmmm?'

'I'm glad Zach forgot about the wedding today.'

His smile is gentle as he folds me into his arms again. As we dance, heart to heart and so close you couldn't slide a feather between us, I hear his, 'Me too,' rumble against my ear.

This day has been so much more than I could ever have hoped for but before I can stop the thought, I'm wondering if Sarah was still here … would George and I have ever even met?

My arms automatically tighten around him and I feel his hands reflexively squeeze back.

Chapter Forty-One

GREAT EXPECTATIONS

Ashleigh

'Ashleigh? You ever going to come out of there?'

George's questions accompany a soft knock on the bathroom door. I lick my lips and stare at my reflection in the small mirror above the sink. I look all lit up from the inside.

What is this stupid giddiness?

This joyfulness?

It's insane, that's what it is.

I should watch myself, right? Because what if—

I go blank.

The fact I can't come up with anything almost freaks me out more.

Almost.

Because, what if I, as Shelley-Ann said, see what happens next?

My imagination ignites.

Normally if I looked this good and there was a Gorgeous George on the other side of the door, I'd confidently open it to stand silhouetted against the frame with a come-hither look in my eyes.

'*Sure you would,*' I imagine Sarah saying with a slow nod of her head, '*because could you look any more sexy dressed in pyjama shorts and tank top printed with dancing pugs?*'

I undo a button. I'm not sure it compensates for the dancing pugs, so I shoot my gaze heavenwards and whisper, 'I didn't invite George here to seduce him.'

'*Also great,*' I imagine Sarah helpfully adding, '*given you're sleeping in your childhood room, with the rest of your family across the hall.*'

'Ashleigh?' George calls again.

'Be out in a minute,' I say, frowning to try and dim the sparkle in my eyes that comes from having a Gorgeous George waiting behind the door.

I guess the question is, is he waiting for me?

It felt like he was, out on that dancefloor.

I breathe in and open the bedroom door.

I lounge nonchalantly.

At least I would have done if I hadn't misjudged completely where the door frame was and stumbled backwards my hands flapping in mid-air like a demented pigeon.

I'm super-glad it's dark as I'm pretty sure there's a gigantic smile on George's face as he reaches forward to catch me. Again.

'I was beginning to think I'd learned your deepest secret,' George says, large hands righting me before dropping away again leaving me bereft.

'Huh?'

'That you sleep standing up in your shower, instead of in a bed?'

Oh. 'Um, right. That's me. A bat.'

'You sleep upside down as well? Does that mean I get the bed?'

'You should absolutely take the bed,' I say instantly. 'Because —' Don't look down. Do not look down. 'Big.' The word comes out on a half swallow as my gaze betrays me to take in a sightseeing tour of his torso in the light from the bathroom. There is absolutely nothing cheesy about the tour.

'Kidding,' he chuckles. 'There's no way you're taking the trundle. I'll be perfectly fine on it.'

For a few seconds it's like we're daring each other not to let our gazes drop again to greedily feast. In the atmosphere, thick with promise, my heart beats crazy fast and it feels like I lean in closer but then he's moving away, leaving me off balance and with no other choice but to cross the bedroom floor to slip into my childhood bed, alone. In the darkness I turn onto my side to stare at him and can just about make out his biceps on arms folded back behind his head. Biceps I remember feeling when his arms wrapped around me on the dancefloor.

'I think I was expecting boy band posters.' His voice is quiet in the dark.

I think I was expecting sex! It takes me a moment to accept that I got it majorly wrong. That while I was in the bathroom with my excited feelings, George was wandering around my room soaking up the teenage atmosphere. 'You don't like my covers of *Interior Design Weekly* and *Best Home*?' I manage to ask.

'Are you kidding? They're a fascinating insight into the younger you. I particularly like the handwritten list of cleaning hacks,' he says. 'Especially the one where you talk about shoving everything under your bed for instant results.'

I can't help a smile forming. 'That might have been more about annoying my mother than flexing my design skills.' I strive for different territory. One where my eyes aren't gawping and my ears aren't straining for the sound of the beat of his heart – is it mimicking mine? Is it steady? Thready? 'What was your room like growing up?'

He's quiet for so long I wonder if he'll answer at all, and then I hear him say, 'It was still and spotless.'

'You already know I crush over spotless, but I guess at frantic times, stillness can be soothing. Healing.'

'I guess.'

'Not so for you?'

There's a heartfelt sigh and then, 'It's hard to feel alive when you have to be so...'

'Still?'

'Yeah. But then, that stillness helped provide a good study environment as I got older.'

'And probably fostered a good imagination.'

He laughs and it gets me all tingly. 'How did you manage to turn that into something dirty?'

He laughs again and I close my eyes and think that along with all the heady anticipation, the closeness and the intimacy on that dancefloor, there'd been something even more syrupy seductive. There'd been laughter.

So much laughter.

As warming as being enveloped in a silk comforter.

Of course, even better would be wrapped up in a silk comforter *with* George.

'I liked hearing more about your friendship with Sarah today,' George says.

I sober instantly and then acknowledge that as much as I loved the dancing and the laughter, I love this too – this quiet late night talk thing we both find so easy to slip into. It makes it okay to admit, 'It was good to talk about her. I guess I haven't let myself.

It's hard to bring something like that into new friendships, you know? But maybe it would be okay to do that a bit more?'

'Definitely okay. So, coming home for this wedding has been good?'

He makes me feel it was fate I got to bring him with me and I wish I could return the favour when he goes back to England for his brother's wedding. I hope he comes back after. But I don't want to think about if he doesn't, so I say, 'Thank you for what you said to my family. I think it's the first time my mother's looked at me and really seen how much I love what I'm doing.'

'I think they'd love you running their company in the future.'

There was thinking longer-term and mapping out my whole future and hadn't I seen what that kind of rigid plan had done to him? 'It'll be years before they retire,' I say non-committedly, but now I'm thinking about Rhonda offering me that promotion. I know why even the suggestion had freaked me out, but could there be some sort of compromise there? I wait for the panic to set in and when it's only very low-level I promise myself to properly think about it.

In the silence I shift position. Restless and reacting again to the tendrils of awareness arcing across the small space between beds.

If I pushed back the covers… If I asked him to, would he climb in beside me? Because at least then if he didn't come back after his brother's wedding, I'd have some hot memories.

Like a moth to a flame and with the want in me needing confirmation I whisper, 'Hey, George?'

'Yeah?'

'You really thought my bunny outfit was sexy?'

There's the sound of his breath leaving his lungs, followed by, 'Ridiculously.'

I grin.

Until he says, 'Night, Ashleigh,' and I hear him turn to lie on his side away from me.

Wow.

But I guess, what exactly did I think was going to happen the minute I told George that Zach and I were no longer a thing? That he would automatically make a move?

'Night,' I whisper.

I close my eyes though it's a long time before I fall asleep.

Chapter Forty-Two

RAIN OR SHINE

George

'Wait.' Ashleigh stops us halfway to the elevator. 'Did you water Ficus-Ficus?'

'I thought we hadn't agreed on Ficus-Ficus?'

She shoots me an exasperated frown. 'But we did agree on not letting it die, right?'

'Right,' I confirm, watching her curiously. Her mood is more than my propensity for forgetting to water the plant, I think. 'How about I water Yet to Be Named. You hold the elevator?'

She sighs and walks off and it takes me a second to remember to look at the lock I'm putting my key into and not the sway of her hips and fit of her jeans.

Two minutes later I'm back out the door, preoccupied with getting to the bottom of what's going on with her, which is why I don't register Mrs. Lundy's, 'Off on another romantic date with Ashleigh?' until I see Ashleigh's head pop out from inside the elevator, expression mildly horrified.

'Hi, Mrs. Lundy,' I greet, slowly turning around.

'Hildy,' she corrects, zeroing in on the picnic hamper I'm carrying. She looks back up at me with an approving smile.

'Hildy,' I say, but nope. Still awkward.

'Why would you think we're off somewhere romantic?' Ashleigh asks, the last word coming out, I want to say, *panicked*, as she joins us.

'Didn't you go to a wedding together a couple of weeks ago? Weddings are very romantic. Then you went out sightseeing last week.'

'Top of the Rock?' Ashleigh scoffs. 'Romantic? Sure. If romance equals vertigo and crowds.'

I watch Ashleigh so studiously avoiding my gaze and wonder at our completely different takes on last week's day out together before looking back at Mrs. Lundy who says, 'Romance is like magic,' and nearly blinds me with the twinkle in her eye. 'If you believe in it, you can find it in everything. All it takes is a look. A touch. Some Barry White.'

'What's a Barry White?' Ashleigh asks suspiciously.

'More *who*,' Mrs. Lundy explains. 'Look him up. Vintage but musical romantical magic.'

'We don't need Barry,' Ashleigh assures, even while I'm wondering about heading back to the vinyl shop to investigate. 'I'm only taking George out because it's not good for him to be couped up in his apartment on the weekend.'

'Woah.' I turn my full attention on her with a look that suggests I don't appreciate my name becoming synonymous with a *six-letters-someone-you-feel-sorry-for* crossword clue answer. 'You've been taking me out on *pity* dates?'

'Of course they haven't been "pity" dates,' she concedes, her gaze sliding away and then back to mine, as her chin tips up. 'They haven't been dates at all.'

And there you have it, ladies and gentlemen.

Somehow between the wedding and now, I've been friend-zoned.

Kind of thought we were heading into a different zone and find myself announcing, 'Thought we'd take the ferry over to Governors Island for the day. Have ourselves a picnic. Catch the sunset.'

'S-sunset?' Ashleigh stutters. 'I have to be back by five.'

'Why, are you a werewolf?' I ask. And then it hits me. Has Ashleigh got a *date* tonight? Now she's no longer seeing Zach, why wouldn't Carlos and Oz be presenting her with new options? I hadn't thought – hadn't considered – had been enjoying too much how the anticipation was amping up between us.

'Funny.' Ashleigh stares at me, her huge brown eyes searching. She licks her lips and when she notices me track the action, swallows. 'The whole day on Governors Island, that's really your pick?'

'Yep,' I tell her, daring her to bail now she knows it isn't a day of headphone-wearing-audio-guides.

A defiant glint enters her expression. 'Can't think of a better way to spend a Saturday *with a friend*.' Turning to Mrs. Lundy, she asks her if the plates she returned were okay and as they start chatting about some Japanese art of fixing things with gold I study her, fighting this new instinct to pull out all the stops for this non-date date and telling myself friendship is fine and I'll appreciate having it when I get back from Marcus's wedding. That I won't have any problem seeing her dating, or having to negotiate spending time with her.

'…Well, babysitting calls,' Mrs. Lundy finally says, waving a hand before knocking on Julia Montford's door. 'I'll let you two *friends* get going.'

We get in the elevator, silence reigning until I can stand it no more. 'Look, would you rather not do this today?'

She looks up warily. 'Why do you ask that?'

'You seem a little…' *Do not say panicked.* 'Tense?'

'That's because it's going to rain and your plan is to spend the day outside.'

I grind my jaws together, adding to the stab of hurt that she feels she has to lie to me. 'It's not going to rain.'

She brings up a weather app on her phone and points to it.

Shit.

'Fine. What do you want to do instead?'

She hesitates and I can tell she's trying to think of something – *anything* – more impersonal than sharing a picnic and a sunset. Finally, she squares her shoulders and says, 'Nothing. You fly out for your brother's wedding tomorrow so it's only fair you pick today's d—'

'Date?'

'Day out,' she corrects.

Outside, in the fabulous rain belying sunshine, we head, in silence, towards Brooklyn Bridge Park and the pier for the ferry.

An hour later, who knew renting a tandem to explore the island would be key to breaking the stilted carefulness we'd adopted on leaving the apartment? But from the moment Ashleigh looked up from the map she'd been studying, clocked me wheeling it towards her and said, 'You're not seriously asking me to mount that beast?' and I'd waggled my eyebrows and replied, 'Just grab onto me tight and enjoy the ride of your life,' and the delightfully dirty laugh had fallen from her mouth, the spell had been broken.

We've spent the morning leaning a little into audio-guide geekery with a look around Fort Jay and Castle Williams before discovering the architecture of the original nineteenth century military officers' houses.

But now, as I watch her, looking not out at the incredible view of the Statue of Liberty in the distance, but instead, the people enjoying the open space of the Hills, I can sense a new quietness, a trepidation, and at the risk of spoiling what we'd recovered, I ask, 'So what are you doing tonight?' Because what it comes down to, as I sit on the picnic blanket with her, the remnants of a feast from Oscars laid out between us, is that I'm not willing to give this up.

This exploring New York City with Ashleigh.

This exploring what Ashleigh and I have.

Whatever it is between us may have got confused since the wedding but there's *something* and a plane ride back to the UK is a long journey to regret not fighting for it.

I catch the unguarded flash of indecision in her eyes before she masks it with a, 'Huh?'

'Tonight?' I probe. 'Sunset? You said you needed to be back so I figured you had a date. That maybe Carlos and Oz had procured—'

'Procured?' She raises an eyebrow in warning.

'Arranged another date for you?'

She seems more fascinated in a couple throwing a Frisbee back and forth than looking at me as she murmurs, 'I don't have another wedding to go to until next year now, so there's no urgency to find another date.'

I remember the bake-date trial and her telling me about why she started going on dates in the first place. That it was more for company than forming a connection. 'So, you're not looking for a relationship right now?' I guess the plane ride is long enough to lick my wounds instead.

'Although maybe I *should* go on more dates,' Ashleigh suddenly asserts. 'Keep expanding my social life. Make some more friends. Did I tell you I'm going for a drink with one of the nurses at the hospital where I volunteer read? She knew Sarah so that's a nice connection.'

'And then there's me,' I say, because our connection is surely deeper than an understanding of loneliness – mine from when I was younger and hers after Sarah died.

'You?'

'Are we not friends?'

'Of course.'

'So why have you been distancing yourself?'

'I haven't.'

'Something's changed since the wedding.'

'You're imagining it.'

'Why did you get so panicked when Mrs. Lundy mentioned romance?'

She starts clearing away the picnic and I'm all for observing outside eating rules but when she starts folding and refolding the napkins like she's in some sort of origami competition before squaring everything back in the hamper like it's on military parade I realise she's cleaning for a reason. I just wish I knew the reason. 'Ashleigh—'

'Oh,' she suddenly says, withdrawing a book from the hamper, 'you bought crosswords?'

Distracted for a second, I glance down at the book. Yes, I bought crosswords. I thought it would be romantic. Sitting somewhere with a view. Fantastic company and some word games – different to the one we seem to be playing right now.

I lay my hand over hers, look her in the eye, and say, 'I don't want to do a crossword right now. I want us to talk.'

'Talk?'

'About what has you so spooked around me.'

Ashleigh stares at me for a while and I think, okay, here it comes, she's going to explain and I brace, but then she looks away and says, 'I spoke to my boss, Rhonda, earlier this week.'

So not where I thought this was going. 'Oh?'

'About a promotion she offered me a while ago. She's been looking for someone to start taking over more of the management and even though I sort of got her to promote Jamal, I don't know, lately I've been thinking there's enough work for two and how it's important to keep a business evolving and—' she breaks off. Shrugs. Looks bashful.

'But that's brilliant,' I tell her.

'It is?'

'It isn't?' If anyone deserves to be able to take all their initiative to the next level, it's Ashleigh.

'I guess I'm nervous about it.' She offers me a tight smile and then looks out to the water. 'I probably won't be able to clean for you anymore.'

My heart skips a beat until I remember I'll be getting another job soon so wouldn't be seeing her while she cleaned anyway. 'Makes sense. But we should celebrate or is that what you're doing tonight?'

'With Carlos and Oz. I thought you'd be busy packing.'

Ask me to come with you. When she doesn't, I say, 'So we'll celebrate when I get back.'

She picks a non-existent crumb off her jeans. 'Sure.'

Is it that she thinks I'm not coming back? She doesn't trust me? How can she not trust me? I've been more open with her than anyone ever. 'You don't sound it. Don't forget we'll be free weekends and evenings,' I assert.

She takes a deep breath, and releases it on a breathy admission of, 'You know how it goes with new jobs, I'll be super busy – stretched. Probably have to work evenings – at least at first.'

I don't get it. Where's my fearless Ashleigh gone? I stare out at the skyline and realise it's got very dark. 'You'll make the effort to get out a little as well, right? On top of all the working? Because otherwise what happened to learning to make room for the important things in life? I thought that's what you'd learned after your experience at *Best Home* and Sarah dying.'

'I'm just trying to explain that it might be hard for us to find time to … chill together.'

'So, it's fine to lecture *me* about making room for the important things in life? Having a balance? Doing things outside of work that I enjoy? All that crap about singing and sport and sightseeing—'

'Well, I'm right about that, aren't I? If you took a job like the one at the hospital, where you made less but it gave you so much more, you could fit in soccer coaching or rock choir or dating.'

What the hell? 'You're worried about my dating life now?'

'I'm worried that to protect your heart you'll use work as a convenient excuse to stop yourself having more.'

I shake my head sadly. 'No, that's not me, that's actually you, right now. *And my heart is fine.* I already told you I want a family and that the next person I got seriously involved with would have to understand that and be up for that too.'

'It's one thing to say that.'

I stare at her, feeling like the dark clouds gathering above are casting a shadow between us like a physical barrier. 'This is such bullshit. Look, I get why you feel the impulse to save people but to be clear – I don't need saving.' I lean forward to tilt her face towards mine. 'I'm more than some bloody project for you. I'm – *we're* – what are you doing?' Disappointment has my heart feeling leaden. Here I am taking the risk, speaking my truth and she's jumping to her feet and trying to roll up the picnic blanket with me still on it.

'It's raining,' she says, folding her arms waiting for me.

I jump to my feet also. 'Who cares about the bloody rain? There's more between us than a job.' I grab hold of her hands.

'What are you talking about?'

'You heard me. A job isn't going to stop you thinking about me any more than it would stop me thinking about you. From day one I've felt you looking at me – stealing glances. I know it because I do it right back. It's how I know the gold in your eyes deepens and turns molten, making the brown richer, deeper.'

'All creative people know how to paint a pretty picture.'

'You know our friendship has deepened. Admit it. What about the wedding? Your heart beat just as crazy-fast as mine when we were dancing. I felt it.'

'B-but you didn't make a move… The whole time after you didn't make one move. Worse, you rolled over to turn the other way.'

'*That's* why you've pulled back? Of course I didn't make a move. The day was incredibly emotional for you. Not to mention you'd had enough alcohol to fell a bison.'

'It doesn't matter now anyway.'

'Doesn't matter?'

'You're going back to—'

'I'm coming back.'

The rain is coming down thick and fast, bouncing off the grass and soaking everything in sight.

'Ashleigh, look at me.'

'I can't, it's raining too hard.'

'One week from tomorrow I will be back here hardly able to wait to spend time with you. You can trust in that.'

'No one can ever be one hundred per cent sure about anything. Some things are outside a person's control. What if—'

'Forget what ifs. I'm not walking away from this because it feels like it might get complicated. How could I when being around you feels like the easiest thing in the world?'

'I—'

'Maybe this will convince you.' My hands move up to cradle her face, and her eyes go wide in surprise. She is easily the most beautiful woman I've ever seen. 'Do you know you have raindrops clinging to your lips?' My last clear thought is that she has me gushing like some bloody poet before I tilt her head, lean in, and at last, lay my lips over hers.

Instant heat.

Exploding fireworks that can't be doused with any amount of rain.

I feel her arms wrap wildly around me, pulling me in close, closer and I love the franticness. Her need to get closer matches mine as my hands drive into her hair.

Our tongues touch, stroke, dance, and the litany of sensation fires off messages in all directions – the biggest of which, is that no one in their right mind ever would or ever could stop kissing Ashleigh Rivera once they'd started.

Chapter Forty-Three

I CAN SEE CLEARLY NOW THE RAIN HAS GONE

Ashleigh

'*All I saw was you…*'

That's what George said when I reminded him to add seeing the Statue of Liberty to his list of landmarks if his family asked.

His gruff admission, sliding into my ear in the early hours of this morning, still has the power to produce a delightful squirm as I sit in Oscars awaiting my promised First Day of Promotion Breakfast Muffin.

It wasn't even a line. I mean, okay it's totally a line, but coming from George, the *way* he said it – despite being over the phone and with a gazillion miles between us – had the same melting properties as if he'd been staring into my eyes at the time. Yeah. George's romance-speak is off the chart written-about-in-books crazy-good. I feel another blush coming on and bring my magazine closer to cover my face.

In the forty-eight hours he's been gone we've been messaging and calling like we're exclusive. And, hello? Why aren't I crazy-fearful that we've both entered this with open arms and open hearts?

I guess after that incredible kiss – correction – *kisses* – so many drugging, dazzling, cause-a-public-spectacle kisses – it's easier to feel we're at the beginning of something special.

Something not to be tainted or disrespected by What Ifs.

I grin to myself and concentrate on reading the next question in a quiz I'm doing when a loud 'Ha!' permeates and I look up to discover Carlos sitting opposite me.

Oops. Totally missed that the morning rush is over.

'What?' I ask when he continues to stare suspiciously before his hand suddenly snakes out to whip the magazine from my hands. 'Hey.' I reach over the table to try and get it back.

'I knew it,' he says, triumphantly separating *Best Home* magazine from the magazine I was *actually* reading. 'I knew from your expression you couldn't have been reading *Best Home*.'

'What expression?'

He ignores me and focuses on the magazine article. 'How to Tell If You've Fallen in Love.' His gaze shoots straight back to mine. 'Seriously?'

'It's a bit of fun to quell First Day Promotion nerves,' I defend.

Carlos regards me with a deep frown before leaning back in his chair to call out in the direction of the kitchen, 'Ozzie, we have a problem.'

'There's no problem,' I whisper and then repeat it again louder as Oz comes out from the kitchen, looks at the article, sighs, and walks over to flip the sign on the door to 'Closed'.

'What are you doing?' I ask. 'With business doing better you can't put the "Closed" sign on the door like that. And where's my muffin?' The request is all indignant as my heart starts galloping.

My confidence from a minute ago shines less brightly as if preparing for pin-popping bubble-bursting.

Oz retrieves the muffin from the counter and sets it down on the table before sitting down next to Carlos. There's a little paper banner he's stuck into the top that reads: *You're Going to Be Great* and I relax. Until I look at the matching serious expression on his face and repeat, 'It's a harmless quiz.'

'Right.' Oz nods. 'So, are you mostly As, Bs or Cs?'

My big toe starts tingling. 'I only got as far as question two,' I lie.

Oz turns to Carlos. 'Look at her. She's Mostly A's – Definitely Fallen.'

Carlos gives a sad shake of his head. 'What the actual, Ashleigh?'

'You know when I was invited to swing by this morning for a Good Luck Congratulatory muffin I didn't expect—'

'Dish or no muffin,' Carlos insists, dragging the muffin to his side of the table.

I stare at them both mutinously, knowing I'm not getting out of here until I do. 'Okay, so … we kissed. George and I.'

'You didn't,' Carlos whispers.

'In the rain.' I stare at the muffin then, unable to help myself, my gaze drifts back up to them and I let out a happy sigh. 'It was like that scene in *The Notebook*.'

'It wasn't,' Carlos says but his words are in that type of hushed tone you use when the details are undeniably epic. He takes a moment to process and then says, 'Yeah, okay, I can see that. The guy's got charisma in spades. All straightforward confidence and sexy earnestness. But don't go mistaking that and a sizzling smooch for something more.'

'He asked for all your favourites when he came in to get the picnic,' Oz says.

Carlos turns to him. 'You didn't tell me that.' He turns back to look at me. 'So, he knew he was going to make a move on Governors Island. It was like a date. A date with moves at the end.'

'No, the kiss was…' I drift off, shivering as I remember the way he drew me in, as if he couldn't not. The incredibly gentle brush of his thumb against my bottom lip. His groan as he lowered his mouth to mine. 'It was spontaneous. We were arguing and—'

'Arguing?' Carlos's voice goes up a notch. 'Your first time with George was after an argument? Arguing and then sex is not a healthy pattern to set.'

'We were arguing about him leaving and we didn't have sex.'

'Why not? That's even worse. What's wrong with the guy?'

'Nothing. He didn't want me to feel like it was going to be goodbye sex. He wants me to understand he's coming back after his brother's wedding. It was romantic.' Gallant. Enthralling. Perfect.

I may not have appreciated him pushing against the confines of being friend-zoned beforehand but I'm so glad he did. Me backing off and giving him a let-out hadn't been a ploy. I'm not into playing games. It had been about saving face. I hadn't expected him to fight for not letting us fizzle into nothing but the fact that he did makes my heart beat faster. I mean, I know he fought for Anya but this is different, right?

'This is so much worse than I expected,' Carlos says.

'Why?'

'Because—' He breaks off and looks at Oz. 'You tell her.'

'Tell her what?' Oz asks. 'I like him for her.'

At least one of them is on my side. Even so, I steel myself to ask Carlos, 'Why don't you like George?'

'I like him just fine. Oz is going to talk to you now, in a calm manner, about you only just coming back to life and falling for something that—'

'*Someone*,' I correct.

'*Something* that may not be what you think it is.'

I want to bolt. 'What do *you* think it is, then?'

'I think it's not casual. I think you're about to get into something super serious when you need to be able to enjoy something lighter, first. You need fun, not scary feels.'

'Why do you think it'll immediately get serious?'

'Please. You've already stopped straightening up everything on the table,' Carlos says, pointing to the sugar granules and screwed up napkin I've left. 'You're happy. Not thinking clearly.'

'You want me to be happily unhappy? You do realise you sound ridiculous?'

'You think we didn't know you only wanted to start dating so you'd have some company on the weekends?'

Damn.

'That's why I want you to know I have other photos. Other guys.'

'What?' Oz swings his head to Carlos.

'Not like that. Never like that. I mean for her,' Carlos says, nodding his head at me.

'I don't want to see photos of other guys,' I tell him.

'Fine – you could still have Zach. There. I've said it.'

'Zach?' I feel like I've been doused with cold water.

'On a super-casual basis, like you've been wanting. On the weekends.'

My eyes narrow because he seems so certain. 'And you know this how?'

'I did a deep dive into his socials.'

'Carlos,' Oz groans. 'You didn't.'

'Hey, *one* of us at least was curious he forgot an entire wedding invite. And I felt responsible, being as it was me who slipped her his photo. Anyways it turns out he's way too busy for random hook-ups because he's moving back home and in with his mother!'

Wow.

Makes a weird kind of sense though.

'So, it turns out,' I say, 'Zach wasn't casual about making decisions so much as he was carefully keeping things casual with me while he made a life-changing decision? You know what? I'm not even mad he didn't mention it. I'm happy for him. I think this will be good for Zach. I think he felt really torn.'

'And it'll be good for you because if he's back home during the week it means he'd now be free on the weekend to see *you*. Whereas George—'

'George?'

'George is just out of a long relationship. He'll have baggage. I know you don't like to talk about losing Sarah and I don't want to define her in any way as baggage but you're already in deeper with George than you were with Zach. What if you both barely get started unpacking your baggage together and George decides to go back to the UK?'

I thought there was some rule about not sticking your friends with their biggest fear? My chin, when I lift it, may portray a fine wobble but I'm determined to stay positive. 'Then I'll have had some fun and let loose with a really decent guy and be happy about that.'

'You'll be devastated.'

I mean, he's not wrong but I'm not going to let the fear of that stop me from having this so I remain silent.

'Ashleigh, come on. Even the fact that you're so calm about George is scaring the bejesus out of me.'

'I am calm. I am positive. I'm…'

'Do *not* say in love with a guy you just met.'

'Happy, is what I was going to say. Maybe I have fallen in love. Or at least back in love with life.'

'So, George is like a reward for you?'

'That shouldn't upset you if all you want for me is fun.'

'It's not all we want for you, Ashleigh,' Oz says gently.

'What happens if your reward is removed?' Carlos asks, like a dog with a bone.

'Or,' I say leaning forward and adding dramatically, 'what if George stays and we fall in love with each other? Become each other's person? Get married? Have a family?'

Carlos is looking at me like he's scared I really think that's going to happen when it couldn't possibly and it hurts. Really hurts. 'We need you to be careful. We need you to be sensible. We don't want to see you get hurt.'

'Are you telling me that if I fall you won't be here to catch me? Because if that would place too much on our friendship I've been through heartache before and managed to pick myself back up.'

'That was different. If Sarah was here, she'd tell you to—'

'Nope.' I stand up, yanking my purse strap over my shoulder. 'You don't get to talk about Sarah. You never even met her. I'll tell you this about her though, if Sarah was here, she'd tell me she was happy for me.' *Wouldn't she?* Feeling panicky, I mutter, 'I should be going. Thanks for the muffin.'

'Ashleigh, wait. Please—'

I pause at the door, my breath locked in my throat. 'I get it. You're looking out for me. I'm okay. See you later.' Wrenching the door open, I step out into the morning sunshine.

I'm shaking a little bit as I walk.

Can feel that horrid, relentless, inevitable feeling of over-breathing.

I don't know – can't fathom – what Sarah would have thought about me and George.

It's okay to be happy, Ashleigh.

That's all I need for her to tell me.

I glance up.

Silence.

I immediately switch to looking down at the ground for a white feather to pick up.

There aren't any.

Chapter Forty-Four

MIDNIGHT CALLER

Ashleigh

'Are you all right, dear?'

I look up from the list I've been making and note the concerned expression on Mrs. Lundy's face.

The short answer is I'm not sure.

You know that thing when you try to stifle a yawn by pretending your jaws are wired together and end up instead making a sort of snorting, hiccupping sound? That.

Blinking rapidly, I reach for the delicate cup of tea she offered me when I arrived this morning. I'm so tired what I could really do with is a gallon of Carlos's super strength expresso blend. Unfortunately, I'm still shy about spending time at the bakery. Not because we aren't talking, because we are. Sort of. In a carefully polite way I hate, although probably not as much as Carlos, and I guess the fact he stopped the 'I Don't Believe in You and George and Here's Why You Shouldn't Either' talk, did give him points with me but there's been damage done.

The dent to my confidence disappears whenever I'm talking to George but in all the other hours of the day and night it's exhausting thinking Carlos will reintroduce his Worry Wagon and convince me to hitch myself to it.

I miss George.

Missing someone is a familiar feeling. It's unsettling and makes having Carlos's 'You're in too deep' as an earworm even harder to drown out but I have to try.

If I could just stop my brain from feeling it's become the Overthinking capital of my body. Especially today when I need to focus on the new service I'm trialling so I can work up a decent proposal to go over with Rhonda tomorrow. It's such a big thing to have reached forward for something I wanted at work and got it. The deepest regret I could have right now is messing that up.

'I'm fine,' I tell Mrs. Lundy. 'A little short on caffeine intake this morning.' I hold up a plate in a different pattern to the ones before. 'What do we think? Keep or donate?'

'Not sure.' Mrs. Lundy looks at the contents of her dining room cupboards currently stacked on her dining table, trying to find the set it belongs to.

'How about I put it in the "keep" section for now and we can make a final decision if we find the full set?'

Mrs. Lundy is my guinea pig for a new curating and decluttering service I'm developing. I scan the area set aside for tchotchkes and fight back another industrial-sized yawn. The last thing I want is to make anyone feel their most treasured possessions are boring or irrelevant. 'Once we have a handle on what you want to keep, I'll work out how much storage you need and give you options for displaying everything so you can see it and use it.'

Cleaners often know the contents of clients' homes better than the clients themselves so I'm hoping offering a way for people to re-engage with what they have will be a big hit. There'll need to be some training on editing collections and displaying them beautifully and tonight I'm going to put all the details together for Rhonda.

I'm so glad I had the conversation with her about developing Sparkle's services. I didn't want to step on Jamal's toes but was honest about feeling ready to formally take on more responsibility. I even explained about what had happened at my last job and she was great about it all.

Of course, I'll have to break it to George that someone else from Sparkle will be cleaning his apartment now. It would be too weird for me to do it if we're going to start seeing each other.

Is that what we're doing?

I bend my head to concentrate on writing an inventory, protective of the grin I can feel spreading over my face. Even though I consider Mrs. Lundy a friend, after Carlos's reaction I don't want any more well-meant friendly warnings to spoil all the trouble I'm in.

The wonderful, heart-pounding, can't-stop-grinning-to-myself trouble.

The kind of trouble that makes colours more intense. Food more delicious. Love songs more decipherable.

'Will it *really* work in the long-term though?' I muse.

'I don't know, dear. Some people aren't ready to let go of their things, but I trust you to work it out.'

I realise Mrs. Lundy thinks I'm talking about the new service but that the same advice applies.

Later, I'm at home surrounded by notes I've made for my work proposal but instead of ironing out details, I'm scrolling through photos George has sent of his brother's wedding. Pretty sure I've a happy-sappy smile on my face because of pictures of George looking super sexy.

I land on a photo of the bride and groom and their children, posing with the Wedding Family Tree I created for them. Yeah, my smile is getting sappier. Heartfelt joy is evident in all the photos and I know how much that will have meant to George.

My phone beeps to signal another message and I immediately open it. This time it's a selfie of George and a little old lady with the text:

They sat me in the corner next to the ringer!

I study the photo noting the wedding posies dotted along the bar, until something else catches my eye. I tap the screen to zero in and wow, not one, not two, but *three* collection cups for heart health charities.

Have I only been seeing what I was expected to see? All the times George talked about it being hard to gain distance from being ill – are his smiles tinged with the strain of being back in the place that kept him in that box?

Without thinking about my hair-up-in-messy-bun-no-makeup appearance I FaceTime him and when he answers, say, 'Didn't you tell them no one puts baby in the corner?'

George chuckles and my heart performs a Happy Dance worthy of being on *Dancing with the Stars*. 'She had me divulging my secrets within moments. But that's more because she's my grandmother and I'm her favourite.'

'Of course you are,' I say, nodding sagely. 'Tell me more.'

'About me being her favourite?'

'About anything you want to.' I settle back to listen to stories about his grandparents and how his grandfather gave him the watch he wears and what it means to him before George circles back to the wedding.

He looks so happy and relaxed. I can tell it's been good for him to be back home with his family for a few days.

Home.

I've been trying not to think of his being back with his family as him being home. It's nicer to think of his feeling that here is home now.

Here where I am.

At least keeping so busy has helped me avoid spiralling into What Ifs but now I need to use his gorgeous face to help keep me present.

'It's good to see you looking so happy,' I tell him.

'I am. Today's been the best day, really. I can't believe I was dreading it and now it's all over bar the clearing up and I've enjoyed every second seeing my brother get himself hitched to the love of his life.'

'Look at us, killing it at weddings when a few weeks ago we would have done anything to avoid them. By the time my cousin Tina's wedding rolls around everyone will see us as the personification of #WeddingGuestGoals.' As I notice the jolt of surprise flash across George's face, I cannot believe what I've said. 'Wow.' I try a laugh. Really not sure it worked so start babbling. 'I would never want to assume – or you to think that I expected – that I'm looking that far into the future and figuring—'

'Ashleigh.'

'Yeah?' God, I love it when he says my name like that, quietly stopping me in my tracks.

'I'd love to go to your cousin's wedding with you. That is, if you're inviting me?'

Wow. I... But what if – no. If things change in the future, they change. It's okay to make plans based on the information you have at the time, right? 'I do,' I reply in a rush.

George's eyebrow shoots up. 'Isn't that what the bride and groom say?'

Crap.

'I mean I am. Inviting you. And you ... accept?'

'I do,' he says, with a wink.

I roll my eyes but laugh along with him.

'I like I can get you flustered.'

I full-on blush but there's also that fiery response in my belly. That sudden and empowering understanding that I could get him all flustered too. I never felt like this with Zach. Had to force all my responses whereas all I have to do is look at George or hear his deep, throaty laugh.

'So how are things going with your folks?' I ask.

'They've really surprised me. Especially Mum. She told me New York must agree with me – that I was looking well. I think that's the first time I've ever heard her say that and look like she meant it.'

'That's so great. It looks like we've both managed to get our families to see us in a healthier light lately.' I wonder if that's down to the two of us connecting and influencing each other or if I'm romanticising. 'Did they understand about your job and Anya?'

'I may have omitted the noodle-dunking and gone with Anya and I realising we wanted different things and that it no longer seemed appropriate to work together. Oh, but, hey, speaking of work, guess what? I got offered a job today.'

The sentence has me feeling sucker-punched. 'Another one?' I whisper, trying to arrange my face into a smile because he needs to know I'm happy for him even if he's just made it sound like he's not coming back.

'Yes. I could practically hear you telling me how perfect I'd be for it.'

'Yeah?' My heart feels like a dumper truck of cement has reversed up and emptied its load into it. I've been so busy trying to keep the what ifs at bay I hadn't realised how far I'd travelled down the road of us being an *us* and if we're not to be an us, well, I know I told Carlos I was all about picking myself up and embracing life but…

'Turns out you were right about the village thinking I should run the pub. That's the job I was offered.'

The photos George sent made The Bedraggled Badger look even better than I'd imagined a centuries-old pub to look like. Cosier. Quainter. With history oozing from the oak beams to the inglenook fireplace.

The interior designer nerd in me had drooled over how it could look at Christmas. Logs hissing in the grate, traditional ornaments dripping from the tree, and boughs of holly, ivy and mistletoe falling gently from the beams.

It's too easy to now picture George behind the bar. 'And – and is that something, you, um, are now considering?'

I guess it could be cool to live over a pub with George, the two of us running it, together. It would be hard work but I don't mind hard work. And it would be an adventure, wouldn't it? I sit up straighter, knocking some of the notes I'd made off the bed and as

I bend down to pick them up, wonder what the hell I'm thinking. I've just committed to a promotion at Sparkle.

Not to mention George hasn't invited me to ride off into a British sunset with him.

'Of course, it isn't,' George says. 'How on earth would I attend your cousin's wedding if I'm over here?'

'We could always fly back for it.' We? Did I just say *we*?

'Being back here has been great,' George says, either not hearing or politely ignoring the fact I've basically said I could imagine the two of us living in the same village as his folks while running a pub. 'I've even enjoyed serving behind the bar. But I love what I do. I think I forgot that for a while. Got myself caught up in competing for accounts. Lost my edge. Then lost all sense of creativity and my confidence took a nose-dive and I guess I've been panicking it would never come back ever since.'

'I've always had faith in you.'

George blows out a breath and says quietly, 'I've got to tell you it feels amazing to have someone believe in me. Champion me.'

'Oh, is that what I've been doing?' I tease. 'And here's me thinking I was just nagging you about the job at Memorial.' Because I do champion him, I add, 'You're sure running The Bedraggled Badger wouldn't be a good stop-gap until you find an opening over there?'

'I'm sure. So how about you? How is your proposal for decluttering services going?'

'Great,' I tell him. I scoop up the pages of notes I've made and show him. 'Just have to ensure I've included these in the pitch to Rhonda tomorrow.'

'Do I need to let you go so you can finish up and get some sleep?'

'Absolutely not,' I say. It's too much fun talking to him. 'But it must be ridiculous o'clock over there, do you need to go?'

'I can sleep on the plane tomorrow.'

'Where are you? Childhood room?'

'Yeah.' He moves the camera around to show me.

'It's … sparse.'

'My mother could do with your decorating advice, I suspect. Also, no trundle for unexpected sleepovers.'

'The deprivation you've suffered! Although the size of your bed in the apartment, you've made up for it.'

'True. And where are you? I don't recognise the bed.'

'And when have you seen my bed?' I flirt back.

'I thought I'd seen it when we went there before the wedding.'

'Oh, that's right.' I sober as I move my phone around to show where I am. 'So right now, I'm in what was Sarah's room. I'd like to admit to being altruistic and say that because she worked shifts, she deserved somewhere quiet to sleep but in reality, we tossed a coin for it.'

'She really liked mint green, huh?'

A burst of laughter erupts out of me. 'She really did. I may change the colour.' The words are only shocking to me for a second before I admit, 'I haven't been able to come in here but after speaking with Shelley-Ann and Jasmine at the wedding I realised I should try and maybe clear it. There isn't much left. After Sarah died, Shelley-Ann came to get most of her things.'

'That must have been a hard day for you.'

'No,' I automatically answer, then correct with a 'Maybe,' before finally confessing, 'Yeah. I spent the day crying on a bench in the park until someone passing by put change in my coffee cup and I realised I was sitting on a bench in the park when Shelley-Ann had the harder job by far. By the time I got back to the apartment she'd already packed up everything and left me a note with a list of the things she thought I might like to keep. The first thing she'd listed was a box I knew contained Sarah's journal. I left the list unread on top of the box and from that moment on, only came in whenever I needed to yank more clothes out of the closet.' I look around the room again. 'You know, I've been in here all evening, using the space to work in, and it's been fine.'

'What will you do, move into it or advertise it?'

'Not sure I'm ready to see someone in what was her space, so I guess I could move in. I'm used to living on my own now so could I cope with someone using the bed in the living area?'

'Sounds like we both have things to think about. Me getting a new job and you getting a new housemate.'

'Yeah.' I feel a little panicky. Why is it as soon as you get comfortable being brave, something new comes along to force you into being even more brave? Clinging to safer ground and not ready to stop talking I say, 'So I'm pretty sure Hildy is breaking her dinner plates on purpose so that I can kintsugi them.'

'Whoa…'

'I know, right?'

'No, I mean, I've no idea what kintsugi is but, whoa, you just called her Hildy.'

'Wow. I guess I finally feel confident enough to. And kintsugi is the Japanese art of fixing broken pottery with gold lacquer. Instead of hiding the cracks you highlight them. Embrace the knowledge that something can be whole again. Stronger even, for being imperfectly perfect.'

'When I get back the first thing I plan to do is knock on her door and casually drop her name into conversation.'

'Really? That's the first thing you plan to do when you get back?'

George's smile turns wicked. 'Well now, maybe not the first thing. Maybe the first thing I'll do is stop by to see you.'

'Yeah?'

'Yeah. Consider it a date. Now, tell me about this kintsugi thing again?'

I grin, happy it's just the two of us, talking late into the night, making the time pass faster until we get to be together.

Chapter Forty-Five

FLYING WITHOUT WINGS

Ashleigh

Nerves and excitement vie for position as I stand looking up at the arrivals board. I press my hand against my belly, hoping to quell some of the jittery tangle inside and realise I'm still in my Sparkle uniform. What can I say, when inspiration struck, I didn't wait to follow through and at least there's no danger of missing me in it.

Beside me Oz complains to Carlos, 'You're not holding your signs up right.'

'Like it matters,' Carlos replies. 'Do you see anyone coming?'

'What's with the 'tude from these two?' Hildy whispers out the side of her mouth to me.

'Oh, it's how their protectiveness comes out,' I whisper back, looking down the line of my support network.

My friends.

And even as it feels bittersweet that I only have them because I lost Sarah, I hold close to my heart, the feeling that Carlos, Oz, and

Hildy *are* standing beside me. I've given them each a sign, the reverse of which contains my pitch notes for Rhonda, which went super-well so if this all goes hideously wrong, at least there's my job.

But this isn't going to go wrong because this is just a casual swing-by. A cute way of welcoming George back.

'Either that or they're hangry?' I add. 'But no time for snacks because, look'—I point back up at the board—'his plane's landed.'

Now what?

I must have said the words aloud because Oz says, 'What do you mean now what? Now you wait. And we wait with you.'

The nerves win out over excitement. 'Yes, but then what?'

Anyone?

Sarah?

I honestly don't know how I got here – I mean, okay, I know how I got to the airport arrivals lounge at JFK because I'm not likely to forget the farce that was the four of us getting into the cab. Not with all the worry about Hildy breaking a hip, Carlos breaking his jaw from whining or Oz breaking the cab with his size.

What's harder to comprehend is how I made it here, out of the void I was in last year. The void that stopped me doing anything to take me out of my comfort zone because I was all good with the hollowness inside me. The numbness.

I'm so thankful for figuring out that rather than healing I was dancing dangerously close to sleeping through life. Numbness can be a seductive companion. It may protect for a while but it pervades and sometimes, if you're not careful, it makes you numb to everything and everyone for evermore.

So, this excited feeling over that numbness?

Even if I have to go through the anxiety to get to it?

Totally worth it.

Except, okay, as I wait, my heart busy dancing inside my ribcage, what started out as a cute way of welcoming George home is turning into second, third and fourth thoughts because what if being here smacks of pushing myself on him, when maybe I was supposed to let him – us – breathe a little?

On the other hand, life is for living and why would I wait to wrap my arms around him and show him exactly how much I've missed him?

On the *other* other hand…!

'The time for overthinking was immediately after coming up with the idea,' Carlos whines. 'Not after dragging all of us here.'

'You didn't have to come,' Oz tells him.

'And what kind of friend would I be if I didn't support her?' Carlos says.

'And George,' Oz says.

'Right,' Carlos sighs. 'And George.'

'*And George*?' I grin, tamping down my need to do a happy dance. Having won Carlos over I don't need to set Oz off. 'Truly?'

'Truly,' Carlos admits. 'You were right to push back at me the other day. I liked seeing you take a stand. Reminded me you're not that lost little kitten we found crying on your doorstep trying to get your boss at the magazine a bizarro kale and kumquat smoothie.'

Oz groans. 'Let's all agree a kale and kumquat combo is wrong not just on so many levels but *every* level.'

'I know you're not in that same place you were,' Carlos adds, 'and some – not all – but some of that's down to George. So, here's what happens now: you'll see him, he'll see you, you'll kiss each other's faces off, then ride into the sunset together. Meanwhile, the three of us will apply for a loan to afford the cab ride back.'

'Quick,' Hildy interrupts. 'People are coming out. Hold your clues up.'

The four of us get into position.

My gaze scans as passengers start emerging to connect with loved ones.

'I don't see him,' I whisper after what is probably only minutes but feels like eons.

'Maybe we missed him,' Hildy muses.

'Impossible,' Carlos says. 'George is the type of guy that crowds part for.'

The first time I'd seen George, in the photo in his apartment, I'd thought the exact same thing. There's no way I'd miss him in this crowd and absolutely no way he'd miss me in my fluorescent white jacket.

More people trickle through.

Seriously though … where is he?

I start pacing.

Up and down.

Back and forth.

Throwing furtive glances at the gates.

Then longer glances.

Then focused glares.

People meeting his flight dwindle to us four. New greeters and loved ones arrive to meet passengers off other planes.

Finally, I look at my friends and force out the thought that has travelled to lodge in my throat like barbed wire. 'He didn't get on the plane?'

'We'll check the passenger manifest,' Oz assures.

'Not sure they make those available to the public,' Hildy explains.

I could call my mother to see if she could use her CIA contacts and then remember she doesn't actually work for the CIA.

'Maybe he's at lost baggage claim?' Hildy suggests.

'Yes,' I say, pasting on a smile, prepared to wait some more, determined to eradicate all catastrophizing. 'That's probably it.'

As we wait, I know it's not only me internally willing him to appear but when he still doesn't, I think I go into shock.

I felt so sure.

So confident.

But now it's as if someone has pressed pause on everything.

If I thought there was the slightest chance he wasn't getting on the plane I never would have let my friends witness this – *me* – dumfounded by stark reality.

'Ashleigh, make the call,' Carlos says.

To do what? Go back to my apartment and clean? I can't stay here waiting indefinitely. 'I g-guess we should leave?' But even as I'm saying it, I know I'd be exiting the cab while they're all getting into it and racing back here to wait for him because there's no way, right? *No way he didn't get on the plane.*

'I mean call George,' Carlos says, getting my phone out my pocket and handing it to me.

Oh.

Right. Of course.

Simple.

With shaking hands, I call him.

He doesn't pick up.

I feel myself going quiet inside. Launching into preparation mode to accept something I hadn't, with all my super-power ability to catastrophize, even once considered.

This was supposed to be simple.

This now feels so far from simple.

And I feel stupid.

So stupid.

'I can't believe I dragged you all here. Made you hold up stupid signs.'

'It's not stupid and neither are your signs,' Carlos says loyally, and I want to hug him fiercely. 'Call him again. Leave a message.'

'And say what?' I ask, wincing at the sympathy on their faces. 'Ask him why he didn't get on the plane? Why he isn't answering his phone? I'm not that girl.'

'It's as good a place as any to start,' Hildy offers.

'Alternatively, Oz and I will get on a plane, hunt him down and make him pay for doing this to you. Or at least Oz will. I'll be right behind him because I haven't finished paying for these veneers yet.'

'I really want to be that girl,' I tell them. 'The one who demands to know what's going on because none of this feels right at all. I mean, we talked all night.' I start pacing again. As if to out-stride the memories and cement myself in this new world where he isn't here. 'You know, I think I will leave a message. Tell him a few things. About how if he didn't want this, he could have just told me. He didn't need to avoid the whole of New York City. It's a big place, right? I'm sure we can exist in it without bothering each other. I know I can. I'm an adult. I have coping mechanisms. I —' Suddenly I'm feeling this horrid un-tethering sensation because what if it's worse than him not getting on the plane because he didn't want to come back?

What if it's that he didn't get on the plane because something happened to him?

My stomach flips and my world tilts and I'm wondering if Oz can move fast enough to catch me because it feels like I'm going to fall … have, in fact, fallen.

Fallen for George.

'Ashleigh, honey, you're shaking,' Hildy steps towards me. 'You shouldn't leave a message this angry.'

It's not anger coursing through me but I can't lend voice to the worry something happened to him. Instead, I think I might be crying. Know it for certain when I raise my head to find Oz, Carlos and Hildy leaning forward as if to catch me.

But I don't need catching.

Because this isn't happening.

Isn't, isn't, isn't.

Pointing to my phone, I look at them all and stutter, 'I-I'll just um… I need some space … privacy … to…' Waving my phone in the air at them, I do what anyone in a state of denial does.

I turn and run.

Chapter Forty-Six

KINTSUGI FOR THE HEART

George

Usually, after a long flight, my first thought would be about doing the *Die Hard* 'fists with your toes' thing but instead of exhausted I'm invigorated.

How quickly life can turn around.

A few months ago, I didn't even realise I was only going through the motions. I mean, I'd started noticing I was lonely in my relationship but refused to look too closely at that. Now, I'm about to embark on an exciting opportunity and I'm in the first clutches of a new relationship that has me falling deeper, quicker, than I thought possible.

None of this was planned.

I can't feel the ground beneath my feet.

Haven't felt this *alive* in a long time.

And I love it.

Exiting into the airport lounge, I'm thinking about buying flowers for Ashleigh to go with my news, so when I see the huge man standing in front of me, I assume I'm imagining it's Oz.

But as I walk forward, I see I'm not mistaken. Oz is with Carlos and Mrs. Lundy. I grin because if they're here then Ashleigh is too. I can't believe she came to the airport to meet me. Except, wait. Yes, I can. It's just the sort of sweet surprise she'd organise.

'Hello,' I greet. 'Are you all here for me?'

'We're your welcoming committee,' Carlos says, his voice tense.

'*Community* – welcoming community,' Oz corrects him, sounding the same.

'Right. What I said,' Carlos insists, his gaze zeroing in on me in a way which is making me think I've got this all wrong.

Is Ashleigh not here, then? My little welcoming committee is about something else? They don't like me for her and are here to head me off at the pass?

Maybe Mrs. Lundy came along as a sort of balancing force because one of them has to be on my side, right – I'm not that bad, surely?

Hours ago, I told Ashleigh I was going to start calling Mrs. Lundy, Hildy. Now, I'm silently promising that if she can help these two understand how great Ashleigh and I could be together I'll call her anything she wants.

I glance at my watch and as well as noting the time, am reminded how patient I've learned to be. Carlos and Oz are important to Ashleigh. I can take the time to explain I intend to be as good to her as she is to me. I'll explain it over and over, if I need to. But when I glance back at them, I'm struck with how immovable they look and just how huge Oz is.

'Oh, for heaven's sake,' Mrs. Lundy says to Carlos and Oz. 'He's got totally the wrong idea. Hold your signs up.'

The three of them shuffle into a line and I see now that Mrs. Lundy – *Hildy's* sign says:

Two words, 7,4: On Your Return

Carlos and Oz are holding up a page each that has hand-drawn crossword grids and Hildy is holding a marker out to me. I relax and my grin re-forms as I reach forward to write in Welcome Home. This is above and beyond the welcome home I used to get when I was with Anya, which mostly consisted of a text along the lines of:

Working. Rain check?

But Ashleigh doesn't rain check anything and I love that about her.

And then, suddenly, Carlos is being pushed one way, Oz the other, and there Ashleigh is, breathing hard, her beautiful big brown eyes drinking me in.

My heart stops mid-beat and then re-starts. It's going to do this every time I see her now and how can I be mad about that when it feels so damn good?

'You're here,' she whispers.

'I'm here,' I whisper back.

'No, I mean, *you're here*,' she repeats and in a split second she's launching herself into my arms to claim my mouth with hers.

Hell yes to kisses first, news later, as I drop my bags to the floor and wrap my arms around her, returning her enthusiasm with my own. No jetlag on earth could win out over the sparks created by her mouth on mine, in turn soothing and wakening every cell in my body and making my heart pound with life.

When she finally draws back, we're both breathing hard. 'Wow,' I finally manage. 'Totally surpasses the *Welcome Home* banner.'

Ashleigh lowers herself awkwardly back down to the floor and clearing her throat, says, 'Sorry – I guess that was maybe a lot?'

'Not sure it could ever be enough, actually,' I tell her, and then, already missing touching her, I reach out to drag my knuckles gently down the velvet smoothness of her cheek. That's when I notice her red eyes. 'Hey, what's this?' I swallow hard. 'You've been crying?' The last time I saw her cry was at Jasmine and Rob's wedding but that was also the time I saw courage that impressed me to my core.

'It's nothing,' she says, flapping a hand dismissively.

'It's not nothing if it made you cry,' I insist. At first my brain can't catch up – it's reluctant to leave Happy Land when I had her in my arms but as I watch her gaze dart away and it finally registers I don't see any of the other passengers from my plane hanging around, my little grey cells start firing. 'You've been waiting here for me but I didn't come out with the others,' I murmur, my mouth dry as it forms the words.

She looks horribly guilty as she admits, 'I *may* have started wondering if you'd decided to stay in the UK and didn't know how to tell me—'

I breathe in deep, preparing to tell her there's nothing that could have kept me from getting on that plane but she's rushing out more words.

'—but then I knew that's not who you are. You said you were getting on the plane. And I believed you. Trusted you.'

My heart expands to accept her trust even while she stares at the floor and murmurs, 'It's just when you still didn't appear…'

'You thought something had happened to me?' Slowly I tip her head up so that our gazes can connect and when she blushes deeply, I know it for certain. Swallowing, I explain, 'I was making a call – that's why I didn't come out with the others. It was quieter where I was and I was so busy concentrating on what I was saying I ignored the call alert then afterwards, I was so wrapped up in when I'd get to see you and tell you my news...' I take out my phone and look at it. Shit. 'I'm sorry, Ashleigh. I see the missed calls. There's a message too. I'm guessing it's from you?'

I go to play it but in a surprisingly fast move given his size, Oz reaches out and whips the phone out of my hands. 'Nope,' he says, making my eyebrows shoot up to somewhere in the vicinity of my hairline. 'You don't need to hear that.'

My gaze slides to Ashleigh, who, if possible, flushes an even deeper crimson, making me guess she left an angry message she's going to want me to delete without playing.

'I hate I worried you,' I tell her. 'I know you have direct insight into how life can change in an instant. I also know that doesn't just go away.'

'I'm mortified,' Ashleigh responds. 'This was supposed to be a simple welcome home. I really thought I'd conquered the what ifs but what if the reality is that brave Ashleigh was only here for a flicker?'

I wonder if she has any idea how beautiful she is when she blushes.

Or when she looks into my eyes like I'm the only guy in the world.

Or when she smiles.

Talks.

Moves.

Exists.

Even when that existence includes extreme cleaning.

I reach forward, taking her hands in mine. 'Well, what if I told you I'm here for the flicker and staying for the fully turned on?'

Behind me, I hear Carlos let out a whistle and I turn in time to see him flap his hand against Oz's ribs. 'That right there? Those words? Total #RomanceGoals.'

Hildy nods and tells them, 'I think he's been dipping into Barry White.'

Carlos and Oz exchange mystified looks and Oz asks Carlos quietly, 'Should we maybe google that?'

Ashleigh reaches out and lays a hand against my cheek to get my attention and her words are low and determined when she says, 'I'll get better at this.'

'We both will,' I promise.

'So, what's your exciting news?'

'Oh. That. I have a job interview. That's what I was on the phone arranging.'

'But that's fabulous, George. We'll go out and celebrate, right everyone?' She turns to the group.

'I'm seeing a rooftop bar,' Carlos agrees. 'Lots of alcohol. You down for that, Mrs. Lundy?'

'Absolutely,' she says.

'While you have no idea how much I love that you all want to celebrate with me,' I tell them. 'I kind of need to get to the hospital.'

'Hospital? Something's wro—' Ashleigh stops and regroups, only to then take a step back from me, her expression turning wary. 'Wait a minute, where is this interview?'

'It's at Memorial,' I reply.

'You're interviewing for the job Kyle Denton offered you? That's who you were on the phone with?'

'Yes. And it's all down to you and the kintsugi.'

'The kintsugi?'

'Last night when you were explaining how it painted over cracks – not to airbrush them out but to celebrate them, I got tingles.'

'You had a panic attack?'

'What – no. I haven't had a panic attack since you helped me look at everything differently. Tingles as in sparks,' I tell her. 'A jolt of electricity. The type I always got when a great idea for a campaign struck. You got me thinking about how people can feel imperfect or not whole after surgery and that led to thinking about embracing surgery scars – highlighting them in a positive way. I spent the plane ride working on my idea and as soon as I landed, I called Kyle and practically demanded an interview so I could tell him all the reasons I was the best person for the job.'

'Right.' She shakes her head in disbelief at me. 'You're taking a job at a hospital and now you "kintsugi" be happier about it?'

Chapter Forty-Seven

FIVE WORDS: 7, 2, 4, 4, 3

George

'Well, I have to get the job first, but yes, that's the idea,' I announce. I don't get it. Instead of looking excited I finally worked out what I want, Ashleigh looks appalled.

'This is because I bullied you into it,' she asserts.

'Bullied me?' I can't help the burst of laughter. 'Come on, Ashleigh. As if.'

'Persuaded you then. Wore you down. It's what I do, isn't it?' Her voice lowers to a shame-filled conspiratorial admission, 'I have form, remember? I—'

'Every time you talked about the job, I got excited about it,' I insist, cutting her off. 'Every time. It's like you knew if I just stopped running away from my experiences when I was younger and instead added it to my skillset, I could help people in a way that really matters.' I close the gap she created between us. Reach for her hands. 'You had faith in me even when I didn't. You push for people to be the best versions of themselves but you push yourself even harder. Do you have any idea how inspiring that is? When I said it wasn't just the kintsugi, I meant it. You inspired me – do inspire me. You said you trust me, right?' I search her face. Watch as she licks her lips nervously. The second I see her nod, I add, 'So, trust that how I react to that inspiration is my choice.'

There's still concern etched over her fine features and if ever there was a time to use my words it's now because no way do I want to be the guy who loses out because he didn't communicate.

And I definitely don't want to be the fool who loses Ashleigh. 'Look, forget about the job for a moment.'

'What? No. You have an interview. I don't want to be responsible for you missing out if it's truly what you want.'

'I have time and this is more important. I don't want you thinking this new energy I have is solely about a job. Not when it's actually for you – *us*. I know that sounds a lot and fast but we came in at a level or two above casual, I think. I need you to know I can't wait to take you out on dates, Ashleigh. Fun dates. Sexy dates. More sightseeing dates. So many dates. All of them creating our *"us."* We can go at whatever pace you want but I want us working on being an us. You came all this way to meet me off the plane.' I lower my forehead to rest against hers. 'I *love* that you did that for me. This is more than casual for you too, right?' God, I'm out of breath. Can feel my heart hammering inside of me. 'Ashleigh?'

'Play the message,' she says.

'What?' Her words have me frowning until she reaches back and grabs my phone out of Oz's hands. Ignoring the look of horror on their faces, she places the phone in my hand and repeats, 'Go ahead. Play it.'

The first thing I hear as I play the message on loudspeaker is the wealth of emotion when she says my name. My hand tightens around the phone and I look to check she wants me to continue. She stares back unflinching and in a way that has me thinking, that right there is my brave Ashleigh.

'I'm at the airport, George,' the message continues 'and you're not here and I have to tell you I'm so bloody bollocksing-mad.'

I wince. 'Not how we use that w—' I see her expression and stop. 'Sooo not relevant.'

'...But as bollocksing-mad as I am, it's not even close to how bollocksed-up unravelling I am at the thought something's happened to you. I don't know what that something is or why you can't get to me but I – I wanted to tell you some things. Big things. Things I've come to know over the course of knowing you. Like how great a human you are! How creative and talented. And decent. Decent is a very underused and underrated word but it's a big part of who you are. It literally gets me gooey inside. I love how you are with your family – I love how you were with my family and I will never forget how you had my back at the wedding.

You got me good, George. Maybe even from Day One. And I wasn't even looking. Specifically, wasn't looking. How could I be when I wasn't fit to offer anything – but then you always make me feel like what I have to offer is enough. In fact, you make me feel more. Seen. Two such incredible gifts.

I can't bollocksy-believe we may never get to finish our crossword book. May never get to stay up talking all through the night again. The thought of never getting to hear you whisper into my ear... or feel your lips on mine again... Or never again seeing those blue eyes of yours sparkle with humour, deepen with kindness, heat with passion...

It's literally the cruellest bollocks ever, George.

You once said I should try stand-up but I'm not sure funny is for me because I realise that if I was standing in front of you today, I'd be taking a giant leap and telling you I want serious with you. Life can be so short *and white feathers on the ground or no white feathers on the ground, George, I have to tell you, at least one time out loud, that my heart's involved and I'm: Five words, 7, 2, 4, 4, 3'*

'To re-record your message, press…'

Ashleigh and I stare at each other.

And then Carlos says 'Hold up because I can't with these crosswords. Did you just ask George to marry you?' He turns to Oz. 'Do we now need to find funds for a flight to Vegas?'

'Get another clue,' Oz tells him. 'That's only four words and it's a question, not a statement.'

'Although I suppose she is already wearing white…' Hildy says, her gaze at full-on twinkle. 'Well George? Do you need another clue?'

'Thanks Hildy, but I've got this,' I confirm, my eyes never leaving Ashleigh's. I pull her into my arms. Smile down at her. 'I'll whisper it into your ear again later but right now, out loud, I'm saying that, Ashleigh Rivera, I am absolutely, five words, 7,2,4,4,3 *falling-in-love-with-you*, too.'

A beautiful, sexy, confident smile lights up her face. 'I think this is the part where I kiss your face off,' she says.

'Oh, I'm so here for that,' I tell her.

'And staying for it.' Hildy adds with a wink.

'At least until we rush you off to Memorial for that job interview – ow,' Oz says as Carlos aims another tap to his solar plexus.

'Hell yes,' I whisper to Ashleigh as the world drops away and it's just the two of us. 'Here for it and staying for it – *for you*.'

'*For "us"*,' she answers.

Epilogue

Three Months Later...

Ashleigh

Oscars is busy, with a line of customers nearly out the door and honestly, it's getting hard to remember a time when it wasn't.

I collect up cups and saucers from the only unoccupied table, getting ready to clean and free it up again and right then, that's when the internal radar that I have for George bleeps madly and I glance to the doorway just as he hurls himself through it. He's out of breath and swaying a little.

Carlos does his parkour thing, flying out from behind the counter. 'Dude! Are you okay? You look like you're having a heart—'

George holds his hand up to forestall Carlos's words. 'There is absolutely nothing wrong—'

'With his heart,' I finish for George.

George peers around the customers to locate me, his expression turning thoughtful as he notes I've been cleaning. Stepping around the line, he walks straight to me and declares, 'I have some things to say.'

'Go right ahead, honey,' the first woman in line says, 'say your things.'

I'm not surprised the crowd, far from baying to be served, has taken one look at the gorgeousness that is George, and become hyper-interested. I even notice Oz walk out of the kitchen to stand behind the counter next to Carlos.

I can't resist asking George, 'You don't think you said enough last night?'

'Depends,' he answers. 'Are you talking about my leaving party at Hildy's, or afterwards? Because I don't recall either of us spending a lot of time talking after.'

I feel myself flush because truthfully, I love it when George says his things, it being equally as sexy as when he uses a more physical form of communication.

But that he always takes time to talk to me is every bit alluring as it is reassuring.

And always makes me want to reciprocate.

With words *and* actions.

George makes a show of clearing his throat before announcing, 'I may have mentioned a time or two how attracted I am to your sexy-clumsy.'

My eyebrows shoot up but I don't tell him to stop.

'Probably because it's uniquely you,' he adds. 'I find it utterly endearing. Enchanting. Authentic.'

'Wow.'

Copy that, I think as Carlos sighs out the word before he turns to Oz and says, 'Again with his words. Why don't you talk to me like that?'

The line of customers turns their attention to Carlos and Oz just as Oz replies, 'I do. It sounds different in his accent. I talk in pastries. You know this about me.'

'However,' George continues, making the line of customers swing their attention back in our direction. 'As attracted as I believe you know I am to it, I am wondering if "clumsiness" is really a good enough excuse *to get out of helping me move all my stuff into yours*?'

'Ours,' I correct him, unable to stop my serious expression from morphing into the biggest grin for him. Because, yes. George and I are moving in together. And it isn't just because Memorial doesn't pay George enough to afford living in The Clouds. Or the fact that his lease is coming up for renewal anyway. He could have got his own place but we did all the crazy-exciting talking thing we keep doing and concluded we wanted this to be the next chapter of our adventure together. 'How's it going?' I ask, excited. 'Are you nearly finished? How many more boxes?'

'Am I...?' His mouth drops open a little. 'Three flights of stairs with each box. Three. And many boxes thanks to you making me get all the "things-that-make-a-place-a-home" paraphernalia.' He looks over at Carlos and Oz. 'And you two were supposed to get some assistance in here so that you could shift boxes for us.'

'Can we help it if all your advice over the months has paid off and we're run off our feet 24/7?' Oz mumbles. 'Besides, we kind of assumed Ashleigh would use it as an excuse to trial a new service at Sparkle.'

'Hey, I resent that,' I chide. 'Life's not all about work, you know.' George and I share a secret smile for each other because as much as we both love our jobs, we're both loving spending time together even more.

Me and him.

Him and me.

We walked into this – *us* – open-hearted.

And it keeps on feeling so right.

'I can't believe you're complaining about carrying a few scatter cushions up three flights of stairs,' I tease. 'You're really worn out from last night?'

His grin turns wicked. 'I was hoping "many hands make light work" would leave us free for...'

'Round two of "after"?'

'More, free for all the rounds for evermore.'

'Wow.'

This time I look over to see, not Carlos sighing, but Fourth-In-Line guy, who now appears to be getting busy recording George's romance speak in a little notebook.

'But despite promising to round these two up,' George tells me, jerking his thumb to indicate Carlos and Oz, 'you instead got here and have been cleaning ever since?'

'Well, they were super-busy and, in my mind, I too was thinking the quicker I helped the quicker we'd get to finishing up.'

George stares intently at me and with a softer voice asks, 'The cleaning isn't because you're scared? Because we can—'

I reach out to put my fingers to his lips and stay his words. 'I'm not scared, George. But even if I was, I'd still be in this with you. Even if I *had* to clean. But that doesn't scare you either, right?'

'Not even a little bit.'

'Good, because you're not getting rid of me that easily. For one thing we have Robert to co-parent now.'

'Robert?' Carlos interrupts. 'Who's Robert? Are you getting a fur-baby? *We're* getting a fur-baby. Do not be stealing our thunder on the fur-baby.'

'It's not a competition,' Oz insists. 'Although, who names a dog Robert anyways?'

'Robert is our Ficus.' I explain.

Carlos looks disgusted at our name-choosing capabilities. 'Who names a Ficus, Robert?'

We both turn and say, 'Six letters: Lead singer of Led Zeppelin.'

A muttering goes up and down the bakery crowd until Corner-Table Guy says, 'I think I know this answer. Robert *Plant*?'

Carlos shakes his head at us. 'I knew it all along.' He takes out his phone to take our photo. 'Ashleigh, I'm sending this to your mom – clearly you two are just weird enough with your kinky-crossword-Ficus-sharing to work.'

'There's one more thing I want to say,' George tells me. 'As well as doing all the moving boxes on my own I picked up a little something for you...'

I watch as George reaches into his back jeans pocket.

Carlos emits a sort of shriek. 'Oh my god. *You're getting out a ring?*'

I've a feeling the startled expression on George's face matches mine.

'I don't have a ring,' he whispers.

'Good,' I whisper back. 'Because no offense to our friends, but should this ever come up in the future I'd be looking to be somewhere a little bit more'—I nod my head to the crowd—'intimate.'

'Good to know,' he whispers back.

And then, because his grin is so sappy-sweet I find myself ridiculously bravely adding, 'Although a pub could maybe work. Possibly in the UK, when we go to visit your folks next year!'

'Also, good to know,' he says, the grin turning deeper and sexier.

'No ring,' Carlos pouts, turning to Oz. 'I felt sure he was about to ask her to marry him.'

'All right, fine,' Oz suddenly grumbles. 'I hear you, okay, and will you?'

'Huh?' Carlos asks.

Oz throws up his hands in defeat, 'Jeez, I have to spell it out for you?' and muttering under his breath he disappears into the kitchen and comes back with a piping bag and starts furiously icing the counter.

Carlos stares at him like he's gone mad. 'Oz, what the hell are you…?'

Oz keeps on piping before finally finishing with a flourish that has him flinging down the bag and gesturing with his hands to his work. His ears have gone bright pink and I open my mouth to speak but First-In-Line Lady beats me to it with, 'Well, honey, what does it say?'

'It says,' Carlos tips his head to the side to read the countertop and then swings his gaze sharply to Oz: 'It says, will you marry me?'

'Damned right that's what it says. This is me,' Oz says. 'Using my words. I may not have the accent like George but I figure you and I? We've worked hard on our sh—' He breaks off, to acknowledge the customers and rephrases. 'We've worked hard on our stuff. We're building something special and, you know, the cockapoo isn't far off and so, Carlos,' his voice turns gruff with emotion. 'You have my heart and will you marry me?'

Carlos's communication skills have been reduced to endless eye blinking and I want to scream to the bakery crowd, 'This is an emergency, people, can anyone interpret the language of Repetitive Blinking?'

And then, into the silence, George answers, 'And that would be a *hell, yes*, he'll marry you.'

With a nod Carlos finally says, 'Right. Uh-huh. What he said. That is – hell yes, Ozzie-Baby, I will marry you.'

In one easy motion Oz swoops Carlos into his arms and lifts him off the ground in celebration. 'Sorry if we stole your thunder,' Oz tells us and then with a nod to everyone, adds, 'You can go ahead and do the dancing-clapping-your-hands-with-glee if you have to.'

As Oscars erupts into congratulations, I look at George through happy tears. 'We are going to crush it as their wedding guests.'

'Totally. So,' he says, taking something small and delicate out of his back pocket and holding it out for me. 'This is what I actually got you. It drifted down onto Robert while I was carrying him upstairs. I figured it was a sign.'

I reach out to take the white feather from his hand. '*A great sign*,' I whisper, stepping into his arms, my heart fuller than I ever thought possible.

'Robert is so wrong for a plant,' I hear Carlos, still in Oz's arms, say. 'But hey, what do you think about the name "Thunder" for our fur-baby?'

'Shush, Carlos,' I reply, grinning up at George. 'I'm about to kiss my boyfriend.' And reaching up on tiptoes I press my lips against his. As always, from the briefest brush of our lips against each other, the spark ignites, almost as if signalling us to buckle-up for the best adventure ever. But even as we deepen our kiss, I know that it's so much more than that.

It's the fact that on this crazy-exciting scary-amazing adventure our hearts beat as one.

It's life changing.

Magic.

It's us.

Acknowledgments

Some characters stay with an author longer than others. From the moment Ashleigh and George appeared on the page, they stole into my heart (with sleeping bags!) and set up home. They continue to light up my heart and I think a lot of that is because they're formed from all of us who put one foot in front of another and go about navigating our lives, despite anxiety.

My heartfelt thanks to everyone who shared with me their own experiences of dealing with anxiety. Modern life contains myriad experiences and stresses, and particularly, these last few years have been tough and I appreciate so much your honesty, courage and strength.

To my readers who've been with me from the very beginning and to new readers who've taken a chance on me in choosing to read this book, a great big squishy thank you – you all make my heart gooey! It's immensely heartwarming when people take the time to contact me or leave a review that says something in my book has touched them, or that I've written about an issue they can relate to, or that they've shed a tear, or had a good giggle, or a bit of a swoon... It makes all the creating, plotting, writing and re-writing worth it and I'm very grateful.

To my incredibly amazing husband, Andy. You just get it! Thank you for keeping my heart full and my sanity safe!

Thank you to Suzi and Rachel – for the listening, for the

understanding, for the *hard relates* to all the weird life stuff, and for all the laughter.

And lastly, thank you to my wonderful editor, Charlotte Ledger, and all the team at One More Chapter, HarperCollins. You've always worked hard and smart but in the past few years you've had to work even harder and even smarter and it's much appreciated.

ONE MORE CHAPTER

YOUR NUMBER ONE STOP
FOR PAGETURNING BOOKS

The author and One More Chapter would like to thank everyone who contributed to the publication of this story...

Analytics
Abigail Fryer
Maria Osa

Audio
Fionnuala Barrett
Ciara Briggs

Contracts
Sasha Duszynska Lewis

Design
Lucy Bennett
Fiona Greenway
Liane Payne
Dean Russell

Digital Sales
Hannah Lismore
Emily Scorer

Editorial
Kate Elton
Dushi Horti
Arsalan Isa
Charlotte Ledger
Bonnie Macleod
Jennie Rothwell
Caroline Scott-Bowden

Harper360
Emily Gerbner
Jean Marie Kelly
Emma Sullivan
Sophia Walker

International Sales
Bethan Moore

Marketing & Publicity
Chloe Cummings
Emma Petfield

Operations
Melissa Okusanya
Hannah Stamp

Production
Emily Chan
Denis Manson
Simon Moore
Francesca Tuzzeo

Rights
Rachel McCarron
Hany Sheikh Mohamed
Zoe Shine

The HarperCollins Distribution Team

The HarperCollins Finance & Royalties Team

The HarperCollins Legal Team

The HarperCollins Technology Team

Trade Marketing
Ben Hurd

UK Sales
Laura Carpenter
Isabel Coburn
Jay Cochrane
Sabina Lewis
Holly Martin
Erin White
Harriet Williams
Leah Woods

And every other essential link in the chain from delivery drivers to booksellers to librarians and beyond!

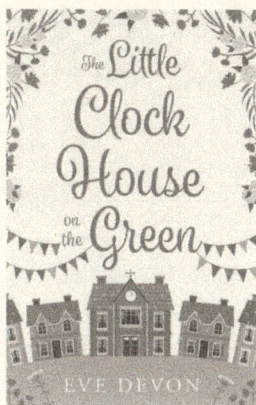

Welcome to the little village of Whispers Wood and one glorious summer when friendships are forged, secrets are revealed and romance delightfully bursts into bloom…

Kate Somersby has finally returned home after years of running away. She's heard that Old Man Isaac is selling the clock house on the green and she's determined to make him an offer – the very bricks that make up the little clock house hold precious memories for her.

Only gorgeous entrepreneur Daniel Westlake is standing in her way.

Their rivalry is the talk of the village and soon rumours are spreading thicker than jam on a scone…

Available now in paperback and eBook!

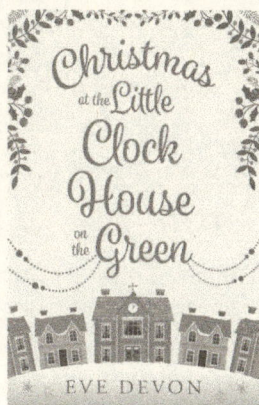

Welcome back to the village of Whispers Wood, where Christmas magic is in the air...

After giving his heart last year only to have it given away the very next day, Jake Knightley is opting out of Christmas permanently! But then a beautiful new village arrival sets mayhem in motion, upsetting all his carefully laid plans.

Emma Danes has said goodbye to Hollywood and will do anything to help make the clock house a success, even working closely with the tempting Mr Knightley.

Now, as snow starts to fall and romance starts to bloom, Emma and Jake may just find themselves repeating Whispers Wood history beneath the mistletoe...

Available now in paperback and eBook!

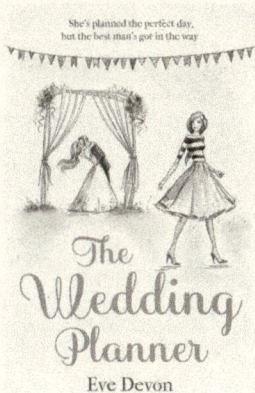

She's planned the perfect day,
but the best man's got in the way

The **Wedding** *Planner*

Eve Devon

Wedding bells are ringing and gossip is spiralling in Whispers Wood...

Single mum Gloria Pavey has a bad habit of saying exactly the wrong thing at the wrong time. Determined to make a positive change she can't say no when her best friend, Emma, asks her to take on the role of her wedding planner. The only problem? Gloria's co-planner – best man Seth Knightley.

Gloria is on a self-imposed man ban but pulling together the most beautiful wedding Whispers Wood has ever seen alongside gorgeous Seth is pushing her to her limits.

As every interaction increases the tension between them Gloria finds herself wondering...could the happy ever after she never thought she'd have be in her future after all?

Available now in paperback and eBook!